DOCTOR·WHO

Quiz Book

BBC

CONTENTS

COULD YOU BE... THE DOCTOR?

Have you ever dreamed of journeying through time and space? Do you long to fight monsters and right wrongs? How great is your appetite for danger? Not many people can do what the Doctor does. Take this test, tot up your scores, and measure your true Time Lord potential!

1. **The TARDIS lands on an alien planet. The scanner shows nothing but sand and rock. Do you:**

a) Go out and explore – you never know what you might find.

b) Take off again for somewhere more interesting.

c) Empty the TARDIS bins on the abandoned planet – you've been meaning to clean up for centuries.

2. **You are walking along the street when a UFO flies overhead. Do you say:**

a) Oh no, not another alien invasion!

b) Fantastic!

c) I'd better look it up in my UFO-spotters handbook to check if it's friendly or not!

3. **You decide you would like a companion on your journeys through time and space. What qualities do you look for?**

a) Someone brainy, brave and strong who can help you out of tight fixes.

b) Someone who will ask lots of questions and need rescuing a lot.

c) Someone who will help you see the universe in a different light.

4. Hostile aliens are roaming the streets of London wreaking destruction. Do you:

a) Advise the army how best to destroy the menace.

b) Confront their leader and warn them to leave – or else.

c) Set up a force field around London so the monsters can't take over anywhere else.

5. You accidentally find yourself at a conference of very important aliens from all over the galaxy. Do you:

a) Convince them that you have a right to be there so you can hang out for a while.

b) Point and giggle at all the funny species.

c) Take off immediately and leave them to it.

6. The TARDIS starts malfunctioning during flight. Do you:

a) Land immediately and check all systems, one by one.

b) Hit the console with a hammer.

c) Ignore it and hope for the best.

7. One of your companions steals rare gemstones from the king of an alien planet, hoping to sell them on Earth. Do you:

a) Take them straight back home and kick them off the TARDIS.

b) Insist they give the money they make to charity.

c) Make them put the gemstones back and warn them not to be greedy again.

8. You are very, very bored one night. Do you:

a) Speed-read a thousand books in one go – all that extra learning might be handy.

b) Add several thousand extra settings to your sonic screwdriver – it could help you get out of trouble in future.

c) Give the TARDIS a full overhaul – so it takes you exactly wherever and whenever you want to go.

9. While flying through space, a hideous alien creature appears inside the TARDIS and advances on your companion. Do you:

a) Rig up a device that will send it straight back where it came from.

b) Run from the control room with your companion and hope it goes away.

c) Try to communicate with it.

10. Which of the following do you find the most frightening:

a) A Slitheen.

b) A Dalek.

c) Your companion's mum joining you in the TARDIS.

COULD YOU BE THE DOCTOR?

Results:

1.	a) 4	b) 1	c) 0
2.	a) 1	b) 4	c) 2
3.	a) 3	b) 1	c) 4
4.	a) 2	b) 4	c) 1
5.	a) 4	b) 0	c) 2
6.	a) 1	b) 4	c) 1
7.	a) 3	b) 1	c) 4
8.	a) 3	b) 4	c) 0
9.	a) 1	b) 0	c) 4
10.	a) 3	b) 4	c) 8

How Did You Score?

36—44 You have true Time Lord potential, with an instinctive grasp of the dos and don'ts of time-space travel. One day the Doctor may regenerate into someone like you!

25—35 You are like the Doctor in many ways, but sometimes prone to panic and over-reacting. Take time out to assess each situation before acting – in case you regret what you do!

18—24 You have much to learn about travelling the universe, and your actions could cause disastrous consequences. If you hear of an imminent alien invasion, stand well back, leave it to the Doctor and pick up some tips!

17 or under You wouldn't know a TARDIS from a traffic light. Are you sure you're not a Slitheen in disguise, trying to mess up the universe at large? You should come with an intergalactic health warning!

WHEN PLASTIC ATTACKS!

TRUE OR FALSE?

The Earth was nearly invaded by living plastic...but were you paying attention? Say whether the statements below are true or false.

1. **The Nestene Consciousness can control all plastic.**
   TRUE/FALSE

2. **Its servants are living plastic mannequins known as Autons.**
   TRUE/FALSE

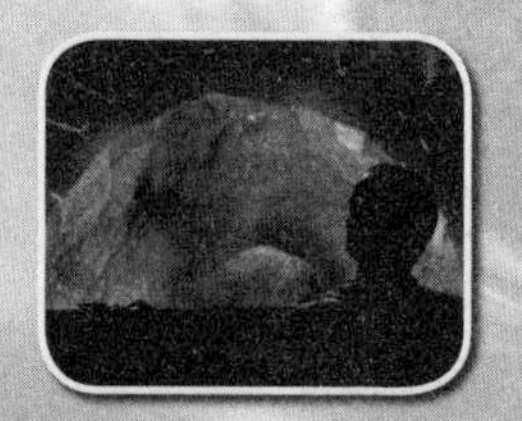

3. **The Nestene Consciousness was a kind creature that wanted to leave the Earth in peace.**
   TRUE/FALSE

4. **It used Buckingham Palace as a transmitter.**
   TRUE/FALSE

5. **Rose's boyfriend, Mickey, was snapped up by a living wheelie bin.**
   TRUE/FALSE

6. An Auton stops working if you pull off its head.

TRUE/FALSE

7. Autons can disguise themselves as shop window dummies.

TRUE/FALSE

8. The Nestene Consciousness wants to turn the Earth into an enormous plastic factory.

TRUE/FALSE

9. Its world was destroyed in the Time War.

TRUE/FALSE

10. It infiltrated Earth's civilisation using warp shunt technology.

TRUE/FALSE

WHEN PLASTIC ATTACKS!

Answers:

1. True. 2. True. 3. False. 4. False. 5. True.
6. False. 7. True. 8. False. 9. True. 10. True.

Scores:

8–10 You're clearly an expert — no plastic's going to take you unawares.

5–7 Not a bad score, but you may be at risk if the Autons invade again.

0–4 If a vicious wheelie bin eats you up, don't come running to us!

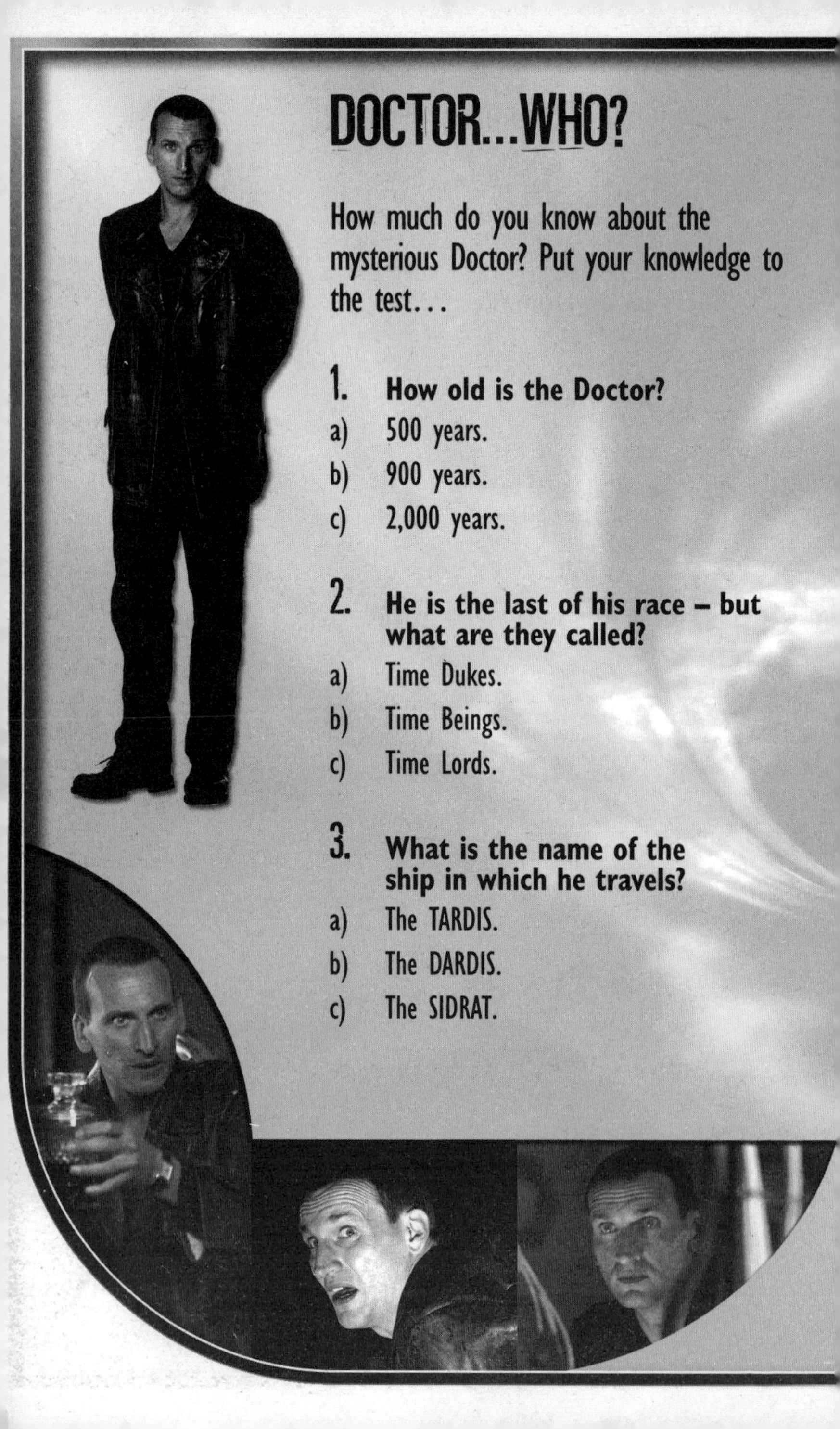

DOCTOR...WHO?

How much do you know about the mysterious Doctor? Put your knowledge to the test...

1. How old is the Doctor?

a) 500 years.

b) 900 years.

c) 2,000 years.

2. He is the last of his race – but what are they called?

a) Time Dukes.

b) Time Beings.

c) Time Lords.

3. What is the name of the ship in which he travels?

a) The TARDIS.

b) The DARDIS.

c) The SIDRAT.

4. To get past locked doors he uses:

a) A sonic spanner.

b) A sonic screwdriver.

c) A laser lance.

5. The Doctor fought in a terrible war, usually referred to as:

a) The Hyperspace War.

b) The TARDIS War.

c) The Time War.

6. How many hearts does the Doctor have?

a) One.

b) Two.

c) Three.

7. When the Doctor is excited he often shouts:

a) Splendid!

b) Cosmic!

c) Fantastic!

8. When the Doctor's body is damaged to the point of death, something extraordinary happens to save him...but what?

a) He regenerates into a new person.

b) He grows an extra heart.

c) He forms a chrysalis around himself to help him heal.

9. How many languages does the Doctor speak?

a) Five hundred.

b) Five thousand.

c) Five billion.

10. When asked for official identification, what does the Doctor show?

a) Slightly psychic ID, which shows people what they expect to see.

b) Universal Express card.

c) TARDIS driver's licence.

DOCTOR...WHO?

Answers:

1. b)	2. c)	3. a)	4. b)	5. c)
6. b)	7. c)	8. a)	9. c)	10. a)

Scores:

8–10 Fantastic! You know the Doctor like an old friend, and are clearly a loyal companion.

4–7 The Doctor remains a mystery to you but one you're keen to crack.

0–3 Wake up! There are adventures in time and space to be had – don't miss them!

THE END OF THE WORLD.
TRUE OR FALSE?

In five billion years the expanding sun will finally destroy the Earth. The Doctor and Rose witnessed its destruction...did you? Say whether the statements below are true or false.

1. **Alien VIPs gathered on a space station called Platform One to watch the Earth end.**
TRUE/FALSE

2. **The stewards on board the space station were bright pink.**
TRUE/FALSE

3. **The TARDIS was dragged off to a cloakroom and the Doctor was given a cloakroom ticket to get it back later.**
TRUE/FALSE

4. **The full name of Cassandra, the last surviving human, is the Lady Cassandra O'Brien Dot Delta Seventeen.**
TRUE/FALSE

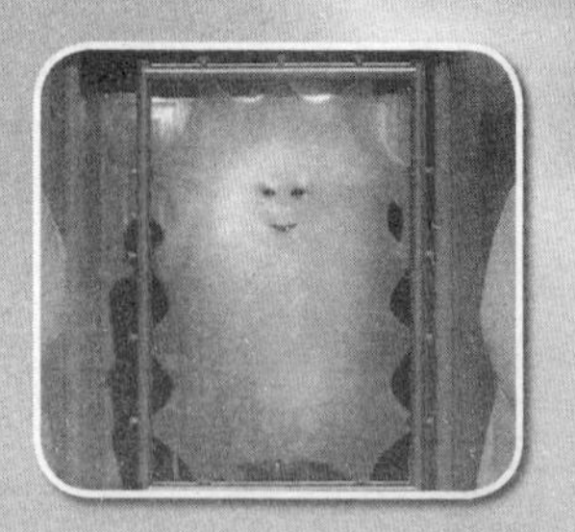

5. **The Earth was being kept alive by funding from English Heritage.**
TRUE/FALSE

6. **Cassandra released robotic slugs into the workings of the space station.**
TRUE/FALSE

7. **She had a transmat booster-feed hidden in an ostrich egg.**
TRUE/FALSE

8. **A super-advanced tree helped the Doctor save the space station.**
TRUE/FALSE

9. **Cassandra has had 708 cosmetic surgery operations.**
TRUE/FALSE

10. **Cassandra escaped justice by fleeing in a spaceship.**
TRUE/FALSE

THE END OF THE WORLD.

Answers:

1. True. 2. False. 3. True. 4. True. 5. False.
6. False. 7. True. 8. True. 9. True. 10. False.

Scores

8–10 You know loads about the end of the world – you didn't stow away in the TARDIS, did you?
5–7 You weren't watching as closely as you could have been, but it's not the end of the world...
0–4 Would you even notice the world ending around you?!

ALL ABOUT ROSE.

Rose is the Doctor's top companion, and they are the closest of friends. But how well do you know her? Take the test and see if you're a best mate or a total state!

1. **What is Rose's surname?**

a) Wyler.

b) Tyler.

c) Smiler.

2. **When Rose first met the Doctor she was working:**

a) In a bank.

b) In a fast food restaurant.

c) In a department store.

3. **What is the name of the place where Rose lives?**

a) The Watt estate.

b) The Powell estate.

c) The Thyme estate.

4. **Rose's mum is called:**

a) Wendy.

b) Rachael.

c) Jackie.

5. **When the Doctor is held prisoner by the living plastic Autons, how does Rose save him?**

a) She shoots them with a space gun.

b) She sprays them with a fire extinguisher.

c) She knocks them into a vat of molten plastic.

6. **What happened to Rose's father?**

a) He was killed in a car accident.

b) He ran away with Rose's English teacher.

c) He was kidnapped by aliens.

7. When did Rose first meet Captain Jack?

a) In a spaceship orbiting Earth.

b) Hanging from a barrage balloon above war-torn London.

c) In a pink Cadillac.

8. What is the name of Rose's former boyfriend?

a) Ricky.

b) Dickie.

c) Mickey.

ALL ABOUT ROSE.

Answers:

1. b) 2. c) 3. b) 4. c)
5. c) 6. a) 7. b) 8. c)

Scores:

6–8 You could be part of the Powell Estate posse — well done!

3–5 You know a bit about Rose, but clearly aren't too bothered.

0–2 What do you mean, "Rose who?"!

ODD ONE OUT.

Look at the different groups of people, places and things below. In each case, which is the odd one out – and why?

1. Mickey, Rose, Jackie, Captain Jack.

2. Cassandra, The Face of Boe, Charles Dickens, The Moxx of Balhoon.

3. Mr Sneed, a Dalek, Gwyneth, the Gelth.

4. Cardiff, London, Platform One, Utah.

5. Adam Mitchell, a Slitheen egg, Harriet Jones, the head of an Auton.

6. Joe Green, Margaret Blaine, General Asquith, the Prime Minister.

ODD ONE OUT.

Answers:

1. Captain Jack – the others all come from 21st century London.
2. Charles Dickens – the others are all VIP guests on Platform One.
3. A Dalek – the others met their doom in Victorian Cardiff.
4. Platform One – the other landing sites are all on Earth.
5. Harriet Jones – the others have all travelled in the TARDIS.
6. The Prime Minister – the others were all used as Slitheen disguises.

Scores:

5–6 Excellent. Your powers of reasoning are almost as good as the Doctor's!

3–4 Pretty good going, but you know you can do better than this...

0–2 The mind is like a muscle – it needs exercising or it wastes away. When was the last time you exercised, then?

MONSTER MANIA!

Wherever the Doctor goes, there are normally monsters close by. He's an expert on aliens – how about you? Come out from behind the sofa and put your knowledge to the test...

1. Where does an Auton conceal its deadly blaster?

a) In its head.

b) In its leg.

c) In its wrist.

2. What was the name of the 'lipstick and skin' creature who called herself the last surviving member of the human race?

a) Cassandra.

b) Miranda.

c) Baccanda.

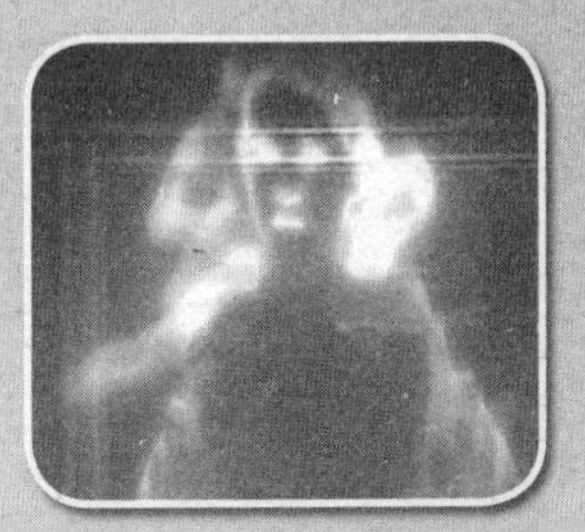

3. The Gelth were creatures from another dimension who had an affinity with:

a) Coal.

b) Cornflakes.

c) Gas.

4. Which kind of animal did the Slitheen turn into an unlikely space pilot?

a) A pig.

b) A cow.

c) A prawn.

5. Where do the Reapers come from?

a) The planet Reapos.

b) Inside the mind.

c) Outside time and space.

6. Which of the following is the full title of the evil Jagrafess?

a) The eternal Jagrafess of the Immense Jagulon Empire.

b) The mighty Jagrafess of the Holy Hadrojassic Maxarodenfoe.

c) The endless Jagrafess of the Jurassic Minidrivafriend.

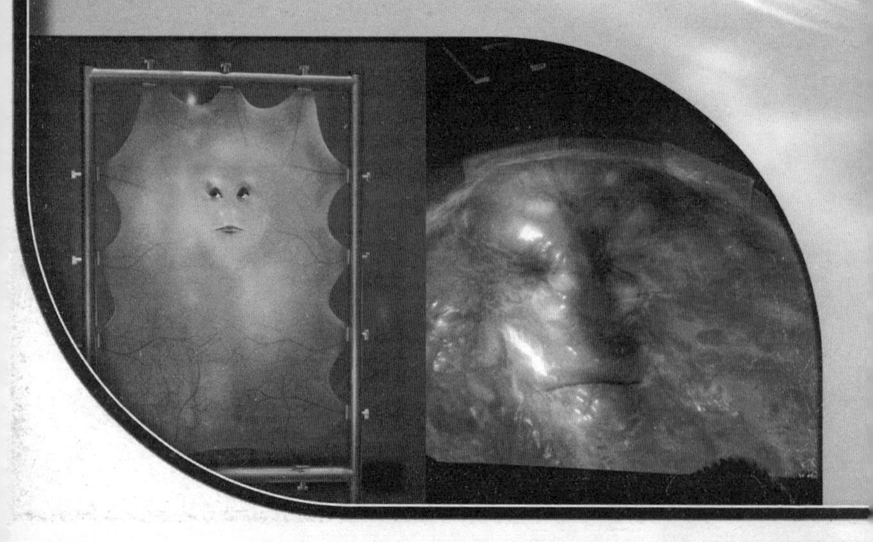

7. Which hideous creatures fought a time war against the Time Lords?

a) The Slitheen.

b) The Daleks.

c) The Autons.

MONSTER MANIA!

Answers:

1. c) 2. a) 3. c)
4. a) 5. c) 6. b) 7. b)

Scores

6–7 You are a monster maniac - just make sure your brains don't mark you out as a target for alien invaders!

3–5 Not bad, but don't try to tackle monsters by yourself - you'll come off worst!

0–2 A monstrously bad mark - go and swot up on your alien races before it's too late!

TARDIS TRAINED.

The TARDIS is a miracle of alien engineering. It makes doing the impossible seem easy. But how easy will you find this quiz about the Doctor's trusty time-and-spaceship?

1. **What does TARDIS stand for?**
a) Trim And Regulated Driving In Space.
b) Time And Related Disturbances In Space.
c) Time And Relative Dimension In Space.

2. **What does the TARDIS look like from the outside?**
a) A police telephone box.
b) A police station.
c) A big fridge.

3. **Which of these phrases best sums up the TARDIS?**
a) Bigger on the outside than the inside.
b) Bigger than the inside of the outside.
c) Bigger on the inside than the outside.

4. How does the TARDIS 'take off'?

a) Its light flashes as it fades away.

b) Its rockets fire and it shoots up into the sky.

c) It spins around until it vanishes.

5. What does the TARDIS key look like?

a) A flat disc.

b) An ordinary key.

c) A metal tube that glows.

6. What is housed beneath the TARDIS console?

a) A drinks machine.

b) A nuclear reactor.

c) A living power source.

7. How does the TARDIS locate the lair of the Nestene Consciousness?

a) It uses an Auton head to trace the Nestene signal back to its source.

b) It scans London for alien energy emissions.

c) It follows an Auton who is heading back home.

8. When the Doctor tries to take Rose back to Naples in 1860, where does the TARDIS actually land?

a) Paris, 1865.

b) Cardiff, 1869.

c) Swansea, 1870.

9. What is the name of the device that would disguise the TARDIS wherever it lands – if it was working?

a) The chameleon circuit.

b) The invisibility shield.

c) The cloaking mechanism.

10. What fuel can be used to power the TARDIS?

a) Petrol.

b) Crushed hydrogen.

c) Radiation from a rift in time.

TARDIS TRAINED.

Answers:

1. c)	2. a)	3. c)	4. a)	5. b)
6. c)	7. a)	8. b)	9. a)	10. c)

Scores

8–10 A TARDIS-tastic result!

5–7 You have a good working knowledge of time-space craft, but you're not yet an expert.

0–4 You wouldn't know a TARDIS from a telephone kiosk! Better be careful where you make your calls…

THE UNQUIET DEAD.

TRUE OR FALSE?

Almost 140 years ago, the world nearly ended, invaded by the Gelth. So. . .how is your history? Say whether the statements below are true or false.

1. **Going to Cardiff in 1869 was Rose's first trip through time.**
TRUE/FALSE

2. **Charles Dickens was reading from his novel *A Christmas Carol* on a theatre stage when a walking corpse interrupted him.**
TRUE/FALSE

3. **Rose was kidnapped from the theatre by an undertaker named Sneed.**
TRUE/FALSE

4. **The Doctor chased after them on a penny-farthing bicycle.**
TRUE/FALSE

5. **Sneed's servant girl, Gwyneth, was a powerful psychic medium who could read minds.**
TRUE/FALSE

6. **The alien Gelth had the power to inhabit dead bodies.**
TRUE/FALSE

7. **The Gelth used Charles Dickens' mental power to propel themselves into our dimension.**
TRUE/FALSE

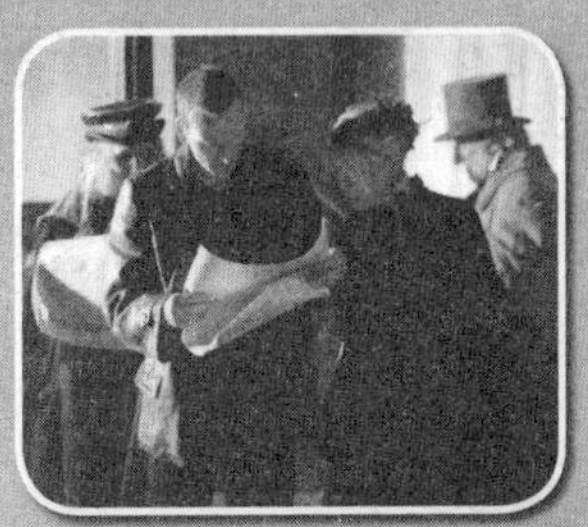

8. **The Doctor and Rose found themselves menaced by an army of zombies.**
TRUE/FALSE

9. **The Gelth were destroyed when Sneed's funeral parlour exploded.**
TRUE/FALSE

10. **Charles Dickens wrote a book based on his adventures with the Doctor.**
TRUE/FALSE

THE UNQUIET DEAD.

Answers:

1. False. 2. True. 3. True. 4. False. 5. True.
6. True. 7. False. 8. True. 9. True. 10. False.

SCORES:

8–10 Your masterly mind is almost as great as the late Charles Dickens'!
5–7 You are a fair student with potential to do well – but you must try harder than this!
0–4 Your brain is so dead, a Gelth could take it over – watch out!

THE DREADED DALEKS.

The Doctor's greatest foes always have a few tricks up their sucker arms...you never know where or when they might strike! Test your knowledge of all things Dalek with this quiz...you never know when the information might come in handy!

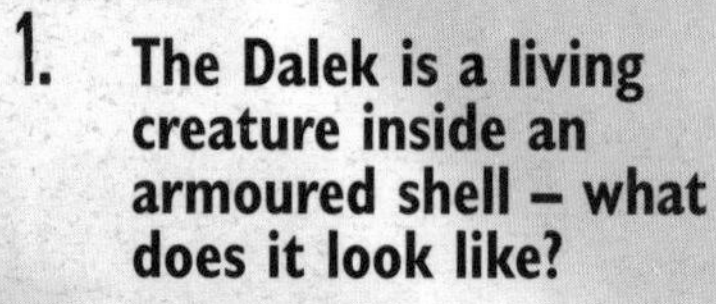

1. The Dalek is a living creature inside an armoured shell – what does it look like?

a) A pulsating crab with three eyes.

b) A one-eyed octopus with a big brain.

c) A giant yellow blob.

2. Who is the leader of the Daleks?

a) The Master.

b) The Emperor Dalek.

c) The Dalek of Daleks.

3. How was the Doctor led to the Dalek being held prisoner in an underground museum?

a) The Dalek sent a distress signal that drew the TARDIS off course.

b) He was hot on its trail and followed it to Earth.

c) He was invited to the museum's opening.

4. What made-up name did Henry Van Statten give the Dalek he had captured?

a) Metaltron.

b) Roboglider.

c) Bernard.

5. What is a Dalek's most famous catchphrase?

a) Annhilate!

b) Conquer the world!

c) Exterminate!

6. How quickly can a Dalek calculate a thousand billion lock combinations?

a) One second.

b) One minute.

c) One microsecond.

7. What does a Dalek do when faced with a flight of stairs?

a) It flies up them.

b) It panics.

c) It blows them up.

8. By what name is the Doctor known on the Dalek homeworld?

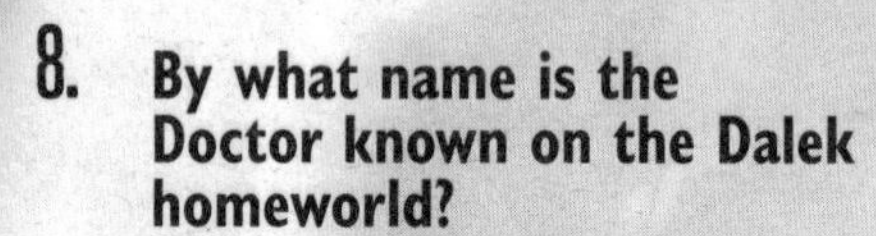

a) The traveller from beyond time.

b) The oncoming storm.

c) The Doctor.

THE DREADED DALEKS.

Answers:

1. b) 2. b) 3. a) 4. a)
5. c) 6. a) 7. a) 8. b)

Scores:

7–8 Your knowledge of the Daleks will serve you well should they invade the Earth again.

4–6 Should the Earth's Dalek experts get wiped out, the world will turn to you for help…so get ready!

0–3 It seems like your brain has already been exterminated! Go and have a lie down.

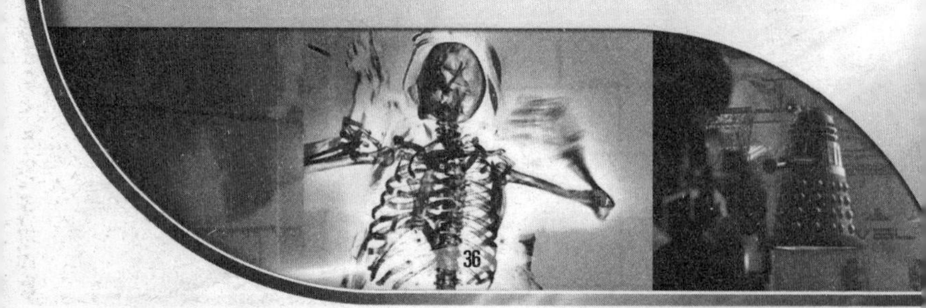

THE SLITHEEN.

TRUE OR FALSE?

How much do you know about these terrifying green meanies? Say whether the statements below are true or false.

1. **The Slitheen come from the planet Slitheron.**
   TRUE/FALSE

2. **A female Slitheen can fire poison darts from her claw.**
   TRUE/FALSE

3. **Slitheen are made of slime.**
   TRUE/FALSE

4. **The Slitheen planned to sell Earth to property developers.**
   TRUE/FALSE

5. **'Slitheen' is only a surname, not the name of an alien race.**
   TRUE/FALSE

6. Slitheen love to hunt.
TRUE/FALSE

7. Slitheen in disguise have zips in their foreheads.
TRUE/FALSE

8. Some Slitheen have personal teleport devices.
TRUE/FALSE

9. A Slitheen can be killed by concentrated vinegar.
TRUE/FALSE

10. A Slitheen feels the pain of another Slitheen.
TRUE/FALSE

THE SLITHEEN.

Answers:

1. False.	2. True.	3. False.	4. False.	5. True.
6. True.	7. True.	8. True.	9. True.	10. True.

Scores:

8–10 A superb score. You're not a Slitheen by any chance, are you?

5–7 Not bad, but you could still be caught out by a large person with wind problems and a zip in their forehead.

0–4 Let's hope that if the Slitheen come back, the defence of Earth doesn't depend on you!

TOUCHED BY THE TIME LORD.

This quiz focuses on the ordinary humans who have been drawn into the Doctor's hectic, dangerous life. How much do you know about them?

1. **What is the name of the man who started his own website devoted to investigating the Doctor's life?**
   a) Rupert.
   b) Mickey.
   c) Clive.

2. **What happened to him?**
   a) He was killed by a Dalek.
   b) He was killed by a Slitheen.
   c) He was killed by an Auton.

3. **Who hacked into the Royal Navy's computer systems and fired a missile at 10 Downing Street with the Doctor's help?**
   a) Adam Mitchell.
   b) Rose Tyler.
   c) Mickey Smith.

4. What childhood act confirmed that Adam Mitchell was a boy genius?

a) He rewired a computer in thirty minutes flat.

b) He almost started World War Three when he was eight.

c) He beat a grandmaster at chess, five times in a row.

5. What hideous creature nearly killed Jackie Tyler in her own flat?

a) A Slitheen.

b) An Auton.

c) The Jagrafess.

6. Which MP for Flydale North helped the Doctor and Rose fight the Slitheen?

a) Millicent Smith.

b) Joe Green.

c) Harriet Jones.

7. How does Rose keep in touch with her mum when she is travelling through time and space?

a) By email.

b) She uses a modified mobile phone.

c) She uses a space communicator.

8. How did Jackie help Rose expose the power source within the TARDIS?

a) She found it in a locked room hidden in the centre of the ship.

b) She borrowed a lorry and used it with a tow rope to drag the console away.

c) She answered a series of logic puzzles to open the console.

TOUCHED BY THE TIME LORD.

Answers:

1. c)	2. c)	3. c)	4. b)
5. a)	6. c)	7. b)	8. b)

Scores

7–8 Your knowledge is suspiciously good — are you a spy?

4–6 You have an eye for detail but it spends too long closed!

0–3 You wouldn't notice if the person next to you was abducted by aliens — wake up!

CAPTAIN ON DECK!

He's the flashiest maverick in space – but does Jack's reputation go before him, or does the Captain leave you clueless? Find out by taking this test...

1. **What is Captain Jack's surname?**

a) Jones.

b) Ittin.

c) Harkness.

2. **Captain Jack used to be a special operative for a secret organisation. They called themselves:**

a) Time Agents.

b) Space Patrollers.

c) Time-Space Generals.

3. **Why did Captain Jack leave this organisation?**

a) He was bored with the lifestyle.

b) He was thrown out for breaking the rules.

c) He quit when his bosses stole two years of his memories.

4. What did he become instead?

a) A space-traffic policeman.

b) A con-artist.

c) A space smuggler.

5. What type of gun was Captain Jack using when he first met the Doctor?

a) A sonic blaster.

b) A glitter gun.

c) A demat gun.

6. In Cardiff, while the Doctor ate dinner with a Slitheen and Rose talked with Mickey, what was Captain Jack doing?

a) Dancing at a disco.

b) Converting an alien device into a fuel source for the TARDIS.

c) Watching videos.

7. What type of ship was Captain Jack flying when he first met the Doctor?

a) Chula.

b) Hula.

c) Hawksmith Vanguard 2000.

8. When Captain Jack was killed by the Daleks, who brought him back to life?

a) The Doctor.

b) The Emperor Dalek.

c) Rose.

CAPTAIN ON DECK!

Answers:

1. c)	2. a)	3. c)	4. b)
5. a)	6. b)	7. a)	8. c)

Scores:

7–8 Your knowledge of Captain Jack's life story is impressive. Were you ever his senior officer?

5–6 Not bad – you might just scrape into the Time Agent academy.

0–4 You're more of a regimental mascot than a captain – next time, try harder!

DALEK UNDERGROUND!
TRUE OR FALSE?

Thanks to the TARDIS, we know that in just a few years from now, a Dalek is due to break out of a very special museum... forewarned is forearmed – but do you remember enough of what you saw to tell true statements from false?

1. **The alien museum was owned by billionaire Henry Van Statten.**
   TRUE/FALSE

2. **It is buried deep underground in Utah, North America.**
   TRUE/FALSE

3. **One whole floor has been converted into a prison for aliens.**
   TRUE/FALSE

4. **The Dalek prisoner was treated with kindness and respect.**
   TRUE/FALSE

5. **When the Dalek saw the Doctor it tried to exterminate him.**
TRUE/FALSE

6. **The Dalek absorbed DNA from Adam Mitchell to start regenerating its damaged casing.**
TRUE/FALSE

7. **A Dalek can kill people with its sucker stick.**
TRUE/FALSE

8. **The Dalek became infected with human emotion.**
TRUE/FALSE

9. **Towards the end of its life, the Dalek wanted to feel the sunlight on its skin.**
TRUE/FALSE

10. **The Doctor shot it with a large alien gun.**
TRUE/FALSE

DALEK UNDERGROUND!

Answers:

1. True. 2. True. 3. False. 4. False. 5. True.
6. False. 7. True. 8. True. 9. True. 10. False.

Scores:

8–10 You are a very observant Dalek expert!
5–7 You must be easily distracted – or perhaps you were hiding behind a cushion when you should have been watching!
0–4 EXTERMINATE!!!

THE SLITHEEN SCENE.

It's harder to rid yourself of a Slitheen than you might suppose... Like bad pennies, they keep turning up. But how much do you know about the Slitheen scene?

1. What is the name of the Slitheen's home planet?

a) Rexapelagoallabeedoshus.

b) Ruxalossophocalicawilberry.

c) Raxacoricofallapatorius.

2. What was the full name of the head of the Slitheen family group on Earth?

a) Jocrassa Fel Fotch Pasameer-Day Slitheen.

b) Bronco Fel Fotch Pasameer-Day Slitheen.

c) Narcissus Fel Fetch Pasameer-Night Slitheen.

3. What are the Slitheen made of?

a) Living calcium.

b) Living nitrogen.

c) Living potassium.

4. Why do Slitheen burp and fart so much in their human disguises?

a) To distract their enemies.

b) Because the Earth's atmosphere gives them wind.

c) The compression fields they use to shrink themselves create excess gas.

5. Why did the Slitheen want to destroy the Earth?

a) So they could sell chunks of it as scrap.

b) So they could sell chunks of it as fuel for spaceships.

c) So the people of Earth would never expand into space.

6. How did Blon Fel Fotch survive the destruction of Downing Street?

a) She teleported out of danger.

b) She burrowed a hole in the ground.

c) She hid inside a cabinet.

7. How can a female of the Slitheen species defend itself when in extreme danger?

a) Bite and scratch.

b) Manufacture a poison dart within her finger and exhale the excess poison through her lungs.

c) Hypnotise her enemy with her eyes and spray acid from her mouth.

8. What happens if a Slitheen child fails to carry out its first kill?

a) It is thrown out of the family.

b) It is fed to the venom grubs.

c) It is tortured for five days and then sent out to kill again.

THE SLITHEEN SCENE:

Answers:

1. c) 2. a) 3. a) 4. c)

5. b) 6. a) 7. b) 8. b)

Scores:

7–8 A remarkable score! Have you been watching alien wildlife programmes?

4–6 You display a good working knowledge of the Slitheen. Keep studying and you could be an expert some day.

0–3 You must take more interest in modern alien menaces...before they take an interest in you!

POLICE

WHAT ARE YOU LIKE?

Imagine if you got the chance to travel with the Doctor...just how would you cope with the dangerous situations that come with the TARDIS lifestyle? Take the test below and find out...

1. **You find yourself on a busy space station where the Doctor suspects something is wrong. Do you:**

a) Stay close to him, wanting to be where the action is so you can fight evil together.

b) Go off exploring on your own to see if you can find any clues.

c) Pocket a few pieces of technology – they'll be worth a fortune back home!

2. **You find a badly injured alien creature trapped inside a prison cell. It pleads for help. Do you:**

a) Enter the cell and try to help the alien, unable to stand by while it is in such pain.

b) Look it up in your electronic alien database to see if its hostile – it might be in prison for a reason!

c) Ignore it – the thing's probably dangerous.

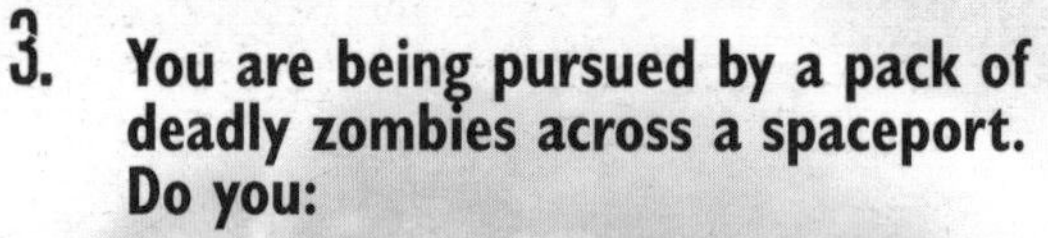

3. You are being pursued by a pack of deadly zombies across a spaceport. Do you:

a) Run for it, keeping an eye out for terrified innocent bystanders so you can help them.

b) Teleport out of danger, grab a sonic blaster and deal with the zombies single-handed.

c) Hide somewhere until they've gone, then sneak back to the TARDIS.

4. Autons are invading London, attacking a shopping centre. What do you do?

a) Phone your mum and check she's safely off the streets.

b) Track down the Nestene Consciousness and challenge it to a duel – if it loses, it calls off the invasion.

c) Wait till the Doctor defeats them, then help yourself to some living plastic – an invention like that's worth a fortune.

5. You travel back fifty years in time on a sightseeing trip. Do you:

a) Look up past relatives to see what they were really like in their youth.

b) Stock up on some trendy retro fashions and hope some action comes along soon.

c) Open a high-interest savings account – when you're back in your own time, it'll be worth loads.

6. The Doctor takes you to an alien cocktail party. Do you:

a) Check it out and marvel at the weirdness of it all.

b) Flirt with all the guests and party all night.

c) Ask the cleverest guests about science and technology, to see if you can use their ideas when you get back home.

7. The Doctor is in trouble, held prisoner by two robots on a scaffold. Do you:

a) Swing on a scaffolding rope, Tarzan-style, and knock the robots aside.

b) Blast the robots with a gun and carry the Doctor to safety on your back.

c) Distract the robots so they start to come after you – allowing the Doctor to overcome them.

8. The Doctor takes you to the planet Woman Wept, where the beaches are a thousand miles across, and where frozen waves a hundred feet high rise up from the endless ocean. Do you:

a) Walk with the Doctor at midnight, enjoying the moment, knowing it will stay with you for ever.

b) Hold a beach party and get out the barbecue.

c) Faint.

WHAT ARE YOU LIKE?

Mostly As

Your approach to time and space travel is a lot like Rose Tyler's. You realise you've been given an incredible opportunity, that it's a privilege to travel with the Doctor, and you're determined to get the most out of your time together. Whether you're fighting monsters on Mars or sightseeing on a far-distant moon, you realise that life is a great adventure and throw yourself into every new situation that comes along – while never forgetting that the universe doesn't revolve around you, and that the people around you may need your help. You're sensitive, caring and always ready to lay your life on the line for others.

Mostly Bs

You're a laid-back, devil-may-care kind of character, a bit like Captain Jack. You live for adventure, dashing and smashing your way through life with a lot of laughs and a great deal of style. For you, space is a playground and you're determined to enjoy yourself. But when unpleasant aliens are about and people's lives are in danger, the playing around ends – you make it your mission to save the day, often with the help of handy high-tech gadgets (that's what they're there for, right?). But remember, there's a serious side to the universe, and one day you may have to grow up a little and face up to that...until then, party on!

Mostly Cs

You have a lot in common with sneaky Adam Mitchell. While Rose sees time travel as a way of making a difference, and Captain Jack breezes through life being outrageous, you are always thinking of what the universe can do for you. You are not brave, and have a strong instinct for self-preservation – after all, it would be terrible if someone as clever as you was killed while sticking your neck out for somebody else. You have a genuine interest in the culture and science of other planets, but at the back of your mind you're always imagining how you might profit from it back on Earth. If you want to stay travelling with the Doctor, you must learn to put others first now and then.

THE LONG GAME.

TRUE OR FALSE?

Travel to Satellite Five in the far future, where the broadcast news is far more important than anyone can guess. Say true or false to these statements about the story, and hope that no one is influencing your answers…

1. **The TARDIS takes the Doctor, Rose and Adam to the year 200,000.**
   TRUE/FALSE

2. **Everyone on Satellite Five uses beads and necklaces instead of money.**
   TRUE/FALSE

3. **All the news from every planet is collected in a rush of data called an info-spike.**
   TRUE/FALSE

4. **News-gatherers have little doorways in their heads that open up to receive the info-spike.**
   TRUE/FALSE

5. When workers are 'promoted' they are secretly killed.
TRUE/FALSE

6. The Editor is a kindly figure who looks after everyone aboard Satellite Five.
TRUE/FALSE

7. He is the ruling intelligence of Satellite Five.
TRUE/FALSE

8. The Jagrafess is a hideous monster that lives on Floor 500.
TRUE/FALSE

9. If the Jagrafess overheats, it explodes very messily.
TRUE/FALSE

10. The Editor escapes the destruction of Floor 500 by rushing to the lift.
TRUE/FALSE

THE LONG GAME

Answers:

1. True. 2. False. 3. True. 4. True. 5. True.
6. False. 7. False. 8. True. 9. True. 10. False.

SCORES:

7–10 You have a lively and inquiring mind – unlike most humans on board Satellite Five!

4–6 You need to ask more questions and pay attention to the answers – you've got a good mind, use it or lose it!

0–3 No point putting an info-spike in your head – there's no brain inside! Pay more attention in future (and in the past for that matter...).

FUTURE HISTORY.

The Doctor's travels have given us a precious peek into the future of the human race...but how much can you remember from his excursions into the years yet to come?

1. What, according to the Doctor, will future Prime Minister Harriet Jones one day be the architect of?

a) Britain's Golden Age.

b) Britain's Dreadful Decade.

c) Britain's Silver Empire.

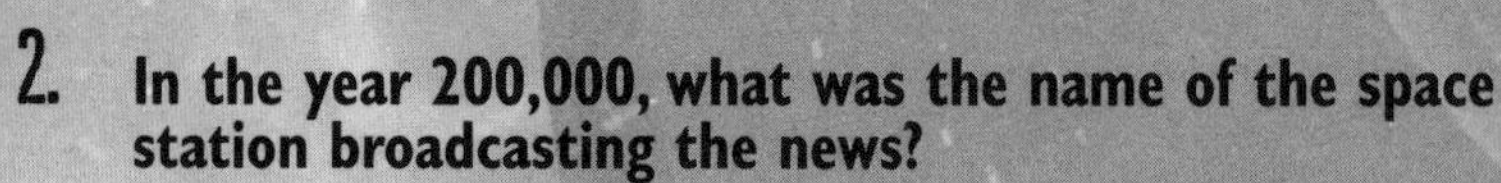

2. In the year 200,000, what was the name of the space station broadcasting the news?

a) Platform One.

b) Satellite Five.

c) News Station 247365.

3. By what name is it known a hundred years later, when the Doctor returns?

a) Satellite Seven.

b) The Game Station.

c) Game-show World.

4. The year 12,005 AD falls in which period of human history?

a) The Second Roman Empire.

b) The Third French Quango.

c) The Rootless Era of Forest-Dwellers.

5. What is the precise year in which the Earth is destroyed by the Sun?

a) Five zillion AD.

b) Five-point-five-slash-apple-slash-twenty-six.

c) Fourteen billion, seventeen million, two thousand and three.

6. In what year did Adam Mitchell board the TARDIS?

a) 2012.

b) 2112.

c) 3000.

7. What happens to evicted housemates on Big Brother in the year 200,100?

a) They are executed.

b) They are put in prison.

c) They are secretly teleported away and turned into Daleks.

8. How did a Dalek from the far future end up on 21st century Earth?

a) It fell through time.

b) It rode there in a time machine.

c) It stowed away in the TARDIS.

FUTURE HISTORY.

Answers:

1. a)	2. b)	3. b)	4. a)
5. b)	6. a)	7. c)	8. a)

Scores:

6–8 Well done! You know your history all right – even the stuff that hasn't happened yet!

3–5 Not bad, but you've got a lot more studying to do if you want to be a future historian.

0–2 Oh dear – your future as a Doctor Who mastermind isn't looking too bright with a score like this! But remember, the future can be changed...it's up to you!

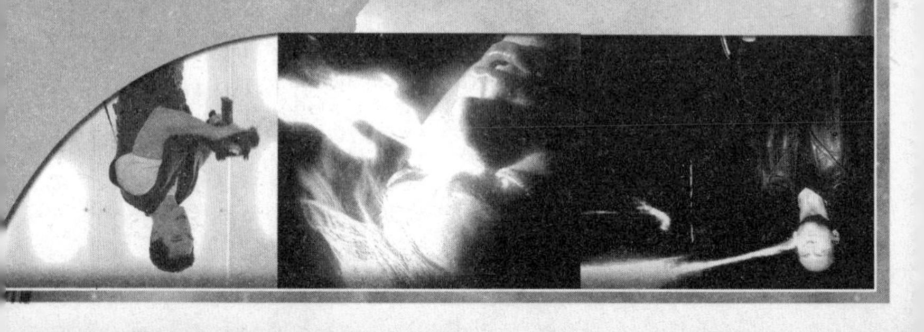

REAPER ALERT!

TRUE OR FALSE?

If you mess about with time, terrible things can happen. Say whether the statements below are true or false.

1. **Rose's dad died in a hit-and-run accident in 1987.**
   TRUE/FALSE

2. **Rose secretly wants to save her dad from being killed.**
   TRUE/FALSE

3. **When Rose saves her dad, it has no consequences for the planet Earth.**
   TRUE/FALSE

4. **The TARDIS is pulled through a wound in time and ceases to exist in our world.**
   TRUE/FALSE

5. **The Reapers are predators from outside this universe.**
   TRUE/FALSE

6. **Everyone they catch is locked up in a big, dark room.**
   TRUE/FALSE

7. The Doctor leads people to the safety of a church.
TRUE/FALSE

8. They wait inside until the Reapers give up and go home.
TRUE/FALSE

9. The Doctor is stronger than the Reapers, and survives their attack on him.
TRUE/FALSE

10. Rose's dad sacrifices his life to put history back on course.
TRUE/FALSE

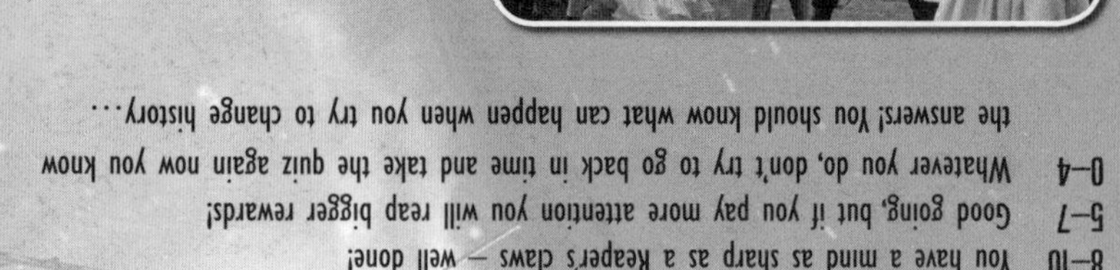

REAPER ALERT!

Answers:

1. True. 2. True. 3. False. 4. True. 5. True.
6. False. 7. True. 8. False. 9. False. 10. True.

Scores:

8–10 You have a mind as sharp as a Reaper's claws – well done!
5–7 Good going, but if you pay more attention you will reap bigger rewards!
0–4 Whatever you do, don't try to go back in time and take the quiz again now you know the answers! You should know what can happen when you try to change history...

TAKING THE MICKEY!

Mickey Smith is Rose's ex-boyfriend, and a reluctant ally in the Doctor's fight against alien aggressors. How well do you know him?

1. **The Doctor often pretends to get Mickey's name wrong. What does he call him?**

a) Sicky.

b) Ricky.

c) Nigel.

2. **What kind of car does Mickey drive?**

a) A blue BMW.

b) A clapped-out green Ford Escort.

c) A yellow VW Beetle.

3. **Why did the Nestene Consciousness make a living plastic replica of Mickey?**

a) To test a new plastic process.

b) So it could use it to find out what Rose knew about the Doctor.

c) Because Mickey knew too much about its plans.

4. Where was the real Mickey held prisoner while his replica was at large?

a) In the Nestene Consciousness's lair beneath the London Eye.

b) In his flat.

c) In a plastic spaceship orbiting the Earth.

5. Why was Mickey taken in for questioning by the police when Rose first joined the Doctor?

a) She was gone a year and they thought he'd murdered her.

b) They wanted to know about the Doctor.

c) They thought he had committed a robbery.

6. Why did Mickey choose not to go with the Doctor and Rose on their adventures?

a) The Doctor is too rude to him.

b) He knows he can't handle their dangerous lifestyle.

c) His passport is not valid.

7. Who did Mickey start going out with when he broke up with Rose?

a) A movie actress.

b) A model.

c) Trisha Delaney from the shop.

8. What alien creature does Mickey help the Doctor catch along with Rose and Captain Jack?

a) A Dalek.

b) A Reaper.

c) Blon Fel Fotch Pasameer-Day Slitheen.

TAKING THE MICKEY!

Answers:

1. b) 2. c) 3. b) 4. a)
5. a) 6. b) 7. c) 8. c)

Scores:

7–8 You must know more about Mickey than Trisha Delaney!

4–6 A fair score — but you're clearly not Mickey's biggest fan.

0–3 Mickey would get in a right hump if he knew how little you know about him. Show some respect and do better next time.

THE EMPTY CHILD.
TRUE OR FALSE?

When the Doctor and Rose pitched up in London during the Second World War, a terrifying adventure lay ahead... If you shared it with them, you should be able to sort the true statements from the false!

1. **The TARDIS followed an unidentified alien capsule to Earth with no trouble at all.**
   TRUE/FALSE

2. **Rose found herself dangling from a barrage balloon high above London.**
   TRUE/FALSE

3. **She was rescued by the Doctor.**
   TRUE/FALSE

4. **The Doctor was taken to an eerie hospital by Dr Constantine.**
   TRUE/FALSE

5. **All the patients had the same injuries and wore gas masks.**
   TRUE/FALSE

6. **They were being controlled by a strange, scary child looking for his mum.**
TRUE/FALSE

7. **The child had been brought back from the dead by alien nanogenes.**
TRUE/FALSE

8. **The Doctor couldn't find the child's mother.**
TRUE/FALSE

9. **The Doctor couldn't save everyone and turn them back to normal.**
TRUE/FALSE

10. **Captain Jack decided not to join the Doctor and Rose on their travels.**
TRUE/FALSE

THE EMPTY CHILD.

Answers:

1. False. 2. True. 3. False. 4. True. 5. True.
6. True. 7. True. 8. False. 9. False. 10. False.

Scores:

8–10 Your skills of recall are remarkable.
5–7 Not bad – though you could use a few nanogenes to rebuild your brain cells!
0–4 Never mind the Empty Child – you have the Empty Head!

USEFUL THINGS TO HAVE...

The Doctor is never short of ingenious solutions to terrifying problems, Captain Jack has a useful gadget for every emergency, and alien creatures excel at using lethal devices. But at the end of the day, a quick mind is the most useful thing to own of all – test out yours right now!

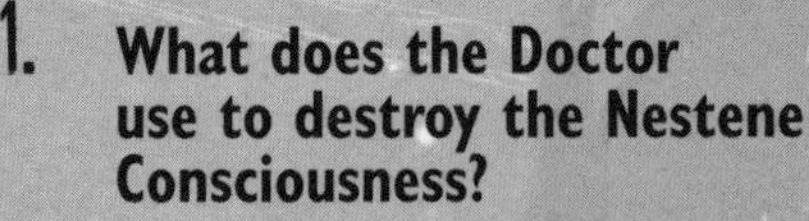

1. **What does the Doctor use to destroy the Nestene Consciousness?**

a) A bottle of paint stripper.

b) A sonic blaster.

c) A tube of anti-plastic.

2. **What does Captain Jack use to heal Rose's cut hands in 1941?**

a) Antiseptic cream.

b) Sub-atomic healing robots.

c) Chula cough drops.

3. **The cheapest way to interface with the computers on Satellite Five is a Type One Head-chip inserted into the back of the skull. How much does it cost?**

a) One hundred credits.

b) One credit.

c) One million credits.

4. **In war-torn London, the Doctor instructs Rose to use the sonic screwdriver on setting 2,428-D. What does this do?**

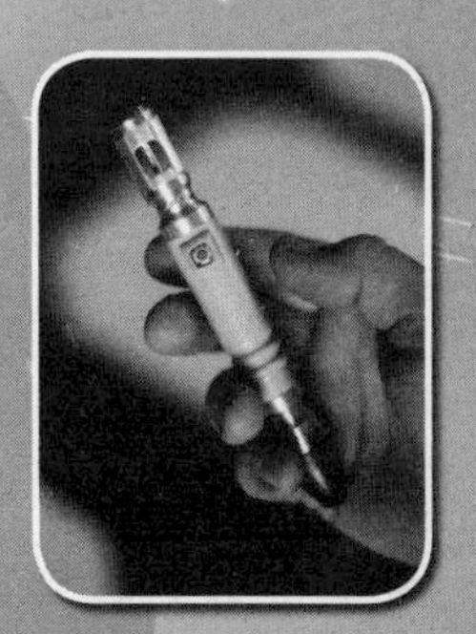

a) Ignites marsh gas.

b) Sends a distress signal.

c) Re-attaches cut barbed wire.

5. **What is special about Captain Jack's handcuffs, as worn by Blon the Slitheen?**

a) They dig into her wrists if she tries to escape.

b) They can be magnetised, pinning her to any metal surface.

c) They zap the prisoner with ten thousand volts if she tries to escape.

6. **How does Captain Jack keep his spaceship hidden from public view?**

a) He parks it underground.

b) It has a cloaking device.

c) It is coated in chameleon skins.

7. **What does the Doctor entrust to Mickey at the end of the first Slitheen attack on Earth?**

a) A special computer virus that will wipe out all trace of the Doctor from the Internet.

b) A special Slitheen detector.

c) A spare TARDIS key.

8. **Blon planned to escape Earth using a 'pan-dimensional surfboard' – but what, according to Captain Jack, is its full technical name?**

a) A tribophysical waveform macro-kinetic extrapolator.

b) A super-advanced motion-field wave-rider.

c) An enhanced shockwave-energy mass-extractor.

9. **What happened when this device was connected to the TARDIS console during a Dalek attack?**

a) Nothing.

b) It generated a powerful force field.

c) It turned the TARDIS invisible.

10. **How does the 'vomit-o-matic' work on Satellite Five?**

a) If you're sick, microscopic cleaning robots clear up the mess.

b) If you're sick, nano-termites in the lining of the throat freeze it to avoid mess.

c) It allows you to fake sickness so you can skive off work or school.

USEFUL THINGS TO HAVE...

Answers:

1. c)	2. b)	3. a)	4. c)	5. c)
6. b)	7. a)	8. a)	9. b)	10. b)

Scores:

8–10 You know your neutron flow from your proton exchange all right! A score worthy of a true mad scientist!

4–7 Your knowledge of weird science is quite impressive, but there's scope for improvement.

0–3 Have you sold your brain to medical science? If so, run, before they want their money back!

ODD ONE OUT.

In each of the groupings below there is an odd one out... Seek it out and exterminate it!

1. The Anne Droid, a Slitheen, Trin-E, Zu-Zana.

2. The Emperor Dalek, one of Cassandra's sabotage spiders, the Nestene Consciousness, the Jagrafess.

3. Cassandra, The Doctor, Captain Jack, Van Statten's Dalek.

4. Clive in a shopping centre, Lynda on Satellite Five, Suki on Satellite Five, Harriet Jones in 10 Downing Street.

5. A bicycle pump, a seat, a kitchen sink, a hammer.

6. Gwyneth, Rose's dad, Jabe the tree, Dr Constantine.

ODD ONE OUT.

Answers:

1. A Slitheen – the others are deadly robot hosts on the game station.
2. The sabotage spider – the others are all monsters who rule.
3. Captain Jack – the others all believe they are the last of their kind.
4. Harriet Jones – the others were killed by alien monsters.
5. The kitchen sink – the others can all be found in the TARDIS control room.
6. Dr Constantine – the others all sacrificed themselves to save the lives of others.

Scores:

6–8 A fantastic score in a very hard quiz! You are a true expert on the Doctor and his adventures.

4–5 Still a pretty impressive result. You are a bright spark, and are bound to get brighter still.

2–3 Not bad – at least there's no danger of Henry Van Statten asking you to join his underground museum staff!

0–1 Oops. Better luck next time – meanwhile, give that brain cell of yours a good rest!

BOOM TOWN.
TRUE OR FALSE?

The Doctor wasn't expecting to run into the Slitheen again after the last time they tangled – but life is full of surprises. Can you say whether the statements below are true or false?

1. **The Doctor took the TARDIS to a rift in space and time in Cardiff for refuelling.**
   TRUE/FALSE

2. **He found that one of the Slitheen family, Blon Fel Fotch, had survived the explosion in Downing Street.**
   TRUE/FALSE

3. **Blon Fel Fotch had set up a hamburger stand in the Millennium Centre Square.**
   TRUE/FALSE

4. **When she was found by the Doctor, she gave up without a struggle.**
   TRUE/FALSE

5. **She had planned to escape Earth by setting off a nuclear reactor on top of the rift and riding the shockwave to a different planet.**
   TRUE/FALSE

6. **The Doctor planned to take her to a space prison where she would be locked up for 100 years.**

TRUE/FALSE

7. **The Doctor and the Slitheen went out for dinner together.**

TRUE/FALSE

8. **Blon Fel Fotch didn't try to kill him once.**

TRUE/FALSE

9. **She sneakily used a high-tech gadget to open the rift in an attempt to escape.**

TRUE/FALSE

10. **The power at the heart of the TARDIS reversed her time-stream, turning her back into an egg.**

TRUE/FALSE

BOOM TOWN.

Answers:

1. True. 2. True. 3. False. 4. False. 5. True.
6. False. 7. True. 8. False. 9. True. 10. True.

Scores:

8–10 An explosively good score – almost good enough to open a rift in time and space!
5–7 A fairly impressive result – good enough to start a medium-sized explosive reaction.
0–4 Fairly feeble – you might just ignite a paper bag with a score like that. Better luck next time!

FOLLOW THE BIG BAD WOLF.

Wherever the Doctor and Rose go, the words BAD WOLF seem to crop up. Different times, different places...like it's written across the universe. But just where exactly did all those references crop up...?

1. **Where was the phrase first heard?**
a) In Victorian Cardiff.
b) On Platform One.
c) In a tent in Naples.

2. **On Platform One, who spoke of a 'bad wolf scenario' taking place?**
a) The Face of Boe.
b) The Steward.
c) Jolco and Jolco.

3. **Who said they could see the big, bad wolf when the Gelth tried to cross into our dimension?**
a) Gwyneth, the servant girl.
b) Sneed, the undertaker.
c) Charles Dickens, the author.

4. The words 'Bad Wolf' were seen scrawled as graffiti in the Doctor's next adventure – but where?

a) In a hospital.

b) On the TARDIS.

c) On the door of 10 Downing Street.

5. 'Bad Wolf One' was the call-sign for which vehicle?

a) The Steward's shuttle on Platform One.

b) Henry Van Statten's helicopter.

c) A barrage balloon in 1940s London.

6. What was showing on Badwolf TV on Satellite Five?

a) Coverage of a war on Vortis.

b) Coverage of a famine on Earth.

c) Coverage of the Face of Boe expecting baby Boemina.

7. Where did the phrase appear when the TARDIS landed in 1987?

a) On a wedding invitation.

b) Nowhere.

c) In graffiti.

8. What was written on the German bomb Captain Jack took into his spaceship?

a) Bad Wolf.

b) Schlechter Wolf.

c) Achtung Wolf!

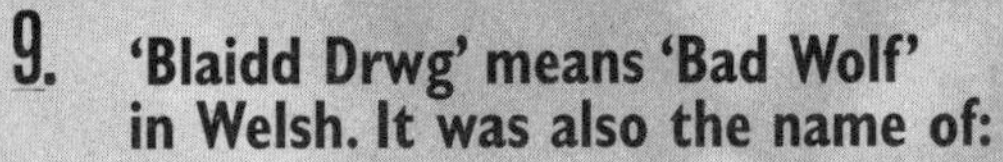

9. 'Blaidd Drwg' means 'Bad Wolf' in Welsh. It was also the name of:

a) The restaurant in Cardiff where the Doctor and a Slitheen had dinner.

b) The hotel in Cardiff where Mickey was staying.

c) The unstable nuclear power station in Cardiff.

10. Who runs the Game Station?

a) The Bad Wolf Corporation.

b) The Bad Wolf Syndicate.

c) The Bad Wolf Gaming Programme.

11. When do the Doctor and Rose first realise the words BAD WOLF are appearing wherever they go?

a) In Van Statten's museum.

b) In Cardiff Town Hall.

c) In a tent in Naples.

12. Who spread the words 'Bad Wolf' through the universe as a kind of trail for the TARDIS to follow?

a) The Daleks.

b) The Editor.

c) Rose.

FOLLOW THE BIG BAD WOLF.

Answers:

1. b)	2. a)	3. a)	4. b)	5. b)
6. c)	7. b)	8. b)	9. c)	10. a)
11. b)	12. c)			

Scores:

10–12 You clearly love a good mystery – not much gets past you!

6–9 You have an enquiring mind but to keep it sharp you must keep your eyes open.

3–5 You will get more out of life if you pay attention to the little details as well as the big ones!

0–2 Better watch out – with a score like that, the Big Bad Wolf will be coming for YOU!

QUALITY QUOTATIONS.

Who first said the following memorable words? Clear out your ears and see if any of these quality quotations stick in your mind...

1. **"I can feel it – the turn of the Earth... The ground beneath our feet is spinning at a thousand miles an hour..."**

a) Jackie.

b) The Doctor.

c) A Dalek.

2. **"You're just skin, Cassandra. Lipstick and skin!"**

a) Jabe.

b) The Moxx of Balhoon.

c) Rose.

3. **"This is not life. This is sickness. I shall not be like you! Order my destruction! Obey! Obey! Obey!"**

a) The Doctor.

b) Henry Van Statten.

c) A Dalek.

4. "D'you think it's cheap, looking like this? Flatness costs a fortune."

a) Cassandra.

b) Blon Fel Fotch.

c) The Editor.

5. "The Doctor is a legend, woven through history. When disaster comes, he is there. He brings the storm in his wake and he has one constant companion...death!"

a) Captain Jack.

b) Mickey.

c) Clive.

6. "Let me tell you something about the human race. You put a mysterious blue box slap bang in the middle of town – what do they do? Walk past it."

a) The Editor.

b) The Doctor.

c) Harriet Jones.

7. "See you in hell!"

a) Captain Jack.

b) Jabe.

c) The Editor.

8. "EXTERMINATE!"

a) The Moxx of Balhoon.

b) The Nestene Consicousness.

c) The Daleks.

QUALITY QUOTES.

Answers:

1. b) 2. c) 3. c)
4. a) 5. c) 6. b)
7. a) 8. c)

Scores:

7–8 Either you have a good ear for memorable words, or you're a brilliant guesser! Either way – congratulations!

4–6 Pretty good, but your score will improve if you listen more carefully in future.

0–3 Here are some more memorable words you need to hear: PAY ATTENTION!

THE PARTING OF THE WAYS.

TRUE OR FALSE?

In the gripping conclusion of the Ninth Doctor's adventures, nothing was safe and there was nowhere to hide. Say if the statements below are true or false – if you dare!

1. **The Doctor, Rose and Captain Jack were all abducted from the TARDIS and placed in futuristic game shows.**
   TRUE/FALSE

2. **The Doctor found himself playing Can't Cook, Won't Cook.**
   TRUE/FALSE

3. **He soon realized that he and his companions were back on Platform One, only further in the future.**
   TRUE/FALSE

4. **The Doctor learned that the Daleks were the power behind all the game shows.**
   TRUE/FALSE

5. **The Daleks captured Rose to ensure the Doctor would not interfere with their plans.**
   TRUE/FALSE

6. **They planned to invade Mars and turn all Martians into Daleks.**
TRUE/FALSE

7. **The Doctor rescued Rose and sent her back to Earth in the TARDIS, alone, where she would be safe.**
TRUE/FALSE

8. **Rose used the TARDIS instruction manual to fly it back to the Doctor.**
TRUE/FALSE

9. **Rose, possessed by the Time Vortex, destroys the Daleks – then the Doctor takes the vortex into himself before it can harm her.**
TRUE/FALSE

10. **The Doctor suffers no ill-effects as a result of his bravery…**
TRUE/FALSE

THE PARTING OF THE WAYS.

Answers:

1. True. 2. False. 3. False. 4. True. 5. True.
6. False. 7. True. 8. False. 9. True. 10. False.

Scores:

8–10 You were clearly with the Doctor right to the end – a loyal and knowledgeable fan!
5–7 Your memory seems a bit hazy – you're probably still suffering from shell-shock!
0–4 Do you actually have a memory?

THE MEGA CHALLENGE.

This final quiz is designed to test your detailed knowledge of Doctor Who. It's longer, harder and more challenging than the others...and it will separate the Doctor's casual acquaintances from his loyal companions. If you want to make it even tougher, set yourself a three-minute time limit for all 30 questions!

Good luck. Are you ready? Then...GO!

1. **What did the Doctor say when he first met Rose Tyler?**

a) "Hello, I'm the Doctor."

b) "Look out behind you!"

c) "Run!"

2. **The stuffed arm of which old enemy of the Doctor was found mounted in Henry Van Statten's alien museum?**

a) A Cyberman.

b) The Editor.

c) A Slitheen.

3. Why couldn't the Slitheen use the body of the Prime Minister as one of their disguises?

a) He was too slim for them to fit inside.

b) He smelled too much.

c) His body was too badly damaged when they killed him.

4. What is the name given to the age in which Satellite Five operates?

a) The Second Great Human Dynasty.

b) The Fourth Great and Bountiful Human Empire.

c) The Third Imperial Human Space Network.

5. What password does Mickey use repeatedly when hacking into secure military websites?

a) Blue Box.

b) Buffalo.

c) Bible.

6. What were the names of the TV presenter robots who wanted to change Captain Jack's image on Satellite Five?

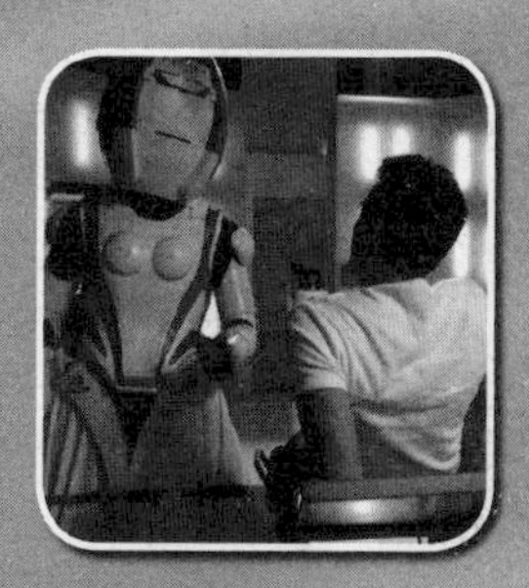

a) Ethel and Beryl.

b) Trin-E and Zu-Zana.

c) Zog and Zug.

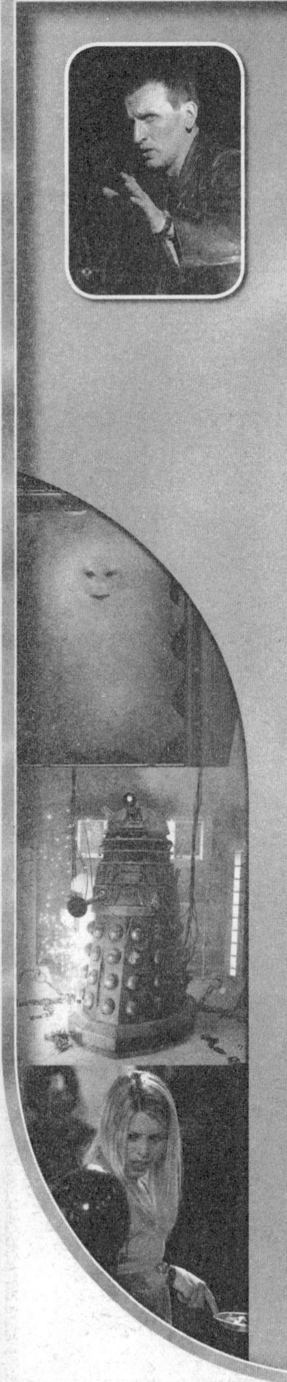

7. What piece of old-fashioned technology does Cassandra, the last surviving human being, mistake for an iPod?

a) A jukebox.

b) A fridge.

c) A vacuum cleaner.

8. Whereabouts on Earth did the Dalek crash-land before it was acquired by Henry Van Statten?

a) The Ascension Islands.

b) Russia.

c) Spain.

9. Why does everyone seem to speak English on the planets the Doctor and Rose visit?

a) Because they are English.

b) Because the TARDIS's telepathic field gets into Rose's head and translates.

c) Because the Doctor gives his friends special translating hearing aids.

10. Cassandra's father was a Texan, but where did her mother come from?

a) The Arctic desert.

b) The Sahara ice caps.

c) Luton.

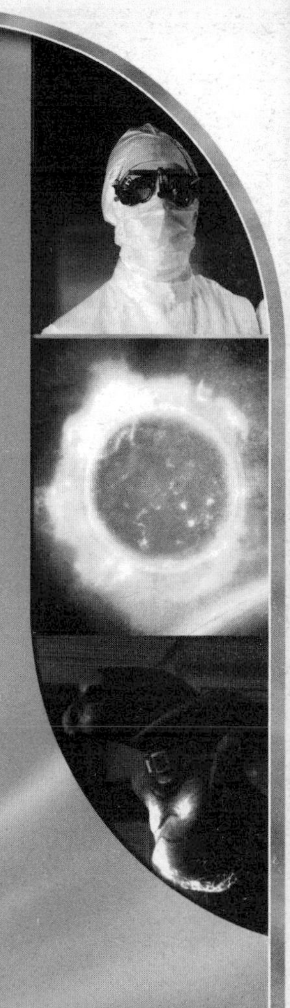

11. What sort of star will the Sun turn into when it expands?

a) A red dwarf.

b) A white midget.

c) A red giant.

12. How are criminals executed on the Slitheen's planet?

a) Hanged, drawn and quartered.

b) Shot by a firing squad.

c) Boiled alive in acid.

13. How many times was Mickey taken in for questioning by the police about Rose's disappearance?

a) Three times.

b) Five times.

c) Four times.

14. What does the Satellite Five snack 'zaffic' taste like?

a) A beef flavoured slush-puppy.

b) A sweet-and-sour sticky bun.

c) Chicken curry with lemons.

15. What was the name of the military doctor who examined the Slitheen's pig pilot?

a) Dr Ghoulash.

b) Dr Sato.

c) Dr Hoo.

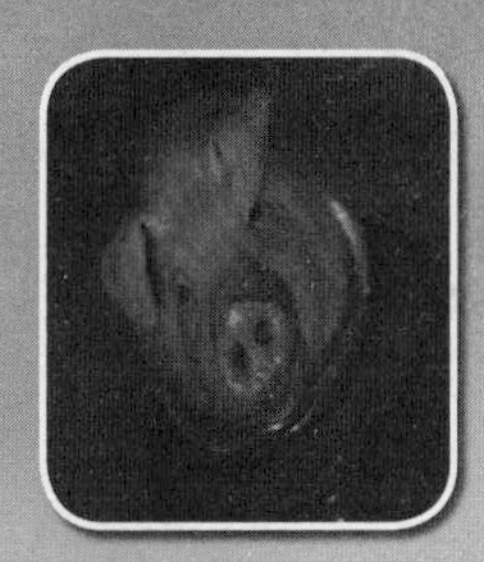

16. What did Rose mistake the Autons for when they first attacked her?

a) Students.

b) Security guards.

c) A street gang.

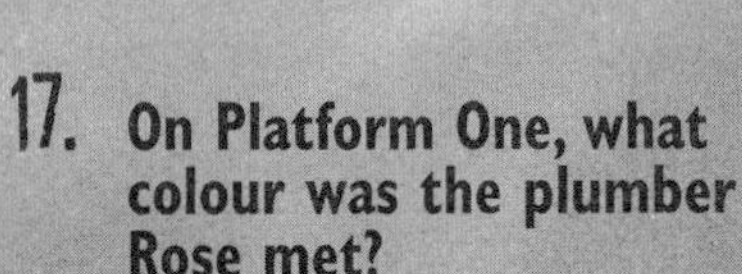

17. On Platform One, what colour was the plumber Rose met?

a) Purple.

b) Yellow.

c) Blue.

18. According to Henry Van Statten, where did the technology for Broadband come from?

a) The crashed UFO at Roswell.

b) An alien computer.

c) The Dalek.

19. What is the name of Rose's dad?

a) Paul.

b) Russell.

c) Pete.

20. To which anarchist organisation did Satellite Five worker Suki Cantrell belong?

a) The Red Fist.

b) The Freedom Foundation.

c) The New Justice Alliance.

21. What hardly-human creature was in charge of programming on the Game Station?

a) The Controller.

b) The Director.

c) The Game Vendor.

22. In the time of the Game Station, what storm has been raging on Earth for the last twenty years?

a) The Pacific Whirlpool.

b) The Great Atlantic Smog Storm.

c) The Towering Torquay Tornado.

23. What was the name of the department store where Rose used to work?

a) Henrik's.

b) Ibsen's.

c) Finch's.

24. What does Trin-E and Zu-Zana's defabricator do?

a) Measures how truthful you are being.

b) Removes clothing completely.

c) Removes stains from clothing.

25. What does a Slitheen egg resemble?

a) A small, blue cube.

b) A round, black ball.

c) A smooth oval with dreadlocks!

26. What does the Emperor Dalek believe himself to be?

a) The god of the Daleks.

b) The ruler of the whole universe.

c) A lumberjack.

27. What did Rose ask Mickey to bring to Cardiff for her?

a) Some magazines.

b) Her passport.

c) Her favourite shoes.

28. When the Doctor and Rose are trapped in 1987, which of the following helps bring the TARDIS back into existence?

a) A church pew.

b) Jackie's big hairdo.

c) A mobile phone battery.

29. What is written along the top of the TARDIS?

a) Police Public Call Box.

b) Police Telephone Box.

c) Police Free For Public.

30. How many legs do Cassandra's sabotage spiders have?

a) Eight.

b) Six.

c) Four.

THE MEGA CHALLENGE

Answers:

1. c)	2. c)
3. a)	4. b)
5. b)	6. b)
7. a)	8. a)
9. b)	10. a)
11. c)	12. c)
13. b)	14. a)
15. b)	16. a)
17. c)	18. a)
19. c)	20. b)
21. a)	22. b)
23.a)	24. b)
25. c)	26. a)
27. b)	28. c)
29. a)	30. c)

Scores:

26–30 A truly impressive demonstration of Doctorish knowledge. Have you cheated and had an info-spike installed in your head?

22–25 Your remarkable powers of memory recall mark you out from the crowd. You can be proud of this result.

17–21 A solid foundation upon which to build your knowledge of the Doctor and his universe.

10–16 You were guessing a lot of these questions, weren't you?

5–9 There must be a malfunctioning data chip in your head!

0–4 Report to Floor 16, Medical, at once!

POLICE PUBLIC CALL BOX
POLICE TELEPHONE
FREE
FOR USE OF
PUBLIC
PULL TO OPEN

CHAPTER I

The Godless College

WHEN JOSEPH LISTER'S FATHER WAS bout ten years old an incident occurred which, trivial as it eemed at the time, had a lasting effect upon him and, in-irectly, on the Lister family.

The boy had been writing in his copybook, and while he 'as waiting for his father to inspect his lesson he happened to ɔok out of the window. It was then that he made a remark-ble discovery. Due to a defect in the glass, a kind of bubble ad been formed, and when he looked through the bubble he ould see everything outside much more clearly than he could 'hen he looked through the rest of the pane, or even when e window was open.

Just then the boy's father entered the room; Joseph Jack-on turned quickly away from the window, so that he would ot be tempted to look through the magic bubble until his ther's inspection was finished. John Lister was quite strict ith his only son, who had come to him when he had given p hoping for a boy, almost twenty years after the birth of seph Jackson's two sisters.

"All finished with thy task?" John Lister asked.

"Yes, Father," Joseph Jackson answered, handing the copy-ok over.

"It is well done, in the allotted time," his father pronounced last. "There should be no more complaints from thy school bout slowness, and no more plum cakes withheld on that count! And, even more important, I am beginning to ink we need no longer fear that thee has any traces of thy ousin Steven's slothful disposition, which caused him to lie ed and come late to meals, so I could no longer keep him my house."

man, friend of Ruskin, Thackeray, and Mark Twain; and his little story was published under the title of *Rab and his Friends*. Countless numbers of people cried over it, moved by what the poet Swinburne referred to as Dr Brown's "love of children and the dead."

But though they cried over Ailie and James and Rab, they did not question the inevitability of her death. They did not ask themselves, "Why did Ailie have to die?" That, they knew, was to be expected when people were operated on. In those days entering a surgical hospital was often the equivalent of signing one's death-warrant.

The man who changed all that was born three years before Ailie died, the son of a Quaker couple named Isabella and Joseph Jackson Lister. He too was touched by the story of the old woman, but he did more than sympathize; he resolved not to rest until he had eliminated the disease which caused her death.

It was a tremendous task. Something like half the patients operated on in hospitals inevitably died, usually from septic diseases. This was true despite the fact that only the simplest surgical procedures were attempted, few surgeons being reck-less enough to operate upon the chest, abdomen, or brain. Compound fractures—fractures in which there was an external wound leading to the break in the bone—usually meant that the limb had to be amputated, and thus accounted for a large number of the deaths. If an epidemic of gangrene or some other hospital disease broke out the mortality soared, and not half but all of the patients in an infected ward might die.

That was the way things were when Ailie entered Minto House Hospital—and for many years afterwards. Surgeons had become excellent craftsmen, operating rapidly and with great technical skill, but surgery itself was closer to its primi-tive state than to the science it has become to-day.

By asking why Ailie had to die, and finding the answer to that question, Joseph Lister defeated an enemy so powerful that no operation, no matter how simple, was considered safe. Within a few years after Lister's discovery five times as many operations were performed, many of them procedures no one had dared to attempt before, and the mortality dropped to one-tenth of what it had been. For about a hundred years before Lister practically every mother undergoing a Cæsarean section died; immediately afterwards only one in ten failed to survive, then one in every twenty, until to-day the operation only rarely causes the death of a healthy woman.

During the American Civil War the number of soldiers who died of wound-infection was so great that figures are almost unobtainable. As Major Albert Gaillard Hart, a Union surgeon, put it, "What we term pyæmia or blood-poisoning has always been the scourge of armies, and ours was no exception. At the field hospital the cases were very frequent. Statistics are unnecessary; they proved uniformly fatal." Now all of that is changed. Blood-poisoning is no longer a scourge, and 97·5 per cent. of the men wounded in battle recover. Perhaps even more important is the fact that the overwhelming majority of these men are able to lead normal, useful lives, whereas the few Civil War casualties who did survive were usually helpless invalids and cripples.

It is actually not strange that Lister is not better known, for few great doctors achieve the popularity of heroes from other walks of life. Compared with other doctors, the name of Lister is by no means obscure; it has a more familiar ring than those of John Hunter, Ignaz Semmelweis, Rudolf Virchow, or Robert Koch. If it is less familiar than such names as Newton, Faraday, Darwin, and Curie, we must remember that the history of medicine is not taught anywhere except in a few medical schools: it is supposed to be interesting and valuable only to certain physicians.

It is only very recently that people have begun to realize that discoveries which have increased their chances of living are just as interesting as those which may cause their death. The number of people who visited the Wellcome Historical Medical Museum in London—where the wards in which

Lister worked his miracle have been reprod
instruments and apparatus preserved—is ve
pared with the numbers which flock to visit
military weapons.

There is another reason why so little is know
Lister, in spite of the many honours which wer
him, and that was his own modesty. By ke
remarkable personality as far out of the limelig
he made his work seem almost anonymous. Th
tude of his discovery, which opened the way to
discoveries, helped to create this anonymity.
assumed that anything so important must h
long ago. It is, indeed, difficult to realize
women are living to-day who read the story of
it for granted that infection must follow the su

This book, then, attempts to describe List
birth of modern surgery and its rapid developm
long and active life. And, in addition, it atten
personal story of Joseph Lister, the story of a m
woman he so deeply loved.

"Yes, Father." It was all right to talk about the bubble now, and Joseph Jackson Lister asked about it eagerly, ending with, "Why is it, Father, that I see so much better through that part of the pane?"

"The bubble acts as a magnifying glass," John Lister told him. Much as he cared about his only son, it did not occur to him that he might be short-sighted if he needed help in order to see figures on the other side of the narrow London street. Instead, he concentrated on trying to answer the boy's questions, which seemed to him to be sensible and intelligent ones, and a little more than he could cope with by himself.

"I fear I do not know enough about the subject to explain it all," he said honestly. "But I will look about for a book on optics for thee."

"I should like that very much," the boy said seriously.

"First I shall wait a few months, to make certain thy interest is a lasting one, and then I shall buy thee a good book. And glad to do it, for, since we Friends cannot go to the universities, our higher education depends upon ourselves, and thee cannot learn too young to study by thyself. Some day thy drawing and painting and perhaps a hobby like the study of optics will bring thee far more satisfaction than others derive from hunting or dancing or the theatre."

John Lister was right, except for the fact that the interest aroused in Joseph Jackson Lister by a glass bubble which had the power to magnify things grew until it became far more than a hobby. He soon went on to study the microscope, working so diligently that his father rewarded him by presenting him with a microscope of his own, which became his most prized possession. Eventually he made improvements which raised the microscope from "little better than a scientific toy to a powerful engine of investigation," and earned the title of "the pillar and source of all the microscopy of the age."

His major contribution was the achromatic lens, which solved the troublesome problems of iridescence and blurring, and transmitted a pure white light. He not only worked out the theoretical basis for this lens, but ground the lenses himself. He also made some important discoveries, notably concerning the structure of zoophytes. For his discovery of the achromatic lens he was made a Fellow of the Royal Society, and the name of Lister is still remembered in the field of optics. But it is best known because of his second son, whose interest in science was stimulated by his father's microscope.

In his early twenties Joseph Jackson Lister married Isabella Harris, youngest daughter of Mrs Isabella Harris, the widowed superintendent of a school which the Society of Friends maintained for its poorer members. The ageing John Lister turned over his flourishing wine-business to his son, who ran it competently, managing somehow to find time for his scientific work and his growing family as well.

Joseph was the Listers' fourth child, the 'middle one,' for there were to be seven children. The oldest was Mary, who was born in 1820, followed two years later by John. Then came Isabella Sophia, Joseph, William Henry, Arthur, and, in 1832, the baby, Jane. Joseph was born on April 5, 1827, at Upton House, a quaint Queen Anne mansion where the Listers had settled down after having lived for three years at Tokenhouse Yard, in the City, and four at Stoke Newington.

At that time Upton was a quiet country village, still far beyond the limits of Greater London, which was later to engulf it. The Eastern County Railway was not to be built until 1839, and visitors came to see the Listers, if they came at all, by coach or carriage or on horseback, along the winding lanes which led from the Romford road towards Plaistow. It was a pretty road through meadows and fields, bordered by a dozen or so comfortable houses and attractive gardens and lawns. It was not at all unusual to find that a deer had created havoc in one of the flower-beds, taking advantage of his safety from hunters, for this was a Quaker neighbourhood.

Although the Friends were no longer persecuted as they

had been in the past, they remained a clannish group, since the rules of the Society prohibited 'marrying out.' As they were more or less barred from the professions by their unwillingness to conform to the Established Church, as was required by the universities, they devoted themselves to business and trading, making an avocation of philanthropy if they were prosperous. One reason why the Listers had bought Upton House was because it adjourned the estate of Sam Gurney, the wealthy Quaker banker who had been Joseph Jackson Lister's friend since their boyhood days.

Sam Gurney's sister was Mrs Elizabeth Fry, who was to become famous as the originator of reforms among the female inmates of Newgate Prison, where conditions had been so bad that it was generally referred to as "that hell above ground." Her interest in the tragic lot of the insane led her to establish what was probably the first charity organization in England. Later, having visited Pastor Fliedner's Deaconess Hospital at Kaiserswerth, she returned with such enthusiasm that she persuaded her sister-in-law, Mrs Sam Gurney, to introduce into England the nursing sisterhood which was to be the inspiration of Florence Nightingale.

This was the atmosphere in which the Lister children were brought up. And yet there was plenty of gaiety and fun. Joseph Jackson Lister's boyhood, spent in London with parents who were old enough to be his grandparents and sisters a generation older than he, had been a quiet and lonely one. He was delighted to help make things as different as possible for his own children.

Upton House had plenty of room for them and their friends to play in, but they liked the outdoors better, for there were almost seventy acres of ground, offering them unlimited opportunities for a good time. A stream, excellent for skating or wading, was only a few hundred yards from their door. The gardens, which Isabella Lister loved, contained all kinds of flowers and shrubs, including some imported specimens which had crept over from the Gurney estate, and Epping Forest, which was near by, was made for minor excursions and picnics. Then, too, there were the Barking Marshes to encourage the collecting of specimens, which the children found particularly fascinating because they could be examined through their father's microscope.

Joseph Lister did well at the private Quaker schools which he attended, although, as his master at Hitchin reported, he was "full of spirits, which sometimes cause him to overstep the rules and bring him a little into disgrace." When he left Hitchin for Grove House, Tottenham, he became one of the top boys there, which pleased his mother a great deal, although she could not help hoping that it would not elate him too much. She need not have worried; none of the honours which Joseph Lister was to receive ever succeeded in turning his head in the slightest degree.

Although Joseph did well in the classics, he was particularly interested in botany and zoology. The subjects he chose for his papers—"The Similarity of Structure between a Monkey and a Man" and four essays on "The Human Structure—Osteology," for example—showed the direction of his interest. They were well written in a stiff, schoolboyish manner—his writing was always precise and formal—and illustrated with ink and water-colour drawings which were accurate and skilfully executed.

In his teens Joseph Lister developed a passion for dissecting, and his brothers and sisters frequently found it a little difficult to get him to join in their games in the holidays. But schooldays came to an end, and by the time Joseph left he had made up his mind about his career. He was going to be a doctor.

University College, in London was non-sectarian—some people for this referred to it as "the godless college"—and so Quakers were not barred from attending it. Joseph Lister entered in 1844, when he was seventeen, working first for his B.A. degree, since his father wanted him to have a good academic training, as long as they could afford it, before he entered the medical school. Though he passed his examinations with distinction, getting honours in classics and botany, he failed to win a scholarship or a gold medal. In 1847 he received his degree without honours.

Passing his college courses, which placed emphasis on memorizing and learning by rote, was easy for him, but he did not find it stimulating. He could understand why John Hunter, the great surgeon of the past century and his greatest hero, had protested against formal education—not entirely, as some people claimed, because he lacked it himself, but because he realized that it often prevented people from observing for themselves and frequently perpetuated mistakes which had been made in the past.

It shocked Joseph Lister to realize that physicians had studied and memorized Galen's works for centuries, until Vesalius, preparing a new edition in 1542, made the astonishing discovery that the organs which Galen described as human were really the quite different organs of sheep, goats, and other animals.

It was true that during the second century after Christ, when Galen had done his work, strictly enforced laws had made death the penalty for dissecting the human body, and the following generations of anatomists were no better off, since Christianity concentrated upon spiritual well-being and banned experiments which would contribute to physical health. Yet it seemed incredible to Lister, who was never content to accept anything blindly, that physicians should have perpetuated Galen's mistakes for fourteen hundred years.

It had taken a long time and a great deal of effort to legalize the dissection of the human body, which was so vital to the progress of medicine and surgery. Not until the Renaissance did the body's structure begin to receive much attention, and then the secrets of its construction were of more interest to artists like Leonardo da Vinci than to medical men, who were floundering about in a sea of scholasticism.

As the need to study anatomy became apparent the bodies of certain executed criminals were turned over to surgeons to dissect; in the middle of the sixteenth century one such body a year was assigned to the surgeons of Edinburgh. That was not nearly enough, and anatomists obtained bodies illegally, the law obligingly looking the other way. Public sentiment, however, was less lenient than the law, and mobs frequently took things into their own hands, attacking doctors and wrecking laboratories where dissections took place.

Still the illegal traffic in corpses continued until it became an organized system. When it was too much trouble to rob graves men like the notorious Burke and Hare provided corpses by the simple method of murder. These conditions were finally ended by the legalization of the use of certain bodies for dissection in 1832, when Great Britain passed the Anatomy Act, following on the heels of a similar measure in the United States.

Not only were medical students able to dissect the human body by the time Lister entered the medical school, but other important changes in medical education had also taken place. William Hunter, who was born in 1718, helped to establish London's first real medical school, and placed the teaching of anatomy and surgery on a firm foundation. His younger and even more famous brother, John, completed the revolution by founding experimental and surgical pathology and teaching surgery in such a way that a student was given a general view of the subject and its principles rather than simply instructions as to what to do in specific cases.

The apprenticeship system was being modified, that method of instruction whereby a student learned as much or as little as his mentor cared to teach him, which usually consisted of "much shrewdness, more humbug, and no science."

In order to get a degree under that system students had to pay approximately twenty guineas to 'walk the hospital' and observe hospital cases, frequently seeing next to nothing because of the large number of people who had paid for the same privilege. So lax had things become that students would impersonate one another at examinations, and sight-seers crowded the operating-theatre (where the spectacles were considered almost as exciting as those to be seen in the bear-pits) to such a degree that many a student became a doctor without having witnessed an operation except over the top of a sea of top hats.

About 1825 Thomas Wakley decided to expose the evils of this system and to campaign against them. He founded a medical journal called *The Lancet* for this purpose. He also wanted to eliminate another evil, the monopoly on medical discoveries which was held at that time by a clique of London doctors. His habit of sending reporters to lectures was sometimes so resented that fist fights resulted. John Abernethy, one of John Hunter's many famous pupils, was a kind man, but so shy, nervous, and irritable that he could scarcely endure the presence of reporters who scribbled down every word he said, and tried to outwit them by lecturing in pitch darkness.

Although Wakley may have been exasperating, his efforts, which were supported by other reformers, did bring results. By the time Lister entered the medical school a well-ordered system of teaching had been established at the University College. Professors had been appointed, and regular courses were given in medicine, surgery, chemistry, and other subjects, although a great deal still depended upon the student's ability to collect information in the wards during the hours he could spare from his chemistry laboratory and dissecting-room.

Good students could learn a great deal from watching the doctors on the wards. They learned how to take the pulse, timing it with a watch, a practice recently developed by Louis in Paris and by the Dublin school. The thermometer, however, was still a novelty with which they did not bother much. Percussion, or 'thumping,' was used a great deal as an aid to diagnosis, and auscultation, which had been discovered by Laënnec some thirty-five years before, was no longer considered a joke. Most medical students owned their own stethoscopes, which were modifications of Laënnec's *baton*, and were twelve inches long—just long enough to prevent fleas from jumping on to the physician from the patient's chest!

The old attitude towards surgeons and surgery was also undergoing a change. For centuries it had been a humble art, relegated to ignorant barbers, while medicine, which was considered a philosophy was something mysterious for the learned to debate about. A surgeon was literally one who worked with his hands, as the derivation of the word from the Greek *cheir*, or 'hand,' and *ergon*, or 'work,' suggests. Even Ambroise Paré, whose accomplishments were so great that he had been elevated from Barber Surgeon to the rank of Surgeon of the Long Robe—despite the fact that one of the qualifications for that position was the passing of an examination conducted entirely in Latin, a language with which he was totally unfamiliar—could scarcely have thought that surgery would some day be considered a profession.

As late as 1820 articles appeared on the Continent emphasizing the fact that doctors were entitled to more respect than surgeons, since they came from a higher social stratum. Laws were still in existence prohibiting surgeons from prescribing medicine for patients to take internally, even though there might be no doctor within many miles.

Gradually, however, the situation changed. People began to expect a surgeon to know more than simply how to cut. He must be a physician as well, and as such he was entitled to increased respect. As a rule he practised medicine as well as surgery, for specialization had not reached the stage where a surgeon could afford to ignore medical cases.

A few signs of the old attitude persisted. Surgeons were still referred to as 'Mr' rather than as 'Dr'; but this had gradually become an important title, and a doorplate announcing MR JONES became as impressive as the one which graced the door of DR SMITH. Lister's plate, when the time came for him to put it out, would have nothing on it but JOSEPH LISTER, for the Quakers used no titles, and even the servants, if they were members of the Society, called Lister, as he called them, 'Friend.'

Joseph Lister was in his first year at medical school when, on December 4, 1846, Robert Liston, who was teaching surgery at University College, decided to try out a method which, according to reports from the United States of America, had been successfully used to deaden pain during surgical operations.

For centuries men had been searching for ways to alleviate human suffering, particularly the excruciating torture of surgical operations. In ancient days the shamans of the Incas had put chewed coca-leaves, which contained cocaine, on wounds, and herbs were frequently employed, although they were known to produce a sleep from which there was no awakening. Laudanum, or tincture of opium, had been popular for a time, and in the early part of the nineteenth century morphine was obtained from opium. Occasionally patients stupefied themselves with alcohol before an operation, and some surgeons bled their patients to insensibility, particularly when they were setting dislocated joints. Even hypnotism and extreme cold had been tried, but none of these methods could be relied upon.

Ether, or sweet vitriol, had been discovered in the thirteenth century, and two hundred years later Paracelsus noticed that it made chickens sleepy. Many years later Humphry Davy, when he was only seventeen years old, experimented with nitrous oxide, which Joseph Priestley had discovered in 1772 and, since inhaling it made him gay and happy, christened it 'laughing gas.' Subsequently his assistant, Michael Faraday, discovered that ether could put people to sleep. None of these men, however, pursued his discoveries any further.

Henry Hill Hickman did. He was not interested in chemistry so much as in preventing pain, and he experimented until he was able to make animals insensible during operations. Only Larrey, Napoleon's beloved surgeon, was interested, but he could not prevail upon his colleagues to do anything about Hickman's ideas, and Hickman himself died at twenty-nine without having been able to help humanity as he had hoped. Ether and laughing gas came to be known simply as agents which would produce pleasant sensations akin to intoxication.

Among the many people who observed that participants in the newly fashionable 'ether frolics' used to bruise themselves without being conscious of any pain, was an American doctor, Crawford Williamson Long, of Georgia. He tried ether for an operation, and it worked, but he gave it up when the opposition it aroused threatened to ruin his practice.

A little later Dr Horace Wells, a dentist from Hartford, Connecticut, tried to introduce laughing gas for pulling teeth, but his demonstrations were unsuccessful. The first time he gave too little, and the patient bellowed with pain, and the second time he gave so much that the patient died. After that he abandoned his plans in despair.

His former partner, a man named William Thomas Green Morton, was more persevering. An ambitious young dentist, he was studying medicine in Boston while he continued to look for a pain-killer more effective than the apparently undependable nitrous oxide. He, too, knew that ether had a stupefying as well as intoxicating effect, and he tried it out with some success and many disappointments. Finally, without saying why he was interested, he consulted the chemist Charles Jackson, and discovered that he had been using impure ether. With a purer form of the drug, his experiments were uniformly successful.

The next thing was to get a reputable surgeon to try out his discovery. It was not easy, for so many men had made extravagant claims that people had grown sceptical. Finally John Collins Warren, chief surgeon at the Massachusetts General Hospital, was sufficiently impressed with Morton's conviction and intelligence to agree to make the test. But he was not too optimistic about it, and when Morton did not appear in the operating-room at the appointed time he almost began without him. Breathless, Morton arrived just as Dr Warren was picking up the knife, and the experiment proceeded after all.

The ether, which Morton had disguised with perfume and christened 'letheon,' was given to the patient to inhale, and after a moment Morton turned to Dr Warren and announced, "Your patient is ready, sir." The elderly surgeon proceed to remove a tumour from the patient's neck, and though the young man partially recovered consciousness before the operation was over he said that he had felt no pain. Turning to the interested spectators who filled the operating-room, Dr Warren announced, "Gentlemen, this is no humbug."

A little less than two months later the students at University College Hospital, London, watched Robert Liston operate, and gasped with excitement as the big, powerful, handsome surgeon cut into the body of a patient who lay strangely still. The operation over, Liston cried in his rough, irascible manner, "This Yankee dodge, gentlemen, beats mesmerism all hollow!"—and Joseph Lister felt a tremendous relief surge over him as he realized that patients need no longer suffer the tortures of an operation.

At last it had been found: something better than poppy or mandragora or cold or alcohol or mesmerism, something to numb the senses and to conquer pain.

This was the greatest triumph for surgery since the sixteenth century, when Ambroise Paré had solved the problem of bleeding by introducing the use of the ligature to tie off severed blood-vessels. Now the second great problem had been solved, the problem of pain. No longer need a surgeon work under tremendous strain on a suffering, struggling patient; no longer would people put off, through fear of pain, operations until they were too late and only hastened death.

Before anæsthetics—Oliver Wendell Holmes, who wanted "to have a hand in a great discovery," suggested that term for agents which produced insensibility, and it caught on—few operations except absolutely essential ones were performed: cutting for stone in the bladder, amputations, the repair of aneurysms—blood-filled sacs caused by the dilation of the walls of an artery—which might burst and cause a fatal hæmorrhage, and the removal of tumours such as those of the jaw and tongue, which prevented the patient from swallowing.

Speed had been the first consideration of the surgeon. The one question all patients asked was, "How long will it take?" and the man who had the reputation for operating rapidly was the one to whom they would go. The leading surgeons had trained themselves until their manual dexterity was miraculous. They sharpened pencils and shaved with their left hands in order to become ambidextrous. They devised all kinds of exercises to increase their speed and skill. Civiale, for example, used to go about the streets of Paris picking up nuts in his coat-tail pocket with a lithotrite, an instrument for crushing stones in the bladder. A good surgeon was a virtuoso of the knife.

Watching these surgeons operate was like trying to follow the tricks of a magician. Sir William Fergusson used to warn his audiences not to wink or they would miss the operation entirely, and one of the jokes which made the rounds concerned the surgeon who, with one sweep of his knife, cut off the limb of his patient, three fingers of his assistant, and the coat-tail of a spectator.

The facts themselves were astonishing enough. William Cheselden used to perform the lateral operation for bladder-stone in fifty-four seconds while James Syme could perform an amputation at the hip-joint in one minute flat. When performing an amputation Robert Liston would compress the artery with one hand while he used the knife with the other, which, since the patient was invariably struggling, was a feat that required remarkable manual strength. He used to claim that his left hand was so strong that it was better than any tourniquet.

Of course there were some absolutely essential operations which could not be performed rapidly, and they were dreaded by humane surgeons almost as much as by the patients themselves. Almost inevitably, however, many surgeons became callous, and it was no wonder that many people regarded them as though they were akin to hangmen.

Now, in 1846, all that was going to change, for surgeons would no longer have to cause suffering. Anæsthesia would make it possible for them to operate slowly, with careful attention to detail, to devise operations which would immeasurably benefit people who had previously regarded surgery as a last resource.

This was the prospect for the future rather than for the period immediately following the discovery of ether. While Lister was a medical student the operations he witnessed did not differ from pre-anæsthetic surgery except that the patient no longer suffered agonizing pain. Yet that alone made a tremendous difference to a sensitive young man like Joseph Lister, who might otherwise not have been able to become a surgeon. Before anæsthesia he would probably not have written home that "truly the practice of surgery is a glorious occupation."

CHAPTER II

Bachelor of Medicine

JOSEPH LISTER WAS NOT ONLY SENSITIVE but extremely shy: just how shy neither he nor anyone else had noticed until he went out into the world where Quakers were considered, at the least, very queer. At home he had been happy and gay, but although he still enjoyed himself at Upton, or when he was travelling with his family on holidays, he gradually grew more and more serious while he was at medical school. He liked his fellow students, and they liked him; yet he never became sufficiently intimate with them to make any close friends. There seemed to be a barrier between him and other people which prevented him from coming close to them, and made him seem quite aloof.

The fact that Lister was boarding with a high-minded, gloomy member of the Society contributed to his developing a depression which became intense following the death of his brother John.

It was a severe blow not only to Joseph, who had been devoted to his older brother, but to the entire family. Joseph Jackson Lister never completely recovered from it. After his eldest son died he gave up the research which had interested him for such a long time, and leading members of the scientific world gradually ceased to visit him at Upton House.

Not very long after John's death Joseph was stricken with smallpox. Fortunately the attack was not severe, and he recovered from it without scars, but he went back to work too soon and studied so hard that he broke down completely.

At his family's suggestion he took a long holiday from his classes, travelling in Ireland and trying to follow the advice which his father sent him in one of the long letters which passed between them.

The House where Lister was born

Agnes, Lady Lister
By courtesy of the Clarendon Press

IGNAZ PHILIPP SEMMELWEIS

James Syme

Sir James Young Simpson

Mrs Janet Porter—Head Nurse

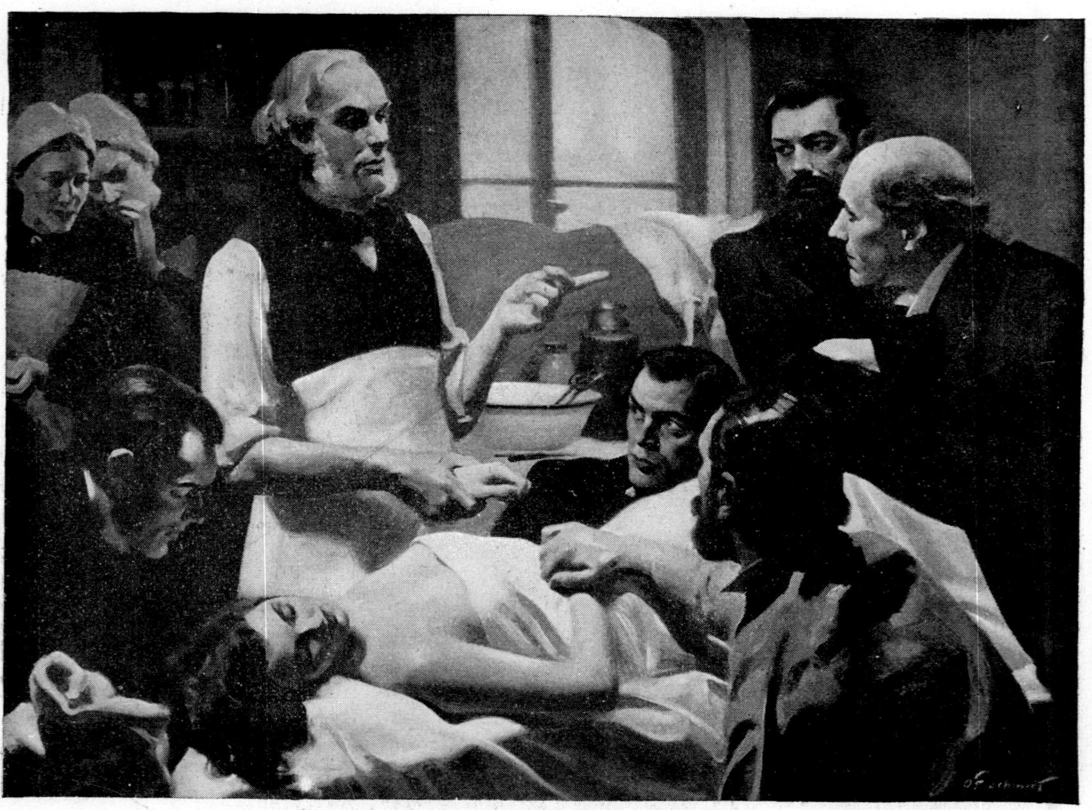

Lister operating

LOUIS PASTEUR

By courtesy of the W. B. Saunders Company

Joseph Lister, 1896

UPTON. 7mo. 1. 1848.

... The things that sometimes distress thee are really only the result of illness, following too close study . . . it is *indeed* a mistake, proceeding from *the same cause*, to believe thyself required to bear burthens on account of the states of others, while in fact, thou hast to suspend even the pursuit of thy own proper avocations. And believe us, my tenderly beloved son, that thy proper part now is to cherish a pious cheerful spirit, open to see and to enjoy the bounties and the beauties spread around us:—not to give way to turning thy thoughts upon thyself nor even at present to dwell long on serious things. . . .

Do not consider thyself required to answer this which contains some things I should not generally advert to.

Although he was not able to follow his father's advice completely, Joseph managed to shake off his depression and returned to his work, fully recovered, in the winter of 1848.

At this time he became a resident in the hospital, where the atmosphere was more cheerful than it had been in his boarding-house. He entered wholeheartedly into the activities, joining the debating and medical societies as well as winning high honours for himself and his college. But he was still unable to make any close friends. And he was continually depressed by the suffering and misery which, despite the introduction of anæsthetics, he saw on the surgical wards.

In those days patients hardly ever recovered uneventfully from operations. Emaciated, visibly sick, and in pain, they either died or fought their way slowly back to partial health. A surgeon in a large hospital seldom saw a wound healing by first intention—that is, cleanly, without inflammation or suppuration.

Putrefactive discharges accompanied by inflammation were regarded as inevitable after an operation. The wounds became swollen and painful, the patient feverish. If nothing worse than that happened the surgeon could congratulate himself or his lucky stars, and the wound would eventually be replaced by a thick, wide scar. This was the best surgeons could hope for. Convinced that "the impurities must be got out of the wound," they spoke of these discharges as "laudable pus" and referred to the process as "kindly suppuration."

Unfortunately the septic diseases frequently followed this process. As John Bell, the well-known Scots teacher and surgeon who died in 1820, put it, the suppuration often "went wrong," and "one foul sore or gangrenous limb, one unlucky fever, makes a whole hospital exhibit everywhere the same dismal scene."

Take, for example, the case of a boy named Joiner, belonging to the ship *Triumph*, whose picture Bell drew to illustrate his description. Joiner had entered the ward with a "slight and superficial wound, no bigger than the palm of his hand" and yet it

> became in two days as big as the crown of a hat. The whole skin of the thigh was destroyed, the muscles stripped of skin and fascia from the hip to the knee, the trochanter was laid almost bare, the hamstring muscles exposed to a considerable extent, and all the muscles of the thigh dissected in a manner no drawing can express.

Another boy from the *Triumph*,

> a lad by the name of Handling, who had at first but a slight wound of the thigh, had the cellular membrane in the course of a few days so destroyed that . . . you could have counted each muscle as in a dissection . . . for three nights he lost two or three pounds of blood each night; it would have been almost cruel to stop the hæmorrhage, had it been possible, so desperate was his situation; on the fourth day he died.

This rotting away of the flesh of people who were still alive was known as hospital gangrene. There were three other diseases, not counting tetanus, which hovered so constantly about surgical wards that they were called hospital diseases, or referred to simply as 'hospitalism.'

One of these was erysipelas, known also as St Anthony's fire because of the redness and burning sensation which accompanied it. Starting as a skin-infection, it spread to the tissues, attacking the membranes of the heart, lung, and brain. Accompanied by a high fever and rigors, or shivering fits, it was frequently fatal and extremely contagious. Most hospitals had erysipelas wards; while Lister was at the University College Hospital a patient with erysipelas was placed by mistake with the other surgical cases, and although he remained there only two hours it was long enough to infect the entire ward. The disease seemed to prefer certain periods of the year, and doctors bowed before its whims; at the Blockley Hospital, in Philadelphia, for example, no operations were performed during the 'erysipelas season,' which was said to last from the latter part of January until the first of March.

Pyæmia was the term applied to that form of hospital disease in which, it was presumed, septic clots or pus formed in the blood, causing abcesses and suppuration in various, often vital, parts of the body. Septicæmia referred to forms of blood-poisoning where there were no clots in the blood. Both of these diseases could result from even minor operations, and were associated with a high mortality. And, even worse, the patients who recovered were frequently invalids as well as cripples for the rest of their lives.

What was there to do when these hospital diseases struck? John Bell recommended amputation if the wound was on an extremity.

> The wan visage, the pale and flabby flesh, the hollow eyes and the prominent cheekbones . . . the long bony fingers and crooked nails, the quick, short breathing and small, piping voice, declare the last stage of hectic and debility; the natural powers are then sunk so low, the appetite for food and even the desire for life so entirely gone, that we would believe the patient past all help did we not know by experience that it is never almost too late to amputate.

But amputation was no guarantee that the whole dreadful story would not repeat itself, until the surgeon could amputate no further and the patient died.

And when gangrene became epidemic John Bell admitted complete defeat. "Then no operation dare be performed," he said, "and every cure stands still, every wound becomes a sore and every sore is apt to run into gangrene."

His advice in those circumstances was simple.

> Let [the surgeon] bear in mind that this is a hospital disease, that without the circle of the infected walls the men are safe; let him, therefore, hurry them out of this house of death. . . . let him lay them in a schoolroom, a church, on a dunghill or in a stable; let him carry them anywhere but to their graves.

No one knew just why a hospital should be a house of death, but there were plenty of explanations, the most popular of which was that miasmas, or gases, hovered about hospitals, entering the wounds and causing them to rot. Where these miasmas came from nobody could say. It was easy to lay the blame on something vague and general, like a 'cosmic tellurgic influence.'

Some surgeons thought that hospital diseases were caused by the action of oxygen, which set up fermentation in the juices of the wounds. John Eric Erichsen, whose dresser Joseph Lister became, did not agree with this theory, for, as he pointed out, there was just as much oxygen in the air in country homes, where wounds generally healed far better than they did in hospitals. In his opinion miasmas arose from the wounds themselves and, becoming concentrated in the air, caused septic diseases. He had even estimated the amount of miasmas which the atmosphere could hold without becoming overcharged. If there were more than seven patients with large wounds in an average-sized ward holding fourteen beds, the air would become saturated with dangerous gases and gangrene would result.

Lister was not entirely convinced. The first case which he attended as a dresser was one in which gangrene occurred, and it immediately aroused his interest in the subject.

There was an epidemic of gangrene in Erichsen's wards, and Joseph Lister helped him put the patients under chloroform, scrape away the sloughs, and cauterize the wounds afterwards with acid pernitrate of mercury. The fact that some of these patients recovered made Lister suspect that something *in* the wound, rather than a gas or evil atmosphere, had been burned away.

It must be a purely local poison, he thought, and got to work with his microscope, examining material from the gangrenous wounds. Carefully he sketched what he saw: "bodies of pretty uniform size" he wrote, "which I imagined might be the *materies morbi* in the shape of some kind of fungus."

He also sketched the corpuscles of pus in a case of pyæmia that followed the excision of a little boy's elbow, wondering at the "solid constituents" which he observed but could not identify.

The paper which he wrote on gangrene and one which advocated the use of the microscope (a controversial subject, as some doctors were afraid that the microscope would compete with clinical observation) showed the direction of his thoughts. Even in those days, when students accepted gangrene and other hospital diseases as inevitable, Lister tried to find out just what these diseases were and how they were caused.

In addition to Professor Thomas Graham, from whom he got a training in chemistry which was to be invaluable to him throughout his career, he was fortunate enough to study under Wharton Jones, the ophthalmologist, and William Sharpey, the father of modern physiology. Influenced by them and stimulated by his father's microscopical work, Lister made some experiments which were far above the level of even those exceptional students who attempted original research.

His first experiments were on the muscular tissues of the iris of the eye, and the way it dilated and contracted in order to regulate the size of the pupil.

Although the work was incomplete, as he was too busy with his examinations to "carry the inquiry further at present," it was considered important enough to be published in a leading microscopical journal.

A little later he investigated the tiny muscles in the skin whose involuntary contractions cause what we call goose-skin, verifying and adding to the observations which had previously been made by Kölliker in regard to the contraction of the small bundles of unstriped muscles which thrust up hair-follicles and depress the intermediate portions of skin. His method of preparing sections of the scalp were ingenious, his observations accurate, and his drawings excellent.

This paper, too, was considered worthy of publication. To his father's delight, it, along with the previous one, received attention and approval and was highly commended by important men, such as Joseph Jackson Lister's friend Sir Richard Owen, the zoologist.

Lister also conducted some original experiments on the flow of the lacteal fluid in the mesentery of the mouse, the results of which were not published for several years.

Because of these experiments his father and many of his acquaintances thought he would devote himself entirely to research. However, he possessed the "feeling heart," which he used to say was one of the prime requisites of a physician, and it inclined him in the direction of clinical surgery.

It was nine years since he had entered the University College of London, and he had what was considered an excellent medical education. In 1852, the year he received his M.B. degree, he was made a Fellow of the Royal College of Surgeons of England. He had served as house surgeon to Walshe and Erichsen, and all that was required to put the finishing touches to his training was a visit to some foreign clinics and doctors. After a short visit to the Continent he would return to London and settle down to a practice which, because of his education and ability and the connexions of his family, was bound to be a successful one. That, in general, was the course which Joseph Lister's future might be expected to take.

As a rule, the young doctor who was conscientious enough to feel he needed more experience before plunging into practice—or pretended to be, so that he could have a vacation before settling down to work—made a tour of the Continent, spending most of his time in Paris, which was still the leading medical centre. Although Germany, which placed its emphasis upon learning as opposed to observation, was beginning to attract many students, surgeons were still flocking to Paris, where Velpeau, Malgaigne, Magendie, and other prominent men still lived, and where the influence of Larrey, Dupuytren, and Lisfranc was still felt through the men whom they had recently trained.

But Professor Sharpey suggested that Joseph Lister should first go to Scotland instead.

"Edinburgh has a great deal to offer," he said. "I think it would be well worth your while to visit Syme's clinic there. There are two hundred surgical beds in the Infirmary, you know, and large, stimulating classes, with all the teaching grouped about one centre. And in addition there are private classes, like those Mr Syme used to offer at Minto House before he received the Chair at the University. Those classes keep the University teachers on their toes, and furnish excellent material for the University to draw upon.

"You won't find better operative procedures anywhere than those which Professor Syme has developed, and he's really a pioneer in the teaching of clinical surgery."

"It sounds wonderful, and I should like to go there for about a month," said Joseph, stammering a little as he added, "If you th-think he—I mean, I know my attitude towards certain matters of tradition is sometimes . . . well, questioning, to say the least."

"It is true that James Syme cannot brook opposition, even from his friends," William Sharpey admitted a trifle ruefully. But he was reassuring to the young man who was standing before him.

Joseph Lister was a very likeable person as well as an able one. Although he was fortunately entirely unaware of the fact he was also extremely handsome, with clear, regular features, plenty of brown hair, and a twinkle in his hazel eyes which counter-balanced his serious manner. Just under five feet eleven inches tall, he looked shorter, although he was quite slim. His co-ordination, which had always been good, was so excellent now that people were almost invariably struck with the easy, effortless way he walked and moved about his work.

Professor Sharpey knew what Joseph meant when he referred to his questioning attitude towards certain matters of tradition. It had disturbed the young man's instructors in the past, including Dr William B. Carpenter, the Professor of Medical Jurisprudence, who had on one occasion placed Lister's name low on the honours list.

What Joseph Lister did not realize, Professor Sharpey thought, was that it was a tribute to him that he should have been put on the honours list at all by a professor with whose theories he had disagreed. Not only that, but Dr Carpenter had felt impelled to write him a long letter of explanation, verging on apology, for not having given him a higher place. That was by no means routine procedure on the part of the University's rather autocratic professors.

But even more important, where James Syme was concerned, Joseph Lister possessed a certain quality—self-contained was the way Sharpey described it to himself for lack of a better word—which made it hard to picture his ever giving offence.

"I wouldn't worry if I were you," he said at last. "It takes two to make a quarrel, even with Professor Syme. And somehow I have a feeling that you and he will get along very well."

CHAPTER III

The Formidable

JOSEPH LISTER HAD GOOD REASON to wonder how he would get along with Mr Syme, who had reached his place as "the Napoleon of surgery" after a stormy journey studded with so many quarrels, lawsuits, and polemics that he was frequently called "the formidable."

No one, perhaps not even the principal parties concerned, knew what had caused Syme to quarrel with Robert Liston. Possibly it was jealousy, for Liston was the faster and more popular operator, though Syme's patients were apt to lose only a foot and Liston's, in similar circumstances, usually lost a leg. At any rate the quarrel was bitter enough while it lasted, and it lasted for fifteen years, during which time the two surgeons caused many disturbances, blocking each other's hospital appointments and those of their respective friends. However, they were reconciled in 1840 and remained on good terms until Liston's death, seven years later.

Syme's relationship with James Young Simpson, Professor of Midwifery in Edinburgh, was even stormier. For a time he had opposed Simpson's suggestion that chloroform be used as an anæsthetic, but he was finally won over, and a truce was established, during which Simpson went so far as to allow Syme to operate on him when he was in need of surgery. But the period of harmony was short-lived, and new and more intense quarrels soon began, with Syme publicly denouncing the "male midwife's vulgar insolence."

Shortly before Lister went to Edinburgh Syme had a try at London, having resigned his Chair to accept the position of Professor of Clinical Surgery there. He very soon discovered that he was expected to do more teaching than he had anticipated, and he also witnessed the bad behaviour of the students, who heckled one of his colleagues while the authorities made absolutely no effort to enforce discipline. Remarking that he did not care "to assume the onerous obligation of a double charge, in opposition to the hostility which would probably be transferred to me," he turned on his heel and went back to Edinburgh.

By disposition James Syme was a reserved and taciturn man. According to his friend Dr John Brown, he "never wastes a word, a drop of ink, or a drop of blood." He could, however, find plenty of words when he wanted to put some one in his place. Once, when the audience at an operation he was performing for cancer of the tongue—an operation which he had devised and which had been severely criticized —burst into spontaneous applause, he first pointed to a sign calling for SILENCE, and when that did not have any effect he remarked very pointedly, "Gentlemen, permit me to assure you that I have reached an age and a position in the profession when I care neither for censure nor commendation."

When a distinguished American physician asked him to autograph his photo he wrote on it the words "James Syme" and nothing more.

"Now please add 'Professor of Clinical Surgery in the University of Edinburgh,'" the visitor prompted him.

"No," he said.

More than a little surprised, the American asked him why not.

"That is supposed to be generally known," remarked Professor Syme.

In a preface to an American edition of Syme's works the editor, who was a great admirer of his, quoted from John Brown, who had called Syme "verax, capax, perspicax, sagax, efficax, and tenax," adding, "his mental eye is achromatic, and admits into the judging mind a pure white light . . . and he has the moral power, courage, and conscience to use and devote such an inestimable instrument aright."

Consulted about the book, Syme looked it over and remarked, "Your preface seems to me to be a little 'loud,' but I dare say it will do for your side of the Atlantic."

In addition to his quarrels with Liston and Simpson, Syme battled with Sir William Fergusson, Dr J. Argyle Robertson, Mr Lizars, and a host of others. Libel suits, 'open letters,' recriminations, and reluctant apologies flew thick and fast. That, however, was quite in the spirit of the times when doctors provided a good living for a number of lawyers, and the code of medical ethics did not restrain physicians from airing their grievances.

The Lancet was violently partisan. It used to publish facetious accounts of operations, referring to certain surgeons as "the owl," "the oyster," or "the fish," instead of by their proper names, and the books written by doctors whom Wakley disliked provided splendid opportunities for his bitter and sarcastic reviews. When a certain doctor, for whom the editor had no respect, moved his office, the notice appeared under the heading, "Metastasis of an Extraordinary Fungus."

Dupuytren, who was considered "the first of surgeons and the least of men," always referred to his rival Lisfranc in an uncouth and insulting manner, one of his favourite remarks being that, in "*une enveloppe de sanglier on portrait parfois un cœur de chien couchant,*" while Lisfranc countered by calling Dupuytren "*le brigand . . . l'infâme du bord de l'eau.*"

And at that, things had improved since the days of the Hunters. Even though John Hunter was suffering from angina pectoris, a disease which made any excitement dangerous—as he put it, "my life is at the mercy of the first rascal who chooses to annoy me"—it was simply impossible for him to control his temper, and he died after a fit of rage due to an argument.

Surgeons of pre-anæsthetic days were on the whole a short-tempered lot, usually irascible or brutal or both. It was not at all unusual for a doctor to order two bottles of whisky before an operation, one for his patient and one for himself. Few surgeons failed to show signs of the strain they laboured under as they repeatedly, almost constantly, caused intense suffering. When a particularly difficult operation was to be performed a patient would occasionally manage to break the straps which bound him to the operating-table, and bolt from the room before the surgeon could make the initial incision. Sometimes this would come as a relief to the surgeon, who had been dreading the ordeal almost as much as the patient, but as a rule he would find the laughter of the audience too much for his nerves and indulge in a fit of rage.

Despite their short tempers many of the leading surgeons were kind-hearted men. Although they belonged to the school of rough-and-ready surgery they were exceedingly able, and, in addition to being skilful operators, possessed an extensive knowledge of anatomy and devised operations which are still performed to-day. Here, and in the field of diagnosis, James Syme ranked with the best. He had originated many difficult operative procedures, including an amputation at the hip-joint which was a modification of Lisfranc's technique. Lisfranc had been famous for his thigh-operations, and, as Oliver Wendell Holmes remarked, probably mourned the passing of the Empire because the Guardsmen had such magnificent thighs to cut!

As a young man Syme had invented a means of rendering material waterproof, but as he failed to patent the process it was called 'mackintosh' after a subsequent inventor.

He was also famous for his phenomenal memory. In 1821 he removed a huge disfiguring tumour from the jaw of a youth, and after thirty-five years, when there appeared in his office a middle-aged man with a big beard completely covering the lower half of his face Syme called him by name immediately. Once he failed to recognize the face of a distinguished patient upon whom he had performed an operation for anal fistula, but the moment he saw the scar he remarked, "Oh, now I remember you, Mr ——" a story which, with variations, has been going the rounds up to the present day.

Syme had an excellent sense of fair play and was willing to go to a great deal of trouble to see that justice was done. He once procured a stay of execution for a criminal who had assaulted his wife when they were both drunk, for it was Syme's belief, based upon the post-mortem, that the woman had died of delirium tremens rather than from her injuries. He objected to the fixing of medical fees, saying that he wanted to render his services "available to all who required them," and though he had a wholesome respect for money he never toadied to his rich and distinguished patients. He seldom cultivated them socially or invited them to his home, where he preferred the company of his family and his assistants.

As Sharpey had anticipated, Syme took a liking to the young man who had come to him so highly recommended, and Lister was tremendously impressed with Syme, not only because of his ability as a surgeon and teacher and his knowledge of pathology, but as an individual.

Lister had planned to stay about a month in Edinburgh, but when Syme offered to make him his assistant at operations and a supernumerary clerk, or house-officer, as well, Lister jumped at the chance, for it was a non-resident post which would give him plenty of opportunity for research as well as surgical experience. Later, when Syme's resident house-surgeon was called away, Lister agreed to take his place temporarily. He held it for over a year, because, although it did not seem like an important position for a man with his educational background, it was actually an excellent one, as Syme established a relationship with him which was less like that which usually existed between a professor and his assistant than like that between two surgeons, with the older man acting as consultant. Lister had complete charge of all but a few exceptional cases, and these it was his responsibility to write up for publication, in addition to the weekly *résumés* of Syme's lectures which he prepared for *The Lancet.* Lister's acquaintances referred to him as a "super house-surgeon," and Syme's twelve dressers took to calling him "the Chief," a title which stuck to him the rest of his life.

Gradually Joseph Lister's depression disappeared. He was completely happy, not only in his work, but when he visited Syme's home, Millbank, where to his surprise he never felt in the least like a stranger. Perhaps it was because it reminded him of Upton House.

It was a beautiful estate, very much in the country, although it was only half an hour's walk from Syme's consulting-rooms in Princes Street. Like the Listers, Syme was devoted to botany; he had many greenhouses, including a pineapple-pit, a banana-house, and two hot-houses containing nothing but orchids. Lister liked nothing better than to be turned loose in the greenhouses or gardens, either by himself or with a member of the Syme family.

James Syme had been married twice. By his first wife he had nine children, some of whom died in early childhood, in about nine years. When Mrs Syme died following the birth of the last baby, he wrote to a friend, "What is to become of me and my poor children, God only knows!" A little over a year later, in 1841, he married Jemima Burn, a "quiet amiable, dark, comely damsel." Despite her devotion to her stepchildren, only Agnes and Lucy were still living when Joseph Lister arrived in Edinburgh. Five children were born to James and Jemima Syme, but only two of them, a girl and a boy, survived their childhood.

It was a warm and friendly family, and it took Joseph Lister a little while to realize that there was one member of it in particular who was responsible for the good times he had at Millbank and for the happiness to which he could scarcely become accustomed—Syme's oldest daughter, Agnes.

Lister had liked her from the first. He had been unable to make friends all the time he had been in college, and yet he had felt from the very beginning that he and Agnes Syme were friends. Everything was different; people did not seem to be so far away, and he was not even shy in the presence of Syme's many friends who came to Millbank. Something about Agnes seemed to change everything, and it was not only the fact that she was sweet and beautiful, contented and gay.

When the time came for him once more to leave Edinburgh the assistant surgeon at the Royal Infirmary died in the Crimean War, and, after thinking over the matter carefully and discussing it with James Syme, Lister decided to apply for the place. In the twenty pages which he painstakingly wrote his father explaining his reasons for wanting to stay in Edinburgh he did not mention Agnes Syme. He was certain that the desire to be near her had not influenced him in making up his mind.

Yet when he received the appointment and went to Paris for a month, to perfect his surgical technique on anatomical specimens, he realized how much it meant to be away from her, and he longed to be with her again.

Back in Edinburgh he discovered that she was still constantly on his mind. The only thing he could think about was Agnes, and as far as preparing for his lectures was concerned he realized that he might just as well be on holiday at Upton for all he was accomplishing. The time had obviously come for him to propose.

And so, with Syme's good wishes, he asked Agnes to marry him, and without hesitation she said, "Yes."

It was absolutely perfect except for one thing, and Agnes spoke of it to him some days later, when they were walking on the lawn waiting for dinner to be announced. It was the fact that his 'marrying outside the Society' must lead to his disownment by the Friends.

"I know it has caused the family some unhappiness," he said, walking slowly because it had been a hot day, and, even though the sun was almost setting, it was still very warm. "But they love me enough to understand. You know, one of the Society's epistles says that true religion stands neither in forms nor in the formal absence of forms. So when, or if, I do join your Church, it will be with a clear conscience and no regrets."

The following spring, in April 1856, they were married in simple, Scottish fashion in the Millbank drawing-room, which was decorated with their favourite flowers for the occasion. Then, for four months, they travelled about Europe, combining their honeymoon with trips to leading European medical men and centres which Lister had planned to visit almost four years before.

Unlike many woman Agnes Lister scarcely noticed the inconveniences connected with travelling, and, to Joseph's great joy, she seemed to enjoy it as much as he did. Like himself she lacked the British conviction that every one ought to speak English, and joined with him in the study of foreign languages.

Even happier than when they left Joseph and Agnes returned to Edinburgh in October, and, taking a house on Rutland Street, near Syme's consulting-rooms, they settled down to married life.

Lister's position as a lecturer and assistant surgeon at the Infirmary was a fairly responsible one. For long periods he had complete charge of Syme's wards, making rounds with the students and performing almost all the operations. Yet he managed to find time for research, and, with Agnes to help him, he intensified his work on several problems which had interested him for some time.

One of these was concerned with the coagulation of blood. Why should it clot when it was outside the body, or when a piece of inert material like a silver wire or glass rod was introduced into a blood-vessel, or when it came in contact with an inflamed vascular wall? Lister spent a great deal of time on this subject, returning to it frequently. His research removed many false conceptions, including that of Sir Benjamin Ward Richardson, who believed that blood clotted when it was shed because of the loss of ammonia. He also helped to accumulate a great deal of information which was of use in later work.

The other problem was not unrelated to the question of the coagulation of blood, and was concerned with an attempt to discover exactly what took place during the process known as inflammation.

This was the first stage of the dreadful post-operative syndrome which so frequently ended in death. It was a subject which, as a teacher of surgery, he would have to discuss constantly, and it bristled with so many theories that only a scientist would notice that it was practically bare of facts. It seemed to Lister that here, if anywhere, what he called "the beacon light of correct pathology" was badly needed.

His paper on the subject, in which he incorporated "An Inquiry regarding the Parts of the Nervous System which regulate the Contraction of the Arteries" and "On the Cutaneous Pigmentary System of the Frog," written earlier, was read on June 18, 1857, and published a little later. It was an important scientific contribution and laid the basis for all of his subsequent discoveries. He called it "An Essay on the Early States of Inflammation."

It seemed important to Lister to concentrate upon the early stages of inflammation, because so many complications set in later that the picture soon became confused. Besides, he always liked to start at the beginning. He wanted to know what happened in the simplest forms of inflammation, such as chafing or blistering, for example. He frequently got blisters on his hands when he was rowing. How, exactly, had they been caused? He poked at the reddened spot, he removed the loosened epidermis of a blister and pressed against the scarlet surface underneath, studying the action of the blood in the capillaries.

Because it was more practical and easier, and because the frog's reactions to inflammation in its early stages appeared to be similar to that of man, Lister began to concentrate on that animal, occasionally examining a bat's wing under the microscope to check the effects of irritation on the circulation of a mammal.

His experiments had to be carefully performed, as frogs could not long endure the warmth of human hands. He had to avoid touching the creatures as much as possible, keep them in wet, cold lint, and use a forceps to tie the threads he fastened to the toes so that he could spread them and observe the circulation in the web through the microscope. As a general rule the frogs were chloroformed, but he sometimes destroyed the sensibility and motion of the limbs by dividing the junction between the brain and the spinal cord with a tenotome, an operation easily and rapidly performed.

"Comparatively dull though we know sensibility to be in an animal so low in the scale as the frog," he wrote, "it is a comfort to feel that this method must be attended with exceedingly little pain. . . . The creature cannot feel the tying of the naturally sensitive toes or the subsequent dragging upon them."

Through the microscope he saw that irritation due to heat caused the blood-vessels to contract and the part to become pale. Next the vessels dilated and the part turned red, and then some of the blood in the most injured parts slowed down and coagulated. Redness occurred which persisted even when you pressed upon it. Then fluid passed from the blood-vessels through their walls and formed a blister.

His earlier work on skin-muscles and on the muscles of the iris helped him now to recognize similar contracting and dilating muscles in the blood-vessels. He saw that "blood flowing through an irritated part approaches . . . the condition which it assumes when separated from the tissues."

In his study of the pigmentation of the frog he noticed that prolonged irritation caused it to lose its power to change from dark to light, which was like that of the chameleon except that it resulted entirely from the effect of light upon the eyes rather than from direct contact of rays on an exposed part. He called this diminution of function a paralysis, or temporary death. Sharpey questioned his use of the term, but that was what it was. He wrote his father on December 7, 1857:

> I incline to write a few lines to thee this afternoon to tell thee of some observations I made a few days ago upon the frog, although I dare say thee may wish I could tell thee of having done with that animal for good and all. . . . Thee may remember that the observation of the *paralysis* of the pigment cells in the inflamed part was a very important portion of my labours; as it seemed to show certainly that, so far at least as *that* issue (*viz.*, of the pigment cells) was concerned, inflammation consisted in *paralysis* of tissue . . . but I felt very desirous, if possible, of showing in some simple way that agents which cause inflammation do really paralyse.

He then went on to describe the details of experiments he had made with chloroform vapour on the cilia of the frog's mouth, which produced a condition similar to that following irritation, which he had brought about by other means. His letter continued:

> Now there can be no question, I imagine, that the effect produced on the cilia in these cases is one of paralysis, and therefore we need not any longer scruple about speaking of the effect on the pigment cells as of a similar nature. . . .
>
> I believe my paper will be very much improved by remodelling the last section on the plan suggested by Dr Sharpey, adding this additional matter about the cilia. I am also not at all sorry to omit the historical sketch (which, if I had followed thy advice, would never have been written) and also the concluding remarks, which were much too hurriedly put together.

The experiments which he made to determine the effects of irritation were many and varied. He used mechanical violence, galvanic shock, dissection of the tissues, dry heat, warm water (100° F.), intense cold, caustic ammonia, a strong solution of common salt, carbonic acid, acetic acid, tincture of iodine, chloroform, oil of turpentine, tincture of cantharides, and croton oil. From these experiments he came to the conclusion that, while different tissues appeared to "differ in the facility with which they are affected by irritants," it seemed probable that "all the vital processes are liable to similar temporary arrest."

In his summary of the fourth section of this paper Lister stated that various physical and chemical agents produce

> a condition bordering upon loss of vitality . . . in which the tissues are, for the time being, incapacitated for discharging their wonted offices, though retaining the faculty of returning afterwards, by virtue of their own inherent powers, to their former state of activity, provided the irritation have not been too severe or protracted.

Wherever there was inflammatory congestion, he said, "the tissues of the affected parts have experienced to a proportionate extent a temporary impairment of functional activity or vital energy."

That was his discovery: irritation caused loss of vitality, and during this temporary death tissues were as helpless to defend themselves as dead cells would be. He was not yet fully prepared, however, to grasp all the implications of this discovery.

Lister had passed his thirtieth birthday at that time—getting on, as he put it, towards the half-way mark. Despite the fact that he could consider himself a success, having been made a Fellow of the Royal College of Surgeons of Edinburgh and enjoying all the advantages of a good hospital position and of being Syme's associate, he began to wonder whether he should not strike out on his own.

"After all," he told his wife, "it might be better for me if I did not have to depend on your father's guidance. And if we ever plan to leave Edinburgh we really ought to go before my practice gets too big."

"If you're referring to that one patient of yours," Agnes remarked, "I do not think you have very much to worry about on his account."

"Now, Agnes, no slighting remarks about the size of my practice! It is bound to grow, if only on account of your father. That is why I wondered whether we should not think about leaving before too much energy is spent trying to build it up."

"I don't know what to say, Joseph. If you want to go, why, then, I think we should."

"But how about you? Leaving your family and friends, and going to a strange city. . . ."

"You will be there, and I'm sure I can trust you to keep me busy enough so I won't have time to be lonely."

"You would never think my grandfather was an anti-slavery agitator, would you, the way I keep you grinding away eight or nine hours at a stretch?" he said. Although he knew how much Agnes enjoyed working with him, taking dictation or helping him in the laboratory, he could not help reproaching himself for what he considered his lack of consideration for her.

"At least you've never curtailed my night's sleep to only half an hour," said Agnes, "as you did yourself before your first lecture."

"That was stupid of me," he admitted, remembering how he had struggled to finish his speech, going to bed after two in the morning and getting up again at four, when it had seemed as though he had just dozed off. And even then, the last words had scarcely been written before he had to hop into the cab which was waiting to take him to High School Yards. "I've got to stop tempting fate by leaving things till the last minute, as Father tactfully pointed out."

"I'm sorry to say I haven't noticed any marked improvement as yet," she told him sternly. "I never thought we'd get that paper on Spontaneous Gangrene finished in time. You were dictating to me out of one corner of your mouth while you told Mr Craig how to prepare the sheep's feet out of the other—and plied him with quotations from the paper on Inflammation at the same time! And the excitement of getting you and the papers and the sheep's trotters off in the cab. . . . If you'd been one minute late they would have called your name in vain after Dr Haldane sat down. Really, Joseph——"

"Of course you are quite right," said Lister. "But shall we come back to the question of leaving Edinburgh?"

"If you think it will help in your career, Joseph——"

"Frankly, I do. But not so much as to make it worth the while if you are likely to miss Edinburgh very much."

"I don't think it will be any harder on me than it is on you," replied Agnes. "You are very fond of Edinburgh, aren't you?"

"I love it here," he said. "Our friends, and working with your father, to say nothing of the Infirmary—the patients, and even Mrs Lambert's soup—'It's a wee bit better to-day, sirs, than usual'—and Mrs Porter going through the wards asking, 'Wha' says ile, wha' says peels?'"

Agnes laughed at her husband's imitation of the two head nurses. "Do you remember what Mrs Porter said when you hurt yourself climbing with Dr Beddoe? 'Tha's wha' comes w' agoin' abawt wustlin' upo' Sawbath,' she said. When everybody knows you don't whistle!"

"Why, Agnes, I do believe you're still indignant about it!"

"Well, as long as you weren't really hurt, I'll forgive her. And I know I'll miss her, too, if we do leave Edinburgh. And I can see you want to. Have you said anything to Father yet?"

"It was your father who spoke to me," answered Lister. "You see, Mr James Lawrie's death has created an opening, and there's a possibility I might get the position. Your father—though he was kind enough to say he would miss my work as well as your company—thinks I might be appointed Regius Professor at the University of Glasgow."

"Glasgow!"

"Of course," went on Lister, "if I apply there is still a good chance that I shall not get the position. . . . After all, these Crown appointments——"

"Nonsense! Of course you'll get it," Agnes told him confidently.

She was right. After some months of delay the appointment came through in January 1860; and after a series of farewells to Edinburgh the Listers left for Glasgow, where they were to remain for a decade.

CHAPTER IV

The Killer in Glasgow

JOSEPH LISTER DESCENDED THE STEPS of the Glasgow Infirmary and paused for a moment in the hot August sun which penetrated the smoky haze hovering above the great industrial city. Standing in the courtyard, he faced the original infirmary buildings, with the four-storied fever hospital directly at his left; but he did not notice them, nor did he pay any attention to the foppish young student who sailed hurriedly by, high hat balanced precariously on his narrow head, crimson cloak stirring the still air. Lister sighed—the sigh of a man who had at last started on work which he had been anxious to undertake, but which was obviously going to be even more difficult than he had anticipated.

To-day he had taken command of his surgical wards in the Royal Infirmary. It was high time. He had been waiting for over a year, since the position of Regius Professor of Surgery did not, for some reason, carry a hospital appointment with it. Lister liked teaching, and his classes were the largest and probably the most enthusiastic in Great Britain. His articles on amputation and on anæsthesia, which he had prepared for Holmes's *System of Surgery*, had kept him busy enough. Yet he had missed clinical teaching and working with patients in the wards.

Now he was back with them again. Like each of the other three senior surgeons at the Royal Infirmary he had charge of three large wards—one for male accident cases, one for general female surgical cases, and a third, less important one in the old infirmary for chronic male cases. Formerly medical and surgical patients had all been treated in the same building, and even the fever hospital had been used, and was still used upon occasions, when the surgical wards were overcrowded.

The new building was well designed. It was four stories high over a basement, with each floor containing two large wards communicating with a central staircase, and several smaller apartments besides. The wards were spacious, with fireplaces, and windows on two sides to ensure proper ventilation. In fact, conditions were apparently close to ideal.

And yet—conditions were very bad. It was not only because Lister had been more or less out of touch with hospital practice that the suffering of the patients struck him in full force; actually, they were worse off than they had been in Edinburgh.

There he had assisted his father-in-law with some twenty thigh-amputations without losing a single patient: a remarkable record, for thigh-amputations were dangerous. Here, on the other hand, eight out of every ten amputations died. If there were more than a limited number of open wounds the entire ward would 'go bad,' so that the surgeons used to hope they would be able to fill their beds with simple fracture cases, however dull they might be for the students. Pyæmia almost always followed a compound fracture, and as Lister wrote later, "Experience has taught us that it was only in comparatively mild cases that it was justifiable to attempt to save the limb." Syme had been wondering for some time whether it might not be wise always to amputate if a compound fracture had occurred. Of course, septic diseases often followed amputations, but even so the patient had a better chance of surviving than he would if the operation were postponed until he had already undergone a siege of the disease.

There must be something he could do to improve conditions, Joseph Lister thought. If there were only some way he could help the children who lay, two or three in a bed, so weak and listless and patient that it almost broke his heart!

Before he had left Edinburgh he had decided that suppuration—the decomposition or putrefaction of the fluids in the wounds—far from being 'kindly,' was actually the cause of the septic diseases which frequently followed it, and that something from outside caused the suppuration. But what could it be?

Alphonse Guérin of Paris insisted that it was the air, and bandaged his wounds carefully to prevent air from reaching them. Lister still did not think that could be it. He had noticed, as John Hunter and Abernethy had before him, that in cases of traumatic pneumothorax, when a rib penetrated the lung, hospital diseases did not enter with the air. He had also observed that hospital gangrene seldom appeared in medical wards no matter how crowded they were—not even if there should be a patient with an open ulcer, which in a surgical ward, would almost certainly have become the site of a septic disease.

He was growing more and more convinced that it was not the air or noxious gases, but, as he had suspected at the University College, something *in* the wound which caused the damage. However, he could not work out what it could be.

Could it possibly be dirt? In his studies of inflammation in the frog he had observed through the microscope the way bits of dirt and foreign matter caused irritation. Perhaps if he kept dirt out of the patient's wounds it would do some good. At any rate, he did not see how it could do any harm, and cleanliness was certainly desirable in itself.

That was quite a revolutionary idea in 1861. True, there were some sensitive doctors who objected to what their hardy brothers called "that good old surgical stink," but they usually contented themselves with trying to cover it with clouds of eau-de-cologne. Very few doctors were brave enough to face the charge of being foppish, which was what their colleagues called them if they tried to keep clean.

Lack of cleanliness had become a part of the surgical tradition. Men who might be extremely fastidious in their private lives considered surgery a dirty business, and each surgeon kept a special frock-coat for operations and work on the wards. Since it was bound to become soiled immediately, he never bothered to have it cleaned; its very dirtiness advertised the fact that the surgeon operated a great deal and was a success. When at last the garment was so encrusted with blood and filth that it simply could not be used it was just thrown away. As for washing one's hands before an operation—why, that was what one did afterwards. Before operating it was considered enough to wipe one's hands on the greasy tails of the frock-coat.

That was the tradition. Sir Astley Cooper, who was one of the finest gentlemen of his day, in addition to being the surgeon who made John Hunter's teachings understandable, operated on King George IV himself with a knife which he borrowed from the pocket of a friend, and which he did not even bother to wipe. Robert Liston once cut a piece of wood out of the dirty operating-table, and used it to plug up a blood-vessel which he had severed. And the plug was probably no dirtier than the ligatures—bits of whipcord which had been threaded through the lapel button-hole of the surgeon or his assistant, and which had for months been taking on the general complexion of the rest of his coat.

That sort of thing seemed wrong to Joseph Lister, out of keeping with the improvements that were taking place. Splendid new operations were being devised now that the patient need no longer suffer during prolonged surgical procedure. The public was beginning to realize that a surgeon was not a butcher, and it was high time, thought Lister, that surgeons stopped looking the part.

He could not help wondering just how much of an improvement had actually taken place since the discovery of anæsthetics. The patient might be insensible during an operation, but he still had to face post-operative pain and frequently a lingering, agonizing death. The splendid new operations simply created new opportunities for septic diseases. It seemed to Joseph Lister that the operation was the least important part of surgery compared with the results, and he could not see eye to eye with the surgeons who, it was reported, would announce triumphantly, "The operation was a great success. The patient? Oh, the patient eventually died."

"We might as well go back to the old days," one of Syme's dressers had said to Lister in Edinburgh. "What's the use of progress, anyway? Three hundred years ago Paré introduced the ligature to tie off blood-vessels, and we still talk about what a great advance it was over the cruel method of searing with burning oil, and how he solved the problem of bleeding. Yet here we are, right back where Paré started from, trying to think out some way of preventing hæmorrhages after an operation. Only now it's several days after an operation, when the ligatures have rotted out and bleeding has begun again. I think the days of the magic healers were better. They treated the instrument that caused the injury and left the wounds alone, and goodness knows they couldn't have got worse results!"

"That's all true," Lister had admitted. "The solution of two great problems of surgery—the control of bleeding and of pain—aren't going to amount to a great deal until we solve the third problem, the problem of the healing of wounds."

"And the only way to solve that is to go back to the old days. Wounds heal much better in farms and country villages. It's in the big cities with their factories and large hospitals that you find the worst conditions. As Mr Erichsen—or was it Mr Cadge?—remarked, even if a hospital isn't the mother of pyæmia, it is most certainly its nurse; and the bigger the hospital, the better it nurses pyæmia along. Factories are what make people crowd into the cities, and so I say, back to handicrafts and the farms!"

"I don't know. It doesn't seem to me you solve anything by trying to turn back the clock—for one thing, because you never can succeed."

Now, in Glasgow, Lister wondered for the first time whether the clock might not be forced to turn back. Septic diseases were constantly on the increase. Would they not eventually threaten the development of industrial cities like Glasgow, where he could see for himself that conditions were worse than they had been in Edinburgh?

It was hard for artisans and craftsmen to reconcile themselves to the machinery which had forced them to become wage-earners. When they learned that, in addition to depriving them of their independence, factories threatened their lives—for diseases constantly swept through the crowded slums, and accidents sent them to almost certain death in the hospitals—when they fully recognized all this wouldn't they go back to their cottages and starve to death, if need be, on their clean moors?

I know I would, thought Joseph Lister.

But why should hospitals, built to help the needy, turn out to be a curse rather than a blessing? Why should so many evils invade a hospital?

"Good evening, Mr Lister."

Joseph Lister started, for he had been unaware of the presence of the man who addressed him, and whom he quickly identified as one of the directors of the Infirmary.

"Good evening, sir," he said in his low and pleasant voice, stammering a little over the 'g' and the 'd.' He still had trouble with certain consonants, especially when he was tired or embarrassed. It was so slight a stammer and so much a part of him that people were scarcely aware of it, although some of them would have missed it if it had suddenly disappeared.

"Surveying your new kingdom, I presume?"

Lister smiled. Although he looked young for his age, the little fans of wrinkles at the corners of his eyes had grown quite pronounced. "And meeting the new friends whom it will be my privilege to serve," he said.

"Fine building, isn't it? Brand-new, too . . . but then, you know that. The wing must have been finished at just about the time you arrived in our city. We're proud of that building, sir."

"It's a fine structure, sir," Lister agreed, tactfully refraining from mentioning the fact that there were certain disadvantages to it which could, and should, have been foreseen.

For one thing, it was too close to the fever hospital; and for another there was a paupers' graveyard in the vicinity, where it was estimated that five thousand bodies had been buried. If a noxious effluvium or miasma had anything to do with hospital diseases this certainly was no place to erect a new surgical wing.

"It cost a pretty penny, too," the director continued. "I trust you'll keep that in mind and hold the expenses down as well as you can. I'm sure you'll take no offence where none is intended, but we feel newcomers are apt to be a bit reckless with the benefactors' money, especially in little things. And many a mickle makes a muckle, as the saying goes."

Lister's heart sank. "Little things" would mean soap and towels and scrubbing-brushes, so he was certain to meet with opposition when he tried to clean up the wards. If only he could make the directors realize that cleanliness would not merely mean comfort but might even save lives!

"I believe, sir, that we can save money if we can reduce the length of time which patients have to spend in the Infirmary. As you said, little things mount up, and even a day here and there would be quite a bit in a year's time, overcrowded as we are. Now, in Edinburgh I notice that cleanliness encourages the speedy recovery of those patients God wills should survive."

"Yes, indeed; yes, indeed," said the older man absentmindedly. "Get 'em out as fast as you can. We've little enough space. Wouldn't you think they'd be more careful! The way they get injured in the factories and on the streets, you'd think we had nothing to do but take care of 'em! Well, that's the poorer classes for you. We shouldn't have poorer classes if they were careful and thrifty. What was I saying? Oh, yes . . . about cleanliness. Let's not overdo that, either;

some of these people have never been clean in all their lives, and it won't mean anything to 'em. Between you and me, sir—the shock might even give 'em a relapse! Now, don't take it too seriously; it's nothing you need concern yourself about. As some famous surgeon put it, a surgeon is like a husbandman. Once he's closed the wound he's like the farmer who's sown his seed, and can only wait for what the harvest will bring. It's out of his hands entirely."

Joseph Lister glanced at his hands, which were square and strong, with short, broad-pointed finger-tips. Unless one noticed his hands one might overlook the streak of obstinacy in a nature which seemed to be all gentleness and good humour.

"Out of my hands, sir," he said, "if God wills."

It was not until later that the older man wondered why Lister's answer had sounded somehow like a contradiction. Setting his thin lips so firmly that they almost disappeared, he wondered whether they would have trouble with the Englishman. Probably not. Priding himself on his knowledge of human nature, the director decided that Mr Lister might have some foolish, extravagant notions, but he obviously lacked the pugnacity to cause much of a stir either in the Infirmary or in the world.

"You must not take your new responsibilities *too* seriously," Agnes cautioned her husband one evening, soon after he had started working in the Infirmary. "I mean, if you keep on working so hard you simply won't be able to do your best work!"

"You have me there! It's hard not to, when there's so much to be done; and yet, with a problem of this kind it's very important to keep your eye on the wood so that you won't get lost among the trees. This is a very broad problem, you know—as broad as vitality, or life itself."

Agnes shivered. "You make it sound awesome, Joseph. Like . . . oh, like Dr Faustus, trying to solve the mysteries of life and death."

"That should not frighten you, Agnes. After all, you once spent several days in heaven yourself, and have worn the mark of your celestial visit ever since," he said, reminding her of Dr Brown's remarks at their wedding. He spoke jokingly, but in his heart he quite agreed that there was something 'other-worldly' about her loveliness.

"Now, Joseph, just because I was unconscious once for a few days when I was a little girl! You know how Dr Brown romanticizes; it's his literary privilege. You took exception yourself to his using the word 'beauty' in connexion with Ailie's fever after her operation."

"I certainly did! I can't see anything beautiful about any of the hospital diseases. They're all horrible to me! And yet . . . it's a beautiful story all the same."

"I know. Just a poor old woman who has an operation and dies. . . . But he's made you see how lovely she is to her husband, and how much they love each other. Somehow it makes me think of us."

"I think every surgeon ought to read that story once a year, so that he'll be kind to his patients . . . so that he'll think, she may be only a poor old woman, but she's not a *case*, for some one may love her the way Ailie was loved. I don't see how anyone can read that story without resolving to do everything in his power to get rid of hospital diseases once and for all! They're not acts of God—they're something we surgeons have got to conquer! I know it's a herculean task, and yet it can be done. . . . I know it can be done."

"Of course it can—and you're the one who's going to do it!"

"Come, now, you know I haven't any brilliant talent. But perhaps I can make up for it by perseverance. Certainly I love surgery enough, if that's any indication of being adapted to it. But as for my wiping out hospitalism—that's a pretty tall order. Whoever solves those problems is going to win undying fame."

"And wouldn't that embarrass you!"

"I don't think so, my dear," he answered, "because it

would be my work, and not me as an individual, that would be immortalized."

"We can certainly trust you to do your best to keep it impersonal."

"Well, I really do think a man's public life ought to be his scientific work. And much more interesting than his private life, if you ask me. Wouldn't you much rather read about *how* hospital diseases were wiped out than what colour eyes the surgeon had and what he said to his wife at the breakfast-table?"

"Yes, dear. Especially as I know that they are hazel and that he said, 'Darling, am I late again?' But seriously, you don't have to convince me. I can't imagine anything more exciting than reading about the solution of such a mystery. It would be like the story of the dreadful criminal, and how he was exposed and brought to justice at last."

"That's just it—tracking down a clever and relentless murderer and putting an end to his crimes. I'm afraid I met him again to-day . . . and he was wearing one of his most innocent disguises."

That morning two little boys had been brought into his ward—children who had been run over while their parents were at work and they were playing in the crowded streets. The older boy had been hurled against the wall of a house, which had stunned him, broken an arm, and bruised him severely. Lister had given him a whiff of chloroform while he set the bone, and the lad had fallen into an uneasy sleep, exhausted from the pain and the shock of his injuries, the bruises about his face and shoulders already turning into great dark welts.

"Is Jock hurt bad?" the other little victim asked. He too had had a whiff of chloroform while his leg was being set, after which he had immediately taken up his fight to get out of what he referred to as the "pest-house." Not much over four years old, he made Joseph Lister think of a sparrow, a game little street-sparrow with bright dark eyes.

"Jock will be all right, lad," he promised.

Now, at home with his wife, Lister wondered whether he had done the right thing, whether it would not have been better if he had let Andy leave the hospital. For Jock, he was certain, would be all right, but Andy—Andy, who was so strong and full of fight—had a compound fracture. The bone had broken through the skin, leaving an opening for the arrows of the murderer—the killer who stalked the hospitals. Andy might have been safer in his squalid home.

"I really don't know what I should have done," he said to Agnes, after he had told her about the boys.

"You couldn't send the poor baby home, with his parents out all day and no one to take care of him. If only you could have brought him here for me to look after."

"I thought of that, but it wouldn't have been acceptable to the authorities. They think me far too critical of the Infirmary as it is."

"And then you have no way of knowing whether he really would be better off."

"That's just it! If I could only get a clue as to who the killer is, and how he works! What's the use of bolting doors against him, when perhaps he comes down the chimney? If I could only find out why a compound fracture decays, when a simple one, even when accompanied by far more serious bruises, does not! Of course it's the fact that the skin is broken . . . but what can it be that creeps in through the open door? If only I could find that out, and not have to watch helplessly while another little boy goes down into the Valley of the Shadow."

Agnes laid her hand on her husband's arm, and both of them thought: If he were our boy! She sighed, and he said quickly:

"It hasn't been so very long, my dear. Why, one of the old ladies was talking about us the other day—of course she had no idea I was listening—and she said Mr Lister must be fresh from his honeymoon, for people who have seen them say they act like bride and bridegroom."

"And we probably always shall," Agnes said; but she

could not help thinking that five years was a long time to wait for a baby, and it was hard to avoid wondering whether one would ever come. Joseph would make such a wonderful father, and he loved children so! And yet, she thought, it would be something if he could help to save the lives of other children, so that people who had been blessed with babies would not be robbed of them so cruelly.

Aloud she said, "Wouldn't you like to dictate to me for a while? If you put down everything you're thinking it might help to provide a clue as to why compound fractures are so much more dangerous than simple ones. And, as you've said, once you've found that out you'll be much nearer to answering the whole question of hospitalism."

CHAPTER V

The Tragic Hungarian

THAT, OF COURSE, WAS THE PROBLEM in a nutshell—the difference between simple and compound fractures. Jock, whose injuries were severe, was almost certain to make an uneventful recovery, while Andy, who had got off with a broken leg, was probably in for a siege of illness and the loss of a limb. Why should that inch-long wound in his skinny leg, through which the broken end of the bone protruded like the broken bone of a bird, be an open door for disease and death? Joseph Lister kept asking that question over and over again, for if he could find the answer he would be on the right road at last.

Although he never lost sight of the problem as a whole Lister realized that finding the answer to an apparently simple question could furnish the key to unlock a major mystery. Sometimes it was not even necessary to understand exactly how it worked, if one could try the key and discover that it fitted.

Take Jenner and vaccination, for example. Edward Jenner was by no means the first person to notice that English dairymaids had beautiful complexions, unmarred by the horrid smallpox marks which elegant court ladies tried in vain to conceal. Gloucestershire dairymen knew that if one caught a certain disease from which cows suffered one would get a few sores on the hands and arms—nothing serious—and then one would be safe even during a severe epidemic of smallpox. Jenner wondered why. Was it really true, and if so, what did it mean? He went to his teacher, John Hunter, and asked him about it, and his characteristic answer was:

"Don't think; try."

So Jenner tried. Variolation, or inoculation with material from a person suffering with smallpox, made it possible for him to test his theory.

Variolation had been popular in England since 1722, when it had been used on the royal children at the suggestion of Lady Mary Wortley Montagu, who had learned about the custom in the Orient. The purpose of variolation was to enable people deliberately to 'take the pox' in a comparatively mild form and under the best possible conditions for them. It had been observed that the disease varied in intensity; certain epidemics were much less dangerous than others which were accompanied by an extremely high mortality and great disfigurement. Well-to-do people went to elegant sanatoriums to 'enjoy' a light case and put an end to the fear which hung over every one who had not had the disease.

In this way the ravages of smallpox had been somewhat checked among the upper classes, although working people could seldom afford the time or money deliberately to catch a disease which might conceivably pass them by. And it was all on a hit-or-miss basis, as sometimes people got blood-poisoning along with the pox, and, more frequently, variolation without isolation brought about new epidemics.

Variolation provided Jenner with a means of testing what might turn out to be only an old wives' tale. He tried it on some people who had suffered from what he called variola vaccina, or cowpox, and found that the inoculation did not take. None of them had even a mild case of smallpox as a result.

From there it was only a step to injecting material from a diseased cow into a person in order to give him the cowpox, and following that up with an inoculation of smallpox. In May 1796 Jenner tried it on an eight-year-old boy, and in July inoculated him with smallpox. The child remained well. Vaccination, so named because it employed material taken from a *vacca*, or cow, was born.

It met with a great deal of resistance, but it caught on and succeeded in bringing under control a disease which had been so dangerous that mothers did not even 'count' their children until they had survived it.

There was another doctor who, like Jenner, asked himself a question, and it was very similar to the one that Joseph Lister was asking now: "Why should these people die, while those do not?" Ignaz Philipp Semmelweis asked it in relation to puerperal fever, and his answer would have been extremely helpful to Lister, for, as John Bell had written, "Ulcer and gangrene is in an hospital what puerperal fever is in a lying-in ward."

Strangely enough, Lister did not learn of Semmelweis's work for many years, although he must have come close to hearing about it on several occasions.

In 1848 Dr James Simpson had received a letter about Semmelweis's discovery, but he failed to understand its significance and opposed it, perhaps because he was so occupied with the problem of anæsthesia in childbirth. Several years later, after a visit from one of Semmelweis's friends, Simpson reversed his position, but because of the precarious state of his relationship with James Syme he probably failed to discuss it with him. At any rate, it did not get to Joseph Lister's ears.

Lister must have come even closer to hearing about Semmelweis in 1856, when he and Agnes went to Vienna on their honeymoon, which was also a tour of the medical centres of the Continent. There they were entertained by Professor Rokitansky, Dean of the medical faculty and Rector of the University of Vienna. Rokitansky, one of the greatest pathologists of his time, was helping to make Vienna the medical centre of the world, as Salerno, Padua, Montpellier, Bologna, Leyden, and other cities had been at various times. He was credited with having performed 30,000 autopsies, and Lister, who spent over three hours in his museum looking at his specimens, wrote home that the experience was the "best of all as yet."

Professor Rokitansky had visited Joseph Jackson Lister at Upton House in 1842, where, he said, he had been very much impressed by Joseph's two older sisters, although he did not remember Joseph at all.

"That is not surprising," Lister assured him. "Mary and B.—my sisters—were fine girls, and I was absolutely nothing in those days!"

It was quite a feast to which the Rokitanskys invited the young couple, who, knowing that the Viennese had dinner in the middle of the day, had expected a light meal. Agnes described it to Joseph's parents in detail:

> To begin with, a dish of powerfully salted ham, cut in slices, was handed round. Then followed roast goose accompanied by curiously prepared potatoes and French beans dressed in something *very* sour. Lastly came cheese and cucumber. Rye bread and beer formed a not inconspicuous part of the repast. The beer was put on the table in immense glass *jugs* and drunk out of mugs of similar ware, smaller of course though still very large.

After such a meal it was no wonder that Professor Rokitansky did not feel like talking about the young Hungarian revolutionary who had left Vienna so abruptly, without a word even to his friends, and who, half a dozen years later, was doubtless still being watched by the Austrian police in Budapest. Semmelweis was too depressing a person to talk about to a young couple on their honeymoon.

Ignaz Semmelweis had not always been a depressing figure. In 1846, when he was made assistant to Professor Klein in the First Section of the Lying-in Hospital of Vienna, he was a strong, vigorous young man, prematurely bald at twenty-eight, with a florid complexion, industrious and rather excitable, but so frank and cheerful and smiling that it would have been hard to imagine he would ever be referred to as "the saddest figure in modern medicine."

The Lying-in Hospital was divided into two sections, for no reason except that the enemies of the professor in charge of midwifery had got tired of waiting for him to resign or die, and had finally hit upon the idea of splitting the department in two, so that there could be two professors and two heads.

Professor Klein was the head of the first section, in which the students were taught, and he was a tedious bore, supremely indifferent to the fact that far more women died in childbirth in this than in the other section.

Semmelweis was far from indifferent. Like Joseph Lister he felt a personal responsibility for his patients, and he kept asking himself why they should die when the others did not. There must be some way to bring the mortality in his section down at least to the level of the other one; for if Professor Klein ignored the difference between the two sections, the patients most certainly did not. On bended knees women would beg not to be sent to the wards where they were so apt to die.

How did these wards differ from the other ones? Many doctors had looked for an answer, but, like some of Lister's colleagues, they were searching for excuses rather than for reasons.

The 'bad' section, they decided, had a high mortality because it differed in many ways from the other one. In the first place, it was the ward where the poorest and most unfortunate women had their babies, and since they were often immoral, it was only natural that God should take less interest in them. Of course, that did not entirely explain why, if a highly moral woman got into the wrong ward by mistake, she was just as apt to die as one of her less worthy sisters.

There were plenty of other reasons. In the first section students helped to deliver the babies, while in the other midwives were in attendance. Was it not natural for women to succumb easily to disease after such a shock to their modesty? Besides, some of the students were rough—the foreign ones, of course, not the native Viennese—and that might account for a great many injuries. Acting on this theory, the authorities tried excluding the foreign students from the wards, but it did not seem to do any good.

Another possibility: the priest had to pass through the first section whenever he administered the last rites to a dying woman, and he was preceded by a boy ringing a bell. Perhaps it was because their sleep was disturbed in so depressing a manner that so many of these women in the first section sickened and died.

Obligingly the priest co-operated with the doctors. The bell was stilled, and the poor mothers were no longer awakened in the night. But they died just the same.

These were only some of the reasons advanced to explain the difference between the two wards. There were so many of them that it was worse, Semmelweis believed, than having none at all. Everything was confusion, and "only the great number of the dead was an undoubted reality," he said. And he determined to discover how much these so-called differences really meant.

Methodically, systematically, he prepared tables and statistics comparing the two sections, throwing a spotlight on everything that had been blamed, including even diet, ventilation, treatment, and laundry. He discovered a number of interesting facts. For example, women who were in labour for a long time in the first section almost invariably sickened and died, although as a rule they were having their first babies and were younger and stronger than the average patient. Such women did very well in the second section. Even mothers who got to the hospital too late, having given birth to their children in the street, did better in Semmelweis's ward than the young women having their first babies.

Another thing he discovered was that whole rows of his patients went down with puerperal fever, whereas in the other section cases were usually scattered, appearing only here and there. These, and many additional facts, were revealed by what one doctor referred to as "the annihilating force of the statistics of Semmelweis."

When his tables and charts were finished Semmelweis came at last to the conclusion that "the high mortality in the first obstetric clinic was the result of injurious influences originating and operating within the bounds of the first clinic itself." It was not fear, it was not ventilation, it was not a whimsical cosmic telepathic influence; it was something originating in the clinic itself.

What it was Semmelweis discovered by chance, at just the time that a young French chemist named Louis Pasteur was writing, "In the field of science chance only favours the mind that is prepared."

Annoyed by all the commotion Semmelweis was stirring up, Professor Klein obstructed his work whenever he could, and when the time came for appointments he failed to promote him, letting him stay on as provisional assistant for two more years. It was a disappointment to Semmelweis, but it also gave him an opportunity for a vacation which he badly needed, so he went off with a friend to Venice to rest.

While he was away his friend Kolletschka died in Vienna of blood-poisoning, as the result of a small cut made on his hand by a careless student who was helping him perform an autopsy. Being a scientist, Semmelweis read the report of the post-mortem performed upon his friend.

"I was instantly struck," he said, "by the close resemblance of the malady from which Kolletschka died to that from which I had seen countless women perish after childbirth."

Kolletschka had died as a result of getting some decomposed material from a dead body into his system. The poor mothers . . .

Why, that was the answer! The students who examined them came straight from the autopsy room, which, to save their time, was situated next to the lying-in ward. True, the students usually washed their hands before examining their patients, but it had required only the tiniest amount of decayed material, entering the little cut on Kolletschka's hand, to cause his death. The quantity which students carried under their finger-nails would be more than enough to do the damage.

That was why women who were a long time in labour, and were examined repeatedly, usually died, while mothers whose babies were born in the street were so much better off.

That was why the women in the second section, where they were attended by midwives who did no dissecting, stood a much better chance of recovering. Semmelweis's statistics had even shown that during vacation time, when the students were away, the mortality had dropped.

Yes, it was the students—not because there were foreigners among them, or because their presence shocked the modesty of their patients, but because they brought death with them from the dissecting-room.

It would be easy to discover whether he was right, and to stop the slaughter for which he had been partly responsible. "I blame myself," he said, "and others who, when we knew no better than to examine parturient women with hands smelling of the dissecting-room, caused so many deaths." Those unusually fleshy and remarkably dexterous hands of his—how often they must have brought death when they had tried to help a new life come into the world!

Scrub your hands, he said, when you have been working on dead bodies; scrub them until there is no particle left beneath the finger-nails, no trace of odour left, rinse them in a solution of chlorinated lime—and then examine your patients.

The students and the other doctors rather reluctantly humoured him. Immediately the mortality dropped.

There was one setback. A woman with cancer of the uterus had a baby, and all the patients who were examined after her went down with puerperal fever. Semmelweis quickly found the handle with which to turn this defeat into its opposite. Cancerous material was evidently just as dangerous as material from a dead body, so hands should be washed after each examination, and not only after one left the dissecting-room.

Now what did the statistics show? In May 1847 there had been a mortality of over 12 per cent.; during the next seven months the average dropped to 3 per cent., and during 1848 it went as low as 1·27 per cent. For the first time since the two divisions had been separated it was lower than in the second section. There were actually two months when not a single death occurred.

Not only Rokitansky, but Skoda the diagnostician and Hebra the Professor of Dermatology were very much impressed. With the backing of these three leading doctors the way should have been smooth for the acceptance of Semmelweis's discovery. But it was not. Skoda had had his own troubles in the past. His continual thumping of chests was, according to his enemies, annoying to the patients, and they had him transferred to the lunatic asylum, where he could thump to his heart's content. Skoda did not take that lying down, but fought his way back to the position to which he was entitled, making new enemies on the way. One of them was Professor Klein. When Skoda started championing Semmelweis Klein went over from fairly passive to decidedly active hostility.

Then came the Revolution. It was 1848, the time when, as Carlyle put it, "The kings all made haste to go. . . . In city after city, street barricades are piled. . . . From end to end of Europe democracy has blazed up explosive, much higher, more irresistible and less resisted than ever before."

Ignaz Philipp Semmelweis was a Hungarian in everything but his German name. He had been born in Budapest, and always spoke with a Hungarian accent. He never had his photograph taken except in Hungarian dress. Along with the rest of his family he was an ardent patriot, and took an active part in the revolution which he thought would free his country from the Austrian yoke.

Full of enthusiasm, he enlisted in the "Academic Legion" and went to join the Hungarian troops advancing upon Vienna under Kossuth. However, they were forced by superior Imperial forces to retire. Gradually the Revolution petered out, and democracy failed to establish itself in central Europe.

Now it was Professor Klein's turn. A reactionary, he had been infuriated by Semmelweis during the days when the Hungarian had gone about the wards flaunting the plumed hat of his Legion uniform in one hand while he carried his forceps in the other. Semmelweis had even startled the Hebras, who were democrats themselves, by delivering the good Frau of her baby while wearing his revolutionary uniform. It was easy as well as logical for Klein to see to it that Semmelweis did not get the appointment to which he was entitled.

In February 1850 Semmelweis petitioned for the second time for recognition as Privat-Dozent . . . and was kept waiting for an answer until October, at which time he was recommended as "Privat-Dozent for theoretic midwifery, with restriction to the use of the phantom in teaching." This was not only an insult to Semmelweis, for teachers were badly needed, but an effective means of preventing him from doing any worth-while work, as there was very little he could accomplish, especially in connexion with his discovery, if he were kept from the patients and limited to demonstrating upon a dummy.

Convinced that he could not get anywhere in reactionary Vienna, Semmelweis left without a word to his friends, and so hurt and angered Skoda very much. He returned to Budapest, which, like his own family, had been ruined by the defeat of the Revolution. His parents were dead, two of his brothers were refugees, the family money was gone, and, worst of all, Hungary was a conquered nation under absolute administration from Vienna, enduring a state of siege which lasted almost six years. Police spies were everywhere, and for a time it was almost impossible for him even to engage in scientific work.

After a period of enforced stagnation Semmelweis set to work in the obstetrical division of St Rochus Hospital, where his enthusiasm began to soar again as he managed to cut the death-rate down. But once more he met with opposition, and some of it was from important people. Even Rudolf Virchow, the great pathologist, who was just as radical in his politics as the young Hungarian—he had been getting into trouble with the reactionaries in Berlin at the same time that Semmelweis was defending the Revolution in Vienna —failed to understand the importance of Semmelweis's discovery. He referred to him as "*der Kerl der speculiert*," and not until 1864, when it was too late, did he realize that Semmelweis had not been speculating at all.

Although Semmelweis had an "inborn dislike for anything that can be called writing"—and an almost equal distaste for addressing medical societies—he realized that there was nothing to do but put his theory, with all the conclusive evidence to support it, into a book. In 1861 *Die Ætiologie* (of puerperal fever) was published.

Even this book, which proved everything so conclusively, met with a number of attacks. And Semmelweis lost his patience at last. In his 'open letters' to those who had criticized him he said such things as:

> Your teaching, Herr Hofrath, is based on the dead bodies of lying-in women, slaughtered through ignorance. . . . If you go on to write . . . in support of the doctrine . . . I denounce you before God and the world as a murderer, and the history of puerperal fever will not do you an injustice when it perpetuates your name as a medical Nero.

In another letter he estimated the number of mothers who had died of puerperal fever, ending with, "In this massacre you, Herr Professor, have participated. . . . The murder must cease!"

By this time Semmelweis was no longer the cheerful young man he had been when he had first wondered why the mortality should be so much higher in his division than in the other one. His wife, whom he had married when she was only eighteen and he was almost forty years old, had known him to be moody and depressed, or excitable almost to the point of violence. In 1863 she began to suspect that there was something wrong with his mind, although with her and their two children, neither of whom survived very long, Semmelweis behaved, as she put it, "*wie ein gutes krankes Kind*."

She sent for her husband's old friends, and, hoping for a cure, agreed with them that he should go to an institution.

In July 1865, the year that was going to mark a turning-point in Lister's career, Professor Hebra took Semmelweis to the asylum in Vienna. A little cut on his finger, made during one of his last operations, had been neglected by everyone in the excitement. Two weeks later he died from the same disease which had claimed his friend Kolletschka, and which was so closely related to the infection from which he had tried to protect the mothers of the world. The autopsy performed in the same room where the body of Kolletschka had lain, revealed not only indications of blood-poisoning, but also an extensive organic lesion of the brain.

CHAPTER VI

Living Ferments

EVEN IF HE HAD KNOWN OF SEMMELWEIS's work it would not have solved Lister's problem, for Semmelweis had not discovered *why* the introduction of cadaveric or diseased material into an open surface of the body should cause blood-poisoning. Like Jenner, he had worked empirically, observing the facts and using them to eliminate a specific disease, without being able to draw general conclusions.

Oliver Wendell Holmes was one of the other physicians who had observed the contagiousness of puerperal fever. In 1843 he came to the conclusion that if a doctor had to deliver a baby after attending a diseased patient it was important for him to change his clothes and to wash his hands. Less even than Semmelweis, who had recognized puerperal fever as a form of blood-poisoning, did Holmes know just why this should be so; but some people listened to him, because he had a gifted pen and a calmer disposition than the frustrated Hungarian. Where Semmelweis had cried "Murder must cease!" Holmes had said, "I will fight with no man over the counterpane which covers a dying mother," and that helped to lessen the instinctive antagonism with which many eminent physicians reacted to the suggestion that they should wash their hands.

Although Joseph Lister was as calm and as tactful as Oliver Wendell Holmes, the directors did not take kindly to his ideas about cleanliness. Another issue on which they disagreed was his finicky attitude towards overcrowding, for, although Lister did not subscribe to Erichsen's theory that septic diseases were caused by too many patients with serious injuries being in one ward, he recognized the fact that jamming in patients until they were practically on top of one another increased the incidence of disease.

"At this period," he said, "I was engaged in a perpetual contest with the managing body, who, anxious to provide hospital accommodation for the increasing population of Glasgow, for which the Infirmary was by no means adequate, were disposed to introduce additional beds beyond those contemplated in the original construction."

He held out against this practice so firmly that, although conditions were frequently bad, "none of my wards ever assumed the frightful condition which sometimes showed itself in other parts of the building, making it necessary to shut them up entirely for a time."

Because Lister was in many ways satisfied with his work and his opportunities in Glasgow it came as rather a surprise to some of his acquaintances when he applied for the professorship of systematic surgery in Edinburgh in 1864, a position that had been left open since the death of Professor James Miller.

It was true that he would be reluctant to leave his students, who seemed fully to appreciate him, having previously backed up his application for the surgeoncy at the Infirmary with a spontaneously organized petition to the authorities, which 161 of them enthusiastically signed. Yet this surgeoncy, which meant so much to him, would last for only five years, when he would be up for appointment again; and two consecutive five-year terms were all that were allowed, whereas in Edinburgh, where the surgeoncy went with the professorship, it was a permanent position. There were also, Lister believed, better opportunities for research and less routine work in Edinburgh than in Glasgow, where, he said, he felt as though he were working in a corner with a bushel over any light he might be able to shed. Altogether, it looked like too good an opportunity to miss, and so he applied for the position.

To the surprise of his Edinburgh friends he failed to get the appointment. Rather strangely, this did not weaken his position in Glasgow, perhaps because it had made the authorities realize that he was not completely satisfied with things as they were.

He would not, he knew, be completely satisfied anywhere until he could solve the problem to which he was dedicating himself with increasing devotion.

The subject was never far from his thoughts. It was in the back of his mind as he sat preparing some notes for a lecture in his retiring-room, which adjoined the surgical classroom in the western turret of the south side of the college quadrangle. Here Lister kept his books as well as the drawings, models, and preparations that he used to illustrate his lectures. Although he no longer made many notes for his talks, and scarcely consulted the cards on which he had jotted them down, he always made careful preparations whenever he was to speak. Sometimes he prepared so carefully that lecture-time would come while he was still busily engaged in tracking down some piece of evidence he wanted to present, completely unaware of the fact that his class was waiting for him.

From his window Lister could see the three-storied brick buildings, interrupted regularly by turrets of the same height. Looking down, he could watch the students crossing the brick-paved inner quadrangle, flanked on one side by the houses of "Professors' Court," where some of his colleagues lived.

He and Agnes did not live there. They had taken a house at 17 Woodside Place, and she had made it very comfortable and pleasant, a home which their new friends were always glad to visit. Still, they could not help missing the beauties of Millbank; for there were no tropical plants or greenhouses filled with orchids here, and no deer ever grazed recklessly on the lawn. Glasgow was too big and crowded and commercial a city for that. The Clyde penetrated to the heart of the city, but it was laden with vessels which were picturesque only at a distance, and the river's banks, were lined with shipbuilding yards instead of gardens and parks.

There was, however, a charming little park at the edge of the town, a green oasis which could be reached in two minutes. Lister liked to go there to think out his problems, alone or with Agnes or one of his associates.

One afternoon in the summer of 1865 Lister was visited by Professor Thomas Anderson, who held the Chair of Chemistry at the College. They left the Infirmary together, and almost at once Dr Anderson spoke of a paper that he was sure would interest Lister.

This paper, he explained as he and Lister walked along the crowded streets, dodging the loaded carts which were the cause of so many accidents, was in a bound volume of the *Comptes Rendus Hebdomadaires*, the paper of the Académie des Sciences in Paris. It had been written by a young French chemist, Louis Pasteur, the man who had shown that there were two kinds of tartaric acid, each of which had the same chemical formula but whose atoms were so arranged that one kind rotated the plane of polarized light to the left and the other to the right.

"This article, however, is concerned with a problem which interests you—I should say, the problem which interests you most. It's called 'Récherches sur la putréfaction.' Fortunately you know French, so you won't have any trouble reading it."

"I should very much like to see it," said Lister.

"I think you'll find a great deal in the article," went on Dr Anderson. "Pasteur has done some very thorough research, and has come to the conclusion that putrefaction is caused by living ferments. . . ."

"Living ferments!" Instantly Lister recalled the 'fungus' which he had seen in University College Hospital, London, when he had examined a piece of gangrenous tissue under a microscope. "Where did you say the article is?" he asked the Professor of Chemistry.

"In the volume I told you about. It's the issue of June 29, 1863, bound at the end of the year; and since the processes of publication have kept it from you for over twelve months, don't you think you can put off reading it a little longer—at least until after you've finished eating your dinner?"

"I can," admitted Lister. "But I assure you it's going to be difficult and even a little painful."

If he had known what Pasteur's article contained even Agnes would not have been able to persuade him to waste his time eating. For in this article Louis Pasteur provided Lister with the information for which he had been waiting so long—the information which enabled him to alter the whole course of surgical history.

Pasteur had proved that living ferments cause putrefaction; and what was suppuration, what was gangrene, but the decay of tissues which, although not actually dead, had lost their vitality as the result of injury and irritation?

What were these living ferments which Pasteur identified with putrefaction?

As long ago as the early part of the seventeenth century van Leeuwenhoek had seen through the recently invented microscope tiny rod-shaped organisms swimming in a drop of water, and had called them 'animalculæ.' Other scientists had seen them later and had christened them 'microbes,' from the Greek words meaning 'small' and 'life.'

These tiny creatures were mainly interesting as curiosities, although from time to time some one, like Jakob Henle, caught a glimpse of their relationship with contagious diseases. The overwhelming majority of investigators assumed that these microbes were created by molecules coming together and forming themselves into living creatures.

This was spontaneous generation, concerning which a controversy had been going on for years. Some people were convinced that the world was full of raw particles, or molecules, which, when they happened to unite according to certain unknown formulæ, became fungi, earthworms, or even larger vegetables and animals.

In the sixteenth century van Helmont, who gave impetus to the chemical remedies suggested by Paracelsus, produced a recipe for 'making' mice out of "dirty linen, a few grains of wheat, or a piece of cheese." Just leave them alone—you did not even have to shake well—and the particles would form themselves into mice. An Italian scientist named Buonanni 'proved' conclusively that certain wood, after rotting in the sea, would produce worms, and the worms would turn into butterflies, and the butterflies would become birds. And many scientists agreed that a horsehair would turn into a snake if you left it in a pool of rain-water, while cheese-mites would develop from a piece of cheese, and eels from mutton-gravy.

But all was not plain sailing for the supporters of the theory of spontaneous generation. Abbé Spallanzani used the microscope and a lot of common sense to refute the evidence in favour of spontaneous generation prepared by Father Needham.

Then came Charles Darwin, who in 1859 published *The Origin of Species*. Here, clearly, was evidence that plants and animals descended from ancestors of a similar species. Changes throughout the centuries were due to the "survival of the fittest" and to "sports," or mutations, which persisted when they were adapted to the environment in which they appeared.

Yet many scientists, some of whom were willing to agree with Darwin regarding plants and animals, did not see what that had to do with microbes. Here the believers in spontaneous generation had things pretty much their own way, for it seemed as though microbes must create themselves: one minute none would be visible, and when you returned to your microscope you would see them swarming there. Such tiny, simply formed creatures could surely come into existence by the union of raw particles, or molecules!

Pasteur decided to find out. Born in 1822, five years before Lister, he had won recognition as a chemist for his work on tartaric acid crystals and for his solution of a problem which had threatened to ruin the wine-makers of his native France. He knew that yeasts caused beer to ferment, for he had confirmed the work of Cagniard de La Tour and Schwann regarding the part played by these tiny plants in alcoholic fermentation. He discovered that they were also responsible for the fact that milk turned sour and butter rancid (in these cases the tiny organisms lived without air) and for the fact that wine 'fell sick.' By heating the wine he destroyed the microbes and prevented it from souring—and saved the fortunes of many of his countrymen.

But what he wanted to know was: where did these microbes come from? Were they produced spontaneously, or was their existence governed by the same laws of birth and life and death that governed the existence of their larger brothers?

Most people felt that Pasteur would be wasting his time if he tried to solve that problem. J. B. Dumas and Professor Biot, two well-known members of the Académie des Sciences who were interested in his career, cautioned him against tackling something on which so many scientists had burned their fingers.

"You'll never find your way out of this maze!" old Biot told him testily, to which Pasteur replied, despite his respect for the professor, "I shall try."

"Don't dwell too long on such a subject," was Dumas's warning. Pasteur dwelt upon it just long enough to find the answer.

In the course of his experiments he found microbes everywhere. That might mean they created themselves, or it might mean that they were hovering about in the air, waiting to land upon something on which they could feed and multiply.

In order to settle that point Pasteur devised an experiment so simple that anyone could understand it, so clear-cut that it was impossible to refute.

He took flasks with long, curving necks, placed some good microbe food in them, and boiled them to destroy any living creatures which might already be present. Then he let in the air. The necks of the flasks were curved in such a way that, as the air passed through them, all the particles in it —dust, germs, whatever there might be—would settle into the curve, and only clean air would continue on its way to the food at the bottom of the flask.

Pasteur waited for the food to become sour or decay. He watched for germs to appear, searching for them diligently through his microscope. He found no souring, no microbes.

Then he took some of the flasks and tipped them carefully, so that the liquid food came in contact with the curve in the flask's neck, where he thought the microbes would collect if they had fallen in with the air. In a short time the food began to change, to decay. Microbes, he discovered, were growing in abundance.

He made many other experiments, testing the air in cellars, in courtyards, on the tops of the Alps. Nothing was too much trouble for him; he even wanted to go up in a balloon to test the air up there, but finally compromised on the mountain-tops as being more practical. When he had finished he had proved conclusively that microbes did not just 'happen.' They came from other microbes, just as flowers came from other flowers and animals from other animals. Their means of reproduction, however, was different, and it was so rapid that one microbe alone was enough to start a large family in a few hours if it landed on suitable material.

At last Pasteur said, "Never will the doctrine of spontaneous generation recover from the mortal blow of this simple experiment."

It did not. It died hard, but eventually it died, and Pasteur's discoveries opened the way to the solution of many mysteries which otherwise could not have been understood.

If Semmelweis had learned of Pasteur's experiments he would have realized that they provided a scientific proof of his theory of the etiology of puerperal fever. He had demonstrated in a practical manner that it was correct: decomposed material caused childbed fever, just as it caused blood-poisoning, when it was introduced into the body. But he had not known why. Pasteur supplied the answer: because this material was swarming with microbes, and microbes caused disease.

This was precisely the information for which Joseph Lister had been searching, and it came at exactly the right time. Perhaps the element of chance entered into it, but it played only a minor part. Even if Thomas Anderson had not directed Lister's attention to Pasteur's experiments he would have learned about them very soon, as the ensuing controversy attracted the attention of all scientists.

The important fact was that Lister immediately recognized the significance of Pasteur's discovery. As one of his friends put it, "He was watching from the heights, and he was watching alone." By understanding the germ-theory and applying it to his own field Joseph Lister solved the problem of wound-infection and founded modern surgery.

CHAPTER VII

The Killer Revealed

PUTREFACTION IS CAUSED BY LIVING ferments. There is no spontaneous generation."

Walking in the little park which Lister called his "*academia* for peripatetic study," he repeated the sentences over and over again, reaching in his pocket from time to time and pulling out a note-book to jot down something that occurred to him. The sun, slanting against the row of fine elms which he and Agnes had frequently admired, indicated that it was getting late, but now, if ever in his life, he was completely unaware of time.

Every one knew that blood which was exposed to air at body-temperature soon decomposed. Within twenty-four hours after an accident the serum ooze already betrayed the acrid odour of decay. And yet, as John Hunter had pointed out, pneumothorax with emphysema, resulting from the puncturing of a lung by a fractured rib, permitted the air to enter, and yet no inflammation resulted. Now Lister knew why. Now he knew it was not the oxygen nor any other gases in the air, not a miasma, but, as he had half guessed, half reasoned, something real and alive which caused the wound to putrefy. The "germs of various low forms of life" which had been revealed in decayed material by the microscope were not accidental concomitants of putrescence, but its essential cause!

Microbes fell on to tissues which, as Lister had demonstrated, had lost their vitality, become temporarily dead as a result of injury, and these tiny creatures caused the tissues to putrefy just like dead meat.

Microbes swarmed in the air, doing no damage until they gained access to material upon which they could feed. Then they got to work—useful work in some cases, he realized, for the great picture of life could scarcely be painted without including decay. But decay had no place on the bodies of the living, where it caused the horrible septic diseases that made surgical wards places for men to shun. Microscopic creatures were to blame, creatures which lived and multiplied and which could be killed or rendered powerless—if one knew how.

Now Joseph Lister understood why hospitals should be such excellent breeders of septic disease. As Pasteur had shown, microbes were thick in the air in some places, scarce in others; and in a hospital, particularly one built so close to a cemetery, they would be certain to abound. No wonder wounds healed better in a humble cottage than in a hospital, where surgeons spread these minute seeds of death like a farmer sowing a field.

What could the surgeon do? Lister smiled at the first solution which entered his mind: take your patients to the mountain-tops, where the air is clean, and operate upon them there. Perhaps, after all, there was something in the idea of moving patients away from places where contamination had occurred—the pavilion system, as advocated by James Simpson, who had recommended building villages of iron huts each housing two or three patients, huts which could be pulled down and re-erected periodically. This plan had won some powerful supporters, who were clamouring that infected hospitals should be destroyed, but Lister had never liked the idea. It seemed a little like burning down a house in order to roast a pig.

Now he considered it again, and finally decided that you could never win that kind of a race, for some of the patients would be sure to bring with them, deep in their wounds, the germs of disease. Where could you retreat to then? Sooner or later you would have to do battle with your tiny enemies.

How could you fight these creatures which you could not even see without a microscope? Lister realized that he faced unknown foes, some of which, according to Pasteur, did not even require air in order to survive: in fact, like fish, they died when they were exposed to it, which explained to him the reason why attempts—such as those of Alphonse Guérin—to promote the healing of wounds by excluding air had not met with any success.

How could you get rid of microbes, how could they be destroyed? Pasteur knew a little about their habits. . . . What did he suggest?

He had kept microbes out of his flasks by making curves in the necks of the bottles to trap them, along with the dust, and he had filtered them out by plugging the bottles with cotton-wool, through which the air could pass and the microbes could not. Without discarding the information Lister decided the immediate answer to the problem lay in another direction, for he could see no practical way of keeping microbes out of wounds. No wonder it had not done much real good when he had insisted upon his dressers washing their hands before and after examinations; no wonder that the piles of clean towels which, at his orders, always stood on a table for the use of his assistants, had not succeeded in eliminating hospital diseases! Cleanliness might help a little, but to Joseph Lister, plunged suddenly into a world in which microbes had been revealed, as dust-specks are exposed by a ray of light, it did not seem possible to keep germs out of open wounds.

So they would have to be killed, in the air, if possible, or on the wound after they had gained access to it.

Heat destroyed microbes. That was why Erichsen's cautery had been moderately successful in the old London days. But heat was painful to the patient and retarded the healing of wounds.

What else was there? Lister recalled the advertisements of the owners of dissecting-rooms, who used to claim that they had perfected antiseptic processes which would keep anatomical specimens from rotting and so prevent the odour of decay. As far as he knew they had never perfected anything. All they did was to sprinkle some deodorant like charcoal powder round the room, and it had practically no effect either on the odour or on the rats which used to drag off the specimens as soon as the students were out of the way.

Yet for centuries men had known how to embalm dead bodies, keeping them in perfect condition for the souls which might inhabit them again on Judgment Day. Chemicals had been used with great success for this purpose, which had inspired some surgeons to try chemicals for limiting the foul-smelling decay of living tissues.

Professor Polli, of Milan, had experimented with sulphite of potash on dogs, and had recommended it as a prophylactic because of its anti-putrescent properties. But although Lister had given it a try he had not found it helpful. He had not really hoped for victory as long as he was fighting an enemy whose nature he did not even suspect.

Most surgeons believed that putrefaction was a result of hospital diseases, but he had considered it the cause. While they had been smearing everything from filthy salves to antiseptics on wounds in order to make them heal he had been trying to find out what made them putrefy.

Now he knew; he had what they had lacked—a principle to guide him in his search for a proper agent. Limiting decay was not enough. It must be eliminated. He must find something to kill microbes, and kill them quickly, before they could damage the helpless, injured cells.

Many antiseptics had been tried in addition to sulphite of potash—benzoin, alcohol, salt water, chloride of zinc and of lime, carbolic acid. . . . In the city of Carlisle, Lister knew, carbolic acid had been successfully used to get rid of the smell of the city's garbage and to destroy the entozoa which grew in it and sickened the cattle grazing on the near-by meadows. Perhaps carbolic acid, which was known also as phenic acid and German creosote, was the thing he wanted.

"I'll go to Carlisle and see for myself," Joseph Lister decided.

Meanwhile, he would himself, of course, repeat Pasteur's

experiments himself, although he had little doubt that he would verify Pasteur's results. Lister had studied every piece of the puzzle so carefully that when the missing section was revealed to him he recognized it immediately and felt sure that it would fit. What he must do now was to try and try again until he found the correct way to apply his theory, and then present his answer to the world. He had chosen carbolic acid at random, and if it did not work he would find something else.

This was the spring of 1865, the year in which Ignaz Philipp Semmelweis died of blood-poisoning. It had been a cold winter in Glasgow, with a great deal of snow. A number of people, including the police, thought of it as the year of the snowball riots, which had started as a students' prank and had assumed serious proportions when the police entered the college yard against orders.

Other residents of the city, especially members of the medical profession, remembered it as the year when Dr Pritchard murdered his wife and mother-in-law, and, despite the fears of many people that his position would enable him to get off, was finally hanged. There were very few people who knew, or would have cared if they had known, that it was the year when Joseph Lister first treated compound fractures with German creosote.

His decision to test his theory on compound fractures was logical. The analogy between Pasteur's corked and uncorked bottles on the one hand, and simple and compound fractures on the other was obvious. He felt that it was justifiable to try a new method on these cases, as they came into the wards already contaminated and were so frequently fatal. His over-all mortality hovered close to 50 per cent., and compound fractures were among the worst cases.

If only he had been able to think of something to help poor little Andy, who had left the hospital after a year of illness—a weak and drooping little sparrow, scarcely able to hop along on his one tiny leg. Poor Andy! Poor little boys and girls who tossed so restlessly in their hospital beds or lay much too still, staring into space, their fingers plucking everlastingly at their quilts as though they had nothing else to hold on to in the world. Please God, who had not chosen to give him and Agnes any children of their own, please God he would be able to save the children now!

From Thomas Anderson he obtained some carbolic acid—thick, tarry stuff, insoluble in water, but the best that could be procured. In March he used it on his first patient, a man who had come into the hospital in such poor condition that Lister believed his recovery would be positive proof of the value of the new theory.

Agnes, who had shared his hopes and enthusiasm, knew the moment he entered the door just what had happened.

"He's gone," she said. "I suppose it doesn't really help to know there was nothing you could have done."

"It helps a little not to have to think that, but for me, this man might have been alive," he replied. "All the same, the case wasn't properly handled. I know that now. Don't worry, though; I'm not going to allow the failure of any case to discourage me. The theory is so new that I'm bound to make mistakes."

"And you're bound to succeed eventually."

"You believe that even more firmly than I do."

"I'm not sure about that. But I can boast, because I always knew you'd be the one to wipe out hospitalism some day. Only I must admit I didn't know it would be so soon."

"It's a long way from being wiped out as yet," said Lister.

It was five months after his first failure before Joseph Lister tested his theory again.

On August 12 an eleven-year-old boy was brought into the Infirmary, after he had been run over by an empty cart which passed over his left leg, a little below the middle. Both bones had been broken, and at the end of the tibia there was a wound, one and a half inches long and three-quarters of an inch wide, close to, but not exactly over, the fracture. It was not a serious wound, perhaps not severe enough to provide a real test for Lister's method; yet it must certainly have been contaminated by Glasgow's dirty streets.

On Lister's instructions his house-surgeon, Dr Macfee, covered the wound with a piece of lint soaked in carbolic acid, making certain to cover it completely and overlap its edges for a safe margin on all sides. Then, after splinting the leg, Lister waited to see what would happen.

For three days everything went well, which was not unusual. The first three days were usually uneventful if the injury was not too severe; it was on the fourth day that suppuration usually occurred.

Joseph Lister felt a definite anxiety as he visited the ward on the fourth day and stood at the foot of the bed, his back to the little circular table built about one of the posts supporting the ceiling, looking down at his little patient. The boy seemed well, his first glance assured him—a glance which years of practice had trained to grasp the essential features of a picture and add them together almost before his mind was able to record them individually.

"How are you to-day, Jaimie?" he asked in his low, reassuring voice.

"Me leg hurts," answered the boy candidly, watching the doctor's face as he added questioningly, "It's supposed to hurt, isn't it, when it's getting well?"

Lister's heart sank as he gave the boy a non-committal answer. Had this test, also, failed? What had he done wrong? Was this day, the critical day, going to reveal the fact that this wound, like the ones upon which microbes had been allowed to thrive, had started to suppurate?

It seemed strange to him, for the boy had reported that his appetite was good, and the tongue which he obediently thrust out seemed healthy. The pulse indicated no trace of the fever which always accompanied a septic disease. It might be worth while, he thought as he rechecked the pulse, to use a thermometer, since fever was one of the criteria by which he could judge the success of his method. The instrument might cause some commotion, for it was ten inches long and, carried like a gun, looked formidable enough to make some patients object to having it thrust under their arms; but he thought it would not be long before its use in a hospital became a matter of course.

Carefully he removed the outer bandages from the injured leg, which, the knee slightly bent, was resting on its outer side. Lister was perspiring freely. That was not surprising, because it was a hot day, but he wished there were some way he could prevent it. It was bad enough even in cool weather, but when he operated on a hot day he required the undivided attention of a nurse simply to mop his brow.

Gently he raised the inner pasteboard splint which covered the wound. There was no offensive smell.

Carefully he raised the lint dressing, which with the serum ooze and dried blood had formed a kind of crust over the wound. No suppuration, no inflamed, oozing sore . . . A clean surface, already commencing to granulate and heal. Then what had caused the pain?

In a moment he discovered what it was. The skin about the edges of the wound was pink. At once he realized that this was not the angry blush which surrounded the shiny greyish slough of the early stages of hospital gangrene. It resembled, rather, a superficial irritation, as though the skin had been burned about the edges of the wound. Yes, that was it! Creosote was strong, and, having been in direct contact with the boy's delicate skin for over thirty-six hours, it had caused a surface burn.

"What is it, sir?" young James asked anxiously. "Is it very bad? Are you . . . are you going to cut it off? Oh, please, sir, don't cut it off!"

Quickly Joseph Lister reassured him. "Nothing like that, Jaimie. It's only . . . let me see how I can explain it. The medicine I put on your sore to make it heal was a little too strong, and it's made the skin round the edges hurt a little. I'll make it weaker this time."

Just how, he wondered, could he best do that? It was difficult to dissolve carbolic acid. But if he put a lump of creosote into some water, it would be diffused throughout, even if it did not dissolve. He could soak a piece of lint in this water, and then re-dress the wound with that.

He looked up, startled, for the boy had commenced to cry.

"Oh, no, doctor!" he implored. "Don't make it weak. I don't care if it hurts. It doesn't really hurt. I was just pretending that it did. Make it strong, doctor, make the medicine stronger so that it will cure me leg. I've got to have me leg, doctor! I've me mither and the little yins to take care of, and who's to give me work if I don't have me leg?'

Lister laid his hand on Jaimie's tousled head. It was a moment before he could speak, but even in that short space of time the boy relaxed, his eyes on the calm, kind face.

"Don't worry about that, my boy," he said. "It doesn't have to be strong enough to hurt the skin in order to help your wound. Your leg—with God's help—is going to be all right."

CHAPTER VIII

Test Cases

JAIMIE'S RECOVERY WAS UNEVENTFUL. At the end of six weeks the bones had mended and the splints could be discarded; two days later the sore was completely healed. In short, a compound fracture had recovered as though it were a simple one, for a chemical had protected the bruised tissue almost as successfully as did unbroken skin. It was most encouraging, although Lister was the first to admit that this was a favourable case which might have done equally well under ordinary treatment.

Yes, it might have—but how seldom did the average surgeon see a wound heal as Jaimie's had—the way the wounds of animals usually healed, granulating tissues growing rapidly under the protection of a scab! The carbolic acid and lint which Lister had applied directly to the injured area had clotted with the serum ooze and blood to form a crust which acted as a protecting scab did in slight, superficial injuries. The stage of "healthy inflammation" and "laudable pus" had been eliminated.

This same kind of crust protected the wound of a patient who had been admitted while young James was still in the Infirmary. Patrick F——, a healthy young labourer, had been kicked in the shin by a horse, and suffered a compound fracture of the right tibia. Mr Miller, the house-surgeon, had dressed the wound with carbolic lint, changing the dressing in the evening and covering it with waxed paper. This treatment was repeated for five days. On the third day the ooze ceased, and on the critical fourth day the patient's pulse had dropped to sixty-four and his appetite was excellent. His only complaint came after a week, when the acid irritated his skin, as it had done in Jamie's case.

When the crust was removed on the eleventh day the wound was revealed free from suppuration and inflammation, and water-dressings were substituted. A little over two weeks after the injury the entire sore, except for one spot where the bone was bare, was a mass of healing granulations. Lister, who had to leave the hospital at that time, went away confident that his patient would be well and back at work by the time he returned.

But instead, a little sore which had been neglected as unimportant provided an entry for the microbes of hospital gangrene, which established themselves so securely that, in the end, poor Patrick lost his leg.

After that no important cases came into Lister's wards for some time—just several compound fractures with small wounds which healed readily. From them he learned several things: that one could, if necessary, place a splint directly over a wound which had been treated with carbolic, and ignore it, confident that the sore would be healed when the splint was removed. He also worked out a means of covering the carbolic crust with a metallic layer—he first used sheet-lead; later, tin—to prevent the volatile acid from evaporating. This covering also made it possible for him to apply hot fomentations to soothe the injured limb.

Although no suitable cases came in for almost eight months, the three which followed proved to be extremely important.

The first one entered the hospital on May 19, 1866, when John H——, a moulder in an iron-factory, was brought in with a badly crushed leg. An iron box containing sand for a casting was being raised by a crane when the chain slipped, and the load, which weighed almost half a ton, fell from a distance of four feet on to the inner side of the man's leg.

By the time Lister saw the wound three and a half hours had elapsed. Both bones were fractured, and the contusions were severe; on a level with the fracture of the tibia there was a deep wound an inch and a half by three-quarters of an inch in size. This was a serious case indeed.

Treatment was commenced very much as in the other cases, except that on the second day Lister substituted a splint made of tin for the pasteboard one on the leg's inner surface, so that he could more easily apply hot fomentations to ease the swelling. By the end of the fourth day the limb was free from pain, the calf less tense, and the swelling had greatly diminished. The pulse was eighty, and the patient was eating and sleeping well. Because of a discharge caused by the irritation of the carbolic acid on the skin the size of the tin protecting the antiseptic crust was reduced until there was only a narrow flat rim in contact with the edges of the wound.

The sore healed rapidly. A swelling over the fracture turned out to be, as Lister hoped, due to serum only, and soon disappeared. Where the edge of the crust became softened he chipped it away, so that the carbolic scab, along with the wound beneath it, grew steadily smaller.

Three weeks after the operation he made an interesting discovery.

He had been removing a portion of the crust when, as he put it,

> I exposed a little spherical cavity about as big as a pea, containing brown serum, forming a sort of pocket in the living tissues, which, when scraped with the edge of a knife, bled even at the very margin of the cavity. This appearance showed that the deeper portions of the crust itself had been converted into living tissue. . . . Thus the blood which had been acted upon by carbolic acid, though greatly altered in physical characters, and doubtless chemically also, had not been rendered unsuitable for serving as pabulum for the growing element of the new tissue in its vicinity. The knowledge of this fact is of importance; as it shows that, should circumstances appear to demand it, we may introduce carbolic acid deeply among the blood extravasated in a limb, confident that all will nevertheless be removed by absorption.

These were his immediate conclusions from noticing that live tissues had eaten away a crust of clots and carbolic, but he did not let it go at that. Rather, he added this information to his arsenal of facts, using it subsequently to develop absorbable ligatures, and thus make another important contribution to surgery.

Despite the severe contusions the bones united within six weeks, as rapidly as though there had been no wound, although the sore was not completely closed until some time later.

The day after Lister had noticed that live tissues were absorbing portions of the clot, and while the moulder's leg was healing rapidly under its protecting crust, an accident took place in a turner's factory. The arm of a ten-year-old boy who was tending a machine was caught between a strap and the shaft which was turning it. Although he screamed for help it was a good two minutes before the machinery—the factory was a modern one, employing steam—could be halted. By that time the child's arm had been badly mangled.

Such accidents were not unusual. Machinery frequently behaved in an unpredictable manner, and, as many of the leading citizens of Glasgow were quick to point out, people were naturally careless.

And no wonder, thought Joseph Lister, hurrying to his little patient. Ten-year-old boys went to work day in and day out, after a hasty breakfast of bread or watery porridge, inadequately cared for by parents whose entire energies were devoted to trying to support themselves and their families. Unless they were seriously ill children did not dream of staying away from work and losing a day's pay, but stood from morning till night, tending machines which, like the ancient gods, demanded their human sacrifices.

How could you call it carelessness, how could you dismiss it as an act of God, when a child's attention wavered and an accident occurred? A ten-year-old boy who, at the age when Joseph Lister and his brothers had been thinking of bowls and cricket, faced the loss of a limb with the one thought: how am I going to earn a living if they cut off my arm?

It was two hours after the accident that Joseph Lister

looked at the mangled little arm, and wondered whether it could be saved, as Jaimie's leg had been, by the new treatment. This boy's name, incidentally, was also James. His was a far more serious injury. Tags of torn muscles, two or three inches long, dangled from the lacerated wound, which occupied half the circumference of the limb. Since they hung as if by a thread there was no chance that they would grow again, and they had to be clipped away. About an inch of the fractured end of the ulna, which protruded from the wound, had to be sawn off. The radius had suffered a green-stick fracture, and the lower end of the humerus, Lister discovered later, was broken also.

Yet once again the crust of carbolic acid protected the badly torn flesh. Within two weeks the boy's uneventful recovery had proceeded so far that when Lister removed the nearly detached crust he saw, instead of a deep and ragged wound, a granulating surface nearly level with the skin, except in the centre, where he could see the ulna, bare and pink, in a little depression. Again the crusts of blood and carbolic had been absorbed, and the dead tissue also. Seven weeks after the accident James was well again, although the loss of a piece of the ulna had made the union of the bone imperfect. Even if Lister's efforts to remedy that condition should fail the other fractures had knitted perfectly, and the boy had a useful arm, with fingers that functioned normally.

These successful cases gave Joseph Lister courage to tackle his fifth case, which entered his ward on June 23. Not that he hoped for success this time: he started his treatment as a last resource, for an amputation would undoubtedly have been fatal to seven-year-old Charlie, who was already at the point of death.

The child had been run over by a heavy omnibus, loaded both inside and outside with passengers. Either one or both wheels of the vehicle had passed over the tiny leg, breaking both bones and causing a frightfully extensive injury. When Lister saw him, three hours after the accident, the boy was completely prostrated by shock and loss of blood.

At first the surgeon did not see how he could avoid amputating, even though he was convinced that the child would not survive the operation. Then his sure fingers detected an artery pulsing in the child's foot, the tibial artery. That meant that the circulation had not been entirely cut off, and so there was a chance, a bare chance, of saving the leg and the life of the child, which was hanging by so slender a thread.

For thirty-six hours the child hovered at the point of death, his feeble pulse climbing to a hundred and sixty-eight, periods of stupor alternating with delirium. On the third night the clouds lifted just enough to enable him to take his first nourishment, a little milk. There was no doubt in Lister's mind, as there would have been none in the mind of any competent surgeon, that Charlie would be unable to survive the fever which would accompany the suppuration of his wound. But Lister alone knew that this stage of the healing-process might be eliminated—would be eliminated if his treatment succeeded, as it had in the past, in combating the microbes contaminating the wound.

And it did succeed. Steadily the pulse dropped, and the delirium faded away. The child's appetite returned, and, although he occasionally awakened, screaming, in the night, his sleep on the whole was sound. Within two weeks he was on the road to recovery.

Then, on the outer side of his leg, gangrene found a tiny untreated sore, and clutched at it tenaciously with slimy fingers. Despite Lister's efforts the new danger-zone began to spread, and he feared it would merge with the larger one where he was waging so successful a battle.

Placing the child under chloroform, he scraped away the soft grey slough which ran under the skin to the very edge of the carbolic crust which he had counted upon to act as a bulwark against all invaders. Had the enemy penetrated this defence? As the crust was loose Lister decided to look under it and find out.

To his relief he found no trace of the greyish slime which

indicated the presence of gangrene. Yet, before he could congratulate himself on this good fortune, Lister saw something which filled him with horror.

In the wound's cavity the lower fragment of the broken tibia, bare and white like a macerated bone, was freely exposed for a full two and a half inches. The upper fragment was also bare, but for only half an inch, and it was covered with granulations.

Lister had good reason to be disturbed. It was an accepted fact that a dead bone, or any portion of a bone that was dead, must exfoliate, or scale off, a process which was invariably accompanied by suppuration. This was something Charlie was in no condition to survive; and even if suppuration could be controlled to some degree by the use of carbolic acid, the loss of two and a half inches of bone would make the tiny limb absolutely useless.

Lister's only consolation lay in the fact that Charlie was in much better condition now than he had been when he was brought to the Infirmary. If he must amputate he could at least be fairly certain of saving the child's life.

Anxiously he waited. Once more Charlie improved—and once more gangrene threatened to wipe out the gains which had been made.

Once more, however, the disease was fought to a standstill before it could gain access to the major wound, which by the eighth of August was an inch by two inches smaller than it had been at first. The appearance of the bone, also, was encouraging. Although he was still certain the outer portions were dead and must exfoliate, Lister could detect a pinkish tinge which told him the dead layer was thin enough to be transparent. New tissue outside the bone had coalesced with that within, absorbing the dead stratum.

Lister had to leave the Infirmary, and, during his absence, the dead portion of the bone, being loose, was removed without difficulty. He examined it curiously on his return, for it was a strange-looking fragment. In the first place, it was only an inch long, and not two and a half inches, as he had expected. At one end it was nearly the full thickness of the bone, but the lower part was as thin as tissue-paper, and even at the thickest spot it had been scooped and bevelled as though the granulating tissue had been eating it. When there was no sepsis even portions of dead bone could be eaten and absorbed!

Just when Charlie's leg was healing as though it were a simple fracture with a healthy, granulating sore the scourge of hospital gangrene struck once more. This time there seemed to be no way to halt its progress. The fine, intelligent child of whom Lister had grown so fond, and who clung to him with such devotion, would have to lose his leg after all.

Although Joseph Lister had no intention of letting his affection for the child keep him from taking a step which he felt was necessary to his safety, he could not bear to give in while there was still a chance to save his leg.

He knew there was not much hope as long as Charlie had to remain in the overcrowded surgical ward. The entire hospital was overcrowded, with 700 patients crammed into space designed to accommodate a maximum of 572 beds. Not only the patients but the doctors themselves suffered as a result of this condition, particularly those who lived in the hospital; several fever clerks, or residents, had died of typhus, which was bringing into the open the question of reducing the number of patients. Meanwhile, it did not seem to Lister as though any space could be found where a little boy would have a fair chance of winning his battle against infection.

However, to his great relief, a room was offered to him in a different department of the Infirmary, some distance away from the main breeding-grounds of the microbes of septic diseases. Once more Lister put Charlie under chloroform and treated the slough, and then, in the new, airy room, waited and watched, and was rewarded by victory. The battle was won at last, and little Charlie, whom even Lister had been tempted to give up as lost, would run about again on two sound little legs.

There were other cases, too, some of them extremely serious. All of them demonstrated the soundness of Lister's theory, although, as he put it, "I have had *some* rather sorrowful experience in bringing the new method of treatment to a trustworthy state."

One of the sorrowful experiences concerned John C——, who had been crushed by rocks while working in a quarry. Lister would have saved the man, despite his severe injury, but for an accident which occurred just as he was beginning to recover. The sharp edge of the fractured bone cut an important artery, causing a bad hæmorrhage. Lister wanted to try a transfusion: indirect transfusions of defibrinated blood had been attempted for the past thirty years, but the results were not by any means uniformly successful. The patient refused to give his consent to the venture, and died as a result of the loss of blood.

Yes, some of Lister's experiences had been sorrowful. Of a series of eleven patients one had died, one had lost a limb, and gangrene had struck on two occasions, reminding Lister that it was never safe to ignore a sore, no matter how trivial it might be.

He had learned many things from these eleven patients, and most important of all, he had answered the question: why do simple fractures heal while compound ones do not? By answering the question he had demonstrated the soundness of his theory. Wounds would not become inflamed and suppurate if one destroyed the microbes which had fallen into them at the time of injury, and carbolic acid was an excellent agent for performing this function—at least in the case of wounds connected with compound fractures. That much, Lister believed, he had proved conclusively.

CHAPTER IX

Presenting the Evidence

BECAUSE THE RECOVERY OF THE IRON-moulder with the badly crushed leg had created a great deal of excitement around the hospital, Lister had thought of publishing this single case. The uneventful recovery of so severe and extensive a wound should convince people of the value of his new method.

But James, the factory boy, had come into the Infirmary very soon after the moulder, followed in a few weeks by little Charlie. Both were cases of interest and importance, and Lister postponed publication in order to include them also.

By October he was convinced that his antiseptic treatment had sufficiently demonstrated its value in cases of compound fracture so that he could use it elsewhere, and he turned his attention not to the simplest cases—it was not until the following April that he used antiseptics in the removal of a tumour—but to psoas abscesses.

These were abscesses arising in connexion with tubercular spines, usually forming in the psoas muscle of the groin. They were the despair of surgeons, for if they were opened the results were invariably fatal, and if, as most doctors advised, they were left alone, they eventually burst. Then the condition known as hectic set in. In Erichsen's words this was "essentially a fever of debility, conjoined with irritation. Emaciation and general loss of power invariably accompany it; . . . the patient rapidly wastes, and at last dies from sheer exhaustion. . . ."

Lister turned his attention to these cases partly because of the challenge they offered him as a surgeon. If abscesses of this kind should heal after being opened—if they, like the severely contused and lacerated wounds he had treated so successfully, responded favourably to antiseptic treatment—then it should be "obvious that its application to simple incised wounds must be merely a matter of detail."

His decision to try his method on psoas abscesses was not based solely upon scientific considerations. The victims were usually young people and children, whose suffering had always touched him deeply. There was something particularly sad about these cases, for the disease brightened the children's eyes, reddened their cheeks, and gave them a fragile beauty which, combined with a characteristic obedience and patience, made their slow wasting away heartbreaking for him to witness.

Like other surgeons, Lister believed that psoas abscesses were caused by the "excited action of the nerves." He could not see how pus, in these cases, could have been caused by the action of microbes, as there had been no opening in the body to admit any germs. At that time no one suspected that tuberculosis was caused by a micro-organism. In his opinion the dreadful consequences of opening psoas abscesses were due to the fact that the matter they contained was highly putrescible. Hence, when germs entered the opened abscess they immediately caused decay. If microbes could be kept out, he thought, the abscesses could be emptied without danger; and while his theory of the origin of psoas abscesses was incorrect his treatment was based upon a sound practical principle: keep microbes out of abscesses when you open them, create, by means of antiseptics, an aseptic wound, and healing would result.

Having first tried carbolic on carbuncles and simple acute abscesses, he decided to use it when he opened a psoas abscess which was obviously about to burst.

This "bottle of putrescible material" he "uncorked" with extreme care. Carbolized lint had been placed over the site of the incision before the operation. Lifting it carefully, he made a slit with his lancet, which had been dipped in carbolic, and a pound of matter was allowed to flow away under the protecting 'curtain' of the lint.

The contents of the abscess he mixed with crude carbolic oil to form a paste, which he applied to some lint and placed about the wound, covering it with a cap of block tin.

The next day when he removed the dressing no matter flowed from the abscess, and he was momentarily at a loss, as he had planned to use it for his antiseptic paste. However, he thought of glazier's putty. Why shouldn't he make something like that? Quickly he sent to the dispensary for some whiting (carbonate of lime) and boiled linseed oil. Making a solution of one part of carbolic and four of linseed oil, he rubbed it with the whiting in a mortar, and, spreading this putty over block tin, applied it to the abscess.

This antiseptic putty worked very well. It guarded the opening in the abscess, being too firm to be washed away by the discharges which oozed from beneath its edges, where they were absorbed by rags.

Four days later the entire discharge for twenty-eight hours was only one-fourth of a dram, quite odourless, and almost transparent. This did not deter Lister from continuing to treat his patient with meticulous care, for, until healing was complete, no germs must be permitted to enter the uncorked bottle and start the process of decay.

As these cases mounted up Lister began to wonder whether, instead of publishing a paper, he ought to write a book. But the idea was abandoned; he was never to write a book in his life.

Although he did not hate writing as Semmelweis had, it was not easy for him, and he was too conscientious to write carelessly. Sometimes he would spend hours trying to find a word which would convey his exact meaning, to replace one which he thought might be misconstrued. Should he, for example, refer to the 'conditions of suppuration' or the 'causes of suppuration'? He wrote about it to his father, whose advice he still found extremely valuable, and finally decided to use the phrase 'conditions of suppuration' in his title.

Some surgeons would have preferred him to wait until he

could present his discovery to the world in two expensive volumes, complete to the last detail. They did not want to hear about it until it was 'done,' for even with his guidance and leadership they were reluctant to follow a new trail.

Lister could not help that. He was constantly modifying his technique and making new discoveries, and if he waited until he could offer the world a blueprint complete in every detail he would never publish anything.

And he ought to publish, for his work had progressed to the point where it did not "seem right to withhold it longer from the profession generally." Although the figures themselves were not conclusive the cases were. Other surgeons might boast of seven successive recoveries of compound fractures, but it was quite another matter for seven severely lacerated wounds to heal without suppuration or pain. As he wrote to his father, "I now perform an operation . . . with a totally different feeling from what I used to have; in fact, surgery is becoming a different thing altogether."

Having decided against writing a book, Lister finally wrote a series of papers for *The Lancet*. He planned to divide his paper into three sections, dealing with compound fractures, abscesses, and suppuration in general, but he altered his plan so that the series was actually in two parts.

In the first, headed "On Compound Fractures," he took his readers with him along the journey he had made. He told them of his theory, how it had been based upon the discoveries of Louis Pasteur, and how he had developed it. Following this, he gave the case-histories of the patients upon whom he had worked out its practical application. In the second section, "Preliminary Notice on Abscess," he described his treatment of these cases, mentioning a few of them without giving the histories of each in chronological order. It was a paper typical of Lister: precise, somewhat stilted, free from the popular rhetoric of the period, modest, honest, and clear.

The first article of the series appeared in March 1867, and the last in July of that year. Before the final issue appeared

James Syme urged his son-in-law to discuss his discoveries at the British Medical Association meeting which was to be held in Dublin that year.

Lister agreed that he should not neglect such an opportunity, although preparing a speech meant one of those last-minute rushes to which Agnes had grown accustomed, and during which she was, as usual, invaluable.

This speech, although it followed close on the completion of his articles in *The Lancet*, already contained some changes —an example of what some people considered Lister's irritating habit of refusing to let well alone and insisting, instead, on mentioning every improvement which had resulted from his experience and experiments. It also placed emphasis upon the theoretical basis of his work, being entitled "On the Antiseptic Principle in the Practice of Surgery," which irritated the many surgeons who wanted only to be given something that would make wounds heal.

How, Lister wondered, was the world going to react to his discovery? He had solved the third major problem of surgery, the problem of the healing of wounds, without which the two other major contributions—the control of bleeding and the elimination of pain—could not be fully utilized.

Would the world accept or reject his contribution? The adoption of a discovery was as important as the discovery itself, particularly in medicine, where human lives were hanging in the balance. Unfortunately it was frequently more difficult to obtain recognition for something new than it was to discover it. Semmelweis was not the only doctor whose work was rejected instead of being used to benefit mankind. After all, Cagniard de La Tour and Schwann had shown in 1837 that fermentation was caused by vegetable cells which split up a sugary solution into alcohol and carbonic acid, but Liebig had insisted that both fermentation and putrefaction were slow combustion, caused by the action of oxygen upon the molecules, and Liebig's views had prevailed.

Discoveries of a limited but important nature were constantly being made and ignored and made again. In 1827, for example, a young French doctor named Melier wrote a paper saying that the condition which was called, among other things, the iliac passion, was not just another variety of stomach-ache, but a disease caused by the inflammation of a small appendix on the intestine. Dupuytren, the famous tyrant of surgery, laughed him down, and for sixty long years the last hours of the victims of appendicitis were made miserable by strong purges, enemas, and bleeding.

The road travelled by many major discoverers, such as the men who had discovered anæsthesia, had been marked by many detours. Now Lister wondered whether his own contribution would be accepted readily, or whether he, too, would reach his goal only after a long and tortuous journey.

He had presented his case against the killer to the jury. What the verdict would be would depend a great deal upon the jury itself. Was it composed of men who were his peers, or of those who could not understand, did not want to understand, or, understanding, preferred to ignore the evidence for reasons of their own?

One of the gentlemen of the jury was James Simpson. Quite capable of understanding, a man who had himself fought a good fight for scientific progress, Simpson was from the very first a leader in the opposition to antiseptic surgery.

James Simpson was born in 1811, the eighth and youngest child of a baker whose finances reached rock bottom the day that James was born. After that Mrs Simpson took a hand, and business picked up; but she died when James was nine, leaving him to the care of his only sister.

Meanwhile his brothers were working hard, determined to give the 'baby' the opportunities which they had been denied and to which they believed he was entitled because of his ability and diligence as a scholar. With their help he embarked on a career which was to bring him many honours, including that of being the first Scottish professor and doctor to receive the distinction of becoming a baronet.

It was an extremely stormy career. Simpson was a

quarrelsome man, and he was convinced that some of his colleagues lacked cordiality towards him because of his humble origin. Probably that was one of the few things James Syme did not hold against him, but they quarrelled about almost everything else, agreeing briefly on one occasion when they attacked the new fad of homœopathy. According to one of Simpson's close friends "there was a morbid touchiness about both parties which led them to take offence at the slightest cause."

Considering the importance of the antagonists, one finds it sometimes difficult to understand the pettiness to which they descended in their quarrels. In a letter to Dr Beilby, President of the Royal College of Physicians at Edinburgh, Dr Simpson wrote:

> Mr Syme states, "he [Dr Simpson] admits having intercepted me at the chamber door of the patient." Now, Mr Syme knows perfectly well that I never did in any way admit of such a thing. . . . When we met Mr Syme had not, in truth, "nearly reached" the patient's bedroom door (as he avowed to you in his first letter) and far less was he actually "at" it (as he next inadvertently asserts in his second) . . .

and so on for over 1500 words.

Although it was waged at a low level the battle raged furiously, with distinguished allies coming forward to support each claim and counter-claim. Neither of the men ever lacked staunch partisans and friends, whose devotion was a tribute to his good qualities.

Upon Simpson's death Dr Horatio Storer of Boston referred to him sincerely as "not merely an eminent and learned Scotch practitioner, but a philanthropist whose love encircled the world." This must have been a slight exaggeration, since Simpson's circle of love certainly excluded Syme and his son-in-law. But there is no doubt about his being a learned man and a humanitarian.

Not only was he moved, as so many other doctors had been, by the suffering of patients during surgical operations;

but he included in his sympathy the suffering of women in childbirth, accepted as inevitable and right by most of his colleagues in the field of midwifery. For a short time he had investigated mesmerism in the hope that it might do some good, and when Robert Liston successfully tried out the "Yankee dodge" which "beat mesmerism hollow" Simpson immediately considered its use in childbirth.

There were certain disadvantages, he found, particularly in protracted labour, because of ether's unpleasant, nauseating odour and irritating effects. Experimenting continually on himself, Simpson came to the conclusion that chloroform was better. He never claimed to have invented chloroform, although he claimed all the credit for its introduction as an anæsthetic. He was undoubtedly a pioneer in the field, and entirely responsible for the use of chloroform in childbirth.

He did not succeed in gaining recognition without a struggle. Almost every innovation met with opposition, usually on the ground that it was sacrilegious and would destroy the home and family. The latter argument appealed particularly to people who were quite indifferent to the squalor and suffering in the homes they were determined to preserve.

When Edward Jenner informed the world that he could keep people from catching smallpox by inoculating them with a bovine disease he was immediately denounced as a beast of the Apocalypse. Smallpox was heaven-ordained, and trying to prevent it, especially by giving people a disease which God had intended for animals, should be severely punished.

There was no lack of evidence to prove that God would punish people Himself. Doctors exhibited proof—a sickly girl covered with scales and a boy with a horn were much in use as evidence of God's anger at those who tried to interfere with His plans—while artists depicted the tragic transformations of human beings into cows; although sometimes, as in the case of the cartoonist Rowlandson, they drew with their tongues in their cheeks.

Every invention had to be tested for impiety, and even the winnowing machine was frowned upon because only God should have the power to raise the winds. This time, however, the sanctity of the home did not appear to have been invoked, as it most certainly was against the doctrines of Darwin, whose theory of the origin of species was considered a contradiction of the Bible and an invitation to pattern one's behaviour upon that of the apes. Referring to these and similar controversies which people regarded as battles between science and religion, Joseph Lister later remarked, "I have no hesitation in saying that in my opinion there is no antagonism between the religion of Jesus Christ and any fact scientifically established." But his point of view was not shared by the majority of his contemporaries, particularly where motherhood was concerned.

Anything dealing with this sacred subject was suspected of threatening the sanctity of the home. This was particularly true of Simpson's plan to lessen the pain of childbirth; for if women did not suffer when they were having children what was to prevent them from having them illegitimately? And anyway, it was pain which engendered mother-love. How could a woman have any affection for her baby if it were born while she was in a drunken stupor—and how, with such a start in life, could it help but be an immoral drunkard?

Did not the Bible specifically state that women should bring forth their young in suffering? Heaven only knew what the penalty for tampering with the primeval curse would be! Certainly the impious would be consigned to the eternal fires of hell, even though it was no longer possible, as it had once been, to burn them at the stake.

Large sections of the clergy, including those of Simpson's own Church, led the attack, as the clergy of the devout Catholic Pasteur was later to attack him on similar ground.

Simpson was a very pious man, although it was not until 1861 that he actually started on his "apostolic work." Educated on, as well as in, the Bible, he was as familiar as any of his adversaries with the territory over which the battle raged. Medical arguments were sandwiched in between Genesis iii, 16, and Isaiah xxvi, 17, while Simpson answered text and verse with text and verse, and managed to emerge triumphant.

The opponents of painless childbirth, he claimed, had misinterpreted the Bible regarding the bringing forth of young in suffering. The word should be translated to mean labour, or toil, not pain: Adam must labour and toil for his food, not suffer. Simpson's thunderbolt was, "And the Lord God caused a deep sleep to fall upon Adam, and he slept: and He took one of his ribs, and closed up the flesh instead thereof," which proved that God himself had been the first anæsthetist, and had used anæsthesia, moreover, during the first birth!

When people insisted that this sleep had occurred before the original sin, at which time God had not insisted that people must suffer as He did later, Simpson replied, "*Your* Bible differs from mine," if it said that pain entered the world with sin.

He was quite as ready for doctors who argued that anæsthesia in childbirth interfered with natural functions and might, by accident, cause death. "Why do you ride, my dear doctor?" he demanded. After all, there were plenty of accidents connected with trains and carriages which interfered with the natural function of walking. "Chloroform 'does nothing but save pain'? A carriage does nothing but save fatigue," he argued.

He had plenty of reason to agree with one of his patients who wrote him reassuringly that he "need not be afraid that there will not be enough suffering in the world." Like so many of the parents of his day, Simpson knew from experience how much suffering there was in trying to raise a family.

He had lost one baby in infancy. He had sat, helpless, by the bed of his four-year-old Maggie, his "little marmoset," while her throat closed for ever after an attack of measles. He had watched his poor Jaimie die at fifteen after a life of half-blind invalidism. Most tragic of all, he had seen his eldest son, David, a promising young physician, stricken with a fatal attack of what was probably appendicitis. Jessie, whom they all called "Sunbeam," had survived her beloved brother by only a month. Yes, there was suffering enough to go round, no matter how much of it one managed to prevent.

As Simpson had predicted, it was the mothers themselves who helped him win the battle to spare them pain; in particular, it was the royal mother. After Queen Victoria took chloroform during the birth of Prince Leopold, there was not much that could be said without slandering a family which was certainly a model of British middle-class sanctity.

Winning this battle did not place James Simpson for ever on the side of the angels.

He had his own reasons for opposing antiseptics, and they seemed like very good ones to him. He was by no means indifferent to the dangers of hospitalism—it was a word of his own invention. On the contrary, he had attempted to arouse the profession to its dangers by compiling and publishing statistics which showed that of 2089 amputations performed in hospital practice 855 patients died, while a similar number of operations in private practice had resulted in only 226 deaths. "Must hospital surgeons ever remain content with losing one-third to one-half of *all* their amputation cases, and nine-tenths of some?" people asked. To drive home his point Simpson added, "A man laid upon the operating-table in one of our surgical hospitals is exposed to more chances of death than the English soldier on the field of Waterloo!"

He sincerely wanted to do away with hospital diseases, but he wanted to do it his way. One of his suggestions was that hospitals should be replaced by the pavilion system. This idea was becoming popular, and might have resulted in the destruction of many of the fine buildings which had been erected at great expense.

As late as 1874 people who had not heard of Lister's

method, or who had dismissed it as unsound, agreed that "when once a hospital has become incurably pyæmia-stricken it is as impossible to disinfect it by any known hygienic means as it would be . . . an old cheese of the maggots which have been generated in it. There is, in these extreme cases, only one remedy left," the writer continued, "which the Governors and Staff of the Lincoln County Hospital have so generously, so disinterestedly, so nobly, resolved on—*viz.*, the demolition of the infected fabric."

Simpson had another plan for combating hospitalism, which was even dearer to him than the pavilion system. This was the replacing of ligatures, which helped to cause sepsis, by acupressure, or needles which compressed the arteries. The best that Simpson's friend and biographer Duns could say for the position which Simpson took in regard to antiseptics was that "nothing, he thought, should be tolerated whose tendency was to continue the use of the ligature in amputations after the superiority of acupressure had, as he believed, been established."

At the meeting of the British Medical Association in Dublin, at which Lister had spoken of his new principle, Simpson had reported on the success of his acupressure, and had noted with satisfaction that he received a more enthusiastic reception than the newcomer.

However, he was very much annoyed to discover that favourable comments followed the conclusion of Lister's series of articles in *The Lancet.* The paper itself commented editorially, "If Professor Lister's conclusions with regard to the power of carbolic acid in compound fractures should be confirmed by further experiment and observation, it will be difficult to overrate the importance of what we may really call his discovery."

This was the opinion of James Godchild Wakley, youngest son of the founder of *The Lancet.* Things might have developed in quite a different manner if Thomas Wakley had not recently died, for when he defended some one it was with a vigour which, backed up by his ready fists, had made him a figure to be reckoned with. His son was of a milder and more equivocal nature. Not only was James Wakley's championship of Lister rather weak, but it was also confused. He placed far too much emphasis upon carbolic acid and too little upon the theory behind its use. Lister's choice of the word 'antiseptic' was also rather confusing; later it became obvious that it would have been better if he had made it clear that he was attempting to create an aseptic wound, one free from sepsis, by means of an antiseptic, or decay-combating, agent.

Following Lister's speech to the British Medical Association, Professor Simpson said candidly, "I am rather hopeless of the evils of hospitalism being cured by any such agent as carbolic acid"—which showed that he, too, placed more emphasis upon the drug than on the principle.

With so much importance being attached to carbolic acid it was quite natural for doctors who read about Lister's success to give his method a chance by daubing some carbolic on to a wound. If an instrument dropped on the floor they would pick it up, wipe it on their coat-tails in time-honoured fashion, and continue to use it as a matter of course. It was many years before the average surgeon remembered that he must not absent-mindedly run his hand over his hair during an operation or hold his scalpel in his teeth for just a minute, and even longer before he restrained his curiosity and stopped peeping under bandages or poking at wounds to see how they were getting along. It was quite natural for many surgeons to think they had tried antiseptic surgery and, when infections followed their operations, decide that it did not work.

For years Lister struggled to make himself understood. Carbolic acid and antiseptic surgery were not identical: carbolic was merely the weapon for a surgeon to use in his battle against germs. In order to get good results, Lister insisted, "You must be able to see with your mental eye the septic ferments as distinctly as we see flies or other insects with the corporeal eye." Unless surgeons could do this they could not successfully practise antiseptic surgery. The method was based upon the germ-theory, and "without a belief in the truth of that theory," he explained over and over again, "no man can be thoroughly successful in the treatment."

"The injured tissues do not need to be 'stimulated' or treated with any mysterious 'specific,'" he wrote in a pamphlet describing the antiseptic system of treatment. "*All that they need is to be let alone.* Nature will then take care of them: those which are weakened will recover, and those which have been deprived of vitality by the injury will serve as pabulum for their living neighbours."

It was, however, extremely difficult to interest surgeons in a theory, for most of them prided themselves on being good, practical men, with no time for philosophical nonsense. Too long, they insisted, had metaphysics and medicine been confused. It was time to get away from all that. Theories were for philosophers, who, for their part, were proud of being above practical matters.

It was quite true that considering medicine as a philosophy had retarded its progress for centuries, but opposing theory did not remedy the situation. Lister himself never made the mistake of separating theory and practice. He would spend hours shopping for a suitable material or devising a surgical instrument, and hours delving into the problem of vitality. For him theory and practice were so closely connected that he could never say where one began and the other left off.

Soon after the publication of Lister's articles letters began to appear in *The Lancet.* One, reprinted from the *Daily Review*, was signed "Chirurgicus," but was undoubtedly written by Professor Simpson. Possibly because some one had recently claimed that his method of acupressure was not original, he attacked Lister by insisting that he was not offering anything new. A French doctor, Jules Lemaire, had used carbolic acid for several years, and was entitled to whatever credit the system might deserve.

Instead of rushing into print to claim priority, Lister

wondered whether there was any truth in the letter, and, after a great deal of difficulty, managed to locate Lemaire's book.

Although Lister himself had not heard of carbolic acid being used except on sewage Lemaire had, he discovered, actually employed it on wounds, and had grasped at least some of the implications of Pasteur's work on putrefaction. But Lemaire had used carbolic acid indiscriminately, even putting "a few touches with an *extremely* weak watery solution of the acid" on cancers, and looking through "rose-coloured spectacles at the results of his experiments."

Lister had "never thought of such a thing as any merit attaching to happening to be the first to *apply* carbolic acid." To him it was not a question of finding a drug that would work like a charm—another disinfectant might have done just as well, and if carbolic had not seemed satisfactory he would have searched for something else—but of discovering that injured tissues had the power to recover when protected against microbes that caused putrefaction.

Whether or not he suspected Simpson's arguments of disingenuousness, Lister never permitted himself to take a subjective view of the situation. He always referred to his opponent courteously, in 1898 going so far as to praise him without a trace of rancour, saying, "Thanks to anæsthesia—in the promotion and diffusion of which the illustrious citizen to whom you have referred, the late Sir James Simpson, took so large a share—the actual operative procedure is now as a rule painless." Of course, this was after Simpson's death, but even while his opponent was alive Lister never descended to the level on which polemics were usually waged.

As he once wrote to his father when he had been on the verge of getting involved in one of Syme's quarrels, "I am by disposition very averse to quarrelling and contending with others; in fact, I doubt if I could do it, though I have never tried much." Subsequently he remarked that he was relieved when no men of importance appeared at medical congresses, because he had discovered how frequently the time was apt to be "monopolized by the squabbles of some great ones."

Nothing seemed more wasteful to Lister than to consume one's time and energy in a personal battle, such as the one which raged for years over the question as to who deserved the credit for the discovery of anæsthesia, a struggle which ended disastrously for all of the contenders. Horace Wells had taken to sniffing chloroform to console himself for the loss of the glory to which he believed himself entitled, and committed suicide while he was in gaol after one of his sprees. William Morton and Charles Jackson (the chemist who had given him advice) devoted themselves exclusively to fighting about the credit for the discovery, and, like stags with locked antlers, fought almost literally to the death: Morton succumbed to a heart-attack brought on by reading an account of what Jackson had said about him, and Jackson, whose mind had been failing, went completely insane while he was staring at a monument erected in Morton's honour, and had to be placed in an asylum.

Lister had no intention of joining in such a battle with James Simpson. Yet his letter had to be answered, so he wrote briefly and with restraint, explaining what he was trying to do and contrasting his theory with Lemaire's haphazard use of carbolic acid.

Simpson replied with a signed letter in which he gave himself away by remarking, "Prof. Lister . . . seems actually to believe that the use of carbolic acid may lead to the absorption of a piece of necrosed bone or a silk ligature," and wanted to know why Lister did not use acupressure as he ought to, instead of trying to redeem the discredited ligature.

This letter, too, could not be ignored. Lister wrote:

> The elaborate communication of Sir James Simpson in to-day's *Lancet* may seem to require some reply. But as I have already endeavoured to place the matter in its true light without doing injustice to anyone, I must forbear from any comments on his allegations. In the forthcoming numbers of your journal, I have arranged to publish, with your permission, a

series of papers fully explanatory of the subject in question, and your readers will then be able to judge for themselves how far the present attack admits of justification.

I am, sirs, yours, etc.

JOSEPH LISTER

GLASGOW. *November* 2, 1867

This dignified note, so different from the long outburst Simpson had anticipated, gave him no opening for another attack. However, he got hold of some one else to write opposing the new method. Soon two doctors who favoured Lister's treatment wrote in his defence, after which a period of comparative quiet followed.

But Simpson, like Syme, loved a fight as much as Lister disliked one. He had never given in before in his life, and he was not going to now, particularly as Lister proceeded to ignore his advice and continue with experiments and discoveries intended to redeem the "discredited ligature."

CHAPTER X

The Discredited Ligature

LISTER NEVER LIKED ACUPRESSURE. This system of Simpson's was based on the observation of John Hunter and others that an object like a needle did not cause suppuration when introduced into the body, whereas ligatures did. If pressure was applied to a needle thrust under an artery clotting and occlusion would result. The clot thus formed would remain after the needle had been withdrawn and would serve as a stopper to prevent the flow of blood.

Acupressure needles, slender and sharp, made of non-oxidizable iron and headed with wax or glass beads, similar to the needles used in repairing harelips, became quite popular with many surgeons. They were easy to apply, they could be removed without pain to the patient, and, most important, they did not create suppuration or rot away.

Lister, however, never found them trustworthy. "Could you take an acupressure needle out of a man's thigh forty-eight hours after an operation," he asked his students, "and go away home with a mind at ease?"

He certainly could not. A clot was not a safe stopper for an important artery. It might come loose, and then a hæmorrhage, often a fatal one, would result.

But ligatures were not safe either; Simpson was quite right about that. They were left with long ends hanging out of the incision, to act as drains for the poisons generating in the wound; and after a week or so, when they had usually ulcerated through the artery, they were pulled out. Naturally a secondary hæmorrhage frequently occurred, because the ligature, along with the blood-clot and the vessel itself, had softened and rotted away.

It was taken for granted that ligatures must rot. Lister

wondered why, since bullets and needles could "lie for an indefinite period embedded in the living tissues without inducing suppuration." That, he decided, was because those objects were solid, while thread was porous, containing putrefactive germs in its interstices. If the germs could be destroyed the silk would be safe and would eventually be devoured, he reasoned, as blood-clots and other dead material had been, by the living tissues.

He soaked silk in a solution of carbolic acid and tried it on a horse that needed an operation. When the animal died a short time later Lister investigated and decided that the treated silk had lived up to his expectations. He therefore used it on a human patient, and wrote afterwards to his father, "I don't think any case ever excited me so much."

The operation was for aneurysm, a condition which occurred frequently in those days. Kidney diseases, gout, and, especially, untreated syphilis caused inflammation of the arteries which, yielding spontaneously under cardiac pressure, created a sac or cavity filled with blood. Whenever it was possible this sac must be opened and the artery tied off before it ruptured and caused a hæmorrhage.

Lister's patient was a woman of fifty-one who had been suffering for four years from an aneurysm about the size of a large orange, which had lately commenced to cause her agonizing pain. Lister operated, successfully tying the external iliac artery, a difficult task and one which he had never performed before.

Confident of the harmlessness of his treated silk, he cut the ends short instead of leaving them long enough so that the ligature could be pulled out. He dressed the wound antiseptically, which, as he explained, did not "mean merely 'dressed with an antiseptic' but 'dressed so as to ensure the absence of putrefaction.'"

The patient made an excellent recovery, and was able to climb stairs within six weeks. For ten months she remained in fairly good condition. Then as she was sitting up in bed one day she suddenly cried out that something had given way within her and that she was dying. She was right; as so often happened in cases of that sort, another artery had given way, and she quickly bled to death.

Fortunately Lister was able to perform a post-mortem and to examine the silk ligature. The results fell short of the goal which he had expected to reach. Although the noose about the artery had been devoured by the tissues, the knot itself had been only "superficially nibbled, so to speak." In the knot he found a tiny amount of fluid containing a few pus-cells. If the patient had lived long enough these cells might have caused an abscess.

It seemed to Lister that the irritation had been caused by the "sharp and jagged fragments" of the disappearing silk, as he was sure he had been thorough in his antiseptic precautions. So perhaps he should find a softer material.

Catgut, the submucous lining of the interior of the sheep's intestines, had been used without success in the past, but Lister thought it would make a good ligature if he could destroy the microbes on it.

For twenty years he was to continue trying to find the perfect absorbable ligature—an example of the perseverance which he once modestly said he hoped would make up for his lack of brilliant talent. Not that he devoted himself exclusively to that subject; other phases of his work were equally important and received equal attention. In the main his efforts took two directions: trying to improve his antiseptic technique, especially with regard to cutting down the amount of irritating carbolic acid which came in contact with the wound, and reconsidering operations, since, in the light of his discoveries, it was frequently possible to save portions of the body which previously had to be sacrificed.

When he was a boy his holidays at Upton House would never have been complete without scientific work such as the dissection of small animals and fish, the maceration of bones, and putting up of skeletons. It seemed quite natural to him, at forty-one, to want to spend some time during his holidays that way.

Holidays were very important to him and to Agnes. Few doctors took time off in those days, priding themselves on their ability to keep going, a little afraid, in the face of cut-throat medical competition, to turn their backs on their patients even for a few days. A great deal of the irritability, short-sightedness, and lack of perspective of the members of the medical profession undoubtedly arose from their custom of keeping their noses steadily to the grindstone.

Lister was never afraid of losing his patients to a rival or an assistant, and he could confidently leave his practice in the hands of the men he had trained. Although he was frequently tempted to stay indefinitely at his work, he knew how much he and Agnes needed an occasional break in their routine. In the long run it helped him to accomplish a tremendous amount of work.

It was work which required the stamina for steady plodding as well as the ability to sprint: to plan sound strategy as well as execute brilliant tactics. And Agnes's tasks were no less demanding than his own. She was in her own right as remarkable a person as her husband, particularly when compared with the other women of her period and class.

The ringleted, vapid virgin, legless in her hoop-skirts, "half angel, and half bird," helpless and innocent, was being replaced by a pert and frivolous creature whose curves were exaggerated in front with padding and at the back with a bustle. Well-to-do ladies, with the exception of a grim little group of New Women, were dedicated to social pleasures, aiming to achieve a reputation for witty small-talk and seductive charm.

Gifted with a lively wit, Agnes Lister had none of the reformer's disapproval of a good time, but social pleasure consumed only a tiny fraction of her life. No crusader for the equality of the sexes, she already enjoyed a relationship with her husband which was one of true equality.

By no means merely Lister's secretary and housekeeper, she performed both functions perfectly and managed to adapt them to his requirements. Lunch might be delayed until four-thirty in the afternoon, and work in the laboratory might continue through the night, and Joseph showed no signs of reconciling himself to the fact that there were only sixty minutes to the hour—but it was all part of the man and the life she loved.

Their holidays were delightful as well as necessary. They both loved to travel, enjoying the scenery and sight-seeing with their guide-books, locating the sites of famous events which Joseph had hoped to visit ever since the days when he had taken honours in classics.

Their study of foreign languages continued: French and German, Italian and Spanish, and, eventually, Danish, which Lister decided to tackle when he discovered that it would enable him to understand Norwegian and Swedish as well, and which he fancied bore a resemblance to the Scots dialect.

They did not always travel abroad. Frequently they went for a short vacation to some near-by country boarding-house, where they lived very simply and where Joseph was particularly happy if he could fish or swim. He was naturally adept at sports, and he would have liked to have the time to become just a little more than a good amateur fisherman, and to master something more complicated than 'eights' and 'threes' as a skater.

Always interested in botany, he and Agnes devoted more time to the subject after his brother Arthur turned his attention in that direction and became an authority on the higher fungi and myxomycetes. In addition to specimens for their own collections Joseph and Agnes were always on the alert for something which Arthur Lister might find useful.

Together they would walk or rest, discussing an idea which Joseph had tucked aside until he had time to talk it over with his wife. Combining "study with ease," as Joseph Jackson Lister use to put it, they would make simple experiments or correct proofs or jot down notes for future lectures. Agnes used to keep their diaries, and they would alternately record, with Joseph supplying the sketches, the birds which they had seen.

If they were particularly tired they would spend most of their time resting, perfectly content when they found a charming spot such as the one which Joseph described in a letter to his brother. A little garden

> full of bright flowers, the trees in full unimpaired summer foliage, the corn fields golden with the late harvest, the lower hills emerald green, the higher ones purple with heather-blossom. . . . Agnes pointed out to me the scattered scales of a fir cone, no doubt the work of one of thy beloved crossbills.

They always returned from their holidays with new energy and enthusiasm for the work which lay ahead. Both of them particularly enjoyed their visits to Upton House. True, London was getting ready to swallow the little village, which was scarcely country any longer, but it was still the place where Lister had been born and where he had spent his happy childhood.

Time had altered the family as well as the neighbourhood. John had passed away, as had Henry and their mother; and the fact that Isabella Sophia was still alive at Christmas was almost a miracle, brought about by her brother Joseph's skill and his antiseptic discovery.

It had not been easy for him to operate upon his "darling B.," but he had never shirked what he considered a responsibility. Before antiseptics, only small and incomplete—and hence almost useless—amputations had been performed for cancer of the breast, because death almost invariably followed the infection of the tremendous wound which would be created by the removal of the pectoral fascia and glands of the armpit.

Knowing that the operation would not be a success, no surgeon was willing to tackle this case, and Joseph's sister, in despair, had been on the verge of putting herself in the hands of quacks.

Mr Syme, however, felt that Lister's method would deprive the operation of its dangers, and would certainly afford the patient her only chance. She wanted him to do it, for she had complete confidence in her brother; and so, in June of 1867, Lister approached his "*most* formidable undertaking."

His sister's confidence was justified. As he put it, "the operation was done at *least* as well as if she had not been my sister. But I do not wish to do such a thing again."

Now, a year and a half after the operation, there had been no local recurrence, which was in itself cause for rejoicing, although Lister knew that cancer might strike again.

It was good, too, to see his father once more, still in possession of his faculties, although no longer "firm and erect and bright and beautiful." Joseph Jackson Lister had hoped that his son would be able to be near him "during the short time that might remain to me in this changing world," for in 1866 Lister had applied for a position at University College, in London. It had been a great disappointment to the old man when the Chair had gone to John Marshall, who had been waiting for it for eighteen years.

Lister had been more disappointed than he had expected, although he took it very well. Syme, whose opinion of London had not altered since the days when he had given it such a brief trial, was not at all sorry that he was to remain in Glasgow.

"In order to maintain a good metropolitan place," he wrote, "it is necessary to do a great deal of dirty work . . . which I am quite sure you would decline."

And perhaps it had turned out for the best, because Lister's work had almost immediately begun to bear fruit in Glasgow, and he might not have been able to do so well in another city.

So, all in all, the Christmas holiday, the last which Lister was to spend at Upton House, was a happy one.

Arthur and his wife were there, and the children, who, with their cousins, made the house as gay as it had been when Joseph and his sisters and brothers had been growing up. Always at ease with children, Lister was the delight of his nieces and nephews—who perhaps wondered a little when they grew older how they had dared to romp with so distinguished a relative.

Already some of the children were growing up. Mary Lister Godlee's son Rickman John was following his uncle into the field of medicine. A little later he would try to 'educate' Erichsen, under whom Lister had once served as house-surgeon, in the antiseptic method, and find it very difficult; for Erichsen, although friendly towards Lister, was old-fashioned and could not quite comprehend what the younger man was driving at.

Young Godlee—the family called him John—had a real thrill that Christmas holiday: for the first time in his life he assisted his uncle at an operation. True, the patient was only a calf and the operating-theatre was Joseph Jackson Lister's museum—which, being on the ground floor, could accommodate the unwieldy creature—but it was an important operation all the same. Its purpose was to test whether or not catgut would make a suitable ligature.

John was very careful as he helped his uncle cut short the calf's hair and rub a solution of carbolic acid in four parts of linseed oil well into the skin. Lister had begun to perspire the moment he made the incision, but his perfect calmness steadied the boy, who watched his uncle's large hands with fascination. They moved skilfully and precisely even when they performed the finicky little task of threading the aneurysm-needles with the ligatures, which, having been soaked for four hours in a carbolic solution, had softened and swelled until it was almost impossible to get them through the needles' eyes. One ligature was home-made, consisting of three strips of peritoneum from the small intestine of an ox, firmly twisted together, while the other was commercial 'minikin gut.'

Exposing the artery in the neck of the calf, Lister tied it off, and then, with the second ligature, tied it in another place. This ligature broke, and, leaving it about the artery to see what would become of it, he used another, which held. The operation was performed with a meticulous attention to antiseptic technique which Godlee was seldom to see equalled by other surgeons on even the most distinguished patients.

When it was over the calf's neck was bandaged and covered with a towel which, to prevent its slipping, was stitched to a halter.

John Godlee sighed with relief as he looked up from the snoring calf, and then smiled as he noticed his "grandfather's alabaster Buddha on the mantelpiece, contemplating with inscrutable gaze the services of beasts to men."

This beast had performed a very useful service. When it was slaughtered a month or so after the operation the portions in which Lister was interested were sent to him, having been carefully packed according to his directions.

As he examined the ligatures in his laboratory it seemed at first as though they were still intact, for he could see that they had preserved their original shape and colouring. Closer examination, however, revealed the fact that the ligatures were "present in appearance though absent in reality." They had been almost entirely replaced by living cells which had assumed the shape of the material they had devoured; the colour was due to the tiny bits of dirt which had not been eaten.

The very success of this experiment worried Joseph Lister. It was good to see that the ligatures had been absorbed; but if they were absorbed too quickly they might not secure the blood-vessel until the danger of hæmorrhage was past. If the cells gnawed away too much of the knot it might slip even before it was completely absorbed, particularly if it were subjected to an unusual strain.

After a good deal of effort Lister worked out a way of preparing the gut so that it seemed to answer his requirements, but he was not satisfied with it. For twelve years he continued to improve on it, making hundreds of experiments, visiting countless factories, and testing all kinds of samples as he searched for the ideal catgut: supple and thin but strong, thoroughly disinfected by carbolic but not slippery, aged (he learned from an old fiddler the trick of seasoning catgut to increase its strength) without its being tough or inelastic or brittle. It was almost impossible for him to obtain a commercial catgut which suited his requirements as well as the gut which he prepared himself.

Some misunderstandings arose over absorbable ligatures; a number of doctors thought Lister said that catgut was dissolved by the fluids in the body, while others believed he was claiming that it came to life. The latter were in some cases misled by his use of the term 'organized' in describing what happened to the gut—a word which, he explained, was not of his inventing but "ready to my hand."

Despite the confusion the ligature itself was a success, and soon found supporters. In April 1869 Bickersteth wrote to Syme telling him how well it had worked, and ending with, "I wonder what will become of acupressure now!!!"

Obviously acupressure was going, which meant further stepping on Simpson's already wounded toes. But at any rate, Lister thought, he would make the ghost of Ambroise Paré very happy by redeeming his ligature!

Paré had always been one of Lister's heroes. He felt a certain kinship with a man who said fresh air was rather beneficial to wounds, although air in sick-rooms was dangerous because of what he referred to as miasmas. Paré had urged surgeons not to meddle with wounds, but to regard the patient as a whole and build him up with food and medication. "I dressed him, and God healed his wounds," he used to say—for Paré, like Lister, was a religious man, although religious forms did not mean a great deal to him.

Some people said Paré had hedged about his religion because it was dangerous to be a Protestant. He was one of the fortunate Huguenots who escaped the Massacre of St Bartholomew. But Lister thought he was an honest and pious man, this barber-surgeon who had lived through so many wars and intrigues, the personal surgeon of four kings who, no matter how much they might differ from him on religious or political grounds, appreciated his ability and integrity.

Despite his fame Paré was always ready to learn, admit his own mistakes, and urge people to ignore his advice when it was not sound—another resemblance to Lister, who meant it when he said, "Next to the promulgation of a new truth, the best thing that I can see that a man can do is the recantation of a published error."

Now, fresh from his experiments on the ligature, Lister thought of Paré when, as a young man, he had served as military surgeon in the besieged fortress of Villaine and, running out of boiling oil, had wondered what he should use to destroy the poisons supposed to be lurking in the wounds of his patients. In desperation Paré had applied a salve, and when, in the morning, he had approached the wounded soldiers with trepidation, he found that they were in much better condition than those on whom he had used boiling oil. "Never again will I so cruelly burn the poor wounded!" he resolved, and, since heat evidently was not necessary to destroy the poisons in the wound, he saw no reason to continue the practice of searing the stump of an amputated limb. Bleeding could be controlled by tying the arteries with bits of fine string.

And now that Lister had found a way to destroy the microbes which infected ligatures and made them sources of decay they could be restored, on a higher level, to their rightful place in surgery.

CHAPTER XI

Professor of Surgery

ONE DAY IN THE EARLY SPRING OF 1869 Dr John Brown and Syme's assistant, Thomas Annandale, received a frantic summons to come to Syme's consulting-rooms. His servant had found him on the floor of his study, conscious but unable to rise, his left arm and leg paralysed, his speech indistinct.

It was quite obvious that Syme had suffered a cerebral hæmorrhage. That same day Annandale had seen him suddenly and momentarily unable to speak, had noticed him stumble as he got out of his carriage, but had not thought anything serious was wrong, because he had recovered quickly and operated with all his old skill later in the day.

To the relief of his friends Syme was soon able to speak coherently again, and he felt much better after six ounces of blood had been withdrawn, by cupping, from the back of his neck. Anxiously they waited to see whether his paralysis would continue. Would he be doomed to helplessness or the idleness almost as difficult for so active a man to bear?

Fortunately the stroke was not severe. By the end of April Syme was up and about again, able to visit his patients, attend his classes, and even operate. But he would have to slow down; his days of extraordinary activity were over.

He was seventy, an age at which most men, even if they were in excellent health, usually began to think about retiring. It was obviously time for him to resign his Chair. The idea was made a little more palatable to him by the thought that Lister would be his successor. As he said to Dr Brown, with Lister after him the school "may yet revive."

Lister applied for the professorship without hesitation. Not only did Edinburgh offer many more advantages than Glasgow, but his second five-year term in the Infirmary was coming to an end, and the existing rules prevented him from being in charge of the wards for more than two successive terms. Because he had been disappointed before he did not count too much on the Edinburgh appointment, and he also applied for a few beds in the Glasgow Infirmary so that he would not in any event be entirely cut off from hospital work.

It was, however, an almost foregone conclusion that he would get the Chair of Clinical Surgery, although Simpson and some of his followers maintained that it should be abolished, and the subject consolidated under the heading of Systematic Surgery. They implied that Lister's only qualification for the professorship was his relationship to Syme, and nepotism was casually accepted as the decisive factor by people who did not bother to review Lister's qualifications for the position.

There were plenty of them without counting his recent discovery. His ability and his many contributions to orthodox surgery fully entitled him to the Chair.

He had devised an improved method of amputating at the hip-joint: instead of cutting straight across the hip itself, as most surgeons did, he cut through the flesh lower down on the leg and then dissected out the bone, thus creating a smaller wound. Because this operation interfered as little as possible with the circulation it was particularly advantageous if the patients were elderly or threatened with diabetic or senile gangrene.

He had also perfected a method of excising the affected parts in caries, or decay, of the bones of the wrist—a complicated procedure, it was true, and as dangerous as most bone-operations were. In fifteen cases of excision of the wrist which Lister had performed six became ill with hospital gangrene and one died of pyæmia; but the simpler procedure of amputation would also have resulted in a high mortality, and, as he put it, "to save a human hand from amputation, and restore its usefulness, is an object well worthy of any labour involved in it." Syme had been very much impressed with his technique, urging him to publish it, and writing that Lister "should have seen the sensation" he created when he described one of his successful cases.

Lister's radical amputation of the breast for cancer was also a pioneering venture, following no established procedure; but only his antiseptic method made it a safe operation to attempt.

He had made some important contributions to 'bloodless surgery,' for he had never agreed with the surgeons who considered a great loss of blood a value in operations. If a limb that was to be amputated was raised and a tourniquet applied a great deal of blood could be preserved in the patient's body instead of being sacrificed with the limb. As Lister did very little to bring his work in this field before the profession Esmarch's elastic bandages were, some time later, greeted as an innovation, although Lister's method was more ingenious. He had devised a tourniquet to control hæmorrhage from the abdominal aorta, an instrument independently invented by Joseph Pancoast, of Philadelphia, at about the same time; and though he subsequently discarded tourniquets in favour of Esmarch's perfected rubber bands, it was not before his instrument had sensationally demonstrated its usefulness in an emergency.

Some years before, in the spring of 1862, Mr Syme had asked Lister, who was visiting in Edinburgh, to help him with an operation for aneurysm. It was a serious case, and, because such operations were usually thrilling it had more than the average number of spectators.

The patient, having been "carried in a basket, like a carcase from the shambles," was placed on the table, told to close his eyes, masked with a napkin and given chloroform. Everything was ready: knife, aneurysm-needles, sponges. Mr Syme, holding his scalpel as an artist would a pencil, traced a long line with it upon the skin, a line which was immediately vivid with drops of blood. Lister was already perspiring, although his face, unlike that of the spectators, was perfectly calm.

From the patient's story it had seemed as though the opening by which the artery communicated with the sac of the aneurysm was in the lower part of the abdomen, near the thigh, and as soon as he made the incision Mr Syme inserted his finger, expecting to place it upon the opening.

Unable to locate it, he had to enlarge the wound and insert a second finger, then again to admit a third and a fourth, and finally the thumb as well. Now the entire hand was in the wound, and still the opening of the artery had not been located. If Syme withdrew his hand the blood would gush forth and the patient would bleed to death in a matter of seconds.

What, the spectators wondered, was he going to do? They could not hear what he said to his assistant, but they noticed that Lister was reaching for an instrument which they could not identify. It was the abdominal tourniquet he had invented, which he had brought with him in case it should be needed.

There was scarcely room enough to apply it, as the aneurysm extended from the thigh to two inches above the umbilicus. Having felt the aorta by pressing with his fingers above the huge swelling, Lister placed his clamp over it and screwed it tight. With his free hand Syme felt carefully to discover whether the pulsing of the artery would stop.

It did. Syme withdrew his hand while the spectators watched breathlessly for the blood which would gush forth if its flow had not been entirely cut off. There was no hæmorrhage—only some clots which Syme quickly removed, revealing a bloodless wound. Now he could locate the opening of the artery, which, instead of being in its normal place at the floor of the sac, was closer to the head than the patient's history had indicated it would be.

Quickly he tied not only the external iliac, as he had planned, but the internal and the common iliac as well. It seemed to Lister that no one but his father-in-law could have performed this operation successfully in the difficult circumstances; but when it was all over Syme said, with the generosity which was as characteristic of him as his jealousy: "If it had not been for this instrument in the hands of my surgical colleague, Mr Lister of Glasgow, the man before you would ere this have been bereft of his life, as I know not how else we could have arrested the bleeding."

This tourniquet was only one of the many instruments which Lister invented, and which included a wire needle, forceps for extracting stones from the prostatic urethra, an ear-hook, sinus-forceps, bougies, and many other surgical implements. His interest and knowledge of surgical instruments prevented him from accepting casually whatever a manufacturer sent him and enabled him to reject those tools which were not up to his standards. He always personally went over every instrument he was going to use in an operation, after Agnes had first carefully checked them.

Another field in which Lister was an expert was that of anæsthesia; he had been chosen to write on that subject for Timothy Holmes's *System of Surgery*. He urged the use of anæsthetics, not only in order to prevent pain for humane reasons, but because of the shock which, resulting from pain, was frequently a cause of death. In his articles he emphasized particularly the need for strict attention to detail. He refused to accept the comforting opinion that an occasional accidental death was inevitable. In all the time that Syme had used chloroform, which he and Lister preferred to ether, he had not lost a single patient because of it. Lister recommended paying the closest attention to the respiration rather than concentrating on the pulse; it was important, he said, not to be content because the chest was apparently moving rhythmically, but to listen for the first sound of stertorous breathing and to be ready to pull out the tongue forcibly, to prevent the patient from choking to death.

One of the arguments frequently advanced to prove that Lister was not a good surgeon was that he was not a good operator. His enemies and even some of the people who were not unsympathetic to him insisted that he was fitted for the dissecting-room rather than the operating-theatre. It was true that he was methodical and, when judged by the standards which still persisted, slow and lacking in brilliance and style.

He was not slow out of awkwardness. His large hands were extremely steady, and he could perform delicate operations with the same skill as those which required physical strength. He could be fast when it was necessary, as once when he completed a lateral lithotomy, which included the removal of two calculi, in thirty-two seconds. His slowness was relative and deliberate. He felt about the length of an operation very much as Abraham Lincoln had felt about the proper length for a person's legs: long enough to reach from one's body to the ground. According to Lister an operation should take long enough to be performed properly. The surgeon must balance the need for care and attention to detail against the patient's ability to endure a prolonged operation.

When judged by the standards of the day Lister was not a brilliant speaker any more than he was a brilliant operator. His slight stammer, which increased when he was overtired, got on some people's nerves, although there were others who stoutly maintained that it lent weight to his words. His low, pleasant voice was unquestionably better suited to conversation than to working his audience up to a state of enthusiastic excitement during a lecture. More handsome than he had ever been, he had by no means a theatrical appearance; he seemed smaller and less distinguished-looking on the platform than he actually was.

Some people complained that he was lacking in humour, and it is true that he did not brighten his lectures with jokes; but though his wit was not sophisticated and scintillating, his patients and students enjoyed it, for he had a real sense of fun. As one newspaper correspondent put it, he had a "laughing face."

His students and patients never considered him aloof, for they recognized his genuine friendliness despite the reserve and formality which had replaced his shyness. The students found his lectures interesting, despite the lack of fireworks, for Lister always had something to say, and he never failed to give them the best that he had.

Yes, the students liked Joseph Lister. As he said later, "From the beginning I had youth on my side." He was never to lack volunteers to help him with his many experiments.

"On more than one occasion our patience was a little tried by the long hours," said Annandale, referring to Lister's early days in Edinburgh, "particularly when the dinner-hour was many hours overdue, but no one could work with Mr Lister without imbibing some of his enthusiasm."

When the students learned that Lister was being considered for the Chair which Syme had resigned 127 of them signed a letter expressing their hope that he would come to Edinburgh and referring to his capabilities and achievements in surgery, his contributions, researches, and literature which "have caused your name to stand next to that of Mr Syme amongst the living Surgeons of Scotland."

The Edinburgh appointment was duly made, and Joseph Lister's father was especially pleased, hoping that his son would not be quite so busy now and that they could spend some time together. But Joseph Jackson Lister did not live to see him established in his new position. A month after the appointment he was taken seriously ill, and Joseph and Agnes hastened the visit they had been planning to make, arriving at Upton House shortly before he died. He was eighty-four and, as he had hoped, still in possession of his faculties.

It was a real loss to Lister, whose father had been close to him not only as a parent and friend but as an intellectual comrade, with whom he could discuss every phase of his work. No more long letters, no more advice in planning papers and experiments; no more holidays in the house where he was born, for the home was broken up, and Lister was to see it only in his memories and dreams.

Fortunately he was too busy to devote much time to grief. He and Agnes had temporarily rented a furnished house in Edinburgh, and from it they had to move to their new home at No. 9 Charlotte Square, one of a row of terrace houses, fashionable and expensive. They had hesitated a little about taking it, but finally decided that it was worth the money, if only for the West Princes Street garden across the way, which Lister hoped he would have to himself before breakfast.

Not only was there the new home to arrange but, although his routine duties would not be so heavy as they had been in Glasgow, there were adjustments to be made, inevitable to anyone getting established in a new place.

To be certain of starting on a firm foundation Lister devoted his first lecture—which his father-in-law attended, receiving an enthusiastic welcome—to a demonstration of the truth of the germ-theory, using flasks similar to Pasteur's, which he had carefully brought with him from Glasgow.

He was anxious to convince the men who were to be his students and assistants, and also one of Edinburgh's most important professors, Dr Hughes Bennett, who held the Chair of Medicine. Dr Bennett had made some complicated experiments himself and had obtained results differing from those of Pasteur and Lister. It was these experiments which led Dr Simpson to coin the expression "mythical fungi" to describe the tiny creatures which Lister and Pasteur claimed caused fermentation and therefore putrefaction. Lister, however, was confident that any number of experiments which failed to verify his results must seem insignificant in the presence of even one flask of unsoured milk. As he put it, one successful experiment proved that the germ-theory was correct, whereas any number of failures only proved that the experimenter's technique had been faulty.

Not only must Lister convince his new associates of the soundness of his theory, but he must train a new hospital staff in his new technique. Mr Syme had only partially introduced the antiseptic system, and Lister had to cope with the inflexibility of certain members of the staff who, even when they had the best intentions in the world, could not manage to do things a new way. That he succeeded was evident, for within nine months after his arrival there was not a single case of pyæmia or gangrene in the fifty beds in his wards.

Fortunately, nursing conditions had improved a great deal in the last few years. Through the efforts of Florence Nightingale the country had been aroused to an awareness of the terrible conditions existing in the military hospitals during the Crimean War: soldiers crowded together in a rickety, foul-smelling hospital, without food or equipment or medical care. Chaos and red tape had reigned while rats gnawed away at the mutilated flesh of living men, and the wounded prayed for death.

Miss Nightingale, who had studied at Kaiserswerth and had later been superintendent of the "Establishment for Gentlewomen during Illness," was an organizer and agitator as well as a nurse. She fought valiantly to reform the entire military medical system, and though she only partially succeeded, she introduced a new era in nursing.

In 1860 the Florence Nightingale Training School for Nurses at St Thomas's Hospital was opened in London. Gradually the illiterate, drunken 'Sairey Gamps' who had once been considered good enough to care for the sick disappeared, to be replaced by followers of the Lady with the Lamp. Mrs Porter, the old head nurse at Edinburgh, might be a bit sceptical, calling them "bonny-like probationers that canna' mak' a bed," but the poet Henley described them more accurately as "waning fast into the sere of virginal decay, . . . kindly and calm, patrician to the last, . . ." and able to give "at need, draught, counsel, diagnosis, exhortation."

They were certainly a great improvement over the old type of nurse. Some of these, naturally, lingered on, and were a match even for Joseph Lister, as in the case of one slattern whom he tried to shame out of her habit of crawling into an empty bed in the wards to sleep off her hang-overs.

"Aren't you disturbed by the thought of the patients in your charge?" he asked her pointedly.

"Oh, I nae minds o' *them*!" she replied, convinced that he was politely concerned about the soundness of her sleep.

Visitors also made great demands on Lister's time. Before he left Glasgow surgeons—particularly foreigners and men from the provinces—had started writing to him and visiting his wards in order to learn about his method, and their number was gradually increasing all the time. Though he was delighted, realizing that every convert was of tremendous value in spreading the antiseptic theory, these visitors took up a good deal of his time.

So, although there were fewer routine-duties in Edinburgh than there had been at Glasgow, it was hard to see how he could have been much busier than he was.

"Joseph has only just come in from the hospital at 4.15," Agnes wrote her sister-in-law. "He has had to perform two amputations at the Infirmary and on coming home finds people waiting for him . . . whom he is seeing now without having had lunch. He has an operation in private at 4.30! and three patients to see afterwards. . . . Joseph had an operation here before going to the hospital. So it has been a busy day."

It was unusually busy because Lister's assistant happened to be ill, but all of his days were full enough. Many an entry in his notebook was dated after midnight, and on one occasion Agnes's careful writing recorded experiments until 3.50 A.M., at which time she was evidently persuaded to go to bed, for the final entry, at 4.30 A.M., was made by Lister himself.

He visited the Infirmary even on Sundays, when he would give his coachman the day off and, carrying a light cane, walk briskly along with his easy, rapid stride that ate up the miles—a walk that anyone who knew him could recognize from the distance or from the sound of his footsteps. The patients in the upper wards always knew when Lister was coming, for he took the stairs two at a time without effort. He seldom spent less than four hours in the wards on Sundays, for that was his day to take his time and find out whether his patients were comfortable and whether there was anything troubling them. He established a personal relationship with the patients which created an atmosphere of confidence far more real than the evil miasmas that had supposedly lurked about surgical wards.

He usually saved until the last his visit to the small, two-bedded room where a gaunt, russet-bearded man lay, "playing father to a brace of boys" who shared the other bed. This was William Ernest Henley, the poet. Suffering from tuberculosis which had affected the bones, he had already lost one foot, and amputation had been recommended for the other as well. But, having heard of Joseph Lister, Henley entered the Royal Infirmary in order to become his patient, and Lister got to work with all his skill to save him from another amputation. The battle was won after two difficult years, which Henley described vividly in a series of poems entitled "In Hospital," in which he paid the highest tribute to the Chief.

Not only was Lister busy with his patients and the adjustments necessary in a new position, but he had to give his attention to trying to overcome a difficulty which dated back to his Glasgow days.

Lister had left the Royal Infirmary of Glasgow without anything that could be considered recognition, for the Directors were too busy resenting his suggestion that their hospital was not perfect to realize that he was giving it a place in the sun. They were jealous of the Edinburgh Infirmary, which had been in existence fifty years longer than their institution, and when Lister published a paper in Edinburgh, in December 1869, they were insulted by his references to Glasgow conditions.

The paper, entitled "On the Effects of the Antiseptic System of Treatment upon the Salubrity of a Surgical Hospital," contained a number of statements at which they were bound to take offence.

Lister wanted to show that it was not necessary to tear down a hospital when it became contaminated, that it was not "impossible to disinfect it by any known hygienic means." This was a pressing issue, for not only were expensive hospitals threatened with destruction, but the pavilion system which was advocated in their place had great disadvantages. How could nurses possibly give adequate attention to patients if huts, containing only two or three patients apiece, were spread over acres of ground? It was vitally important, Lister felt, to show that a hospital could be made wholesome even when conditions had been very bad, and in order to do this he had to describe the Infirmary as it had been before he introduced his system.

He therefore wrote frankly about the Infirmary. In 1867, he said, the mortality had been so high in the male accident ward, which was separated from his own by only a narrow corridor, that the underlying drains had been investigated to see whether they could be to blame. It was then revealed that the ward itself had been erected directly over a pit containing the bodies of victims of a recent cholera-epidemic. The managers "did all in their power to correct it." As the pile of dead bodies was too large to remove "it was freely treated with carbolic acid, and with quick-lime, and an additional thickness of earth was laid over it." Meanwhile Lister had been practising antiseptic surgery for nine months in his own wards, which were the least well ventilated of all the wards, and his results had been excellent. In fact, there had not been a single case of pyæmia, erysipelas, or hospital gangrene.

Lister also spoke of the contest which had gone on between him and the Directors regarding the number of patients that ought to be admitted, for, although he had only fifty-five beds, he frequently had as many as seventy patients, the children two or three in a bed, while 'shake-downs,' or mattresses on the floor, accommodated the rest of the overflow.

The Glasgow Directors were furious. An indignant letter, inspired by them but signed by a doctor, was dispatched to the *Glasgow Daily Herald*, and reprinted in *The Lancet*. Lister, they insisted, was entirely unjustified in his remarks. Not only had conditions in their Infirmary always been good—

better, in fact, than in Edinburgh!—but great improvements had been made, not by Joseph Lister's little schemes but by their own efforts in the direction of better nursing, ventilation, diet, and cleanliness.

The letter, which appeared in the same issue of *The Lancet* as an article sneering at the germ-theory, had to be answered, for it flatly contradicted Lister's statements.

In his answer he tried to assuage hurt feelings as much as possible. He had not meant to give offence when he used the word 'contest,' for he really believed both sides had worthy motives. They wanted to accommodate as many needy patients as possible, while he was anxious to prevent crowding which might endanger the safety of the patients as a whole.

But as to the claim that the "three years of immunity from the ordinary evils of surgical hospitals" which his wards had enjoyed was due to cleanliness—to refute that, Lister pointed out that his wards had gone without even the annual spring-cleaning for three years, because, as the superintendent had informed him, they did not seem to need it!

It was true that nursing had improved, but he had been fortunate enough to have good nurses from the start. And if some of his patients did stay a long time in the hospital, which had been mentioned to show that he was not so successful as he claimed to be, it was important to remember that they were patients who, if treated by the old method, would have left the hospital rapidly enough, but would have left it dead.

In short, the improvements which had taken place had been due, as any reasonable person could see, to the new method of treating wounds.

The controversy with the Directors of the Glasgow Infirmary disturbed Lister very much, while it provided a source of real satisfaction to his enemies. It was not, however, a satisfaction which James Simpson was long to enjoy.

For a long time Simpson had been suffering from angina pectoris, the painful heart-disease which had killed John

Hunter, to whom he was, temperamentally, somewhat akin. Both men had known that over-exertion was extremely dangerous, yet neither of them had been able to take it easy either physically or emotionally. In May of 1870 James Simpson died at the age of sixty, after an extraordinarily active life.

Simpson's old enemy did not survive him very long. In April Syme had suffered his second stroke, which was followed in May by one so severe that his speech became inarticulate; he could no longer swallow, and had to be fed through a tube. It was obvious that he would not recover this time.

His children attended him devotedly, especially his daughter Lucy, upon whom he had been completely dependent during his illness, particularly since his wife's death the year before. He died on the twenty-sixth of June, when his garden was full of flowers. A potted orchid from his favourite greenhouse had been placed, at his request, beside his bed.

Syme had been almost as good a friend to Joseph Lister as Lister's own father—formal and restrained, slow to express sympathy or affection, but from the first appreciative of the man who was to win his daughter and was heading for a fame that would eclipse his own. An opinionated and jealous man, he had yet never resented his son-in-law, and always defended him against those who tried to "filch away . . . the credit justly due to him." In his last lecture he referred to Lister as one who "is certainly destined in no small measure to revolutionize the practice of surgery."

The last thing he said to Maclean, his friend and biographer, was: "Be sure to keep your eye on Lister and his antiseptic investigations. I feel sure there is something in them. And remember, sir—look forward, do not look backward."

An obituary, which Lister never denied writing, commented:

> As he [Syme] expressed his sentiments with the utmost candour, he not unfrequently gave personal offence. . . . When convinced that a thing was right he considered his own personal

> feelings as little as those of others. . . . The hostility which he excited in a few was greatly outweighed by the friendship he inspired in the many.

These were words which, as Lister would have been the first to admit, could also have been applied to James Simpson.

They were both gone now, but their personalities had been so vivid that it almost seemed as though they and their quarrels lingered on, as though a ghostly Syme continued to insult the ghost of Simpson by tearing up his pamphlets before a classroom full of students.

Yes, Syme still seemed to linger on in that "hospital, grey, quiet, old, where Life and Death like friendly chaffers meet." If anyone showed the slightest inclination to forget him Mrs Porter would remedy that. Many years after his death she rushed up to a surgeon who was about to administer to a patient, crying, "Leave him be, laddie! Mr Syme wouldna have touched him!" And, whether one liked it or not, Janet Porter was an institution herself and not to be ignored.

Perhaps Joseph Lister himself was half afraid of her. Certainly he never protested when she snatched the towels out of his hand if he happened to have some with him as he was leaving the ward, crying, "Gin my towels gang doon below, they ne'er come up again!" But he was very well aware of her worth not only as a nurse but as a woman, for he had long ago discovered her trick of leaving some of her own money under the candlesticks of poor patients who were about to leave the hospital.

And there was no doubt that he held her dear, for she was a bridge which connected him with his first happy years in Edinburgh, when, as a shy young Quaker with a recent degree, he had come to spend a few months in the city which was to give him Syme's help and friendship and a "gift . . . which was to me a source of unspeakable blessing"—Agnes Syme.

CHAPTER XII

Innovations

NO MATTER HOW BUSY LISTER WAS, he never forgot that his treatment was based upon the germ-theory, and that it and the theory of spontaneous generation could not both survive.

Having himself been convinced by the annihilating force of Pasteur's simple experiments, Lister believed that anyone with an open mind would be similarly impressed. So he had devised some experiments of his own to show that materials such as milk and urine, which were known to decay readily, would remain unspoiled even if exposed to atmospheric gases, provided microbes were kept out of them.

He had made some flasks in Glasgow, modifying Pasteur's models a little, and used them as a basis for tests and further study. Carefully he had carried them on his knees during the train trip from Glasgow to Edinburgh, to the amusement of his fellow passengers, and he held them even more carefully in the carriage as it bounced along over Edinburgh's rough cobblestone streets. These were the flasks which Lister had exhibited at his first lecture, after which they continued to be Exhibit A in his case against the killer which had so long stalked the hospitals.

He made a great many experiments trying to find out all he could about microbes and their habits, for there was a great deal—almost everything, in fact—still to be learned. His experiments were usually simple, for, like John Hunter and Pasteur, he possessed the gift of hitting upon simple and useful experiments. There was always a laboratory in his house, but it was never a nightmare of complicated contraptions; the equipment was usually home-made and extremely practical.

For his experiments on milk, for example, he used sterilized wine-glasses, protected by glass covers and placed, as an additional protection, under a glass bell. Later he tied half a dozen test-tubes to rods and used them instead of a single wine-glass. Taking the greatest precautions, he would have a cow whose teats had been purified milked into these tubes, and subject the milk to various tests and experiments.

Taking advantage of their "common love of science," he wrote in his careful French to Louis Pasteur, describing his experiments on *Bacterium lactis*. Pasteur answered with a long and friendly letter, apologizing because he was so "very little acquainted" with Lister's work, and pointing out a possible error in Lister's experiments and the conclusion he had reached. These letters laid the basis for a sincere and lasting friendship.

It was almost inevitable that Lister should make mistakes and that a good deal of his work should be fruitless, for he was dealing with a subject which was new not only to him but to the world. However, he did make some discoveries, the most important of which was that putrefaction was not, as he had believed, the only reason why wounds 'went wrong.' Gangrene was decay, but some hospital diseases were not, and so the odour of putrefaction was not the only indication that microbes were at work. Erysipelas, for example, had no odour. Infection and putrefaction, therefore, were not identical, and both were dangerous.

One of the results of his interest in microbes was the spray, which was to make life miserable for many of his assistants and associates.

On his knees beside the patient's bed the dresser would start pumping as soon as Lister began to remove the bandages. He would hand the old dressings to his visitors, who would examine them carefully. When, as was frequently the case, there were foreign doctors in the crowd, exclamations, gestures, and excited outbursts would follow, until it seemed to the dresser as though a fight was threatening; but it was only the foreigners marvelling because the bandages did not smell. Lister would talk to them in their own language, and the poor dresser would pump away, gasping for breath, sometimes fainting, his hands and lungs and eyes irritated by the carbolic vapour which the Chief had decided was necessary for the protection of wounds during dressings or operations.

Lister thought it was necessary, although he recognized the difficulties connected with it, saying quite frankly, "If we could dispense with the spray no one would rejoice more than myself." No one would be more pleased than he if he could join the German doctors who cried, "*Fort mit dem Spray!*"

He had devised the spray in order to destroy the microbes which, according to some recent experiments of Tyndall, were even thicker in the air than he had imagined. If there were as many of them as all that—and Lister saw no cause for doubting it—they presented a real danger to an exposed wound. He had no reason for suspecting that all germs were not equally contaminating.

He did not want to combat them by washing wounds frequently with carbolic acid, with its irritating effect upon the tissues. But if one could spray carbolic acid into the air, each droplet would kill germs in its vicinity as it evaporated, making it possible to operate "in an antiseptic atmosphere and effectually prevent putrefactive organisms from entering the wound alive."

At first Lister used Dr Richardson's ether-sprayer, which was employed to 'freeze' the skin in minor operations, and which consisted of an indiarubber bulb and a bottle. This Lister worked with one hand while he attended to the patient with the other—obviously an unsatisfactory arrangement, and one which he soon gave up in favour of having the spray worked by his dresser.

Even when a foot-bellows was substituted for the rubber bulb the spray was still unsatisfactory, and Lister next produced the 'donkey-engine'—a combination of wooden tripod, bottle, nozzle, and lever which actually resembled the animal after which it was named, especially when viewed from a distance as Lister carried it back and forth to the hospital in his carriage.

Finally the steam-spray was evolved, and the pressure which was generated by boiling water blew carbolized vapour for a distance of half a dozen feet. At first the drops of carbolic were coarse and far apart, too large to evaporate before they fell, soaking some parts of the surgeon and the operating-field and missing others completely. Finally Lister managed to arrange the tubes so that the spray was "destitute of scattering drops, perfectly trustworthy . . . though little coarser than a London fog."

The steam-spray was a little contraption not much over a foot high, and it was endowed with every kind of perversity known to machines. Sometimes it clogged up, and nothing was produced except a faint fizzle; at other times the surgeon, patient, and visitors might suddenly be flooded by a carbolic rainstorm.

During an operation the spray was placed on a stand level with the table where the patient lay and about five feet from the site of the operation. If all went well it would send vapour over the operating field; the dresser would hand his instruments directly into the vapour, and if the surgeon had to remove his hands from the mist for even an instant he would repurify his instruments by dipping them into the basin of carbolic solution which was close by. If the spray failed a piece of rag called the 'guard,' which was lying in the carbolic solution, was temporarily thrown over the wound. If the wound was large half of it was covered with the guard while the surgeon worked on the other portion, or else two sprays were used. For changing a dressing on a psoas abscess the spray was directed under the gauze as the surgeon lifted it up.

This constant exposure to carbolic irritated the skin of some surgeons, and if they were very sensitive or not particularly healthy the vapour had an intolerable effect upon their lungs.

Many years later, in 1889, a young southern American girl named Caroline Hampton, head nurse of the surgical division of the new Johns Hopkins Hospital, almost had to give up her operating-room duties because the antiseptics injured her hands and caused a severe dermatitis. William Stewart Halsted, a brilliant young surgeon who played an important part in introducing Lister's method to the United States, was worried about the hands of his head nurse.

After a year he found the answer: thin rubber gloves. Although Caroline Hampton resigned her position to marry the surgeon who had shown so much concern about her hands, rubber gloves had come to stay—an added protection for the patient and a boon to surgeons with sensitive skin.

But that was many years later. Meanwhile, if doctors were sensitive to carbolic they had to keep away from it, particularly from the spray. Some of them, careful to observe Lister's principles in every way they could, obtained excellent results without using the spray—a fact which he failed to take into sufficient account when he evaluated its usefulness.

Because of the difficulties involved he never tested the spray scientifically—almost the only time in his life when he was to accept something without experimental proof. Later he said, "I knew that with the safeguards which we then employed I could ensure the safety of my patients, and I did not dare to imperil it by relaxing them." As he remarked when he was discussing the administration of chloroform, "Better a thousand false alarms than one death." With such an attitude it was quite natural for him to use the spray as long as he lacked proof that it was *not* valuable.

From the moment he had seen the way carbolic acid burned Jaimie's skin Lister had been trying to eliminate its use as much as possible. The crude carbolic acid which he used at the very beginning was insoluble in water, but he soon obtained a better quality which dissolved in water as well as in oil. He diluted the acid, and tried constantly to cut down the amount of direct contact between it and the tissues; as early as 1870 he said, "Of all those who use antiseptics, I suspect that I apply them least to the surface of the wound."

The spray was one aid, he believed, in cutting down the amount of carbolic which must be used during an operation; dressings were another. For forty years he was to spend an incredible amount of time searching for satisfactory antiseptic dressings.

It seems incredible, at least until one realizes that the rolls of gauze bandages which are so closely associated with surgery did not always exist. In Lister's day there were no hospital shelves filled with compresses and bandages of every size. A hospital was fortunate if it had an adequate supply of lint and cloths.

Lint was precious and used sparingly. It consisted of the fluff obtained by picking or scraping apart by hand the fine linen threads which had previously been woven into fine material. Cloths were also referred to as rags, which is what they were—pieces of worn-out garments or household linen donated to hospitals when they were of no further use. They were torn into suitable sizes, but no one bothered to remove the elaborate embroidered monograms and coronets which sometimes decorated them. Of course they were used repeatedly as long as there was anything left of them. Usually it was up to the slattern who gathered up the dressings to decide whether they needed washing or whether they were clean enough to do for the next patient.

Fortunately, boiling was in vogue in many hospital laundries, so that most of the germs were eventually destroyed when the bandages were washed. Usually the hospital laundry system was decidedly sketchy—even in those hospitals which prided themselves on their cleanliness and went so far as to suggest that sheets be changed every month whether they needed it or not!

Poor Semmelweis, who had been trying so desperately to prevent the spread of puerperal fever, had to cope with hospital authorities who regarded laundry mainly as a source for graft. Washing was done outside the hospital, or at least, bundles of it were carried out of one door and, after a suitable interval, returned in the same condition through another. In one of his fits of indignation Semmelweis had thrust under the aristocratic nose of the head of the Budapest hospital a filthy cloth which was about to be applied to a woman who had just had a baby.

Lister never had anything like that to contend with, but he was far from satisfied with the dressings at his disposal. He was to have a great deal of difficulty before at last he perfected the antiseptic gauze which was to remain in use until he improved it in 1889.

He had dressed his first compound fracture with lint and carbolic, which had combined with the serum ooze and the blood to form a protecting crust. This gave him the idea of trying to reproduce as well as he could a natural scab, which acted as a flexible shield for the wound, permitting discharges to ooze out under its edges. That was the way the wounds of animals healed, and Lister thought it would be a good thing to aim at. If protected from microbes, he felt, tissues would heal without assistance, and so there was no sense in handling and treating them constantly in order to make them heal.

He made a putty of carbonate of lime in linseed oil which, after trying tin-foil, gold-leaf, and many other things, he spread like a poultice on block tin. Underneath this antiseptic putty was a layer of carbolic lint. It was only moderately successful, since it cracked easily, stuck to the skin, and prevented the egress of discharges, and was heavy and difficult to apply, particularly on wounds in the armpits and other places where flexibility was necessary.

He next evolved the antiseptic lac-plaster, using first a mixture of paraffin and wax, olive-oil, and carbolic acid on calico. When that cracked too easily he made his plaster of a solution of carbolic and shellac on calico, which he painted with a rubber solution to make it waterproof.

Finally he made a protective plaster—the "green protective"—of oiled silk covered with copal varnish and treated with dextrin and starch so that the carbolic solution would wet the silk uniformly. The purpose of these protectives, which were placed carefully along the line of the incision, was to protect the wound from the irritating carbolic vapour given off by the dressings. Having been dipped in carbolic, the protective killed any germs on the wound, while the more powerfully antiseptic dressings continually acted on the discharges to keep them from becoming breeding-grounds for microbes.

All Lister's first dressings were non-absorbent, so that the carbolic acid they contained was not washed off by the discharges from the wound. Lister was very much afraid of germs getting a foothold on dressings if they lost their disinfecting properties. Even the mildly antiseptic protective gave off enough carbolic vapour to create an 'antiseptic atmosphere' between the plaster and the wound.

However, all non-absorbent dressings had one fault: they kept the wound and adjacent areas moist, and Lister was fully aware of the fact that a soggy wound healed more slowly than a dry one. So, although he had finally found a suitable non-absorbent dressing, he began to look round for one which would be just as good and would also absorb moisture.

He had heard of oakum being used as a dressing. It consisted of hempen rope, laboriously picked to pieces and mixed with Stockholm tar, and its main use was for calking the seams of wooden ships. This pitch, or tar, contained antiseptic agents—not carbolic acid, but that did not matter to him, as he had never made a fetish of carbolic—which, being insoluble, would not be washed out of the fibres. Lister thought it had possibilities.

Trying oakum on small sores, he found it worked quite well, absorbing the discharges without itself becoming a source of infection.

But the patients did not like it. It was dirty stuff, and, what was worse, the dockyard odour was so strong that they felt as though they were breathing and eating tar.

So Lister searched for a material which would be as good as oakum; something cheap—for he knew hospital directors would object to an expensive dressing—porous, capable of being impregnated in every fibre with an antiseptic free from objectionable odour, an antiseptic which would not evaporate or be dissolved for at least twenty-four hours.

He finally found a suitable material—book muslin, known also as butter or art muslin. He used paraffin and resin to hold the carbolic acid, soaked the muslin in it, and packed it in airtight containers. Because muslin was the most expensive part of the dressing Lister advised washing it after use and 'recharging' it with carbolic. He made his dressings of eight layers of this carbolic-acid gauze, with a thin layer of mackintosh to prevent the discharges from going straight through and to make them seep out of the sides instead. As an added precaution he used a few layers of gauze soaked in carbolic with his dressing.

This was the antiseptic gauze which was for many years to replace, at least in the proximity of the wound, the old cloths and towels which had formerly been accepted as adequate dressings.

Reading his many papers on this subject, one is shocked to think of the amount of time and energy he consumed on this problem. Yet it was necessary for him to do it himself. He had assistants and students, to say nothing of his wife, who were glad to help him whenever they could; but he was pioneering, and his ideas grew and developed as he went along, sometimes stimulated by the very difficulties he encountered. He might have found a material while he was searching in drapers' shops which would have given him an idea for something quite different from the bandages then being used.

Not that he ever objected to attending to details himself, for he never considered himself too important for any job. In the course of attending to a detail he might be confronted with a problem, the solution of which might mean an important contribution to surgery.

One such problem resulted in a real contribution to the successful drainage of wounds. In the past they had been deliberately kept open so that the 'laudable pus' could escape, and in addition the long ligatures acted as wicks along which the discharges travelled from the interior of the wound.

With antiseptics there was no more laudable pus, and ligatures were cut short and absorbed in due time. Putrefactive discharges had been eliminated, but, as Lister put it, "an antiseptic itself, while it prevented putrefaction, stimulated to suppuration." This was 'an antiseptic suppuration,' a serous ooze which would eventually be absorbed by the body; but as it was apt to cause painful pressure Lister used to insert a strip of lint into the wound to help the serum escape.

Certain cases, such as deep-seated abscesses, could not always be satisfactorily drained with lint. In one such case Lister thought the lint acted as a plug rather than a drain; for when he removed it and the dressing the day after he had made the incision pus again flowed from the wound.

This was not in itself an unusual case, but it was an important one, because the patient was an extremely distinguished person—a fact which would have prevented some surgeons from trying out anything new, no matter how certain they might be that the procedure was indicated. Many important patients have lost their lives because the surgeon, knowing he was subject to scrutiny, was more interested in covering himself than in saving a human life.

Lister was never unduly influenced by the fear of making a mistake. He felt obliged to assume the responsibility of his capabilities, even though he knew that any failure of his would be exaggerated: he was always in a kind of spotlight. But whether the patient were his own sister, a poor charwoman, or the Queen of England, he made his decisions entirely on the merits of the case. Although he often suffered a great deal of anxiety he thought that the rewards of his profession more than compensated for everything.

The patient with the improperly draining abscess was the Queen of England. Victoria had been staying at Balmoral, which she loved in her widowhood even more than in the days when she and her Prince had found *Gemütlichkeit* there together. Albert had designed it with her assistance, and his red-and-grey Balmoral tartan complemented her Victoria tartan on the pine floors; her water-colour sketches shared wall-space with the antlers and heads of animals he had shot.

Sir William Jenner, who was in attendance while Victoria was at Balmoral, was worried about her condition. A medical man who had done excellent work in distinguishing between typhus and typhoid fever, he knew his limitations in the field of surgery; and when he noticed the pain, restlessness, and fever which accompanied the swelling under the Queen's arm, he called Joseph Lister in to operate.

Lister lanced the abscess, after spraying the spot with ether, which, because it evaporated so rapidly, was effective in producing local anæsthesia by 'freezing' the skin. Carbolic was pumped into the air, and when some of the vapour got into the Queen's eyes she registered a mild complaint to Sir William Jenner, who replied half jokingly that he was "only the man who worked the bellows." Quickly she tried to put Lister at his ease by assuring him that she rather liked the odour.

It was a minor operation, but the day after Lister noticed that pus had accumulated, painful and possibly dangerous.

Walking by himself in the lovely Balmoral gardens, so near the beautiful mountains and the famous river Dee, Lister wondered whether there was not something he could do to help the abscess to drain.

Richardson's spray gave him an idea. Its hollow tube was made of rubber: would not that make a perfect drainage-pipe, one which would not plug up the incision the way lint had done?

Lister did not know that rubber tubes had been introduced for drainage purposes ten years before by Chassaignac, for they had never become popular. Quite independently he decided to try a rubber tube on the Queen, in case lint should again be unsatisfactory the next day.

He hurried back to his bedroom, where he cut holes in a piece of tubing to admit the seepage, tied loops of silk in one end to facilitate its removal, cut the end the proper shape, and soaked his little drainpipe overnight in carbolic. In the morning he was relieved to discover that the acid had not softened the rubber. Later in the day he used it instead of the still unsatisfactory lint. To his "inexpressible joy" it worked perfectly. No more pus collected, the pain subsided, and a week after the incision had been made the Queen had completely recovered.

It was to be the only surgical operation Victoria was ever to undergo, and, as she told Lister gratefully, it was "a most disagreeable duty most agreeably performed."

So Lister managed not only to save his Queen from what might have been an extremely unpleasant experience, but to work out a good method of draining abscesses to boot.

CHAPTER XIII

The Vivisection Controversy

FOUR YEARS AFTER LISTER HAD operated on Queen Victoria he received the following letter from her Majesty's private secretary.

BALMORAL

June 15, 1875

DEAR SIR,

You are no doubt aware that a Royal Commission is about to enquire into the subject of Vivisection, but some time must elapse before any legislation is attempted.

In the meanwhile it is to be feared that the unnecessary and horrible cruelties which have been perpetrated will continue to be inflicted on the lower animals.

The Queen has been dreadfully shocked at the details of some of these practices, and is most anxious to put a stop to them.

But she feels that no amount of legislation will effect this object so completely as an expression of opinion on the part of some of the leading men of science who have been accused, she is sure unjustly, of encouraging students to experiment on dumb creatures (many of them man's faithful friends and to whom we owe so much of our comfort and pleasure) as a part of the regular educational course.

The Queen therefore appeals to you to make some public declaration in condemnation of these horrible practices, and she feels convinced that you will be supported by many other eminent Physiologists in thus vindicating the Medical Profession and relieving it from the accusation of sanctioning such proceedings.

Yours faithfully,

[*signed*] HENRY F. PONSONBY

It was not an easy letter for Lister to answer.

For some time rumours had been spreading through the United Kingdom concerning the cruel practices of vivisectors. Visitors to the Continent were almost invariably shocked by the experiments of Amussat, Magendie, Bernard, and other French scientists. It was quite true that even sweet-faced Magendie was carried away by his dislike of speculation and his emphasis upon experiment—he said of himself that he picked up facts like a rag-picker—and possibly he performed experiments which were frequently needless as well as cruel.

Stories circulated to the effect that Magendie's successor, Claude Bernard, used stolen pets in his work on the effects of poisons, of gastric juices, and of sugar in the blood. His discovery that artificial diabetes could be produced by puncturing a part of the medulla oblongata with a needle, and his masterful *Introduction à l'étude de la médicine expérimentale*, published in 1865, seemed far less important than the possibility that stolen dogs might be found in his laboratory.

The veterinary school at Alfort was another source of stories that supplied grist for the anti-vivisectionists' mill. From Dr Bigelow's description of what went on there it is easy to understand why. In a paper read before the Massachusetts Medical Society in 1871 he said:

> My heart sickens as I recall the spectacle at Alfort, in former times, of a wretched horse, one of many hundreds, broken with age and disease resulting from life-long and honest devotion to man's service, bound upon the floor, his skin scored with a knife like a gridiron, his eyes and ears cut out, his teeth pulled, his arteries laid bare, his nerves exposed and pinched and severed, his hoofs pared to the quick, and every conceivable and fiendish torture inflicted upon him, while he groaned and gasped, his life carefully preserved under this continued and hellish torment, from early morning until afternoon, for the purpose, as was avowed, of familiarizing the pupil with the motions of the animal.

This had taken place in France, in an era which had passed; but it helped to alarm some sections of the public concerning practices in Great Britain. People wondered whether their sons were being brutalized by witnessing and perhaps participating in such butchery. There was no doubt that some doctors, particularly those who had been hardened by the sight of the pain they had been forced to inflict in pre-anæsthesia days, were quite indifferent to the suffering of animals in laboratories.

It was a period marked by suffering and brutality, usually accepted as inevitable by large sections of the population. Children were beaten to keep them awake in mines and factories; terrorized, stunted chimney-sweeps could not imagine a world where there were no blows. The insane were whipped for behaving in an insane manner, peasants were flogged for trying to postpone starvation by stealing a bit of bread or poaching a rabbit which had grown fat on their grain, and in the army and navy, in schools or orphanages, in homes—everywhere—the whip was a familiar and respected instrument.

It was hard to tell which was more brutal, virtue or fun. Boxers beat each other to pulp for the entertainment of cheering multitudes; bull- and bear-baiting had not lost their popularity because the law frowned upon them; and horses and hunters as well as foxes were maimed and killed while contributing to the pleasure of the chase.

But if the nineteenth century was one of brutality and injustice it was also one of reforms. Frequently, as in the case of the temperance movement, these reforms concerned themselves with the symptoms rather than the causes of social evil. Efforts to prevent cruelty to animals were extremely popular. People who were indifferent to the death of soldiers would weep over the sad fate of a beautiful cavalry-charger, and, as Pasteur's biographer, Vallery-Radot, pointed out, one had only to mention the word 'dog' and an audience would be conquered. Quite possibly all this had something to do with the fact that animals never exhibited any dangerous Jacobin tendencies to try to help themselves.

All kinds of people flocked to these societies—sincere

humanitarians as well as fanatics who spent huge sums of money trying to win people to the vegetarian cause while half of Ireland starved. There was also the usual quota of cranks who would to-day be labelled sadists or masochists, who evidently got as much pleasure from gloating over and describing the horrors of the laboratory as did the occasional warped experimenter who persuaded himself that he was contributing to science by inflicting pain.

Many a youthful psyche was undoubtedly distorted by the gruesome pamphlets of the anti-vivisectionists, just as many an education in pornography was provided by sanctimonious pamphlets defending the right of women to enter medicine by describing, with illustrations, the licentiousness and lasciviousness of male physicians.

The Royal Society for the Prevention of Cruelty to Animals was composed of all kinds of people, but its publications and programme were more restrained than those of many other organizations. The jubilee of the society seemed to its members an excellent occasion for advocating a Bill designed to prevent cruelty by restricting vivisection, insisting that all animals used for that purpose must be completely anæsthetized and destroyed before regaining consciousness.

A Royal Commission was appointed to investigate conditions and make a report, which was to include a discussion of the need for legislation. It was high time, for people were confused by the *exposés* of the anti-vivisectionists, which quoted hearsay as fact, lumped together past and present practices on the Continent with what was happening in Great Britain, and quoted statements from leading scientists denying the usefulness of any animal experimentation. Many of these leaders were prominent only in the eyes of the anti-vivisectionists; some had long been dead, and others were misquoted or quoted only in part.

Some sort of investigation was necessary. Remembering the days of Burke and Hare and the body-snatchers, people had begun to wonder whether fiendish doctors would experiment on them, particularly if they were poor hospital patients or if their cases were unusual. According to the anti-vivisectionists, a well-known but unnamed doctor had actually attempted to cut up his dying daughter, and had barely been restrained from continuing until she had breathed her last.

Queen Victoria looked with favour on the cause of the R.S.P.C.A., to whom she confided her personal anxiety about the sufferings of animals under experiment. While not suggesting a total prohibition of vivisection, she expressed the hope "that the entire advantage of those anæsthetic discoveries from which man has derived so much benefit himself, in the alleviation of suffering, may be fully extended to the lower animals." Her message to the R.S.P.C.A. was delivered in 1874, the year of the society's jubilee; the letter to Lister followed a year later.

The Queen could scarcely have appealed to anyone less useful in restricting vivisection—or more capable of reviewing the entire subject calmly and convincingly from the viewpoint of a scientist and a humanitarian.

Lister did not like to give offence, but he would have liked dissembling even less, if he ever thought of such a thing. His Queen had made a request of him, and while honesty forbade his saying he was sorry he could not comply, he could say that he would be sorry if he were not certain that agreeing would fail to "promote the real good of the community, which I know to be Her Majesty's only object."

In Joseph Lister's family killing animals for pleasure had been condemned, along with slavery and the cruel treatment of law-breakers and the insane. Not only his training but his nature made him recognize and object to cruelty of any kind. But he was a scientist.

When he experimented upon animals that were not insensible, he wrote to Queen Victoria, he did so "at a very great sacrifice of my own feelings." He had wondered whether one ought to eat the flesh of animals, which was associated with the infliction of a certain amount of pain, but decided that it was all right since it was approved by the Scriptures. But castrating animals or, for example, removing a harmless tumour from a horse simply to gratify "the pride or purse of its owner" seemed to him far less justifiable than causing pain to further the progress of science.

The suffering of animals in the laboratory, he believed, was less than they might be forced to endure in the ordinary course of their lives, and certainly less than that which resulted from "the winging of pheasants in a single day's sport on the *battue* system."

Fortunately the sensibilities of lower animals were not so acute as those of human beings. The way a salmon pulled a hook out of its mouth was an indication of that fact; if it were not so it would scarcely be possible to justify fishing. "And for those," he wrote, "who have no objection whatever to fish being caught in these ways to raise an outcry against scientific experiments upon a few frogs seems to me, I confess, simply ludicrous."

To him the main thing to consider was the purpose for which suffering was inflicted. Not only the making of discoveries, but the teaching and demonstration of facts already ascertained seemed to him to justify causing a certain amount of pain.

All this he wrote to Queen Victoria, and concluded with the uncompromising statement that "I am therefore clearly of the opinion that legislation on this subject is wholly uncalled for."

It was an opinion which he was never to alter and which he frequently expressed. In 1897, at the jubilee of Queen's College in Belfast, he devoted a large portion of his address to a defence of vivisection, saying:

> There are people who do not object to eating a mutton chop —people who do not even object to shooting a pheasant with the considerable chance that it may be only wounded and may have to die after lingering in pain . . . and yet who consider it something monstrous to introduce under the skin of a guinea-pig a little inoculation of some microbe to ascertain its action. These seem to me to be most inconsistent views.

It was most important, he went on to explain, not to judge questions in the abstract but to consider motives and to judge things as a whole. To illustrate his point he reminded his audience that, while it was obviously wrong for a murderer to cut a man's throat in order to take his life, "any one of you medical students may have to cut a man's throat to save his life." In those days tracheotomies frequently had to be performed to prevent suffocation, especially in cases of diphtheria.

> So soon as our poor selves are concerned our objections disappear [he commented]. If a tiger threatened to attack a camp who would care much about what kind of a trap was set for it? . . . When the matter affects only the welfare of others, including generations yet unborn, the good done does not appeal to the individual, and the objector sees only the horrors of modern scientific investigation.

This was the point of view which Lister expressed when he testified before the Royal Commission in 1875, emphasizing the fact that restricting vivisection would prevent people from making discoveries that would benefit humanity. His experiments concerning inflammation, which laid the basis for his antiseptic treatment, were made in the days when, as he reminded them, "I was not a person of recognized scientific attainments." He had no idea what the final results would be when he irritated the tissues of a frog with a touch of acid or the scratch of a needle; he was only seeking to learn.

After stating that he had found animal experimentation absolutely essential to the discovery and development of the antiseptic method he offered the following testimony in regard to his work on absorbable ligatures:

> Q. Had you not made experiments on brutes, you would have had to experiment on man; there was no alternative, was there?
>
> A. There was no alternative.
>
> Q. You could not have discovered such a thing . . . by any *a priori* reasoning?
>
> A. It must be tested by experiment.

When Lister believed in something he gave it his whole-hearted support. Having been appointed to the General Medical Council when Sir Robert Christison resigned (Lister was one of the few surgeons to receive such an appointment), he waged a real campaign in defence of vivisection both through the Council and as an individual.

In the latter capacity he went further than the Council itself. As the Royal Commission had reported in favour of legislation, believing it necessary although stating that the reports of cruelty had been exaggerated, the Medical Council was convinced that legislation would be passed. It therefore decided to concentrate its efforts upon modifying this legislation as much as possible, while Lister continued to oppose legislation altogether.

It was not that he took an uncompromising 'all or nothing' attitude. Although any legislation was bound to open the door for those who wanted to abolish vivisection entirely it would make a great deal of difference what kind of bill was passed.

The various proponents of legislation did not entirely agree. Some of them insisted that vivisection should be completely abolished, while others were concerned only with eliminating pain. Most of them, however, saw eye to eye on certain points.

Chief of these was that, whatever form of vivisection was finally permitted, animals should be completely anæsthetized with a general anæsthetic and should be destroyed before regaining consciousness. It did not matter to the anti-vivisectionists that in many cases local anæsthesia would have sufficed, or that many experiments would have been impossible in those circumstances. Such a restriction would have meant, as Lister had pointed out, that he could not test his catgut on an old horse or a calf bound for the slaughter-house. A human being might have to bleed to death before he could discover whether catgut could be trusted to complete its function before it was absorbed. There could be no more tests for the action of poisons or their antidotes, no more experimental surgery, no more testing of inoculations which might prevent diseases.

If a restriction of this kind had been applied to Louis Pasteur it would have prevented him from attempting to find a cure for rabies, which had undoubtedly caused more canine suffering than the sum of all scientific experiments put together. Strangely enough, it was against Pasteur that many anti-vivisectionists directed their heaviest fire, shrugging aside Darwin's question, "Will not animals be the first to profit" by Pasteur's work?

The proponents of anti-vivisection legislation also argued that vivisectors should be licensed, and allowed to perform experiments only on licensed premises. This sounded reasonable enough: an honest investigator should have had no trouble in getting a licence and no reason for wanting to cut up animals in an unlicensed, hidden spot. Actually, however, this restriction would have decidedly hampered scientists. Lister could not possibly have got a horse or calf into his small laboratory, any more than Pasteur could have transported flocks of sheep from the meadows where they were grazing to licensed premises in order to inoculate them.

Another suggested restriction would have limited vivisection to experiments which would discover new facts useful in saving or prolonging life or preventing suffering. This would seriously have handicapped investigators. As the Royal Commission pointed out, "Knowledge goes before the application of knowledge, and the application of a discovery is seldom foreseen when the discovery is made." Subjecting an experiment to this test was, as Benjamin Franklin was reported to have said at an earlier date, like looking at a newborn baby and demanding, "But what is it *good* for?"

Another point on which most anti-vivisectors agreed was that there should be no experiments or demonstrations for instruction or practice, although a few of them were willing to make certain exceptions for medical students. Evidence had been presented to prove that demonstrations had a demoralizing effect. Lecturers were callous, provoking laughter by their descriptions of mutilated animals; there was quite a furore over a woman teacher, whose name was courteously withheld, who had brutalized the young ladies in her charge by cutting off a lobster's claw without realizing that the creature was not yet dead.

It was true that scientific lectures were not always conducted on a high level. Under the heading of science a volunteer would be taken from the audience and hypnotized or given gas or ether, while the remainder of the audience would howl with delight at his antics.

However, depriving medical students from witnessing or participating in any experiments would certainly have handicapped their education, and there was a tendency to exclude from the restrictions a few demonstrations with unconscious frogs.

There was by no means unanimous agreement as to what was meant by the term 'animal,' anyway. Were frogs to be included—perhaps even oysters—or should there be two sets of rules, one governing experiments on the higher, the other on lower, animals, with cats and dogs and horses entirely exempt?

These were some of the main points under debate.

Knowing that the total abolition of vivisection would drive the leading scientists, and later the students, to the Continent, the Government was apparently not prepared to go to such lengths.

Partly as a result of Lister's efforts the Bill, which was called the Cruelty to Animals Bill and finally passed in April 1876, was somewhat of a compromise. It stated that no experiments causing pain could be performed except by licensed people upon animals rendered unconscious by a general anæsthetic. If pain were likely to continue, or if the animal were seriously injured, it must be promptly killed. Such experiments could be performed only to advance a new discovery useful in saving or prolonging life or alleviating suffering, and not as illustrations of a lecture or to acquire manual skill.

The 'physiologist's animal,' the frog, was included in these provisions, and dogs, cats, horses, and some others were to be completely exempted. However, there was the possibility of obtaining a certificate waiving this and some of the other rules if the experimentor showed due proof that it was absolutely essential in order to perform some important experiment. These certificates, obviously, would be difficult for any but established scientists to obtain. And there could be no lifting of the ban against experimenting in unlicensed premises.

That meant no more experiments for Lister on his holidays, unless he went outside the United Kingdom—not even a simple test in a convenient stable or barn, performed upon a creature already selected for slaughter. As Rickman John Godlee, Lister's nephew, put it:

> The strangest anomaly, as it must appear to our less sanctimonious brethren in the rest of the civilized world, is that our law, while it forbids the granting of a special licence to a distinguished doctor to experiment upon a chloroformed frog in his own study in pursuit of science, allows anyone who can afford it to hunt a stag to death, or set two greyhounds to course a hare and wager money on the result.

In spite of his interest in the Cruelty to Animals Act Lister's work had not by any means been standing still. He had crowded a great many interesting things into his days, not the least of which was a European tour of inspection, from which he and Agnes returned in June of 1875.

CHAPTER XIV

Bitter Opposition

THE EUROPEAN TOUR HAD COMMENCED at Cannes, where Joseph and Agnes joined Arthur Lister and his wife and daughters, who had been waiting for them. They started with a family holiday, most of which was spent in Italy. In Vienna the party split up; Joseph and Agnes went to Germany, where they visited one city after another, receiving a royal welcome from the men who had championed Lister from the first.

They went to Leipzig, the home of Carl Thiersch, who had been horrified by the conditions in his hospital, and, reading Lister's first published papers and immediately grasping the significance of his discovery, had adopted the antiseptic method without hesitation. Now he could boast that in a twelve-month period in a hospital containing three hundred beds he had had only one case of pyæmia.

In Halle Professor von Volkmann had been on the verge of closing his wards, almost emptied by deaths resulting from septic diseases, when he heard of Lister's work. Without visiting him or even sending an assistant to learn the method von Volkmann had introduced it and worked a miracle. During the whole of 1872 he had not lost a single patient who suffered from a compound fracture.

In Berlin Lister saw von Bardeleben, and in Mardeberg he just missed seeing Professor Hagedorn but was enthusiastically received by his assistant. At Bonn he met von Busch; at Munich, von Nussbaum; from city to city he travelled, finding himself already famous—thanks to the efforts of men who had appreciated his contribution, and who, with Professor Saxtorph, of Copenhagen, and Lucas-Championnière, of Paris, had been his first disciples.

The Listers had not, however, made the journey merely to receive the homage of Joseph's admirers, but to visit clinics and explain the details of his method. It was particularly important to see people like the elderly, distinguished Professor Lagenbeck, who, as Lister put it, had a "barren admiration" for antiseptics. Lagenbeck's hesitation vanished when he was able to discuss antiseptics with Lister himself.

Things like that made the tour really worth while. To Agnes it was even more memorable because of the wonderful reception her husband received—the banquets and meetings held in his honour, the tributes from distinguished men who appreciated him as he deserved to be appreciated. No matter how many honours he received later she never forgot the thrill she experienced when she first heard people call him 'great.'

Perhaps the most exciting event of all was the big dinner held at the Schützenhaus in Leipzig, attended by 250 guests, including such notables as Professor von Volkmann and his seventy-eight-year-old father. (Agnes kept forgetting to ask how von Volkmann's gorgeous waistcoats, bespangled with embroidered flowers, his red artists' ties, and his Scots plaid trousers had appealed to Joseph's Quaker taste in dress.)

She was sorry that she and her hostess, who had been entertaining her at tea, arrived at the places in the gallery which had been reserved for lady visitors just as Joseph was finishing his speech. True, they were not expected until after the end of the banquet, and she would not have been able to understand much of the speech anyway, despite the progress she had made with her German. Fortunately she had no trouble in understanding the flattering things people said about her husband, or the cries of "*Hoch*" and "*Hoch soll er leben*" which resounded through the hall, accompanied by several trumpets and a drum. She had also managed to understand the German version of "John Anderson, my Jo," which the students had sung as a compliment, and the jingles they had written to student melodies, one of which, the *Karbolsäure Tingel-Tangel*, was considered quite witty.

The morning after the banquet Joseph attended Professor Thiersch's lecture, which was also visited by the King of Saxony. Agnes assured her husband afterwards that she was certain no one knew how embarrassed he was when the King asked him questions during the operation which followed the speech. Fortunately the King had left before, at Thiersch's request, Joseph performed an operation himself.

At last the tour was over, and they set out for home again, glad—as they always were, even though there were a number of places they would have liked to visit—to be getting back to work.

In 1870 the Franco-Prussian War broke out. Although Britain was not involved Lister at once devoted his energies to an attempt to mitigate the terrible suffering of the wounded soldiers. He described his system briefly in a four-page pamphlet entitled "A Method of Antiseptic Treatment applicable to Wounded Soldiers in the Present War." In this he simplified the method to include only "the employment of such materials as are likely to be accessible to the surgeons of both armies."

Although he wanted to help the wounded of both sides Lister's sympathies were with France. In 1866 he had written to his father that he was not particularly grieved to see the minor German states swallowed up by Prussia, as he thought the inhabitants might be better off in the long run under a single strong government; but he added, "to what extent Prussia may be compelled to disgorge her unlawful plunder . . . or what other calamities may happen who can predict?"

In 1870 he saw some of the calamities occur, and wrote with some concern, "I can't help fearing Bismarck will dally with us till he has made an end of France and then dictate his own terms to us," and the defeats France suffered distressed him very much.

Pasteur was completely occupied with matters unrelated to surgery when Lister's pamphlet appeared. Too valuable a man to be allowed to risk his life in Paris, he had been sent to Arbois where he saved the silk-industry of the district and so enabled his country to pay the tremendous indemnity later imposed by the Germans. It is doubtful whether he even heard of Lister's pamphlet, which was unfortunate, for if he had backed it the French army surgeons might have taken it more seriously.

The French military surgeons needed all the help they could get. The mortality among their wounded was terribly high; of every hundred soldiers who underwent amputations, even minor ones involving fingers or toes, ninety eventually died. The official figures of the Inspecteur-Général, which were probably an under-statement, recorded 10,006 deaths out of 13,173 cases of amputation. During the siege of Paris the hospitals, which could be identified almost streets away by their smell, were places of indescribable horror. One surgeon reported a mortality of 100 per cent. following operations.

Even the Prussians, despite their preparations and efficiency, were not much more successful in their care of the wounded, being forced to report that "scarcely an amputation recovered, death resulting from exhaustion and sloughing of the flaps, and frequently from pyæmia."

Of course it was difficult even with the best of intentions to adapt this new method, scarcely past its experimental stage, to the requirements of military surgery. When Dr Marion Sims, a supporter of the antiseptic method, discussed the ambulance of the Anglo-American Society, he had to admit that at Sedan it "became completely septicized."

That was war. Surely, however, there should be no such difficulties connected with the peace-time adoption of Lister's method; surely after the opposition of Simpson and his friends subsided the antiseptic method would make steady progress.

But it did not. In the eight years that had passed since the publication of his articles in *The Lancet* it had seemed to Lister as though each step towards the acceptance of his method had been immediately followed by at least half a step back.

Personally he had received recognition enough. Since the death of his father-in-law he had been recognized as the leading surgeon of Scotland. Soon after his arrival at Edinburgh he had received his first foreign honour, a diploma making him foreign associate of the Society of Medicine of Norway. His practice and his classes were all that he could desire.

It was not personal recognition that he wanted. As he pointed out, the excellent results he obtained were not due to his surgical ability. "That would indeed be something to be proud of," he said. "But it is not so. It is simply that we are working on a new principle. Mr Rice, my house-surgeon . . . does these things exactly as I do them myself."

Because people would not recognize that fact he was reluctant to publicize some of his successful operations. He refused to let his dresser, young William Watson Cheyne, publish his notes and cases as he had once published those of Mr Syme. If people heard of some of his operations, such as that for repairing a fractured patella, other surgeons would perform them also; and, if they failed to use his antiseptic method they would gravely endanger the lives of their patients. Until the germ-theory was accepted and understood Lister's successes were bound to be attributed to his ability, and his system would make little headway.

After some initial enthusiasm and objections a lull followed the publication of Lister's articles, and it lasted until 1869, when Mr Nunneley, a well-known surgeon of Leeds, attacked the antiseptic system at the annual meeting of the British Medical Association. He disagreed vehemently with Pasteur's conclusions and those of Lister in regard to the cause of decay, and insisted that antiseptic surgery was scarcely in use any more in the city of Leeds.

Mr Nunneley's report was published in eight columns of the *British Medical Journal*, and was followed by a flurry of letters. Since Lister could not afford to remain silent, he wrote one of his short, dignified notes, enclosing a letter from T. Pridgin Teale, another Leeds surgeon, which refuted

Mr Nunneley's claim that antiseptic surgery was no longer practised in that town.

Thomas Keith, the pioneer in ovariotomy, also wrote to deny the insinuation which had been made that he had no faith in antiseptics. It was true that he obtained unusually good results without antiseptics, as did Spencer Wells, who, with Lemaire, had independently recognized the importance of the germ-theory to surgery. Shortly before Lister's discovery Spencer Wells had given an excellent account of Pasteur's work and its relation to surgery, but he had not applied it himself, although he emphasized cleanliness. Both Spencer Wells and Keith were very able surgeons, with large private practices; they operated frequently in private homes, and even were pioneers in abdominal operations.

Because the mortality resulting from Thomas Keith's operations was about half that of most surgeons, and because he was delicate and sensitive to carbolic, he was reluctant to adopt the antiseptic method, especially the spray.

Lister gave the matter a great deal of thought. With the limited amount of information he possessed concerning bacteria he could not completely understand why Spencer Wells and Keith should obtain such excellent results without using antiseptic methods; but he came very close to the answer, especially considering the fact that he had no knowledge of the means by which the body attempts to combat germs.

He had observed that certain parts of the body, such as the face, healed more rapidly than others; this he attributed to the high degree of vitality possessed by those tissues. In abdominal operations he had noticed that the peritoneum absorbed fluids rapidly. If germs should enter this body-cavity, Lister reasoned, they would find very little in the way of suitable juices to feed upon. To this, and to the care and cleanliness of Keith and Wells, and the fact that they seldom operated in contaminated hospitals, he attributed their success in abdominal surgery, and neither he nor they considered it evidence against the antiseptic theory.

Following the skirmish brought about by Nunneley's attack there was another lull, and once more Lister hoped that the opposition had run its course.

In 1871 he gladly accepted the opportunity of addressing the meeting of the B.M.A. at Plymouth. Here he would have an opportunity to explain his methods to the leaders of his profession, who, he assumed, would be glad to have the question clarified. It did not occur to him that they might prefer to listen to the traditional general discussion of surgery and its history, and even consider it bad taste for him to talk about his discovery. Although he was a modest man, Lister was completely lacking in false modesty.

He covered the ground carefully, discussing the theoretical background of his discovery, exhibiting the material he used in applying it in surgical cases, and describing some of the most interesting cases he had treated in this way.

This address was, as usual, got into shape at the very last minute, the second section being completed at three in the morning and the third before breakfast, while certain cases were checked over in the carriage on his way to the meeting.

Lister was very much surprised to discover that some of the members of the association were annoyed because he had implied in his talk that surgery, as it was practised by them, was in need of radical improvements. What gave the greatest offence, however, was Lister's reference to the germ-theory, which he thought had been proved once and for all by Pasteur's experiments.

"I am ready to blush for the character of our profession for scientific accuracy when I see the loose comments sometimes made upon this experiment," he said, in the presence of some of the men whose comments had, to say the least, been "loose."

So the speech which he had counted upon to advance his theory created as much opposition as it did clarity. And, far from dying down, the opposition increased, augmented by many who had turned from indifference to open antagonism. They were beginning to fear the germ-theory, which threatened to topple them from their high places and send them back to school again, as much as the old virtuosos of the knife had hated anæsthesia, which negated the value of their speed and skill.

Doctors cropped up everywhere with elaborate experiments 'proving' that decay was not caused by the action of microbes —but offering no proof that it was caused by anything else. Mr Nunneley's arguments were supported by the experiments of Dr Charlton Bastian, Dr Hughes Bennett, and many others. Expressions like "mythical fungi" grew in popularity, and dignified surgeons went about singing gleefully "There's Nae Germs aboot the Hoose" and "Germs, Busy Germs." Carbolic acid was called "the latest toy of the medical profession," and to sneer at Lister was as respectable as making fun of Darwin and his 'monkey-business.'

Unwilling to continue even a mild championship of an unpopular theory and one he had never understood, Wakley of *The Lancet* allowed himself to be convinced by the experiments of so many important men, and went over to the opposition, exhibiting some of the pettiness characteristic of a change in sides.

In 1873 he demanded editorially, "Would M. Pasteur, in the present state of science, still attempt to uphold his vital theory of fermentation?" He did not, however, wait for an answer from Pasteur, who, having accepted Dr Bastian's challenge, had proved that he was right and then gone busily ahead developing the theory which was soon to eliminate many deadly diseases.

Would Lister, *The Lancet* went on to demand, still give this theory his "unqualified adherence"? Wakley's arguments reached a peak in 1875, when he insisted that if Lister's plan had been any good it would have been unanimously adopted.

Lister had sufficient faith in his colleagues not to come to the conclusion that if *they* were any good they would have adopted his plan. He kept trying to clarify matters, to point out the reasons for failure when, as so often happened, surgeons thought they were giving antiseptics a fair trial.

It happened frequently. One of Lister's supporters remarked, after a trip to Paris, that he had been shown "at various hospitals, 'modifications' of his [Lister's] method in which everything was present except his principles." Even a man like Sir James Paget sealed up the wound of a compound fracture case with collodion, applied carbolic acid on top of it twelve hours later, and then wrote that Lister's method had "failed altogether to attain its end."

Fortunately, Sir James was a reasonable man, and when Lister explained that sealing up a contaminated wound and then, after an interval of twelve hours, applying carbolic acid was not practising antiseptic surgery, he didn't take offence. Instead, he sent an assistant to spend the day finding out what Lister's method really was, which pleased Lister a great deal, although one day, he knew, was not enough.

Other surgeons were not so open-minded. They joined *The Lancet* in demanding not theories, but proof. Where were Lister's statistics, they wanted to know? How could anyone believe he was right when he refused to publish figures to support his claims?

When Semmelweis had compiled careful statistics learned doctors had remained indifferent to them; now they demanded figures of Lister, who had never felt he could spare the time to collect them. The ones he had offered in connexion with the Royal Infirmary of Glasgow had not impressed people greatly, and he was quite aware of the fact that figures could be manipulated, perhaps unconsciously, in whatever direction one wished. The principle, the theory, was what people must understand, and statistics would not help so much as that. Like von Volkmann, Lister believed that any one of a number of his successful cases was more impressive than a volume of tables.

It was true that some people were beginning to understand, particularly the younger men and the provincial surgeons of the United Kingdom and the foreigners who continued to flock to Edinburgh. The latter aroused a certain amount of antagonism among Lister's insular colleagues by their outlandish custom of speaking a foreign language. Lister's assistants would struggle with what they considered French, but usually consisted of phrases like "une excision du elbow-joint," while they wished the foreigners would go away, or longed for the arrival of their polyglot Chief.

Reviewing the situation in 1875, Lister was far from satisfied with the progress that had been made. Must he continue in the same slow way, waiting for the younger men like John Chiene, John Duncan, and Thomas Annandale to climb to positions of importance and spread his doctrine for him?

If that were the only way it could be done Lister would not permit himself to be discouraged. Yet, although he was persevering and patient, he would never content himself with pushing against a stone wall if there were a chance of finding an opening in it, or of locating the main support of the barrier and concentrating his efforts on that.

It was not true, he felt certain, that "there is less antiseptic surgery practised in the metropolitan hospitals than ever there was," which was what *The Lancet* claimed. Yet as long as it was possible for a leading publication to make such a statement Lister could not feel that things were going well. He would continue his work, but he must constantly keep searching for ways of persuading others to give the antiseptic system at least a fair trial.

CHAPTER XV

The Decision

IN 1877, THE YEAR OF HIS FIFTIETH birthday, Lister decided upon an important step which he felt was necessary to hasten the acceptance of his theory.

The more he listed and weighed the factors which were holding back antiseptic surgery, the more he realized that they originated and centred in London. Of all the great cities of the world London had shown the most resistance, and London was the most influential, particularly throughout the United Kingdom.

Why did London hold back? Not only because it disliked theory and was suspicious of change; but largely because Lister's ideas came from the provinces and anything that did not originate in London was regarded as second-rate.

It was ironical that Lister was being ignored because he was a 'foreigner,' a provincial—he who had been born within the shadow of London, had attended London University, and had for some time been suspect as a 'foreigner' in Scotland.

Now, however, he had been associated with Scotland for so many years that reporters were beginning to describe his Scottish appearance; his work was completely identified with Scotland. If it had the prestige of a London background it would be accepted far more readily by the many surgeons who looked to London for leadership.

Wherever he went himself the acceptance of his method was tremendously speeded up. He had noticed that on his Continental tour, when, despite the good work of his disciples, a personal visit had apparently been necessary in many instances.

It had been even more obvious in the United States. He

and Agnes and Arthur Lister had attended the International Congress in Philadelphia a year before, in 1876, the year which marked the centenary of American Independence. The Congress itself had been a great success, despite the competition of the Exposition with its many attractions. Lister was honoured with the position of president of the Surgical Section of the Congress, where his talks received the closest attention. In Boston Dr Bigelow introduced him to a class of enthusiastic students, and in New York City Lister consented to demonstrate his method by opening an abscess before a large and extremely interested group of students and doctors.

But the important thing was that the United States, which had been almost indifferent to antiseptic surgery, seemed to have been waiting for Lister's visit. Immediately it began to accept antiseptic surgery with wholehearted vigour and efficiency.

Of course, a visit would not suffice for London, which was the centre of the United Kingdom and the spiritual, if not the actual, home of its leading professional men. He would have to live there at least for a time in order to do any good.

The main reason why Lister was considering the advantages of transferring to London was because an opportunity had arisen for him to go there. Sir William Fergusson had died in February. He had been for many years Professor of Surgery at King's College, which had been founded as a protest against the non-sectarianism of Lister's University College.

From the religious point of view King's accomplished its aim, but it never seriously competed with 'the godless college' in any other way. The classes at King's remained small, with an annual enrolment of only about twenty-five medical students. Probably because it was felt that the introduction of new blood would make it more popular, Lister, who was now acceptable as a member of the Church of England, was sounded on the subject of joining the staff.

He had always more or less planned to return to London some day, but these plans he had made while his parents were still living and before he had grown so identified with Scotland.

He was happy in Edinburgh; this period of his life seemed to him better and fuller than any previous period, and the thought of going to London had lost its appeal. Actually, he was almost afraid to go, for, as he put it, he had a feeling that he would be "engulfed in a sea of troubles" if he went to London. Yet that was insignificant compared with the fact that he might best advance his theory by taking such a step. If he could then surely it was his duty to go, especially as he would leave an antiseptic centre at Edinburgh where he had trained and capable men to carry on his work.

In addition to the limitations of its size there were other disadvantages to King's College—especially certain practices there connected with the teaching of surgery which Lister felt would handicap him too severely. Feeling that his conditions would not be met, he nevertheless wrote saying that he would accept the offer if certain changes were made with regard to the method of teaching.

Immediately the sea, as he had predicted, began to grow rough. With minor variations history was inclined to repeat itself regarding the filling of vacancies opened by the death of an elderly professor. When Lister had applied for the chair of Surgery at the University College in 1866 he had been turned down in favour of a man who had been waiting for the position for eighteen years. Now, at King's College, there was another man who had taken it for granted that he would step into the vacant place—Mr John Wood, a capable surgeon and anatomist who had taken over some of Sir William Fergusson's duties during recent years.

Mr Wood's friends had apparently not been consulted before the position was offered to Lister, and their resentment against him was not diminished by the fact that he had no way of knowing that his invitation had not resulted from proper official procedure. Their feelings were intensified, and their ranks increased by an event which followed almost immediately.

Hearing that Lister was thinking of leaving them, seven hundred students at Edinburgh signed a petition telling him how much they appreciated him and expressing the hope that he would not go away. When his class presented him with this document, nicely bound, Lister replied with a little speech in which he praised the University with which he was connected, comparing the teaching of surgery in Edinburgh and London to the latter's disfavour.

Clinical surgery, Lister believed, "is, strictly speaking, surgery at the bedside . . . as distinguished from surgery taught systematically in the classroom." But it was difficult to teach large numbers of students in a crowded ward; Syme's classes were enormous, and so he introduced a new method to supplement bedside teaching; he chose interesting and suitable cases, and, having them moved to the lecture-room, delivered his 'bedside' lectures there.

This custom had become established in Scotland, but it was not employed in London, and Lister felt that, as a result, the city's marvellous material for clinical instruction was being wasted. He made this criticism quite frankly, not suspecting that a reporter was present who took down everything he said and sent it to a newspaper, where it was published in garbled form.

London immediately rose up in arms. How dared Mr Lister insult them! How dared he—as *The Lancet* put it—"sit in judgment on his fellows and publicly denounce as impostors those who have the misfortune to differ from him!"

In vain Lister explained that he had not done anything of the sort. When he said he thought it was a poor plan for several surgeons to be appointed, in a semi-honorary capacity, to a Chair of Surgery, he certainly had not intended to imply any criticism of the individuals who had been appointed. His words had been directed against systems and not people.

Unconvinced, the insulted surgeons continued their

attacks, until finally *The Lancet* announced smugly that, although some one had "officiously" undertaken to invite Lister to King's College, it "now appears that this unlawful negotiation has failed."

The Lancet was mistaken. The negotiations continued, and King's College decided to agree to Lister's conditions. An additional Chair of Surgery was created for him; he would have wards of his own. The hospital beds were increased from 172 to 205 by the construction of a new ward and the reopening of an old one. Mr Wood would stay on, in a position of importance equal to Lister's own.

Lister was tremendously popular in Edinburgh, but as he left in the middle of a term no big farewell meetings or banquets were held in his honour. Quietly he and Agnes left the city they loved, and, wondering a little whether they were making a mistake, went to storm the citadel of resistance.

CHAPTER XVI

The Centre of Resistance

GENTLEMEN—IN MAKING MY FIRST appearance as a teacher in King's College, I cannot refrain from expressing my deep sense of the honour conferred upon me by the invitation to occupy the chair which I now hold; and, at the same time, my earnest hope that the confidence thus reposed in me may not prove to have been misplaced."

It was the first of October, and the Lecture Theatre of King's College was filled, the arena with medical men and scientists, the body of the theatre with students. Lister was giving his inaugural address.

Almost without exception the students were too busy looking at him to pay attention to what he said. Curiously they stared at the man who had created such a tempest not only in their school but in the entire city, who had criticized London's teaching methods, called their professors shams, and would probably try to turn the college inside out.

He did not look like a firebrand, this low-spoken, mild-mannered professor. Thick-chested, with iron-grey hair and small side-whiskers, conservatively dressed in greyish trousers, black broadcloth coat, and black tie, Mr Lister seemed disappointingly 'tame' to them.

Having completed his introduction, Lister began to describe the process of wine-making which he had recently witnessed in Italy. The grapes had been trod upon in vats to release the juices which, within twenty-four hours, 'boiled over' from fermentation. This, he said, was caused by the action of a yeast-plant; he had carefully drawn it to scale, and they could see on the chart before them.

He also pointed out a diagram of the rod-shaped micro-organisms which he referred to as bacteria and which he said caused blood to ferment or putrefy—blood which, when kept free of such organisms, showed no more tendency to decay than did grape-juice to ferment if the tiny yeast-plants were kept from it or destroyed by boiling.

The students stirred uneasily, suspicious gleams lighting up their eyes. What was he trying to do? *Teach* them something? That wasn't cricket! Every one knew that an opening address was supposed to be vague and general, entertaining if possible, demonstrating the lecturer's oratorical powers and his ability to tell a good story. It would not hurt if he were inspiring, especially if it provided them with an opportunity to cheer and stamp their feet as he exhorted them upon the honours and glories of the profession which they were about to enter. In this case they had been looking forward to a few good insults to their *alma mater*, which they were prepared to resent publicly and enjoy in private.

But what was happening instead? The table behind which the professor stood was laden with equipment belonging to a laboratory—pipettes, test-tube stands, goose-necked bottles containing milk and blood and other fluids—while coloured charts and diagrams made additional demands upon their attention.

It seemed to him, Lister was saying, that putrefaction was caused by micro-organisms, and yet it was conceivable that it might be due to chemical action, as some people claimed—a process similar perhaps to that caused by the action of ptyalin in the saliva upon starch.

In his experiments he had found various kinds of bacteria, possessing various characteristics; some of them, for example, could move while others remained stationary. It was his intention to try to discover whether different bacteria caused different kinds of changes, and for this purpose he had made many tests with milk, coming to the conclusion that the ordinary process of souring was always caused by the same bacteria, which he identified and called *Bacterium lactis.*

Some people believed that boiling caused the destruction of the chemicals which they thought were responsible for the souring of milk. For this reason he had tried to obtain milk free from micro-organisms so that it would not have to be boiled. After a number of failures he had managed to succeed, by having a cow milked into a sterile test-tube on a drizzly morning, when, as he said, "some of the multitudes of organisms existing in the little orchard might have been washed down, and that the air might thus have been somewhat purified. I got the dairy-woman to milk the cow without drawing the hand over the teat. . . . Her hands were washed with water, and the cow's udder also——"

"Moooo."

In the back of the room some one lowed softly and realistically, and the students laughed in appreciation. Even if Mr Lister was not going to turn out to be a fire-eater they could get a certain amount of fun out of goading him, along with the other old fogies with bees in their bonnets whose lives they enjoyed making miserable. For a start they took to listening carefully so that they could utter an appropriate *moo* every time he mentioned milk; when he referred to the dairymaid an insinuating "Tut, tut!" seemed a good idea.

"The door's ajar! Close it quickly lest one of Mr Lister's microbes should come in!"

That was a good one, deserving recognition. The students stamped their feet until the rumble almost drowned Lister's words.

Lister had not expected anything like this. Having been a student in London himself, he was not unfamiliar with the custom of heckling, which London students had brought to a fine art. One taste of it, even though it had been directed against some one else, had been enough to make Syme turn on his heel and leave London for good. Lister wondered what his father-in-law would have done if he were standing on the platform in his place; something the students would never forget, he was quite certain.

But he was not Mr Syme. He had to do things his own way. People might call him easy-going, but to him the important thing was to keep going, and not to let himself be side-tracked. Some of the audience had made a real effort to be present and hear what he had to say: busy surgeons from other cities and schools, leaders of the scientific world, fellow members of the Royal Society, men like Darwin and Huxley, who had supported and defended him before he had succeeded in reaching the members of his own profession, offering him suggestions when, in the course of their own investigations, they came across something in which he might be interested. They followed his work carefully, reading his lectures in the paper if they could not listen to them in person. These people were entitled to the best that he could offer.

He was never content merely to recapitulate or review. And this was a particularly important point which he was at last able to prove: that a specific organism caused a specific putrefactive process. He and Agnes had worked on these experiments and planned this lecture during their three weeks' holiday in Italy, and, along with Rickman John Godlee, had put a lot of time and energy into the preparation of charts and diagrams which helped to illustrate his points.

He was going to deliver the best talk of which he was capable, despite the rowdies at the back of the hall who had just thought of a new one and were busily engaged in asking one another what time it was, and answering, "Tea-time," in penetrating whispers. The behaviour of the students was a problem for the college authorities. He had made a mistake, which he hoped some day to rectify, by criticizing London's teaching methods so sharply, and he was not going to give offence again.

Ignoring the heckling, Lister went on to explain how he had diluted milk, working out the process mathematically until, by diluting one part of milk with one million parts of boiled water, he was able to obtain an average of one *Bacterium lactis* in each drop of the solution. In this way he weeded out the other bacteria, which were far less numerous than *Bacterium lactis*, but which were usually present in sufficient numbers to cause changes other than souring and so cloud the picture.

Thus he was able to obtain milk free from all bacteria and also milk which contained no micro-organisms except *Bacterium lactis*, so that he could inoculate pure milk with this one strain.

"Where there was curdling and souring," he explained, "the *Bacterium lactis* was present; and in no instance in which there was no lactic fermentation was any bacterium of any sort to be discovered."

This he believed was conclusive evidence that a specific organism, *Bacterium lactis*, caused a specific process of fermentation—namely, souring.

Tasting the milk which he had brought with him from Edinburgh and which he had kept uncontaminated all that time, he remarked that it was still perfectly sweet, and invited anyone who wished to do so to taste it after the lecture.

There were, of course, other points still to consider. "But what I do venture to urge upon you," he said in conclusion, stammering a little because he had been talking for almost two hours and the strain had tired him, "is that you will seriously ponder over the facts which I have had the honour of bringing before you to-day; and, if you do so, I believe you will agree with me that we have absolute evidence that the *Bacterium lactis* is the cause of the lactic-acid fermentation. And thus I venture to believe that we have taken one sure step in the way of removing this important but most difficult question from the region of vague speculation and loose statement into the domain of precise and definite knowledge."

Although Lister was pleased because his lecture was well received by the distinguished visitors and because he had succeeded in not giving any offence, he had committed the crime of boring the entire student body.

He had not expected that. Even those students who had attended his Edinburgh lectures out of curiosity had usually listened and learned at least something from what he said. Young William Watson Cheyne, for example, had enrolled in the surgical course simply because he had a free hour and no place to go except out into the cold, and had been so impressed by the first lecture that he copied it down, and every subsequent lecture as well, verbatim. He finally won the certificate of merit in this fourth-year course although he was only in his third year of study.

It was quite different at King's. Even St Clair Thomson, who had entered the medical school at the advice of his brother, a former pupil of Lister's, was frankly bored. He wanted to hear about surgery, and instead he had been forced to endure a long talk about something that did not even have a name—microscopical horticulture, some people were calling it. As far as he was concerned, he was no more interested in it than he would be in phrenology, which had created a lot of excitement in its time before going the way of all fads.

This was a new experience for Joseph Lister, who had always had youth on his side. When he had first started teaching in Edinburgh his classes had been small. He once commenced to lecture with only one student present, but he had been new to the profession then, and his classes and his popularity had soon increased. By the time he went to Glasgow he could count on an excellent attendance, while after his return to Edinburgh as many as 400 students would crowd the hall to hear him speak. But in London they stayed away.

Sometimes he would address a group of less than a dozen men, including graduate students, foreign visitors, and his own house-surgeons, who came to swell the ranks.

"The utter apathy in my small and irregular audience was sometimes almost more than I could endure," he said.

The students who came usually straggled off before the period was over, and he could never count on lecturing to the same student twice, which made it particularly difficult for him to prepare his talks. Yet he always planned them carefully, even after the time when he went to deliver a lecture on which he had worked very hard and not a single person turned up.

It was not all due to personal animosity by any means. A great deal of it arose directly out of the teaching system which Lister had criticized.

In London medical students were tested for their degrees not by the doctors who had instructed them, but by a special group of examiners, who had their own ideas of what students ought to know. This distracted the attention of students from their own instructors, and directed it towards trying to find out what 'they' would expect them to say. A teacher who could give them tips on what questions might be asked, or 'crammers' who drilled them on points which would be included in their examinations, were much more important to them than an instructor who merely taught.

Many professors strenuously objected to the coach system, but that was usually as far as they went. Scarcely anyone was optimistic enough to believe that 'crammers' could be eliminated or the system which created them could be altered.

To the average student at King's College attending Lister's lectures meant filling one's head with information about which one was not going to questioned. Worse, it might mean absorbing some of Lister's views, which would certainly find no favour with the inquisitors. A student had to care a great deal about pure knowledge to jeopardize his chances of getting a degree by listening to what Mr Lister had to say.

Although the students were indifferent rather than antagonistic towards Lister, there was plenty of real antagonism towards him at King's. One thing which was particularly resented by the staff was the fact that he had brought four assistants with him from Edinburgh—as though he did not think anyone in London was good enough for him!

Lister had considered it imperative to bring with him men whom he had trained in the antiseptic method. Even before he had decided to go to King's College he had asked Watson Cheyne whether he would go with him if he did accept the position. Young Cheyne, who had been asleep when the

Chief came into his room that Sunday morning, had been so excited that he could scarcely wait until Lister had completed his question before he blurted out an excited, "Go to London? I'd go with you anywhere!"

Lister's other house-surgeon, at first his junior assistant, John Stewart of Halifax, was just as enthusiastic as Cheyne, and so were James Altham and William Dobie, the dressers, or clerks—both students who had not yet completed their medical studies. Watching the reaction of the important doctors rather than that of the students at the inaugural address, these young men had been confident that their Chief had made an auspicious beginning, and were subsequently all the more disgusted with the treatment he received. It seemed to them to be a deliberate boycott.

Why, there was not even a patient for him to discuss at his first clinical lecture! Knowing how Lister felt about the value of teaching by demonstration rather than simply lecturing, they tried desperately to beg, borrow, or steal a case. Finally they managed to dig up a Scots tutor who had been sent to Lister from Paris. He was little better than nothing, for the poor fellow was suffering from a psoas abscess on each side, and so advanced a case of tuberculosis that, no matter how skilfully the Chief saved him from death by means of antiseptic surgery, consumption would probably finish him off before people had a chance to see the miracle Lister had wrought.

How could anyone be expected to work in such circumstances? In Edinburgh, where Lister had an average of seventy patients at a time, the crowd which followed him when he made his rounds looked, as Henley described it, "like the ring, seen from behind, round a conjurer." Here there were no patients and no students. The four young men wandered desolately round the empty ward, while close at hand patients rotted slowly away, the odour of suppuration thick in the air.

It was an odour which they, almost alone in their profession, had never known, for they belonged to the new generation which had received its training in wards where hospitalism had been banished, the first of a growing group who would never refer familiarly to "that good old surgical stink." Not until they came to London had they understood what 'orthodox' surgery really was like; here, for the first time, they made the acquaintance of post-operative fevers and "laudable pus," and the trays which were standard equipment in hospitals where antiseptic surgery was not practised—trays placed as a matter of routine beneath the stumps of amputated limbs to catch the inevitable discharges of suppuration.

These things filled them with missionary zeal, and they longed to battle to the death against the authorities who permitted such conditions to exist. Instead, they seemed to be doomed to impotence and idleness.

They had their battles eventually, but unfortunately most of them were with the nursing staff.

Even in Edinburgh they had encountered a certain amount of autocracy among the nurses. Mrs Porter had ruled with an iron hand. However, she was at least willing to recognize the fact that her jurisdiction was limited to her towels, soap, dishes, and similar implements, whereas at King's the nurses' despotism was complete.

Here the care of the patients had been 'leased out' to the Sisters of St John, which was more of a religious than a nursing sisterhood. They were good women, however, and with a different head nurse they might not have become so firmly entrenched in red tape and bureaucracy. As it was they had come to believe that the hospital justified its existence mainly because it provided them with the opportunity to make certain that patients had clean hands and faces and neat beds, spoke politely when spoken to, and said their prayers regularly.

Doctors were almost unnecessary evils, probably inflicted upon them to mar the perfection of their feminine paradise. However, they could be endured, since they seldom put in an appearance more than twice a week; and then, after writing a few prescriptions and saying a few complimentary things about the wards, they hastily retreated and left the nurses to tidy up.

Lister was something they had never had to reckon with before. Authorities on cleanliness, they were as insulted by his instructions as they would have been if a chimney-sweep had invaded their kitchens and started dropping dishes back into the sink because he did not think they had been properly washed. This talk about things being "æsthetically dirty but surgically pure" and "æsthetically clean but surgically dirty" was utter nonsense to them.

In addition, they never knew when to expect this outrageous surgeon. He would casually mention the time of his next visit, and then, when everything was prepared for him, the fire blazing properly, beds in apple-pie order—he simply would not appear. At first they thought he was trying to catch them off guard, and that was bad enough, even though they were confident of out-manœuvring him; but it was worse when they discovered that he had no sense of time. Far from trying to catch them, he did not even notice if some of the patients were not 'decent' when he came in—what was worse, he obviously did not care.

He would drop in any time he felt like it, and stay for an hour or two, talking to the patients, making certain they were comfortable, while the poor Sisters hovered anxiously about, their routine ruined, their nerves so shattered that even a good strong cup of tea could not repair the devastating effects of one of his unexpected calls.

Worst of all, he came on Sundays. Although they had never been able to get any evidence that he failed to attend church with his wife in the morning, they had their own suspicions of a man who had been brought up practically a pagan and who had attended the godless college in Gower Street.

Unable to provoke a fight with the object of their wrath, the Sisters managed to cause plenty of trouble for his assistants. The fact that the skirmishes raged over the bodies of innocent patients seemed of no importance to them.

One day Lister was called in consultation on the case of a boy in one of the medical wards. He diagnosed the condition as osteomyelitis of the femur, and Dr Duffin, the boy's physician, agreed with him that an immediate operation was indicated. Leaving his house-surgeon, John Stewart, and several dressers to bring the patient, Lister went to get the operating-room ready for the operation.

Unable to locate the porters, who had gone off duty—either officially or unofficially—for the afternoon, Stewart found a stretcher and prepared to move the patient himself. At Edinburgh the students had carried patients back and forth to the operating-theatre, and although he knew the job had been delegated to the porters at King's he never considered it the porters' sacred right until he was informed of that fact by the Sister in charge.

"But there aren't any porters here," Stewart explained.

"You may not move a patient without a permit from the Secretary," the Sister announced.

"Where is the Secretary?" one of the dressers wanted to know.

"I'm sure I could not say."

"He's left the hospital; he won't be back till ten o'clock to-morrow," Stewart answered. Addressing the back of the Sister, who had moved away and was basking in the approval of several nurses, he said reasonably, "Look here, Sister, this boy is Dr Duffin's patient, and he and Mr Lister have decided he must be operated upon immediately. They're waiting in the theatre now."

"I'm sorry," replied the Sister, with no perceptible trace of regret in her voice.

"We can't just leave them waiting for us."

"That's not for me to say. All I know is that no patient may be removed from the ward without permission of the Secretary."

She turned away and faced the intruder, supported by her companions, who could not have looked more resolute if they had been preparing to defend their virtue to the death.

Stewart glanced from them to the patient, who was fortunately unaware of what was going on. Then he lost his patience, and decided to act.

As though they sensed his intention the Sister and the nurses closed their ranks, presenting a formidable phalanx of stiffly starched uniforms and even stiffer faces. To Stewart it might have been funny but for the fact that the Chief was waiting and the well-being of a child was at stake. This was a serious case, and a delay of twenty-four hours might make the difference between life and death. The young man swooped down and started to take the child in his arms.

The phalanx moved forward, a menacing array of outraged Amazons. It was too much for the dressers, who broke ranks and fled, with the exception of a brave young man named Addison, who threw open the door of the ward and stood holding it, looking as though he were about to yell, "Run for your life!"

Bundling the boy in his bedclothes, Stewart lifted him quickly and headed for the door, but not before one of the nurses had made a grab, obviously under the impression that if she could not save her patient entirely, she might at least keep a portion of him to propitiate the Moloch of regulations.

All she got, however, was a piece of the bedclothes. Stewart managed to carry his unlawful booty to the operating-theatre, where, according to the regulations, it became Lister's legal property. It was a triumph for Lister's staff, especially as the child, despite his serious condition, eventually recovered.

Towards the end of October Stewart was to come off victorious again in another encounter with the nurses.

When Lister had left Edinburgh a few patients with abscesses from tuberculosis of the bone had remained on his old wards. These patients, who would have died without antiseptic treatment and constant care, were slowly fighting their way to recovery. Although the process was a long one and the cases were without general interest to the staff, it had never occurred to Lister that they would be sent home until they were entirely well, for until the abscesses were completely healed the treatment must continue, or the dreaded hectic would set in.

"I've just heard from Mr Caird, sir," Stewart told the Chief excitedly. "He wants to know whether Lizzie Thomas can be admitted here at King's. You remember her."

"Of course, she was one of my favourites. I've seldom known a better or more cheerful patient. Certainly she can come here. But what's the trouble? Has something gone wrong with her at Edinburgh?"

"They've discharged her, sir, along with some other chronic cases. . . ."

"Discharged them?" Lister asked incredulously. "Why, not a single one of them can be ready to go home. None of the men and boys, and certainly not Lizzie." He paused, and his expression turned from surprise to anger. "Sending patients home to their death in order to make room for more interesting cases—it's an infamous shame!" he cried, with more anger than Stewart had ever seen him show. "Tell Mr Caird that Lizzie may come here immediately. And as for the others—let me see. . . . I'll get them into a nursing-home and ask Dr Bishop to care for them."

Dr Bishop had been the Chief's private assistant in Edinburgh and was fully conversant with the treatment required. He acquiesced to Lister's request, and the patients were duly admitted to a nursing-home, Lister himself paying the bills. His generosity was rewarded, for all of them recovered, one later becoming a doctor in Liverpool.

Meanwhile, in response to Stewart's telegram Lizzie Thomas had left Edinburgh for King's College Hospital. She travelled in one of the wicker baskets which were used to carry patients to and from the operating-theatre. Miss Logan, one of the head nurses, accompanied her from the Royal Infirmary and sighed with relief as they entered King's, which seemed comparatively warm and comfortable after the long train-trip and the journey through the raw October morning from the station.

"Just wait here a moment, sir," said the porter, who had helped John Stewart to carry the heavy basket from the carriage. "I'll notify the Sister in charge."

It was a long time before he returned, and then he looked very perturbed.

"Sister says she can't be admitted without the proper papers, sir."

Stewart and Miss Logan were dumbfounded. Lizzie Thomas was the only one who smiled. Despite a year in bed undergoing treatment for the large abscess which, without Lister's care, would almost certainly have taken her life, she had the brightest eyes and the pinkest cheeks of anyone in the group, although there was no doubt about her being cold and tired.

"There must be a misunderstanding—I'll go and see the Sister," said Stewart, with an assurance he did not feel.

Some fifteen minutes later he was back, in the vestibule again, having come off second best in the encounter. The patient might be exhausted, Mr Lister might have given orders for her to be admitted, but rules remained rules, and no admissions could be made without the proper papers. The Sister was adamant, and reproved Stewart for his "irregular behaviour." The young house-surgeon, infuriated by her superior manner, demanded to know how long he was expected to keep the poor girl waiting.

"When the Secretary comes and draws up the papers," was the haughty reply.

"When will that be?"

"At ten o'clock."

It was not yet eight. Realizing that he had no hope of making headway with this impossible woman, Stewart went downstairs in a temper—on his own confession, "too angry to see the comic side of the affair." Once again he decided to defy the authority of the all-powerful but rarely present Secretary.

The porter, a man named Vaughan and a veteran of the

Crimea, was looking puzzled and unhappy. Stewart wasted no time.

"Now, Vaughan," he said, "an old soldier like you can't stand and see a pretty girl lying on this stone-cold floor—give us a hand!"

Vaughan needed no second bidding.

"I will, sir, if it costs me my place," he replied, and grasped one end of the basket. Stewart took the other, and together they carried Lizzie up the stairs and along to the house-surgeon's own ward. There one of the Sisters stood barring the closed door.

"You can't bring her in here without admission-papers!" she said.

"Aren't you ashamed of your scandalous conduct?" put in one of her colleagues.

"No, but there *will* be a scandal very soon if you don't take the patient in and put her to bed!" replied Stewart. "Because if you don't, we'll take her in and put her to bed ourselves!"

Lizzie Thomas giggled. Vaughan chewed his moustache and tried to look very fierce as the horrified Sister shot a glance in his direction. To talk about undressing a girl and putting her to bed, in front of the porter—and worse, to threaten to do it with his help, while the outlandish Scottish nurse who did not even have the grace to blush took note of everything and prepared to spread the story all over the provinces! The Sister had met her match. Lizzie Thomas could come in.

But, although the porter obviously enjoyed the triumph, and though Stewart was relieved on Lizzie's account, he realized that he had actually increased his Chief's difficulties, since so much of the success of the antiseptic method depended upon the co-operation of the nursing sisterhood.

If he had any doubt about whether he had done right or not, however, these were completely dispelled when Lizzie eventually recovered.

CHAPTER XVII

Storming the Citadel

For a long time London had been demanding statistics from Lister, and *The Lancet* had been urging a test in which his method would be used in one ward or hospital while orthodox surgery would be practised in another, and the results compared. Now it was actually happening, on a small scale, at King's, where Lister had his wards and Mr Wood, who was also professor of clinical surgery, continued in the old way.

True, Lister's ward consisted of only twenty-four beds, which were slowly filling with patients, many of whom were quite unimportant from a surgical or teaching standpoint; yet London felt it would be a kind of test, and watched curiously for the results.

Most of the doctors hoped Lister would fail. Not only were they satisfied with the *status quo*, but they held grudges against him for various reasons.

The established surgeons objected to his casual manner of charging for his services. Like Syme, Lister felt that having set fees for operations was unsatisfactory. Each case was different, and so was the ability of the patient to pay, and he did not want to deprive anyone of his services who really needed them. So he left it to the patient to pay according to his own conscience, which meant that he was frequently taken advantage of, and his rivals thought that he was cutting prices. Lister had never had to think much about money, and the fact that he was quite as willing to see his bank account diminish as to watch it grow was very much resented both by men who had to, and those who wanted to, pursue what Abernethy used to refer to as "that damned guinea."

The younger doctors were annoyed because he would not trust orthodox surgeons or general practitioners with the post-operative care of his patients. This they had always counted upon as a source of income, and they were indignant when Lister turned over his patients to Watson Cheyne or to Rickman Godlee after an operation.

Nor did they like his sending his patients to a private nursing-home instead of to a hospital, for that practice was not yet well established in England. Though many doctors recognized its advantage to the patient they felt that it removed interesting cases from a central place of observation and prevented them from enriching their experiences.

So, although the arrival of this outsider had not created much scientific excitement in London, the doctors were interested personally, and they watched like hawks for Lister to make a mistake upon which they could pounce.

They thought they had found what they were waiting for when Lister operated upon a patient who had been admitted to his ward with a fractured knee-cap.

The man had been thrown from his horse, and, landing upon his knee, had suffered a transverse fracture of the patella. Although the bones were badly smashed there was no open wound, and healing could be counted upon to proceed uneventfully. However, as so often happened in such cases, the bones did not set properly, despite the use of weights and pulleys.

The only way to give him a useful knee, Lister told his patient, was by opening the joint and wiring the bones together. Over six years before he had felt sufficient confidence in his method to "make a voluntary compound fracture of the ulna and a compound dislocation of the elbow-joint" in a case where the fracture and the dislocation had both been simple, but where it had been necessary to create a wound in order to set and repair the injured bones properly. He had performed similar operations successfully many times, although he had not published the cases, for fear that other surgeons would attempt to do the same thing without antiseptics. He could remember his father-in-law discussing fourteen cases of compound dislocation of the ankle, which had been admitted to the infirmary and had all terminated fatally.

The patient, a man in his early forties, knew too much about the usual result of surgical operations to want to risk his life or, at the least, his leg, which would have to be amputated if sepsis set in after operation. Politely he refused Lister's offer, and went home.

Fourteen days after the accident he was back again. He had been thinking over the alternatives. Either he must spend the rest of his life with a useless leg, unable to walk, let alone ride horseback again, or he must put his trust in this calm, modest, confident, and honest surgeon. The patient decided to take a chance.

Lister cut down upon the knee-joint, exposed the broken bones, and, using a silver wire, bound them together so that they would unite properly.

This, the London doctors felt, was going altogether too far. It was the surgeon's function to choose between evils, to sacrifice a limb in order to save a life, to remove a tumour of the jaw which would prevent the patient from swallowing or breathing, to tie an artery which had caused an aneurysm and was threatening to burst. To cut off, to cut out, whatever would endanger life or cause constant unbearable pain was the function of the surgeon. It was not within his province to repair or to attempt to improve a condition which was merely deforming or painful or would prevent a patient from leading a normal life. Performing an operation which was not absolutely necessary was regarded as 'tempting Providence,' and public opinion restrained surgeons from these homicidal adventures.

No reputable man would think of cutting into the unbroken flesh of a fractured knee as long as there was a chance of the injury healing with no worse results than a useless leg. Experience had shown that deep cuts or gashes, particularly in knee- or elbow-joints almost invariably became septic and necessitated the amputation of the entire limb. Only a presumptuous man like Joseph Lister would risk such a thing on the off-chance of obtaining a spectacular result.

"When this patient dies some one should proceed against *that man* for malpraxis," one of London's most distinguished surgeons suggested, and there were plenty of people ready and willing to take his advice.

"It makes me perfectly furious!" said Agnes angrily. "How must the poor man's family feel—how must he feel himself, with every one so glibly discussing his approaching death!"

"Fortunately," said her husband, "he feels well. When I saw him this morning, just after breakfast, the only thing that was worrying him was how soon he would have his lunch. His pulse was 70, his tongue clean and moist, his temperature 98·2.

"Not that I don't agree with you, Agnes," he went on, "I should hate to silence anyone who wants to speak, but surely doctors should be the first to realize how cruel it is to deprive a patient of confidence in the physician to whom he has entrusted his life."

"They ought to be ashamed of themselves!"

Agnes turned to her husband, torn between anger and sympathy for him. Yet it was hard to feel sorry for Joseph, especially when she looked at him. As John Brown had once said, "You have only to look at his face to see how uninjured he has been in his walk through life."

It was, she knew, because he enjoyed his work so very much, despite its difficulties. As he had once told his students, their profession was second to none in interest and pure pleasure; and just because the pleasure was pure, he had remarked to Agnes privately, did not make it any less enjoyable.

"The reason I am feeling so cheerful," Lister informed his wife, "is because I had a most satisfactory experience this morning. A case of severe and spontaneous hæmorrhage. It responded well to my treatment, although it was the first case of its kind I had ever encountered. You can have no idea how happy it made me to give the baby back to her young mother again, as good as new."

"As good as new——" Agnes began. Then she caught the expression in her husband's eyes. "What kind of case are you talking about?"

"A hæmorrhage, almost fatal—of sawdust. The doll came apart and started spilling sawdust into the bedclothes, so the Sister took it away, thereby almost breaking the poor little patient's heart. Fortunately I happened to come along, and we had a fine operation, antiseptic technique and all. Aneurysm-needles are excellent for sewing up dolls, in case you ever need to know. And the little girl was so overjoyed that it has put me in a good humour for the day, regardless of the behaviour of my colleagues."

Her husband's good humour did not, however, alter Agnes Lister's opinion of London surgeons. She knew they considered Joseph a bit of a bore for harping on the germ-theory so constantly, but until they understood it they just could not understand that he was right in opening a knee-joint in order to give a man the use of his leg. They did not like complicated theories, they said! Well, if it was simple and clear to her the leading surgeons of the greatest city in the United Kingdom ought to be able to understand it somehow!

Lister's confidence in his operation on the knee-joint was justified. Eight weeks after the operation he made a small incision in the scar and removed the silver wire, which by that time had fulfilled its purpose. A week later the second wound had healed, and the patient was able to go home. He had already regained some motion in his knee.

Agnes remained indignant because the surgeons who had maligned her husband did not immediately and apologetically come round; but the case made an impression, particularly on account of the publicity which it had received. Some doctors tried to dismiss the whole thing by talking about Mr Lister's luck, but there were others who wondered whether there might not be something to his method after all. As long as he was in London it might be worth while investigating for themselves. Slowly the ripples spread.

Mr Wood was watching Joseph Lister closely. Wood—the grim Yorkshireman with the short, massive frame, the square dark face and piercing black eyes—abrupt and harsh, was the man who had been waiting for years for the chair which he had been unexpectedly forced to share with an outsider. It was no choice of his that he had been cast for the rôle of Lister's opponent in this contest; but then, neither had it been Lister's choice.

It was after Mr Wood had refused to operate upon a patient who had been admitted to the hospital that Lister was asked whether he would care to try.

The man had an enormous tumour of the thigh, for which amputation was clearly indicated; but his condition was so poor that every one was convinced that the first bout of post-operative fever would carry him off. That being the case, the doctors thought it would be kinder to permit him to leave the world in one piece, without their increasing his suffering by an operation.

Lister would have agreed with them if he had not known that post-operative fever and suffering were no longer a necessary consequence of an operation. Untreated, the man would surely die, whereas amputating his leg might save him. Though nothing would please Lister's enemies more than to see him fail in this case, he could not, as he had told his wife, think about that very much or he would be afraid to tackle anything. He decided to operate.

The amputation, as every one expected, went very well. The real test would come later, and Lister knew that Mr Wood would make a point of seeing how it turned out.

Five days after the operation, more than long enough for suppuration and fever to have started their work, Mr Wood appeared at his ward. Lister greeted him courteously, and asked if he would like to see the wound being dressed.

"I might take a look at him," said Mr Wood, and the

two men started down the aisle between the rows of beds. Lister walked with his easy stride, while Mr Wood, who suffered from an old hip-injury, limped along beside him.

Pausing, Lister spoke kindly to a patient who was sitting up in bed reading a newspaper, and Wood champed restlessly behind him. Then, in his harsh Yorkshire accent, he asked suddenly: "Is *this* the man whose leg we all refused to amputate?"

"Yes, this is he."

This was the patient who should have been far along the journey on the road to his death. And he was sitting up, obviously free from fever and pain.

"We shall now change the dressings and we can see the condition of the wound."

As Lister stooped over the bed to remove the outer bandage, one of his dressers started the spray, having previously lighted the alcohol-lamp which provided the heat to create the necessary pressure. Just before Lister cut the outer bandage the spray went into action, and clouds of carbolic arose, giving the scene an eerie quality. First the outer bandage came off, layers of gauze with a piece of mackintosh inside the last layer, the whole of which had been covered with a sheet of waxed taffeta as a protective. The bandage was handed to Mr Wood to examine.

Now the wound was revealed—a clean, healing wound, with no shiny greyish slough to indicate the presence of gangrene, no foul-smelling pus, no inflammation, a wound healing as few wounds had been known to heal without antiseptics. Surely, Lister thought, if Mr Wood is an honest man he will see the difference between this wound and those of the patients on his own ward.

Wood broke the silence. In his rough, abrupt manner, he came at once to the point.

"To-morrow when I operate I should like you to instruct me in your method."

CHAPTER XVIII

The Turning-point

THAT MARKED THE TURNING-POINT. Not that Mr Wood became an ardent disciple and went about proselytizing after his conversion; on the contrary, his support of Lister was extremely mild. Yet he used Lister's method himself. He got Lister to supervise several major operations for him—first, the removal of a large goitre, and then an ovariotomy, the kind of operation which had been banned by the governors of King's because of the tremendous mortality which was associated with it.

Anxious to ensure the Chief's success in this difficult operation, Lister's house-surgeons, reasoning that you could not have too much of a good thing, kept the spray going in the patient's room most of the night before the operation was to be performed, but fortunately the woman did not suffer any ill effects. Both operations were successful, and John Wood was honest enough, and proud enough, to talk about them openly. So it got round that he was using antiseptic methods, and the test had ended.

The real significance of Wood's conversion lay in the fact that it represented a trend which, after two long years, had at last set in. As Lister had hoped, his presence in London was bringing results. Doctors who visited him were impressed with his modesty and intelligence, and began to wonder whether there might not be something in it after all. Many of them were mollified by his open apology for his unfortunate choice of words in Edinburgh, when he admitted that he had not known of all the improvements which had been made in London regarding the teaching of surgery. They were almost willing to admit that there might be advantages in the Edinburgh system which he advocated, especially with regard to the use of patients to demonstrate the points one was making, rather than the simple delivery of a lecture which the students might just as well read by themselves.

Yes, the turning-point had come. Lister had noticed a difference the year before, when he went to Paris for the Universal Exhibition, where he was treated as a celebrity. Personally he was not nearly so interested in that as he was in the long scientific talk he had had with Louis Pasteur, but it was important.

But 1879 was the real year of triumph for him. The high spot was the meeting of the Sixth International Medical Congress at Amsterdam, an occasion celebrated in that city by a musical festival and fireworks and banquets and entertainments. At one of these a series of 'living pictures' was shown. One tableau depicted the old print of Ambroise Paré dressing the wounds of a soldier, only some one representing Joseph Lister had been substituted for Paré. This scene got three curtain-calls, and not until Lister himself consented to take a bow could the show go on.

On the last evening students with bands and torches gathered along the canal outside the building where a banquet was being held, and when the guests went out on to the balcony to greet them it was Lister who received the most enthusiastic cheers.

The real spirit of the Congress was expressed at the formal meeting at which Lister was invited to speak on the antiseptic system. Five hundred of the leading medical men of Europe were present, including Rudolf Virchow, whose *Cellularpathologie* had tremendously influenced all medicine and laid the basis for contemporary pathology. Before Virchow diseases had been regarded as entities in themselves. He showed that the cell is the sustainer of life and that sickness is a form of life under abnormal, modified conditions. As Lister put it, "he swept away the false and barren theory . . . and established the true and fertile doctrine that every morbid structure consists of cells which have been derived from pre-existing cells as a progeny."

When Lister rose to deliver his address the dignified assembly went wild. They threw their hats into the air, waved handkerchiefs, and cheered—something without precedent in the history of medical congresses. At last Professor Donders, the president of the Congress, managed to get a moment's silence, and he said, while Lister stood before him, grave and quiet and a little embarrassed: "Professor Lister, it is not only our admiration which we offer you; it is our gratitude and that of the nations to which we belong."

After that it was obviously an anti-climax when a meeting was finally held in London to acknowledge Lister's contributions. As Dr Ernest Hart sarcastically remarked in the *British Medical Journal*:

"Mr Lister's coming to London has been so speedily followed by a signal triumph of that great principle in surgery which had been accepted everywhere else almost before it was even listened to in London."

But, even though it was late, London eventually came round. The change which had taken place was quite apparent at this meeting, when Sir James Paget said apologetically:

"I can compare my experience at St Bartholomew's Hospital with one of my colleagues, Mr Smith [who practised antiseptic surgery], and it makes me look back to that part of my life with remorse, and I may say that either through ignorance or inattention I had a mortality of which he could justly say he would be utterly ashamed."

This, coming from a surgeon of Paget's importance, indicated quite clearly that the tide had turned.

It was no longer possible for scientists to dismiss microbes as a joke. In 1876 Robert Koch, a busy country practitioner, had written an excellent paper showing that it was a specific micro-organism which caused anthrax, explaining exactly how to obtain this organism from an infected animal, cultivate it, infect other animals with it, or destroy it. The fact that a specific microbe caused a specific disease had been partially demonstrated a few years before in the case of relapsing fever, but the investigator had died before he had been able to complete the proof.

Within a few more years the organisms causing leprosy, gonorrhœa, and malaria were identified, and by 1883 Koch had found that tuberculosis was not caused by a nutritive disorder but by a bacillus. He also located the germ which caused cholera. In addition he made many discoveries about the habits of bacteria, and showed that steam was more reliable than chemicals for general purposes of disinfection, since it destroyed the spores into which some microbes were capable of transforming themselves.

But it was the work of Louis Pasteur which succeeded in convincing even the most sceptical. He had been experimenting with the bacteria of chicken-cholera, which he cultivated artificially and then used in order to give the disease to healthy birds. One day one of those accidents occurred for which his mind was so well prepared. He inoculated a hen with enough artificially cultivated chicken-cholera bacilli to give it a fatal case of the disease; but the hen, although it sickened, did not die.

Puzzled, Pasteur finally decided that the culture which he used, and which had been in the laboratory for some time, had probably grown old and weak. So he inoculated the hen a second time, along with several others, with a good fresh culture.

All the hens quickly died of chicken-cholera—except the one which he had inoculated before, and that bird remained in perfect health.

Pasteur immediately grasped the implications of that fact. Again and again he experimented, until he proved conclusively that aged and weakened bacteria would cause only a comparatively mild case of chicken-cholera, and that a bird into which the bacteria had been injected would subsequently be immune to even the most virulent organisms of the same kind. Just as a sore or two of cowpox would give immunity, at least for some years, to smallpox, so a mild case of chicken-cholera—or splenic fever or swine-fever—would offer animals protection against death from these diseases. The principle of vaccination by means of an attenuated virus was born. (Although the word 'vaccine' referred to the serum obtained from cows the term was applied to material of a similar nature obtained from other animals, just as, Lister said, people had formed the habit of referring to "iron mile-stones.")

This was the third great step in Pasteur's work. The first, which had annihilated the theory of spontaneous generation, had proved that putrefaction and fermentation were caused by microbes, and had made it possible to prevent the spoiling of wine and beer. The second discovery, which followed close upon the first, had demonstrated that infectious or septic diseases were caused by the development within the body of certain microbes. This, in Lister's hands, had made possible the protection of surgical wounds; Pasteur had used it to protect silk-worms from disease and cattle from being contaminated by germs from the bodies of animals which had died of anthrax.

However, disposing of the contaminated bodies of victims was not enough to wipe out the diseases which annually destroyed millions of francs' worth of cattle, swine, and poultry.

Pasteur's third discovery—that the microbes of infectious diseases, cultivated under certain conditions, were weakened and could be used as a protection against disease—made it possible to eliminate certain plagues entirely.

This he demonstrated in a dramatic way at Melun in 1881. On the thirty-first of May two sets of sheep, one of which had previously been inoculated with a weakened virus, were given injections of virulent anthrax germs, sufficient to cause fatal attacks of splenic fever. Anxiously the scientific world waited for the outcome. Pasteur's enemies and the sceptics in general were hoping that all the sheep would be stricken; Pasteur was confident that the sheep he had treated would be safe. By the second of June a large crowd of farmers and delegates from all kinds of scientific societies had thronged to Melun, to witness the conclusion of the test.

There, on the field where the animals had been left, every untreated sheep lay dead, sick, or dying; their vaccinated companions on the other side of the fence grazed away with a placidity possible only to sheep.

The farmers were convinced. Here was a way to protect their flocks from anthrax and themselves from ruin. Just get M. Pasteur to give them a syringe filled with his medicine, and their sheep would not get splenic fever—no, not even if they were injected with enough poison to kill every untreated animal!

Lister was thrilled with this discovery. In August 1880, before Pasteur felt that his theory had passed the experimental stage, he had sent Lister two vaccinated hens, and Lister had exhibited them at the British Medical Association meeting at Cambridge. He was so convinced that Pasteur was on the track of something important that he ventured to make one of his rare prophecies.

"If the British Medical Association should meet at Cambridge again ten years hence," he said, "some one may be able to record the discovery of an appropriate vaccine for measles, scarlet fever, and other acute specific diseases."

Yet in spite of all of the evidence a few diehards still insisted that microbes could create themselves.

In 1881, at a sectional session of the International Medical Congress in London, Charlton Bastian argued against Lister and his theories, claiming that the microbes found in septic wounds had been created by the tissues themselves.

Pasteur, who was representing his country at the Congress, was asked to express his opinion, and, since he did not understand English, he turned to Lister, who whispered a translation of what had been said.

"That's enough for me!" he cried, jumping to his feet, and, like the fighter he was, he defied Bastian to make a simple experiment which he described in detail and which would conclusively demonstrate his error.

Bastian was fighting a losing battle now; the germ-theory, and Pasteur and Lister with it, easily won the day. When Pasteur had entered the gallery for the opening session of the Congress a loud burst of applause and cheers had broken out, causing him to look round nervously and remark, "It is no doubt the Prince of Wales arriving—I ought to have come sooner."

It was hard for him, after so much opposition, to realize that the applause had been for him.

Before much longer he had won the applause of the world.

Preventing splenic fever, chicken-cholera, the diseases of silk-worms, and the souring of wine had interested comparatively limited numbers of people—mainly scientists and the workers and industrialists and farmers whose livelihood he had protected. Hydrophobia, however, interested every one.

Rabies—the term hydrophobia was incorrect, as only in human beings suffering from the disease was the fear of water characteristic—struck terror throughout the world. The actual number of deaths which it caused was not very great. In England they averaged about fifty a year, yet it was more dreaded than the plague.

In the first place, no one was safe from it at any time. Children coming home from school might be attacked by a howling dog with saliva frothing its mouth, a rabid wolf might prey upon the farmers and their flocks, or a beloved pet, in dumb and quiet anguish, might bite a member of the household that did not even suspect it was suffering from the disease.

But it was the course of the disease itself that made it a source of so much dread. Weeks or months might pass, while the victim of a bite would suffer every torture of the imagination, and at last begin to hope that the danger had passed. Even as he began to breathe freely again he might awaken in the morning and imagine that he saw a horrible face peering over his shoulder, and know that the disease had struck at last.

Choking sensations would set in, coupled with extreme

thirst which could not be relieved, for the very sight of a glass of water or a cup of tea would bring on paroxysms of anguish. A period of quiet dejection might follow, but the physician knew it would not last; the paroxysms would come closer and closer together, interrupted by brief moments of terrible restlessness and frightful headaches. No remedies did any good, although bleeding and croton oil, opium, calomel, and strychnine as well as quack medicines might be tried in an attempt to alleviate the terrible agony. In the end death—merciful death—took away the combined mental and physical torment of the victim.

So frightful was hydrophobia that not only were dogs killed if they were suspected of having the disease, but human beings who behaved peculiarly after being bitten—and who, knowing what might be in store for him, would not?—were frequently done to death. This was an added and unnecessary cruelty—unnecessary because rabies could not be communicated by human victims.

All Pasteur's discoveries had been prompted by the desire to solve pressing problems. Now he turned his attention to hydrophobia.

The disease was supposed to lurk in the saliva, but, though he could not isolate the organism causing it, he discovered that it was strongest in the brains of affected animals. Injecting material from the brain of a rabid dog directly into that of a rabbit, he found that he could cut down the incubation period until rabies would result in exactly seven days.

Next he set about weakening this virus, and succeeded in obtaining so attenuated a form that it could be injected without causing any symptoms. Stronger and stronger doses followed, until at the end of two weeks he could give the injection which, if given alone, would cause rabies within seven days. Yet the animal remained perfectly well. Not only was it safe from the strongest injection, but subsequent severe bites by mad dogs were without power to give it the dread disease.

Unfortunately it did not seem possible to vaccinate all the dogs in the world. One injection of serum protected cattle and poultry against anthrax and chicken-cholera, but it would take fourteen injections to protect a dog against rabies, and even then the immunization, for all Pasteur knew, might not be permanent. Even one mad dog or wolf could create terrible havoc.

It was a difficult problem, but Pasteur thought he had a way to solve it. At least a month elapsed between the time of a bite and the first symptoms of the disease. The injections could be completed in fourteen days. Perhaps it would be possible to vaccinate after the bite had occurred, and still be in time to prevent the disease from developing.

Pasteur was not sure. He would have liked to try it out on a condemned criminal, to make certain that it would work on a human being as well as it did upon animals in his laboratory, but that was apparently impossible. He was thinking of trying it on himself. . . .

Then nine-year-old Joseph Meister was brought to him, having been bitten in fourteen places by a mad dog. From what Pasteur could glean about the affair the dog had almost certainly been rabid. If that was so, the child was obviously doomed.

Pasteur could not bear to send the boy home to certain death. On the other hand he was desperately afraid to try his treatment for fear it might not do any good, or that it might actually give the child hydrophobia. The last injection was strong enough to cause rabies in a rabbit or a dog within seven days. How could he dare to thrust a needle into the boy and risk giving him that lethal dose?

Yet Pasteur went ahead and took the only course which might save the boy's life. As he gave injection after injection of increasingly virulent material Louis Pasteur grew more frightened than he had ever been in his life. He could suck saliva from the jaws of a mad dog through a pipette without the least fear that some of it might enter his own mouth, but with the life of a child in his hands he learned what it meant to be afraid. However, even the strongest dose did not cause any harm. The boy had been immunized against hydrophobia.

Pasteur knew fear again when fourteen-year-old Jupille, a brave Alsatian shepherd boy, was brought to him six days after being bitten while protecting his friends from a mad dog. Six days plus the fourteen needed to give the injections made twenty days; that was cutting the margin pretty close. Not too close, however, for again the treatment worked, and the boy was saved.

People learned of these miracles, and from all over the world they came, from tiny villages in Europe—nineteen moujiks who had been bitten by a mad wolf in the province of Smolensk, children from the United States of America—to be pricked by a needle and ask in astonishment, "Is that all?" Yes, that was all—fourteen injections, and the danger of violent madness was past.

No wonder people prayed for Pasteur in villas and cottages; no wonder making fun of him was going out of fashion! Jealous scientists might whisper that he kept his failures a secret, representatives of the Church of which he was so devout a member might attack him on religious grounds, anti-vivisectionists might call him "the laboratory murderer," and doctors might regard him as an interloper because, without a medical degree, he tried to cure humanity; but the people did not care. He had saved the wine-makers, the silk-workers, and the farmers from poverty, and now he was saving their children from the most horrible death in the world.

Just as they were able to appreciate Pasteur people were beginning to understand the benefits of Lister's work. Several years before, an old patient of Syme's had returned after an interval to the Edinburgh Infirmary for a second operation, and, recovering uneventfully in the company of other comfortable patients, had looked round him and remarked, "Ee, but you've made a grand improvement here!"

Lister had been right when he said that even if doctors

refused to accept his principles the public would learn of antiseptics and, as in the case of chloroform for childbirth, would cast the deciding vote. Although there was some resistance to the introduction of Lister's methods in midwifery it was swept aside by the force of public opinion.

People could not help but notice the difference, for surgical wards had completely changed in the course of a few short years. They were no longer filled with suffering men and women and children waiting for death to end their miseries —people who had entered the hospital well and strong except for a compound fracture or a wound "no bigger than the palm of a hand."

Patients no longer considered themselves fortunate if they left the wards permanently crippled and broken in health. Four or five days after an operation if a patient said he felt well enough to go home it was recognized as a sign of returning strength rather than the euphoria of approaching death. No evil stench arose from the patients' wounds at dressing-time, to hang like a pall over the wards, which nurses dreaded because they knew that even the smallest cut on their fingers might be the open door to death. Erysipelas season was no more to be feared than the Ides of March. Patients were more apt to recover from an accident or an operation in a large hospital than they were in a spotless cottage, and no surgeon would have dreamed of begging his colleagues to hurry his patients out of this house of death and lay them on a dunghill or in a stable.

Lister had written to his father from Glasgow that surgery was becoming an entirely different thing, and years later Alexander Ogston summed it up by saying, "You have changed surgery, especially operative surgery, from being a hazardous lottery into a safe and soundly based science."

No matter how many fine hairs some surgeons might continue to try to split, no matter what arguments they might produce, the change had taken place, and the people said, "Amen."

CHAPTER XIX

Antisepsis and Asepsis

LISTER'S OLD TEACHER, ERICHSEN, HAD remarked that "Surgery . . . in its art . . . is approaching, if it has not yet already attained to, something like finality of perfection." At the same time he insisted that it would never be safe to operate upon the abdomen, the chest, or the brain.

Scarcely had he finished speaking when surgery took the tremendous leap from art to science—a step made possible only by the introduction of anæsthetics and the antiseptic method.

Opening the membrane of the brain no longer meant death. Abdominal operations were not only possible but comparatively safe. Exploratory incisions in cases of tumour or cancer could be made with very little risk to the patient. The larynx could be successfully removed, the stomach itself excised, and even a gastro-enterostomy could be performed. Ovarian cysts, which, if left alone, almost invariably resulted in death and which terminated fatally six or eight times out of every ten cases in which operations were attempted, yielded to Lister's method. The mysterious iliac passion, or typhlitis, could be combated, as Dr Reginald Fitz, of Boston, suggested, by operating and draining or removing the inflamed appendix which caused the disease; and when, in 1889, Dr Charles McBurney clarified the question of diagnosing the disease it yielded to the knife.

No longer need a mother make the dreadful decision whether to risk the life of her child or to let it go through life deformed. Club-feet and malformed knee-joints could be corrected, and webs of scar-tissue which, following severe burns, caused disfigurement and prevented the use of limbs could be removed.

In 1883 Lister exhibited at the London Medical Society six patients whose fractured patellas he had successfully operated upon and repaired. Remembering that only four years had passed since some of the men who applauded him now had put their heads together to discuss the suit for malpractice which some one ought to bring against him for performing a similar operation, Lister could not resist finishing his remarks by saying, "Gentlemen, I thank you most heartily for your cheers; for there was a time when such remarks might have met with a different reception."

That same year Lister was made a baronet by Queen Victoria—an honour which many people felt she had put off conferring upon him out of pique because of his stand on vivisection. This was an unwarranted conclusion, because at that time only four doctors were baronets, and only one of these was a surgeon. The Queen had evidently borne Lister no grudge, since she had made him her Surgeon in Ordinary in 1878.

The rumours that Lister had previously been offered the title and had refused it were also without foundation. He was still too much of a Quaker to care about titles, and certainly he disapproved of the practice of chasing after awards of that kind. Scientific honours meant a great deal more to him, such as the degrees which he received from Cambridge and Oxford, the Boudet Prize, and, in 1885, the Prussian Order of Merit. But he would no more have thought of refusing a title than he would any other honour which was generously and sincerely offered him.

More than any honour, however, was the satisfaction of watching the spread of his teachings and the tremendous advances which they made possible.

For a long time a man like Billroth, an excellent surgeon and teacher, but by nature conservative, even reactionary, had held out against antiseptic surgery because he felt it was impossible and unnecessary in a great many operations, particularly those of the mouth, bladder, rectum, and other parts of the body which could not be rendered free of germs.

Now, with an increasing understanding of bacteria, Lister began to see why wounds in some sections of the body healed even when microbes were present.

In the same year (1883) a Russian named Metchnikoff published a paper in which he revealed the fact that certain cells possessed the ability to devour microbes. Studying the process of inflammation under the microscope, he had inserted a sliver into the larva of a starfish, and had noticed that it attracted certain wandering cells. Later he saw these same cells actually eat up a microbe. In a water-flea he saw similar cells fall upon and consume a yeast-spore.

The action of these cells, which he called phagocytes, enabled the body to fight against infection. If the germs were too many or too virulent the phagocytes would lose the battle, and infection would set in.

This explained the partial immunity to septic diseases of certain portions of the body, such as the peritoneum and the face, which Lister had observed. He had always recognized the ability of the tissues to protect themselves, and had emphasized the importance of leaving them alone as much as possible in order not to destroy their vitality.

In a sense he had partially anticipated some of Metchnikoff's discoveries. In 1880 he had made some experiments on the jugular vein of an ass—experiments which he had to make while he was on holiday, since such work was impossible in Great Britain because of the anti-vivisection laws. Trying to discover under what conditions and how long it would take for a blood-clot to become septic, he had introduced short pieces of glass tubing containing septic material into the veins, which he had then tied off.

Putrefaction of the clot, he discovered, varied according to the strength of the dilution containing the septic matter. This surprised him, as he had noticed how rapidly micro-organisms grew in test-tubes, so that it scarcely mattered whether one started a culture with a single organism or a group. Evidently it did make a difference in a living animal; Lister thought it was the serum itself which retarded the growth of bacteria, and discussed his experiments and their results at the Seventh International Medical Congress in London in 1881.

This period marked the approximate end of Lister's intensive work on micro-organisms—a subject which, under the name of bacteriology, was becoming a specialty in its own right.

For a long time if Lister wanted any information concerning the habits of these tiny creatures he had to find it out himself, with the help of Watson Cheyne, who conducted many experiments under his direction. In the same way he had to test upon himself the various chemicals which he considered using on dressings. In those days visitors were often startled, when Lister rolled up his shirt-sleeves to operate, by the number of patches plastered on his arms; it seemed to them that he must have suffered some peculiar accident. Actually he was finding out whether certain dressings would irritate the skin.

Watson Cheyne also practised vivisection upon himself, even going so far as to inject into his own arm some fluid taken from a wound after operation. Usually this material, when examined under the microscope, would be free of micro-organisms; but occasionally some would be present, even though the wound was apparently healing without infection. Could that mean that there was something wrong with the entire theory?

Injecting some of the organisms he found in the wounds into rabbits and guinea-pigs, Cheyne discovered that they did not cause any damage. So he tried them on himself, and got a very sore arm, but no abscess or fever or other signs of septic disease, which led him to the conclusion that certain organisms were not dangerous. Although at first he did not distinguish correctly between the guilty and the innocent, it was the shadow of the coming discovery that there were pathogenic and non-pathogenic bacteria.

Another conclusion to which these early experiments led was to anticipate a discovery which is still not entirely complete:

that something too small to be seen even through the most powerful microscope could cause disease.

Gradually some of the puzzles cleared up as improvements in the techniques for studying bacteria were made. Lister devised some ingenious 'glass gardens' which enabled him to watch the life-process of bacteria for many generations, and Koch recommended Zeiss's oil immersion lenses, Abbé's condenser, and the use of aniline dyes for staining bacteria in order to distinguish them from the tissues. Koch also developed a solid medium upon which microbes could be grown, and this further simplified experiments.

Now that the study of bacteria was coming of age Lister turned his energies in other directions, working on problems such as those connected with the relative pressure in veins and arteries, the effects of chloroform, and matters dealing with other phases of surgery. His knowledge of bacteriology, however, continued to be of great assistance in his constant efforts to obtain better dressings and more satisfactory ligatures.

It also enabled him to draw some useful conclusions from Koch's discovery that while it required a strong solution of carbolic acid to destroy the spores of anthrax, a weak one was sufficient to prevent their growth. Lister called the action of this weak antiseptic *inhibitory*, and realized that it was sufficient to protect the tissues in operations. If instruments were carefully disinfected, and the most dangerous microbes eliminated by the victory over hospitalism, an antiseptic which inhibited growth should be enough, and would be less irritating to the tissues than a stronger one. If germs entered the wounds they were usually either harmless yeasts or moulds or a very occasional dangerous organism which would be destroyed by the phagocytes.

With this new understanding of the comparative harmlessness of the germs in the air Lister reconsidered the spray. From 1881 he had doubted its value, and in 1887 he decided it was unnecessary. Studying its action, he decided it did not actually kill the germs in the air anyway, as they were not exposed to the evaporating carbolic acid long enough to be affected by it. Following his own advice concerning the importance of recanting a published error, he announced at the International Congress in Berlin in 1890, "I feel ashamed that I should have ever recommended it for the purpose of destroying the microbes of the air."

Although it had not fulfilled the purpose that spray had succeeded in keeping the surgeon's hands antiseptic during an operation, acting as "an unconscious caretaker." Eliminating the spray and the washing and irrigation of the wound with carbolic lotion during an operation made it necessary for the surgeon and his assistants to redouble their vigilance, but Lister did not think that this should be too much of a responsibility.

Pursuing this line of reasoning, von Bergmann, an early and enthusiastic supporter of antiseptic surgery, went even further than Lister and worked out techniques which eliminated not only the spray and the use of carbolic acid for washing out the wound, but all chemical disinfectants of any kind.

This was called the aseptic method. Lister had used the word 'antiseptic' to describe his system, meaning by it that he was attempting to obtain an aseptic wound—one free from decay-producing germs—by means of antiseptic, or germ-destroying, agents. In order to prevent germs from entering the wound after an operation he used dressings impregnated with chemical antiseptics.

Von Bergmann, reasoning that since all micro-organisms did not produce sepsis it was unnecessary to kill them all, placed the emphasis upon keeping germs out of wounds rather than destroying them. Everything which came in contact with the wound during an operation could be sterilized by boiling, and germs which might fall into the wound could be washed out with a bland, non-irritating solution of sterile water and salt. He considered antiseptics both unnecessary and, because of their irritating effect, harmful.

When he had first developed his treatment Lister had said, "Of all those who use antiseptics I suspect that I apply them least to the surface of the wound." On certain occasions he had operated without using a chemical disinfectant. Seeing the success of Keith and Spencer Wells, whose technique in fact approached that of the aseptic surgeon, he had been quite reluctant to urge upon them the use of chemicals.

Far from making a fetish of carbolic acid, as some of his followers did, Lister constantly searched for other disinfectants. Chloride of zinc had been suggested to him, and, trying it out, he found it valuable in cases where an antiseptic could be applied only once, as in operations involving diseased bones with sinuses which must be disinfected before the wound was closed. Darwin had recommended benzoic acid and Pasteur boracic acid, which was later again recommended by a Norwegian medical friend. When Lister suffered from an infected finger-nail he substituted boracic acid for carbolic and found it effective as well as soothing. Later he used boracic solutions for skin-diseases such as eczema, and also for ulcers and the treatment of burns. But carbolic acid still seemed to him the best general antiseptic.

To Lister, as to von Bergmann, avoiding chemical antiseptics did not constitute a new system; it was merely carrying Lister's method one step further. Von Bergmann felt that this was possible because the conditions which had necessitated the use of strong chemicals had ceased to exist. Lister had won the battle against hospital diseases, so that operating-theatres and wards, instead of being laden with dangerous microbes of every kind, were far safer than the cleanest country cottages, where wounds had frequently healed without infection. Instruments and operating-rooms were being designed to make life just as untenable as possible for germs. The first round being won, antiseptics could be discarded for the remainder of the fight.

With this Lister did not entirely agree. He thought that the so-called aseptic technique had several serious disadvantages. For one thing, it was complicated. One weak link would cause the chain to snap, one careless act on the part of an assistant or a nurse might place the patient's life in jeopardy. The antiseptic surgeon, however, could call upon a powerful chemical ally in case the wound should accidentally become contaminated.

Equally important, in his eyes, was the fact that the aseptic technique was almost impossible except in a well-equipped hospital. The average student knew that it would be beyond his reach if he practised in a small town or a mining-centre, or even if he relied upon small hospitals which lacked steam sterilizers and other expensive apparatus. Since he probably would not be able to practise aseptic surgery the student who learned no other method while he was at medical school would be handicapped when he went out into the world.

Antiseptic technique, however, was something he could not only easily learn, but could practise in any circumstances. Lister had constantly simplified it, as experience had shown that it was safe to do so.

When he operated in a private home no complicated preparations were necessary. All that was required were some trays and basins containing carbolic lotion in 1 : 20 and 1 : 40 solution, and these he usually brought along himself. The instruments, clean but not sterilized, were placed for half an hour in the strong solution. Sponges, which had undergone a "rough and ready disinfection," were placed in the weak one. While the chloroform was being administered Lister would apply the 1 : 20 lotion to the skin, where, because of the affinity of carbolic for oily substances, it combined readily with the material in the hair-follicles.

Taking off his coat and turning up his shirt-sleeves, Lister would pin on a towel and wash his hands in the strong carbolic, which was too irritating for some surgeons. Throughout the operation his hands and those of his assistants, were frequently dipped in the weak lotion. Towels wet with the lotion were placed about the site of the operation, and the wound was washed with the weak lotion if there were any possibility that contamination had taken place. The catgut he used had been steeped in carbolic for half an hour, as had the sutures of silver wire or silkworm catgut. Following the operation the wound was dressed with cyanide gauze covered with salicylic wool, and the part of the gauze closest to the wound was dipped in carbolic lotion which was firmly wrung out.

Any student could learn this method, and Lister did not think it should be replaced with one which was extremely complicated. "I am sorry sometimes to observe that unnecessary trouble is often taken in some directions while essential points are disregarded in others," he said, but that was about as far as his criticism of aseptic surgery went. He never attacked von Bergmann or his method, nor did the latter ever claim to have done more than to modify and improve Lister's technique.

Unfortunately other surgeons were not nearly so moderate, and rival schools arose, the believers in asepsis calling antiseptic surgeons "old-fashioned," while these responded with indignant cries of "heretics!" Aseptic surgeons made fun of the old fogies who clung to carbolic when every one knew that chemicals were unnecessary and irritating, but they worked out excellent techniques for keeping germs out of wounds. On the other hand, Lister's "faithful followers," as they called themselves, pointed to their own excellent results, and attacked the elaborate rituals of the aseptic surgeons who would not, they insisted, be content until a boiled surgeon could operate upon a boiled patient in a boiled operating-room.

The bland double cyanide gauze which Lister introduced in 1889 seemed to the faithful to be as far as anyone had a right to go in keeping carbolic acid away from wounds.

Although Lister had liked volatile dressings he recognized their disadvantages. They had to be opened while they were still warm, or the layers of gauze would stick together, and the way the manufacturer handled this procedure made a difference in the amount of antiseptic which remained in the bandages. Hospitals had to be extremely careful in storing volatile bandages to prevent evaporation.

Lister had been impressed with Koch's arguments in favour of corrosive sublimate as an antiseptic, and he once more started a series of experiments to obtain better bandages. For years he worked with various non-volatile salts of mercury, trying to solve the problem connected with the chemical action of the sublimate on the albumin in the serum and the blood. At last, in 1884, he produced his "sero-sublimate gauze," which he felt had definite advantages over carbolic gauze.

Although it won a degree of popularity this dressing was not sufficiently absorbent, and the use of horse-serum made it difficult to manufacture and objectionable to some people besides. So Lister tried other salts of mercury, hoping to find one more satisfactory than corrosive sublimate. He first obtained one which was adequate for wounds that healed rapidly, and finally a double cyanide which was not irritating and which was firmly held to the gauze by means of a pretty heliotrope dye.

This gauze met with a favourable response that indicated a new attitude on the part of the profession. Instead of criticizing Lister for changing his dressings doctors praised him for his industry and for not resting on his laurels.

Over the new gauze he used a layer of cotton-wool impregnated with carbolic to filter out any contaminating germs. And there, insisted Lister's followers, was "final perfection." "To 'improve and modify' the completeness of genius is bound to terminate in a medley of confusion," pronounced G. T. Wrench, one of Lister's disciples and biographers.

It was a rather strange attitude for the follower of a man who never felt that he had reached final perfection, and was always anxious to learn from anyone. Once Lister had operated upon a patient whose condition had seemed good to him, although his house-surgeon had found indications of bronchitis. Following the operation the patient died of pneumonia, and at his next lecture Lister spoke on "the medical care of surgical cases," telling the story in detail so that others could learn from his mistake.

Nevertheless, some of his admirers insisted that no improvement upon his work should be attempted. Some time after the Chief was dead Wrench continued to maintain that "man should confirm the inscrutable decrees of Providence, which pick out one man and endow him with supreme genius, by preserving his incomparable value in a firm tradition." Gravely he went on to deplore the "age in which liberty and progress as ideals have jealously destroyed the equally legitimate claims of authority and tradition."

However, despite the attempts made on both sides to keep the issue alive, the distinction between the heretics and the "faithful followers" gradually faded away.

No one is inclined now to question the "elaborate ritual" and "expensive equipment" required by modern surgical technique. A modern surgeon, drilled to the point where it has become second nature for him to touch only the inside of the first rubber glove with the bare, scrubbed fingers he uses to pull it on, while he touches with his gloved hand only the sterile, outer side of his second glove, does not worry in the least whether he is practising aseptic or antiseptic surgery when he uses a chemical like iodine for a preliminary cleansing of the skin before an operation.

A sterile mask covers his mouth and nose, protecting the incision against the germs in his breath, so that in appearance at least he comes close to resembling the "boiled surgeon" that Lister's disciples used to deride. Although his sharp eyes are constantly alert for the smallest break in the chain of his technique, he uses, without confusion and as a matter of course, antiseptics in first aid or when he has to operate under conditions which make adherence to strict aseptic technique impossible or impractical—as, for example, in front-line military surgery.

Since the First World War, when the use of Dakin's solution was considered a triumph for chemicals over the heresy of von Bergmann, the controversy has not been revived. The recent introduction of the use of sulfa drugs and penicillin on wounds suspected of contamination was not even discussed in terms of whether it came under the heading of antiseptic or aseptic surgery.

As the distinction between the terms aseptic and antiseptic was never very meaningful, so the distinction between the two methods lost its importance. The means employed vary according to the circumstances and the improvements which new discoveries make possible. The aim of the surgeon is to keep wounds aseptic, to prevent, in every possible way, germs from entering the body, and to help the body to destroy those germs which have gained access to it. That is the light in which the problem is considered to-day, and that is how Lister saw it and solved it with the best means at his disposal.

CHAPTER XX

The Long Honeymoon

LOUIS PASTEUR WAS BORN ON DECEMBER 27, 1822, and on that day in 1892 the whole world honoured his seventieth birthday. Families he had saved from ruin and given security, ordinary people whose sleep was no longer haunted by the spectre of hydrophobia, joined with the leaders of the scientific world in wishing him a happy birthday.

His jubilee was celebrated officially in Paris at the Sorbonne, the spirit of the meeting being expressed by the words on the commemorative medal which said, very simply, "To Pasteur, on his seventieth birthday. France and Humanity grateful."

The world was very grateful that he had been spared to continue his work, so much of which had been accomplished on borrowed time. In 1868, when he was only forty-six and while he had been working on the epidemic which was destroying the country's silkworms, he had suffered a cerebral hæmorrhage. For a time his life had been despaired of. Looking out of the window from his bed, he had seen the workmen cease their labours on the laboratory which the doctors assured them he would never use. But he had gradually recovered, although a partial paralysis of his left side continued to trouble him.

Twenty years later another stroke made it necessary for him to give up some of his duties, although he continued to work in his Institute, visiting the hydrophobia clinic, supervising the preparation of vaccine, and encouraging the patients who had turned to him as their only hope.

Anxiously mothers prayed that he might be spared to continue his work on diphtheria, which, when it struck in its most severe form, had been known to leave no child under twelve alive in an entire town or village. Already Alexandre Yersin and Pasteur's chief assistant, Émile Roux, were isolating the deadly toxin which the microbe of diphtheria generated; soon they might find an antidote for this poison. Each year that Pasteur lived might save so many lives. From the humblest homes as well as from the highest circles in the world subscriptions came from people who wanted to pay tribute to Pasteur.

It was a notable gathering which filled the 2500 seats of the theatre at the Sorbonne to overflowing. Delegates from important scientific societies in every country, professors in their academic robes, military men in uniform—all brought colour and dignity to the sections reserved for them. The amphitheatre was packed with deputations from various colleges, while the first gallery was reserved for the people who had subscribed to the fund, and the second held the fortunate students who would boast all their lives that they had seen "the most perfect man that ever entered the kingdom of science."

But how old and ill Pasteur looked as he entered, leaning heavily on the arm of the President of the Republic of France! Following him came the Presidents of the Senate and Chamber, Ministers and Ambassadors, all of them humbly taking their places behind the man who served humanity.

The emotion of the audience rose as, after a few words had been delivered by the President of France, the Minister of Instruction, and the President of the Académie, Joseph Lister was introduced.

Representing the Royal Society of Edinburgh and the Royal Society of London, Lister spoke briefly in French, with his characteristic sincerity. Pasteur, he said, had made possible a revolution in surgery, changing it from an uncertain and often disastrous affair to a beneficial science; he had brought about equally great changes in medicine, by having "raised the veil which for centuries had covered infectious diseases." His voice deep with emotion, Lister offered to Pasteur, the chemist, the homage of medicine and surgery.

Profoundly moved by Lister's words, Pasteur could not control himself. The emotional Frenchman rose to his feet, and there on the platform he embraced the restrained and self-conscious Englishman. The two great men stood for a moment "like a living picture of the brotherly unity of Science in the relief of humanity," while all over the theatre, in the seats of honour as well as the students' gallery, the audience went wild. It was not only the French who cried.

Seeing Pasteur and Lister together, it was hard to realize that there was just five years' difference in their ages, for Pasteur was old and infirm, while Lister was the picture of vigour and health. He had grown stockier and his hair was white, but one had only to look at him to see that sixty-five was the prime of life for a man whose father had lived to be eighty-four and his grandfather ninety-eight.

As *The Lancet* put it, Lister was still "as active and able as when, twenty-three years ago, he resigned his chair of Systematic Surgery in Glasgow to become the successor of Syme in the Clinical Surgery chair of Edinburgh University."

But sixty-five was the age of retirement at King's, and Lister had reached that age in April of 1892.

At the request of the hospital authorities he continued on through the summer and would remain in charge of the wards for the next year. Then he would give them up, and, because he had always felt that a physician went stale if he were cut off from the stimulation of hospital work, he would retire from private practice as well.

He had no intention of giving up all his work. On the contrary, as soon as he was relieved of routine duties, and especially the demands which private practice made upon his time, he would devote himself completely to research. The idea had never appealed to him when he had been young; but now, with a wealth of active experience in his possession, he felt that it would have great advantages.

He had never minded working under pressure, but it had

steadily increased, augmented by the load of scientific society meetings, medical dinners, and other duties which were the price of his position, until, as his relatives used to complain, they saw even less of him than when he had been living in Scotland.

It would be a relief to be free of part of the burden. For one thing, he would be able to devote more time to studying the work of other scientists, especially the members of many scientific societies to which he belonged. In March of 1893 he was elected associate of the Académie des Sciences, the highest distinction scientific France could offer, and one which had never before been awarded to an English medical man. He enjoyed his membership in these societies and the contacts which his knowledge of foreign languages made possible for him, and saw in them a step towards the internationalism and peace which seemed so necessary to his logical mind. He looked forward, as soon as he had a little more available time, to making greater contributions to the progress of science.

Perhaps, with Agnes's help, he might even write the book which had so long been demanded of him. Jokingly, he used to admit that he had never got any further than finding a suitable quotation for the title-page—the words of the Psalmist: "My wounds stink, and are corrupt because of my foolishness."

But first he and Agnes would have a real holiday—a long one, not just their usual few weeks' breathing-space from gruelling work. This spring holiday in Italy would be their last short vacation; next year they would stay as long as they liked.

Perhaps they would spend part of the winter here, at Rapallo, on the Italian Riviera. They both loved Italy, and although they were finding Rapallo a little damp in the spring it would be an ideal winter-resort, being situated in such a well-sheltered spot on the east side of the Gulf. There were plenty of beautiful places to visit, including the remains of the castle which crowned the promontory of Portofino, and "Hannibal's Bridge," which had been standing since medieval days, and the ancient tombs of the Dorias. It was only eighteen miles to Genoa, if one took the train, whose tracks seemed scarcely able to find a bit of space between the sea and the steep hillside covered with vineyards, olive-gardens, and chestnut-trees which reached their candles towards the brilliant sky.

Most of the holiday was spent in collecting flowers, which both loved passionately. One morning after breakfast, however, when they were changing the papers of some dried blooms, Agnes began to shiver. Lister was taken by surprise, for his wife had been in apparently excellent health. He sent her to bed, but to his dismay the symptoms of pneumonia appeared shortly after.

There was no English doctor at Rapallo, and no hospital or nurses; but the Italian physician, Dr Piaggio, was most attentive. No nurse could care for a patient the way Joseph Lister cared for his wife. It was doubly hard, having her sick so far from home, but with pneumonia there was not much that could be done anywhere except to give her the best possible nursing care and wait for the disease to run its course.

Agnes's attack was not only acute, but most severe. In order that he could be called at a moment's notice Dr Piaggio took a room at the hotel adjoining the Listers' rooms. Joseph Lister scarcely left his wife's side during the four days and nights in which her condition grew steadily worse.

Sitting by her bed, he thought of all the times in their thirty-seven years together that she had sat beside him while he rested on the couch after dinner. Throwing a shawl over him so that he would not catch cold, she used to read aloud in her lovely voice with the faint burr which he always found so delightful, especially when she was reading their favourite Burns. Or it might be Goethe, whom he knew so well that he would frequently recite with her, in silence, when she reached a familiar passage. Or Dante. He had had a little start on her when it came to languages, but she had managed to catch up with him and more than hold her own.

After an hour of reading he would be completely relaxed and ready for bed or for a session in the laboratory, with Agnes by his side, helping him as only Agnes could. He wondered whether any couple had ever been as close as he and his wife—even the devoted Pasteurs. The very fact that they had no children, which was their only regret, somehow brought them closer together, made them mean everything to each other.

And now she was critically ill. Carefully Joseph Lister moved his chair closer to the bed, so that he would notice if the slightest change took place.

The four days of constant anxiety had told upon him. He was not aware of being tired. He had never been so alert, nor had he ever been less afraid, even when performing the simplest routine, of making a mistake or overlooking something important. Yet it was a strange kind of awareness, almost like that in a dream, completely excluding everything in his surroundings which was not essential to the central issue.

As in a dream, everything seemed familiar to him, as though it had all happened before, a long, long time ago. He looked at his wife's face, and words which he had not read for many years came unbidden to his mind.

"I never saw a more unforgettable face—pale, serious, lonely, delicate, sweet . . . her mouth firm, patient, and contented, which few mouths ever are . . . subdued and beautiful. . . ."

And then more words from their favourite story written by their dear old friend:

> The end was drawing on; the golden bowl was breaking; the silver cord was fast being loosed. . . . The body and the soul —companions for sixty years—were being surrendered and taking leave. She was walking alone through the Valley of that Shadow into which one day we must all enter. . . . Lifting up her calm, clear, beautiful eyes, she gave him a long look . . . as if she would never leave off looking.

He heard a young voice saying, "Ailie was nothing but an old woman to some people, but her husband loved her so much."

And clearly he heard Agnes answer, "Somehow, it makes me think of us."

They were back in Glasgow again, he and Agnes, sitting in the living-room of their home in Woodside Place, talking about *Rab and His Friends*. No one, he had said, could read about Ailie's death without resolving to do everything he could to wipe out septic diseases, and Agnes had assured him that he was going to do it some day.

Had she really known it, then, or had it been the blind confidence of a young girl in the husband she loved? He must ask her. But already he could anticipate her assuring him, with her enigmatic smile, "Why, of course I knew it!"

He started; Agnes had not stirred. He had quite lost track of time; yet, as an old fisherman learns to recognize the moment when the tide is going to turn, he knew it was that hour before dawn when he had seen so many lights grow dim, and flicker, and go out. Joseph Lister leaned over his wife's bed.

The long honeymoon was coming to an end.

CHAPTER XXI

Joseph, Baron Lister

"GOOD-BYE, MY DEAR TWO," JOHN Brown had once written at the close of a letter to Agnes and Joseph Lister. "Good-bye, my dear two, made for each other and for our good."

"Good-bye, my dear two," the train-wheels clacked against the rails as Joseph Lister returned to London with the body of his wife. "Good-bye."

Almost fortunately he was suffering too profound a shock to be able to compare this home-coming with the happy endings to their many other holidays, when any slight regret he and Agnes might have felt because their vacation was over was mitigated by the prospect of them getting back to home and work.

It was terrible, Lister's friends thought, that he should have had to make the difficult and tragic journey by himself. They did not realize that, no matter who had been with him, he would have been alone, would always be alone, from the moment Agnes died.

Joseph Lister buried his wife in a quiet and secluded spot in the large West Hampstead Cemetery.

Then, as he had planned, he went through the summer session at King's, after which he gave up his wards and terminated his private practice as rapidly as possible.

With his release from routine duties he did not, as he had intended, embark at once upon an extensive programme of research. He was free now for the laboratory, yet, with Agnes gone, the place became an unbearable reminder of her absence. For thirty-seven years she had helped him with his experiments, and if he did manage to persuade her to go to bed she would usually wake up when he came in—if she had actually been asleep—to ask him how things had turned out.

Sometimes it seemed impossible for him to make an entry in the "commonplace books," so many of which had been filled with her close writing. Once, for a period of three years—from 1896 until 1899—there were no notes in the book at all. Not only was it painful for him to attempt the work which they had planned together for the days after his retirement, but the spark which she had lighted had gone.

In the same way Agnes had been the catalytic agent which had brought together the people who came to Park Crescent, and made the social gatherings there occasions of warmth and friendliness. Lucy Syme stayed on, and Lister came to depend upon her more and more; but the parties were over for ever.

Not even the passing of time made it possible for him to come close to people again. There had been a gap between him and every one, except children and members of his own family, ever since he had been a boy. During the years it had grown deeper and wider, although he had not been aware of it while Agnes was alive to bridge it for him. Now he was truly remote.

He was as kind as he had ever been, perhaps even kinder since his sympathy had been quickened by his own loss; but, though he could help others, they could not help him. In the face of his aloofness they ceased to try, at least in any personal way.

Impersonally, however, his friends were able to help him a great deal, by seeing to it that he was offered the secretaryship of the Royal Society upon the retirement of Sir Archibald Geikie. In his present mood Lister did not want to accept the position, yet he was persuaded to take it from a sense of duty. His father had been a Fellow of the Society, and it had published his own first papers when he was only thirty years old, and elected him to membership when he was thirty-three. His friends believed that the work would not be too much for him and that it would succeed in arousing his interest.

The correspondence with foreign scientists and the participation in scientific meetings which the position required of him were types of activities with which Agnes had not been very closely identified, and so he was able to enter into them without being constantly reminded of her absence. It was just what he needed to keep him from idleness and brooding, and tide him over the period following his retirement, when he was not forced to keep busy by the duties connected with his position, and he had no heart for original work.

Gradually his interest in the Royal Society and the work of its members increased, and in 1895 he accepted the presidency, a position which had previously been held by only one other surgeon. Although he never completed his original plans for intensive research he was able to make many important contributions in various fields.

The slight change in his orientation which followed from his work in the Royal Society logically increased Lister's interest in public health. In 1891 the British Institute of Preventive Medicine had been incorporated, with Lister as its chairman. Two years later the long-hoped-for antitoxin for diphtheria was perfected. Large sums of money were raised to honour Jenner's discovery of vaccination, which had taken place one hundred years before, and the Institute was given his name. Difficulties, however, resulted because of a commercial firm calling itself the Jenner Institute for Calf-lymph; and, against Lister's inclination, the name was changed again in 1903, when it became the Lister Institute of Preventive Medicine.

That Lister's time was not entirely preoccupied with public-health problems and the work of his fellow scientists was quite apparent in the spring of 1894, when he visited the Medico-Chirurgical Society of Glasgow University. Here he discussed the simplification of the antiseptic method, the activity of phagocytes, and the rapidity with which they devoured anthrax-germs, and experiments which he had made to demonstrate how "greedily epidermis and oily matters take carbolic from a watery solution." He had carefully tested the action of carbolic acid upon hair, and from these experiments he had come to the conclusion that shaving and careful purification of the skin and follicles before an operation were unnecessary.

As usual, he had prepared his talk at the last minute. He wrote his brother Arthur, as he had so often written him before, that he did not think he had ever been so pressed for time.

"More than two-thirds of what I said was without a note to guide me," he added; but, as usual, his thorough familiarity with the subject and the careful attention to detail which marked all his work made his speech a real contribution.

Afterwards, his heart was filled with memories of the past as the students sang *Auld Lang Syne*, and he recalled the days that he and Agnes had spent in Glasgow, searching for and finding the answer to the problems which had made surgery less of a blessing than a curse.

How different this reception was from the coldness which had characterized his departure from Glasgow, when the directors had been so afraid that the improvements he had made might reflect upon them and their management of the Infirmary! He had hoped to improve conditions, when he first went there, by the frowned-upon, extravagant use of towels and scrubbing-brushes and soap—very much, he realized now, as though he had hoped to destroy a horde of wild animals with a pop-gun. Well, antiseptics had reduced the horde in size and strength until even a pop-gun was almost enough to cope with it now.

How pleased Agnes would have been because Glasgow had honoured his work at last! And she would have been amused, he knew, at his discomfiture after the meeting, when he was driving back to the home of Sir Hector Cameron—who had been his house-surgeon in Glasgow twenty-eight years ago—and the students had fallen upon them, insisting on unyoking the horse and pulling the cab by a circuitous route back to the house.

With Agnes gone, Joseph Lister noticed, as his father had before him, that "since his own great loss his friends and contemporaries seemed falling like autumn leaves." His oldest sister, Mary Lister Godlee, had died in 1894, and in September of the following year he, with so many others, mourned the death of Louis Pasteur.

At a ceremony in January Lister paid tribute to the memory of the great man who had been his friend. For once he must have found it hard to suppress a feeling of envy: Marie Laurent Pasteur, who had been Pasteur's wife and companion for almost fifty years, had been at his bedside when he passed away.

Although so many of his contemporaries were going Lister's life was not over. While he might not know real happiness again he was too much of a scientist not to be thrilled by the discoveries which constantly enlarged the medical and surgical horizon.

In 1896, as president of the British Association, Lister discussed various recent contributions to medicine and surgery—anæsthetics, the work of Pasteur, and the newly discovered Röntgen rays, which made it possible to see solid objects through the tissues of the body, and which he realized would open up new vistas in diagnosis and in therapy.

The title of his talk was "The Interdependence of Science and the Healing Art," which was indicative of his attitude in the scientific societies to which he belonged, where he always took the viewpoint of the physician, rather than that of the 'detached' scientist. Sometimes he almost apologized for this tendency of his; but he went on discussing such subjects as Yersin's treatment of bubonic plague, or the 'mosquito theory' of the origin and prevention of malaria. He had favoured a close relationship between science and what had too long been an 'independent art' ever since the days when, as a young man, he had advocated the use of the microscope in medicine, and Sharpey's lectures had, as he put it, inspired in him "a love of physiology that has never left me."

It was because of his accomplishments in science rather than in medicine that he was raised to the peerage in 1897, the year of Queen Victoria's Diamond Jubilee. If he had known about it in advance he might have refused the title; but when he discovered how much it pleased and gratified his colleagues he was glad that he had been singled out.

In the House of Lords Lister took an active part only in the debates which concerned scientific matters. Although he was interested in world and local affairs, it did not seem to him that he had time, at seventy years of age, to acquire a background which would enable him to make any valuable contributions, and it never occurred to him that his distinguished position automatically qualified him as an expert in every field.

Twice he took an important part in questions before the House—once in regard to legislation concerning venereal disease, and once when a Bill dealing with vaccination was introduced.

Compulsory vaccination had created a great deal of controversy in Great Britain. It had been adopted in 1853, since which time it had been far from successful, due to the opposition of conscientious objectors, resisters, and bigoted anti-vivisectionists.

The purpose of the Bill was to see that vaccination was enforced, and at the same time to make it as palatable as possible by extending the age at which a child must be vaccinated from three months to one year, by letting people be vaccinated at their homes rather than insisting upon a public place, and by eliminating 'arm-to-arm' methods which many people found objectionable. A 'conscience clause' had been inserted in the House of Commons in order to protect those conscientious objectors who felt they were being martyred by the law. It was round this clause that the debate centred in the House of Lords.

Lister felt very strongly on the subject of vaccination. In

1889 an epidemic of smallpox broke out in Gloucester, and, referring to it a little later, he had said:

"I have no desire to speak severely of the Gloucester Guardians. They are not sanitary authorities, and had not the technical knowledge necessary to enable them to judge between the teachings of true science and the declamations of misguided, though well-meaning, enthusiasts. They did what they believed to be right; and when roused to a sense of the greatness of their mistake they did their very best to repair it. . . . But, though by their praiseworthy exertions they succeeded in promptly checking the raging epidemic they cannot recall the dead to life, or restore beauty to marred features, or sight to blinded eyes."

Despite his personal convictions Lister had learned enough about politics since the days of the anti-vivisection controversy to realize that compromise was sometimes necessary. He therefore advocated the passing of the Bill despite the insertion of the conscience clause, rather than risk losing it entirely.

"I am rather afraid from what thee say that when thee read it again, thee will not altogether approve," he wrote his brother somewhat apologetically. "But it would have been a very serious thing to leave matters as they are, worse and worse year by year: the only alternative."

Worrying a good deal about whether he had taken the correct position, Lister was very much relieved to find that the medical profession and the general public agreed that he had advocated the soundest course, and the Bill was finally passed.

Of all the celebrations held in honour of Lister's rise to the peerage the one which meant the most to him, and which he really enjoyed, was the dinner given him by the men who had served as his house-officers. Thirty former house-surgeons and one hundred dressers took time from their busy careers to come from all parts of the world and pay tribute to their Chief. Most of them were famous men themselves, but they forgot all that as they relived the old days and told

Joseph Lister about the progress of surgery which his method had made possible in every corner of the globe.

In Canada, where he went with his brother and nieces in the autumn of 1897, to attend some medical meetings, he learned at first hand how highly his contributions were regarded in the New World.

Soon afterwards the city which he loved best of all—Agnes's city—conferred its highest honour upon him, giving him the Freedom of Edinburgh.

Honours and degrees piled up, until he was in possession of some eighty or more diplomas and certificates from nineteen different countries—all of them, of course, requiring formal acknowledgment, if not personal acceptance.

Sometimes it seemed to him as though these occasions were following one another a little too rapidly. As he wrote his brother:

> They seem [to be] going to make a great fuss about my visit to Liverpool on October 8th, as thee will see from the enclosed letter.... Earlier in the month I am to take the principal part in the reception to be given to Virchow; and that will be no sinecure; I could have been well pleased to have been left in quiet for a bit longer.

Lister would have liked to stay longer in the pleasant Welsh countryside where, all by himself, he was recovering from the inroads which fatigue, "absence of appetite . . . the excessive heat, and, last but not least, the real worry connected with the Vaccination Bill" had made into his health. Yet he could not refuse the requests made of him by various committees, and particularly the request that he should participate in a ceremony at which Virchow was to deliver the second Huxley Lecture.

No meeting was ever a sinecure for Joseph Lister. He always felt he must make a real contribution, always added to his general remarks specific information which he had not discussed before and which would help to repay busy scientists for the time they spent attending meetings of a ceremonial nature.

He regarded the honours which were offered him as tributes to his work rather than to him personally, and used the occasions to spread information which he thought would help other people rather than as opportunities to bask in glory, which would have been extremely distasteful to him in any circumstances.

When he accepted the Freedom of the city of Edinburgh he expressed his attitude towards the honours which were being showered upon him when he said:

"Highly . . . as I esteem the honour which you have conferred upon me, I regard that and all worldly distinctions as nothing in comparison with the hope that I may have been the means of reducing in some degree the sum of human misery. And if I am not presumptuous in indulging this hope, I share it with the humblest practitioner who discharges to the best of his ability the sacred duties of our noble profession."

CHAPTER XXII

Another Herakles

IN THE THIRD HUXLEY LECTURE, which Lister delivered in November 1900, a few days before the end of his term as President of the Royal Society, he reviewed his early work as though he knew he was reaching the end of his active career. He had begun to feel that he was growing old. Yet the fact that his mind had lost none of its brilliance and clarity was quite obvious at the Second Tuberculosis Congress.

Robert Koch had recently discovered tuberculin, which, in those days of miracles, had aroused tremendous enthusiasm as a cure for consumption. For a time Lister had shared in the hope. One of his nieces was suffering from the disease, and he took her to Berlin for treatment. Like so many others, he was doomed to disappointment; tuberculin was not a cure. Although his niece died Lister did not join in the attacks against Koch, for he realized that he had been persuaded to publish his discovery "before he himself disposed to do so." And, although tuberculin was of no use in treating tuberculosis, it was of great value in diagnosing it in its early stages.

At the Congress Koch presented the results of his latest experiments, which, he believed, demonstrated that animal and human tuberculosis were two different diseases. He had been unable to infect animals with the bacillus taken from human beings, and he produced arguments which he cautiously but emphatically declared indicated that human beings could not catch the disease from animals. If this were true the elaborate and expensive precautions being introduced to prevent the use of contaminated meat and milk would not be necessary.

Lister recognized the weight of Koch's arguments and all that they implied. As it was up to him to comment at the end of Koch's address he summed up his talk in his clear, logical manner, putting his finger upon the weak places in the argument. While Koch had demonstrated that it was apparently impossible to infect animals with human tuberculosis he had not proved that they were two different diseases. He had not proved that it was impossible to give animal tuberculosis to human beings. For obvious reasons this part of his theory could not be subjected to strict laboratory tests, and had to be deduced.

One of Koch's arguments in support of his theory that tuberculosis could not be transmitted by means of infected milk was the absence of tubercular lesions in the intestines of children who had been drinking such milk. But, Lister pointed out, relatively few people who died of tuberculosis had intestinal lesions, despite the number of tubercle bacilli they must have swallowed in the course of years of illness. This probably proved only that the intestinal mucous membrane was not a favourable site for the development of the bacilli. Even the typhoid bacillus, which flourished in the intestine, occasionally passed through it without producing a characteristic lesion.

Although what Koch had said was both interesting and valuable from a scientific point of view Lister emphasized the danger of jumping to premature conclusions, and urged the continuation and strengthening of precautions against the use of products which might be dangerous.

It was a masterful spontaneous summary. Later Lister suggested experiments to be carried out at the Institute which was soon to bear his name. These experiments, made under his direction, revealed that Koch's conclusions had been incorrect, and supported Lister's warning that it would have been extremely ill-advised to relax the regulations governing the use of meat and dairy products.

Shortly before the Tuberculosis Congress Queen Victoria died. After the period of Court mourning was over elaborate

Coronation ceremonies were planned—only to be postponed at the last minute because of the illness of the man who had been known as the Prince of Wales for so long that it would be hard to think of him as Edward VII.

Lister, who had been Sergeant Surgeon to the Queen since 1900 and, after her death, to her son, was called in for consultation. He advised an operation. Edward was suffering from an appendicular abscess, which, in the days before antiseptic surgery, would have been left unoperated and would have undoubtedly caused his death.

Edward VII was fully aware of that fact. When the Coronation finally took place, in August 1902, he made Lister a Privy Councillor and a member of the Order of Merit, which he had just instituted. And, in order to show how keenly he realized his indebtedness, he shook Lister's hand and said, "Lord Lister, I know well that if it had not been for you and your work I would not have been here to-day."

How many people could say the same thing! How many agreed with Mr Bayard, the American Ambassador, who said at a banquet given to Lister by the Royal Society in 1902, "My Lord, it is not a profession, it is not a nation, it is humanity itself which with uncovered head salutes you."

In December of that year the Royal College of Surgeons was proud to record the fact that fifty years had passed since Joseph Lister had become a member of its organization. The *British Medical Journal* commemorated the occasion by issuing a 'Lister Number.' It was only one of the many honours which were still descending upon Lister, as though to make up by their numbers the fact that some of them were coming rather late.

That Christmas Lister went, as usual, to Lyme Regis, where he and Arthur and a brother-in-law had jointly bought a cottage in 1870. "High Cliff," which was seven miles from Axminster, was a wonderful place for naturalists, and Joseph and Agnes Lister had spent many happy days there collecting flowers.

After Upton House had been sold—the building itself was still standing, but the sixty-nine-acre estate had been cut up as London grew, and houses covered the ground where the Lister children used to play—the family had formed the habit of meeting at Lyme Regis at Christmas.

It was not an entirely happy Christmas for Joseph Lister. His health was troubling him, the more so because he had been counting on his body to give him perfect service for over seventy years. Except for a knee which he had strained long ago he had scarcely known what it was to have to make allowances for himself. Now his knee was almost always painful, and rheumatism joined with other demons of old age to plague him.

He still enjoyed the company of young people, however; with them he made efforts to overcome his infirmities which he would not have attempted to make for older people.

On a recent sea-voyage to South Africa which Lister had taken, accompanied by a niece and the butler, Henry Jones, in order to rest and regain his health, he had never found the children a nuisance. When the time came to award the prizes for the winners of the ship's sports contests he volunteered for the job, although he felt he had to avoid the exertions of other social activities.

Never resigned to illness in others, Lister refused to be resigned to it in himself. With Lucy Syme and the faithful Henry Jones, who had taken to sleeping in his room in order to attend to him in the night, he went to Buxton in the hope that the waters and the climate would be beneficial, but he never met with more than a partial improvement.

Lucy Syme had been a semi-invalid herself for some years, but with Agnes gone she felt that her brother-in-law needed her. She had cared for her own father for many years, and her own ailments receded into the background, even vanished, as she put on again the familiar harness of caring for some one who could not get along without her.

It grew increasingly difficult for Lister to walk, and he had always enjoyed walking so much. Twelve miles had scarcely tired him and Agnes in their middle age, but now . . . For a long time he kept up his daily stroll, but gradually his arm-chair grew more attractive to him than even the Botanical Gardens. Yet he continued active mentally until, in 1904, he suffered a serious illness.

Just what it was the doctors could not determine. They did not agree with his diagnosis of a very slight paralytic stroke. Whatever it was, it was quite serious; though he showed some improvement after about six months, it was obvious that the turning-point had come.

One of the things which troubled him as he strove to regain his strength was the question of his papers. The book which people had been urging him to write since 1869 had never been undertaken, yet every one knew that the writings of Joseph Lister must eventually be published, if not while he was alive then after his death. He had written a great deal, and it had appeared in many different publications; what should be preserved and what omitted must be decided some time.

He was not fit to tackle the problem of editing and arranging his papers himself. As the months passed, and he was no nearer to being able to undertake the work, he grew more and more worried.

His nephew, Arthur H. Lister, was a busy practising physician, and he hated to burden him with such a huge task; but, not knowing where else to turn, he had to ask him to handle it. In order to simplify the work Lister tried to write out detailed instructions to guide his nephew, carefully covering about half a dozen pages of foolscap with instructions; but that scarcely scratched the surface.

As he began to feel a little stronger he thought he might be able to manage a small project, such as republishing the Huxley Lecture which was in a sense a review of his work. That would be something, even though it would not relieve his nephew of the tremendous task which he would eventually have to face.

Meanwhile, Lister's friends and colleagues had been considering the same problem. At last, after many meetings and conferences and the discussion and rejection of all kinds of ideas, they decided to commemorate Lister's approaching eightieth birthday with a volume containing his published papers. A committee was appointed to dig his articles and speeches out of the many journals in which they were buried, to select and arrange them suitably, and prepare an introduction.

Lister was delighted when they told him of their decision. "This new plan will involve full as much work on my part as my poor brain can do," he wrote his brother. "But if I can do *anything*, it will be better than leaving things in the utter confusion in which they would have been left to A.H."

The plan involved a great deal of work both on Lister's part and on that of the committee, but finally it was accomplished.

Although publication was a little late for his eightieth birthday, the two handsome volumes which people had been waiting for so long at last appeared. *The Collected Papers of Joseph, Baron Lister*, contained almost a thousand pages, two portraits, and about twenty reproductions, some in colour, of Lister's beautiful and accurate drawings.

The two volumes were subdivided into five parts—two in the first volume, three in the second. This was an excellent arrangement, as each part dealt with a separate subject, and the papers in each subdivision were in chronological order.

The first series of sixteen articles was devoted to physiology. The first paper, written in 1853, was "Observations on the Contractile Tissue of the Iris," and the last, "On the Coagulation of the Blood in its Practical Aspects," was written in 1891, showing how faithful Lister had been to the subject in which Professor Sharpey had aroused his interest. The second section contained nine articles on pathology and bacteriology. In the second volume were Lister's papers on the antiseptic system and on surgery, and his addresses.

There was only one thing wrong with the handsomely printed and bound collection of Lister's papers: the volumes were too large and expensive to be readily available to the many people who would have liked to own them. As Lister wrote to Rickman John Godlee, "You have no doubt received a copy of the *opus magnum*; my fear is that it is so *magnum* that there will be few who will read much of its contents."

Although Lister's book was not ready in time for his eightieth birthday, the day was celebrated with appropriate ceremonies throughout the world. He himself participated in the festivities for only fifteen minutes, which was all that his physicians felt he should be taxed with, when he received a deputation which went to his house to express the sentiments of his many admirers.

But now there was no stopping the stream of messenger-boys with letters and telegrams and flowers, as well as the callers who wished personally to deliver their tributes to his door.

Hearing the parade of footsteps, Lister thought how far he had come since the days when, as convinced as he was at this moment of the correctness of his theory, he worked without encouragement except from Agnes, his father-in-law, and his students.

And he thought also of Semmelweis, of whom he had only recently learned, despite the fact that he had been in contact with people who had known him or his work—people who must have deliberately forgotten the strange, tragic young man whom they and fate had treated so shabbily.

In 1906, the year before his eightieth birthday, Lister had been asked whether it was true that he had said, "Without Semmelweis my labour would have been in vain," and he had replied that, while it was "extremely distasteful" to discuss the question of his priority, he had to say that he had never made that statement. Even in 1885, when he had visited Budapest, Semmelweis's name had not been mentioned to him, and it was not until some time later that he had learned of his work from a Hungarian doctor practising in London.

"But while Semmelweis had no influence upon my work," he said, "I greatly admire his labours and rejoice that his memory will be at length duly honoured."

Comparing his own life with that of Semmelweis, Lister realized how truly fortunate he had been to live to see the acceptance of his own theories. And if, he thought philosophically, Agnes could not be with him until the end, surely he would not have to wait much longer now.

It did not seem to people as though he would be with them much longer when, in June of 1907, he accepted the Freedom of the City of London—an old man, looking, they thought, like the ghost of the Lister they had known. His voice was so low that they could scarcely hear the words which it cost him such a great effort to utter.

It was the last public ceremony which he was to attend. It was quite out of the question for him to accept in person the Freedom of the City of Glasgow, which offered him her greatest honour in January 1908.

Soon after he went with Lucy Syme to Walmer, in Kent, where he hoped that the sea-air and the drives which he was still able to enjoy would help him to regain his strength.

Part of him was waiting for the end to come, but the vitality which had always interested him scientifically was still strong in him. It prompted him to take to Walmer the papers on suppuration which he had been working on in 1864, when the discovery that microbes caused fermentation and decay had started him on his great work. He still hoped to finish them, for he hated to leave anything incomplete.

In the same way part of him refused to admit that he was not going back to London, where everything remained in readiness for his return.

He never went back, and he never finished the papers which, until the end, remained in his room. He could still write letters, some personal, some concerned with details of his work, such as the use of catgut in operations, but even that was a great strain.

Gradually the twilight was deepening. Arthur Lister died

in 1908, and although Jane Lister Harrison, the 'baby' of the family, was still living, distance prevented Lister from seeing her. He saw hardly anyone. Even though he enjoyed it when his nieces and nephews dropped in it was always hard for him to decide whether he ought to make the effort and suffer the subsequent reaction, if he knew they were thinking of coming.

His eyes and hearing failed him. It was growing very dark. At last, in 1912, quietly, almost imperceptibly, he contracted pneumonia, the same disease which had so cruelly killed his wife, and passed away.

At last he could be laid by her side, his firm request observed even though there were many who wanted to bury him with the great in Westminster Abbey. On the plain granite slab which covered his inconspicuous grave were inscribed the simple words: JOSEPH, BARON LISTER, BORN 5TH APRIL, 1827; DIED 10TH FEBRUARY, 1912.

But though the world observed his wishes in not separating him from Agnes in death, it insisted upon a public funeral service in Westminster Abbey following the simple ceremony for his close friends and relatives the night before.

Some of his friends worried about that second ceremony. Joseph Lister was such a modest man! They remembered that he had once said, as he walked home with Hector Cameron after attending an elaborate funeral ceremony, that he hoped his friends who survived him would see to it "that no fuss of that sort is made when I depart."

However, it was not, they believed, a fuss, but a dignified and solemn ceremony, and they thought that Lister would have been quite willing that it should take place as a tribute to his work. It was a fitting part of the "undying fame" which he had prophesied would belong to the man who solved the problem of the healing of wounds, and which was symbolized by the marble medallion placed in his memory in Westminster Abbey.

Undying fame? Was that, perhaps, going a little too far? Would not Lister's discoveries, however important they were at the time that they were made, be eclipsed by subsequent discoveries in the field of surgery?

It would not matter even if they should be negated by further progress. It was his work which would make that negation possible, just as his antiseptic technique had made it possible to avoid the use of antiseptics. If, some day, surgery should reach its ultimate goal of eliminating itself, it would be at least partially due to the man who made surgery a relatively commonplace affair, multiplying by an astronomical figure the number of operations which could be performed.

In the poem which Henley called *The Chief*, and which he wrote while he was in Edinburgh Infirmary, he described Lister in the following terms:

> His brow spreads large and placid, and his eye
> Is deep and bright, with steady looks that still.
> Soft lines of tranquil thought his face fulfil—
> His face at once benign and proud and shy.
> If envy scout, if ignorance deny,
> His faultless patience, his unyielding will,
> Beautiful gentleness and splendid skill,
> Innumerable gratitudes reply.
> His wise, rare smile is sweet with certainties,
> And seems in all his patients to compel
> Such love and faith as failure cannot quell.
> We hold him for another Herakles,
> Battling with custom, prejudice, disease,
> As once the son of Zeus with Death and Hell.[1]

Another Herakles . . . How strange it seems to-day to compare a brawny fighter with a quiet, modest surgeon like Joseph Lister! Yet it was a comparison which came quite naturally to the mind of a poet seventy years ago. Henley, from his own painful experience, knew that pre-Listerian hospitals were like the Augean stables, filled with the corruption and filth of centuries. The cleansing of these stables

[1] From W. E. Henley's *Poems*. By kind permission of the author's representatives and Messrs Macmillan and Co., Ltd.

had been one of the 'impossible' tasks which Hercules had accomplished.

And Joseph Lister had set for himself, and had accomplished, the impossible task of cleansing the hospitals in which the filth of centuries fed upon the living bodies of the men and women and children who were the victims of man's charity.

Until those stables could be cleansed industrial progress must be retarded by the casualties of city and factory life. Until they were cleansed surgery must remain an art and a skill, and could not become a science.

"It is one of the lessons of the history of science that each age steps on the shoulders of the ages which have gone before," said Sir Michael Foster, the distinguished physiologist, who had accompanied Lister on his last Canadian tour.

Surgery, a science now, rests on the shoulders of the past. The progress it has made and will make in the future depends upon its foundation. And one of its main supports is the work accomplished by the hands and heart and brain of Joseph Lister, with Agnes Lister by his side.

Bibliography

"Anti-vivisection Legislation: Its History, Aims, and Menace," *Defense of Research Pamphlet*, xxv (Chicago, American Medical Association, 1911).

BELL, JOHN: *Discourses on the Nature and Cure of Wounds* (Edinburgh, 1795).

—— *The Principles of Surgery*, abridged by J. Augustine Smith (London, Longmans, Green and Co., 1806).

BILLROTH, THEODOR: *The Medical Sciences in the German Universities* (London, Macmillan, 1925).

BROWN, JOHN: *Horæ Subsecivæ* (Edinburgh, Edmonston and Douglas, 1861).

BROWN, JOHN, and FORREST, D. W. (editors): *Letters of Dr John Brown* (London, A. and C. Black, 1907).

CAMAC, C. N. B. (editor): *Epoch-making Contributions to Medicine, Surgery, and the Allied Sciences* (Philadelphia and London, W. B. Saunders Co., 1909).

CANNON, WALTER B.: "Some Characteristics of Anti-vivisection Literature," *Defense of Research Pamphlet*, xix (Chicago, American Medical Association, 1911).

CHEYNE, SIR WILLIAM WATSON, Bt.: *Antiseptic Surgery, Its Principles, Practice, History, and Results* (London, Smith, Elder and Co., 1882).

—— *Lister and his Achievement* (London, Longmans, Green and Co., 1925).

CHRISTIE, JAMES: *The Medical Institutions of Glasgow* (Glasgow, J. Maclehose and Sons, 1888).

CLENDENING, LOGAN: *Behind the Doctor* (London, Heinemann, 1933).

DANA, C. L.: *The Peaks of Medical History* (New York, Paul B. Hoeber, Inc., 1926).

DE KRUIF, PAUL HENRY: *The Fight for Life* (London, Jonathan Cape, 1938).

—— *Men against Death* (London, Jonathan Cape, 1933).

—— *Microbe Hunters* (London, Jonathan Cape, 1927).

DUCLAUX, E.: *Pasteur: the History of a Mind* (Philadelphia and London, W. B. Saunders Co., 1920).

DUKES, CUTHBERT: *Lord Lister, 1827–1912* (London, Leonard Parsons, 1924).

DUNS, JOHN: *Memoir of Sir J. Y. Simpson, Bart.* (Edinburgh, Edmonston and Douglas, 1873).

FISHBEIN, MORRIS: *Frontiers of Medicine* (London, Allen and Unwin, 1933).

FÜLOP-MILLER, RENÉ: *Triumph over Pain* (London, Hamish Hamilton, 1938).

GARRISON, FIELDING H.: *An Introduction to the History of Medicine* (Philadelphia and London, W. B. Saunders Co., 1913).

GIBSON, THOMAS: "Lister the Man," *The Queen's Quarterly*, vol. xxxiv (1927), No. 4.

GODLEE, SIR RICKMAN JOHN, BT.: *Lord Lister* (London, Macmillan and Co., 1917).

GRAHAM, HARVEY: *Surgeons All* (London, Rich and Cowan, 1939).

HAGGARD, HOWARD W.: *The Lame, the Halt, and the Blind* (London, Heinemann, 1934).

Handbook of the Lister Centenary Exhibition at the Wellcome Historical Medical Museum (London, the Wellcome Foundation 1927).

HENLEY, WILLIAM ERNEST: *Poems* (London, Macmillan, 1933).

LEESON, JOHN RUDD: *Lister as I knew Him* (London, Ballière, Tindall, and Cox, 1927).

LISTER, GULIELMA: "Reminiscences of Lord Lister," *The Essex Naturalist*, vol. xxiv (1935).

LISTER, JOSEPH, BARON: *Collected Papers* (Oxford, Clarendon Press, 1909).

MACLEAN, DONALD: *Personal Reminiscences of Syme*, reprinted from *The Medical Age* (Detroit, William M. Warren).

MORSE, JOHN T., JR.: *Life and Letters of Oliver Wendell Holmes* (London, Sampson Low, Marston and Co., 1896).

MURRAY, DAVID: *Memories of the Old College of Glasgow* (Glasgow, Jackson, Wylie and Co., 1927).

MURRAY, DAVID: "The Scottish Universities," in *Scottish History and Life*, edited by James Paton (Glasgow, James Maclehose, 1902).

PACKARD, FRANCIS R.: *Life and Times of Ambroise Paré, 1510–1590* (London, Humphrey Milford, 1922).

PAGET, STEPHEN: *Experiments on Animals* with an introduction by Lord Lister (London, T. F. Unwin, 1900).

PATERSON, ROBERT: *Memorials of the Life of Professor Syme* (Edinburgh, Edmonston and Douglas, 1874).

POWER, SIR D'ARCY: *A Short History of Surgery* (London, J. Bale and Co., 1933)

—— *Foundations of Medical History* (London, Ballière, Tindall, and Cox, 1931).

ROBINSON, VICTOR: *The Story of Medicine* (New York, Tudor Publishing Co., 1931).

Royal Society for the Prevention of Cruelty to Animals: *Vivisection* (London, Smith, Elder and Co., 1876).

SALEEBY, CALEB WILLIAM: *Modern Surgery and its Makers: a Tribute to Listerism* (London, Herbert and Daniel, 1911).

SHAFTESBURY, EARL OF, and others: *The Vivisection Controversy* (London, Victoria Street Society for the Protection of Animals from Vivisection, etc., 1883).

SIGERIST, HENRY E.: *Great Doctors: a Biographical History of Medicine* (London, Allen and Unwin, 1933).

SIMPSON, EVE BLANTYRE: *Sir James Y. Simpson*, in the "Famous Scots" series (Edinburgh and London, Oliphant, Anderson, and Ferrier, 1896).

SINCLAIR, SIR WILLIAM J.: *Semmelweis: His Life and Doctrine* (Manchester University Press, 1909).

STEWART, JOHN: "First Listerian Oration, under the Auspices of the Lister Memorial Club, Canadian Medical Association, Montreal," in the *Canadian Medical Association Journal* (special number), 1924.

SYME, JAMES: *Principles of Surgery*, edited by Donald MacLean (London, Murray, 1863).

"Symposium of Papers on the Late Lord Lister," reprinted from the *Canadian Journal of Medicine and Surgery* (May 1912).

TURNER, A. LOGAN (editor): *Joseph, Baron Lister* (Edinburgh and London, Oliver and Boyd, 1927).

VALLERY-RADOT, RENÉ: *The Life of Pasteur* (London, Constable, 1901).

WRENCH, GUY THEODORE: *Lord Lister, his Life and Work* (London, Unwin, 1913).

Articles in "Annals of Medical History"[1]

Ashurst, Astley Paston Cooper: "Centenary of Lister, a Tale of Sepsis and Antisepsis" (1927).
Ball, James M.: "The Ether Tragedies" (1925).
Brown, John N. E.: "Syme and His Son-in-Law" (1941).
Carson, Herbert W.: "The Iliac Passion" (1931).
"Centennial of the Death of Jenner" (1923).
Dawson, P. M.: "Semmelweis, an Interpretation" (1924).
Howell, W. B.: "Concerning Some Old Medical Journals" (1926).
Jacobs, Henry Barton: "Elizabeth Fry, Pastor Fliedner, and Florence Nightingale" (1921).
John, Henry J. (translator): "Notes on the Surgical Clinic of Charles University, Prague, Bohemia, 100 Years Ago" (1924).
Krumbhaar, ——: "Early History of Anatomy in America."
Menne, Frank R.: "Carl Rokitansky, the Pathologist" (1925).
Peachey, George C.: "Memoir of William and John Hunter" (1925).
Taylor, Frances Long: "Crawford Williamson Long" (1925).
Thomson, Sir St Clair: "House Surgeon's Memories of Lister" (1919).
Webb, Gerald B.: "René Théophile Hyacinthe Laënnec" (1927).
—— "Robert Koch" (1932).
Weise, E. Robert: "Semmelweis" (1930).
—— "Larrey, Napoleon's Chief Surgeon" (1929).
Wilson, James C.: "Alphonse François Marie Guérin" (1930).
Woolf, A. E. Mortimer: "Personalities of the Hunterian Epoch" (1929).

[1] New York, Paul B. Hoeber, Inc.

Index